THE BONFIRES OF BELTANE

Following St. Patrick Across Ancient, Celtic Ireland

Mark E. Fisher

HERITAGE BEACON

FICTION

THE BONFIRES OF BELTANE BY MARK E. FISHER
Published by Heritage Beacon Fiction
an imprint of Lighthouse Publishing of the Carolinas
2333 Barton Oaks Dr., Raleigh, NC 27614

ISBN: 978-1-938499-52-4
Copyright © 2016 by Mark E. Fisher
Cover design by Elaina Lee
Interior design by AtriTeX Technologies P Ltd

Available in print from your local bookstore, online, or from the publisher at:
www.lighthousepublishingofthecarolinas.com

For more information on this book and the author visit: markfisherauthor.com

Unless otherwise noted, all Scripture quotations are taken from the Holman Christian Standard Bible®, Copyright © 1999, 2000, 2002, 2003, 2009 by Holman Bible Publishers. Used by permission. Holman Christian Standard Bible®, Holman CSB®, and HCSB® are federally registered trademarks of Holman Bible Publishers.

Brought to you by the creative team at Lighthouse Publishing of the Carolinas:
Eddie Jones, Ann Tatlock, Amberlyn Dwinnell, Shonda Savage, Brian Cross, Paige Boggs

Library of Congress Cataloging-in-Publication Data
Fisher, Mark E.
The Bonfires of Beltane / Mark E. Fisher 1st ed.

Printed in the United States of America

PRAISE FOR *THE BONFIRES OF BELTANE*

Mark Fisher has done an excellent job of blending history with fiction in his debut novel, *The Bonfires of Beltane*. Learning of life in a society devoid of Christianity makes me thankful for the ministry of St. Patrick and other people like him.

~ **Carolyn Van Loh**
Author of *A Place of Interest*

Mark Fisher's meticulous research comes to life in these pages. He depicts a struggle both for life and for spirit. The ancient kingdoms of Britain and Ireland appear in vivid detail. With high stakes, intrigue, suspense, and even romance, Fisher weaves a tale worthy of reading and rereading.

~ **Aaron D. Gansky**
Author of *The Bargain*, The Hand of Adonai Series, and *Firsts in Fiction*

The Bonfires of Beltane will hold the reader's attention from start to finish. Mark Fisher has brought the ministry of St. Patrick to life in a new and exciting way and I found myself intrigued and challenged in my own Christian walk. The story's message continues to stay with me long after finishing this book. I look forward to reading more from Mark.

~ **Rebeccah Isaacs**
Freelance Writer

An inspiring adventure through the wild landscape of ancient Ireland, this tale brings to life the remarkable journey of Ireland's earliest Christians. Highly entertaining and engaging.

~ **Cindy Thomson**
Author of *Brigid of Ireland* and *Pages of Ireland*

For Barbara,
the love of my life.

"Look at the nations and observe—be utterly astounded!
For something is taking place in your days that you will not believe
when you hear about it."
—Habakkuk 1:5

TABLE OF CONTENTS

CAST OF CHARACTERS
(BY ORDER OF APPEARANCE)

PART I — ON THE ISLAND OF INIS CREIG

- Taran mac Teague—[TA-run mac TEEG] young seeker of truth
- Laurna—Taran's beautiful, blonde, betrothed, of Gaeadan's *fine*
- Teague—[Teeg] Taran's father and Rí Tuath, leader of the clan of the Carraig Beag
- Bohan—Taran's red-haired brother
- Sileas—[SHEE-lus] elderly mother and servant to all, of Teague's *fine*
- Eadan mac Gaeadan—[AE-dan mac GAE-dan] respected hunter and friend of Taran
- Cormag—[KOR-mak] albino chief druid of the Carraig Beag
- Mungan—[MOON-gun] portly druid follower of Cormag

PART II — IN THE LAND OF ÉRIU

- Kilgarren—boisterous, rowdy leader of merrymakers
- Mùirne—[MOOR-neh] meek, blonde-haired slave of Kilgarren, on loan to Donnach
- Donnach—[DO-nuch] owner of hut where Kilgarren's band is staying
- Coll—follower of Kilgarren, serious, plays the fiddle.
- Dearshul—slatternly servant of Kilgarren
- Amalgaid—Rí Cóicid, or king, of Cruachain and the Kingdom of Connacht, ruler of the Connachta

PART III — IN THE KINGDOM OF ULSTER

- Pátrick—Roman evangelist from Bryton
- Latharn—portly believer, follower of Pátrick from Sabhall

- Servius—a priest and friend of Pátrick's from Roman Bryton

- Armadal—leader of Ulster's armies, second in command to Forga mac Dallán

- Ohran—chief druid of Emain Macha

- Sòlas—[SOO-las] Forga's chief palace guard and executioner

- Forga mac Dallán—Rí Cóicid, or king, of Emain Macha and the Kingdom of Ulster, ruler of the Ulaid

- Beahak—feisty nurse and attendant to Princess Eivhir

- Eivhir—(AY-veer) dying daughter of Forga mac Dallán

PART IV — AT THE GREAT FAIR

- Boodan— druid aligned with Ohran

- Ceallach—[KEL-uch] Coll's master

PART V — IN NORTHERN LEINSTER

- Fedelm—young, red-haired lass lost in the woods

- Eithne—[AY-nyeh] fair-faced sister of Fedelm

- Lóeghaire—[LOO-hair] Rí Cóicid, or king, of Tara and the Kingdom of Leinster, ruler of the Laigin

- Blàr—Lóeghaire's servant

PART VI — IN A FAR NORTHERN SEA

- Angus mac Dughall—young hunter by the cave

- Guaire—[GOOY-ruh] Angus's brother

- Doiurchu—[DOE-ur-choo] druid follower of Cormag

- Gahran mac Madadh—[GAW-run mac MA-dugh] Rí Tuath of the Carraig Beag after Teague, friend of Cormag

- Cailean—[KA-len] son of Eadan mac Gaeadan

- Faolan mac Cè—[FOOL-un mac KEE] pirate leader of the Rathlin

- Cathal—[KA-hul] Faolan's wee sidekick

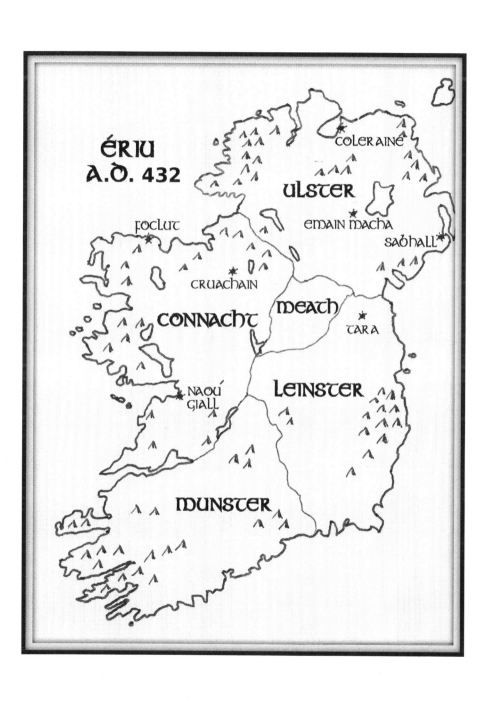

ÉRIU
A.Ð. 432

COLERAINE

ULSTER

FOCLUT

EMAIN MACHA

SAÐHALL

CRUACHAIN

MEATH

TARA

CONNACHT

LEINSTER

NAOÚ
GIALL

MUNSTER

PART I

On The Island Of Inis Creig, A.D. 432

CHAPTER I

Darkness

If Laurna and I were to catch the thieves, we'd no time to lose.

I crept inside the large roundhouse where her *fine* slept and eased the door shut, fearing to wake the forty sleepers sprawled across the floor under furs and rugs. By firelight, I scanned the great room and the spot where she'd be. The air trembled with snoring and heavy breathing. The odor of sweat and animal skins and the sweet smell of pine smoke tickled my nose. By a near wall, I spied her tawny hair spread wild across black fur, then stepped over rugs and bodies, knelt, and gently shook her.

She opened her eyes, focused on mine. "Wh–what? Taran?" A smile spread from her lips to her eyes, blue and sparkling by firelight. "'Tis time?"

"Aye, tonight we'll catch them. I heard footsteps outside, heading toward the pens."

"Sure, and we'll go, but first you must guess what I've made for you." She rubbed her eyes and gave me a lopsided smile. "For every wrong answer, you owe me a kiss."

"A brooch to hold my cape?"

"'Tis na that."

I grinned, leaned over and pressed my lips to hers, feeling their wet warmth against mine. "Lassie, I could play this game, and play to lose, all night. But we've got to hurry."

Smiling, she pulled on a tunic, shoes, and cape, and we tiptoed through the sleepers and out the roundhouse door into the chill of an early spring night. As we hurried over the hard-packed earth between houses, a full moon topped the eastern mountain, lighting the way.

When we passed the farthest house of the village, we saw them. They were leaving the animals' rock pen and entering the forest. One thief led a stolen kid by its tether. A second carried a blazing torch. Both wore white robes.

My heart quickened. I barely whispered the word. "*Druids.*"

They were our healers. Administrators of justice. Advisors to my father, the Rí Tuath, who, along with the *comhairle*, or ruling council, led the clan. They kept the spells of healing and cursing, memorized and passed down from before the days of the Fir Bolg.

They were our priests. They gave their souls to the spirits of trees, streams, and rocks in hope of learning their secrets. Once I was with them. And then I grew cold, dead, and shriveled inside, for they worshiped the darkness. They worshiped the dread idol of gold, Crom Cruach. The Bent and Bloody One. And he owned their souls.

A shiver rippled down my back.

I pulled Laurna behind the trunk of a yew. "This thievery, 'tis druid business."

"There's na good in this. Na good at all." She frowned.

"We must follow them, see what they do."

Laurna caught my glance, put her hands on her hips, and her frown melted into a smile. "Aye, let's follow them."

Thus begins my story of long ago, with Laurna and I sneaking away in the wee hours to solve a mystery of stolen goats. I sit here now, warming old bones by a fire of pine logs, with a pile of vellum parchment and quills. I marvel at how young and brazen we were then. Had we known the trouble to come, the lives we'd upset, we might have returned to our beds.

Instead, we followed the druids' torch down a twisting forest path across the mountain. Never close enough for them to hear or see us, we crept between pines, then oaks, until we reached the rocks above the little falls. They dragged and pushed the goat up a rock face and disappeared over a ridge of boulders. From beyond came the sound of crashing water.

We skirted a patch of loose scree and climbed to the ridgetop. Hiding behind a boulder, we watched the two white-robed men in the clearing below.

Cormag, his hair as white as his robe, knelt by the kid. A knife flashed once in the moonlight. Its throat slit, its strength ebbing fast, the goat kicked against the leather binding its legs and tried to bleat. I squirmed but didn't look away. Over the sound of cascading water came the rhythmic chanting of their spells. Spells I knew only too well.

"Taran, what if they find us out?"

"We're safe in the shadows. Let's watch a bit. Then we'll leave."

She gave me another lopsided smile. "Only if you make another guess."

"A brass ring for my finger?"

She shook her head, and a sassy smile spread across her lips.

I leaned over, held her head with both hands and pressed my lips to hers, lingering. "I like this game. I don't think my guesses will improve."

"'Tis fine with me. But what's this spell they do? Do you ken its secrets?"

Still enjoying the warmth of her lips, I stared into her eyes, silent, smiling.

"Three years you were with them. Sure, and you ken their ways."

I sighed. Once she set her mind to a thing, Laurna wouldn't give it up. "I ken the spell. The goat must bleed its life out beside a falls, for 'tis a gateway to the Otherworld. The animal must be stolen. And the deed must be done in secret."

"Sure, and what kind of spell would that be now?"

"A spell to increase power. Cormag's power. To steal power from the spirits beyond."

As if the chief druid of Inis Creig had heard his name, the tall, gaunt man stood from his kneeling position and turned toward us. Torchlight glinted off his shiny scalp. Thin white hair fell in lonely strands over his pale forehead. His eyes glinted red by torchlight, appearing to stare straight at me. Cormag's dead, pink eyes always troubled me.

I froze. Had he seen me in the shadows?

Oblivious to his movements, Laurna sat behind a boulder. When she whirled her head toward me, her tawny braids, wrapped in strips of blue and gold-dyed leather, swung in the moonlight.

"What if the spell's no longer secret? What if they discover us?"

Motionless, alert to Cormag's every move, I said nothing.

"Taran mac Teague, speak to me!"

Cormag arched his back, stretched, and knelt again by the dying goat. He mumbled more of the spell, then dragged the kid toward a woodpile they'd built. Mungan carried a sword on his belt.

Safe to move again, I turned to Laurna. "He nearly saw us. We mustn't let him find us. If someone breaks the secrecy of this particular spell, it works the opposite way. Cormag's power would then *decrease*."

She shuddered. "He'd never let that happen."

"Never. To preserve the magic he'd kill us first."

Her eyes widened. "Sure now, and would he really?"

"If he thought he could do the deed in secret, aye."

Laurna shuddered again.

Up the slopes in the pines, the hoot of an owl echoed—haunting, lonely. From the mountain came a scent of pine, and from the pool below, an occasional whiff of rotting leaves.

"'Tis what I've been saying and what you haven't wanted to hear. Tonight they've stolen a goat to kill. Granted, a goat's a small thing. Yet if we're discovered, Cormag would rather kill us than give up any of the power he imagines he'll gain by his ceremony. This is evil, Laurna, and it's a symptom of the deeper evil they serve. It's not just about them. It's what they're doing to the entire *tuath*. They're leading the clan into darkness. I feel it. I sense it. I fear for us. Not only for you and me but for everyone."

"Stop, Taran! You're thinking too much."

"You remember what happened last year. You were there. You saw them smash the head of Gormal's baby, then burn the body. And you danced before Crom Cruach's crooked stone, didn't you? We all did. What did you feel then? Did you sense his presence pouring darkness into your soul, filling you with something wild and impure? At the Circle of Stones during that dance, I actually *wanted* them to kill the child. I couldn't wait for it to happen. Think about what's going on here. The druids kill a child and the sun god makes me *want* it. What's happening to us?"

She frowned.

Often, she spent half the morning with the children, telling stories or playing hoops and sticks. Yet, with the sacrifices, like everyone else, she seemed blind.

"I . . . I know what you're saying. I didna like giving him that baby. At first, that is. Such a tiny thing. But after a while, it seemed . . . almost . . . normal. I know how you feel. At first, I was troubled. Very much so. I didna like it, but only at first. Then, with everyone dancing and me joining in, I gave myself up to him. I threw my hands in the air like everyone else. I got used to it. We all get used to it. Sure, and I admit I *did* enjoy it. We're supposed to. All my life 'tis what we've been told. Taran, we must sacrifice *someone*. It's the price we pay for his protection, for milk, a bountiful harvest, good fishing. 'Tis simply how it is."

I shook my head. "Don't you see? Crom Cruach has poisoned your heart. And he's done the same to all of us. To everyone in the clan."

She gaped at me. "He has not. It canna be." Her head was shaking no, but her widened eyes said something else. "'Tis simply how it's always been." She remained silent a while, then blurted, "I know you can sense things others can't, especially when it concerns the spirits, but I think you're wrong. Did Dughall give you these ideas?"

"Dughall's only spoken of a vast world beyond our own. Ruled by great peoples. Where great events occur."

"You think enough already. You donna need more strange ideas from Dughall."

"He's only told me the truth. In Bryton where the Romans held him a slave, Dughall heard of many things beyond our ken. He even tells of a new God they worship, of one God above all others. Laurna, they speak of a God who *loves*. Think of it. One God, not the many who confound and bedevil us, and a *loving* God. Would that I could learn more of *Him*!"

"But donna all peoples everywhere worship Crom Cruach, he who protects us? Is he na the spirit of the sun, the giver of all life?" Her words were strained, coming too fast. Looking back now, I think they were meant for her, not me. "He even begat Danu, mother of the earth. He's greater than the spirits of beasts, forests, and streams. For without the sun, everything dies. Have you forgotten everything the druids taught you?"

"You know I haven't. But someday, someone must speak up to warn the clan. The druids' power grows, as does their evil. Perhaps tomorrow, I—"

"Taran, you'll say nothing about this tomorrow night at your ceremony to join the *comhairle*. If you even hint of what you just told me, you'll na join the high council. Your father might protect you, but you mustna think such dangerous thoughts. You must never speak them."

In the clearing, flames engulfed the goat atop the woodpile, illuminating the falls and the rock face, and releasing the acrid smell of burnt flesh mixed with pine smoke. I glanced at Laurna. Her cape had fallen open.

"A leather armband."

"What?" She looked down at her waist, at the leather band tied with string to her belt. Her eyebrows dipped, and she hit me lightly on the arm. "You cheated, but I forgive you." She untied the leather cuff and presented it to me. Etched with expert, tiny, red and yellow interlocking swirls, it gleamed with oil.

I slipped it up my right arm and secured it with the leather thongs she'd also made. "Thank you. I'll wear it always." I smiled.

"Now it's my turn." Beaming, she leaned over, wrapped her arms around my neck, pulled me close, and pressed her lips to mine. But when we parted, a trace of frown returned.

"And sure, you canna put me off by solving my riddle. If you say anything tomorrow, I donna ken what they'll do. Have you forgotten we're to be wed at the next full moon? Have you even *thought* about us? If Cormag turns against you— well, look what happened to old Bearach."

"I remember." Old, touched in the head, Bearach foolishly spoke the truth against the druids. Mad as he was, they banished him to a death in the sea.

Laurna shifted her feet. A rock tumbled and clattered down the slope behind us—loud, too loud. Alarmed, I spun toward the clearing.

By flickering firelight, Cormag now looked straight at our boulder. Beside him, peering into the darkness, stood Mungan, sword unsheathed. Then Cormag spoke in a voice I heard clearly, even above the crackling, hissing fire and rushing falls. "Go left by the boulders. I'll go straight. They'll na live to see the dawn."

They started running.

"We're found out. *Run.*" I grasped Laurna's elbow and edged her away from the boulders, down a flat, sloping rock face. Half sliding, half racing, we ran until the pitch ended in a graveled clearing. Pebbles scattered. Combined with my racing heart, the noise nearly deafened me.

I glanced back, but they hadn't yet topped the rise.

I ran in front, my feet glad to leave the rough stones, falling instead into the squishy loam of the forest path. I stumbled over a root, then recovered. Panting now, I looked back to see Laurna close behind, her face contorted, eyes wide. Soon the treetops closed, blocking the moonlight and embracing us with blackest night. I'd hunted this way many times, but it was dark, and at first the path eluded me. Finally, I found the narrow trail. Young saplings appeared from nowhere, ragged branches scraping our arms, wads of leaves slapping our faces. I stubbed a toe on a rock. Now smothered in darkness, I stopped, glanced back. Laurna leaned over, grabbed her thighs, and tried to catch her breath.

Cormag and Mungan were fifty yards behind, wild and intent silhouettes under cold moonlight. Unused to the trail, they stumbled and groped off the path.

"Stop!" cried Cormag in our general direction. "Halt and present yourselves to your druids!" We were now in the thickest part of the forest. I didn't think he could see us. Still, his voice sought us out. "I call the forest spirits down upon you."

A chill rippled through me.

We ran farther, finally pulling ahead. Then Laurna tripped over a root and went down. I helped her up, and pulled her forward, but her hand slipped from mine. She leaned against my shoulder, wincing in obvious pain. She looked at me, then down at her injured foot. I glanced back along the path. Any moment now, the druids would be upon us. "Laurna, *hurry*."

"I can't. My ankle."

Looking around, I spied a large black mass. Ahead and to the right, the root ball of a giant, fallen oak. The rotting carcass of its huge trunk stretched at an angle into the dark. I cradled her shoulders, held one of her hands, and nearly carried her off the trail toward it. From the darkness, two yellow circles stared up at us, began to move toward us. We froze. Laurna's glance locked with mine. Druid magic?

Some animal—I knew not what—burst from its hiding place and fled through the trees. Not magic. Just a dumb forest creature. I heard Laurna's breath release, felt her shivering. I pulled her close, and for a moment, just held her. Then came the sound of feet blundering down the trail. I crouched first behind the root ball, and drew Laurna down beside me, our backs hitting a spongy wall of dirt and roots. At my feet, the moonlight caught some long, silvery, multi-legged insect slithering away. We tried to still our labored breathing and waited.

I heard feet straying from the path, rustling leaves and cracking twigs. The druids were inexpert, clumsy woodsmen.

"Did you see them?" said Cormag. "Did you see *anything*?"

"Nay, my lord," said Mungan. "Only two shadows."

"What good are you, druid? You've young eyes, yet you canna see what's afore you."

"One might 'ave been a woman. But . . . I donna ken."

"No matter. We'll find them in their beds tonight, I'll wager, pretending to be asleep. If I find them out . . ." Then their feet carried them away.

When they'd left, I asked Laurna if she could walk. She stood and tried out her ankle. She favored it heavily, but she could at least walk.

"Now what will we do?" She put a hand on my shoulder for support. "They're in front of us."

"We'll get to the village. Somehow, we must reach our beds without being discovered."

I found a fallen branch, a crutch for Laurna. But now we traveled at a much slower pace. We traversed two miles across the slopes, through the forest, and up a steep trail to our high valley. After a time, she managed to put more weight on her ankle. It wasn't sprained. We ran, walked, then ran again. I was breathing hard and sweating from the climb, even though a deep chill had settled over the night. I smelled old, wet leather. My tunic.

We burst out of the upper pine forest into our valley in time to see the druids walking the course between the six large roundhouses. They entered the first house, opposite the building where my *fine* slept.

"They'll be checking everyone's bed." Laurna's voice was a whisper.

"Go quickly to your bed before they come out again. They mustn't see us."

We ran, our feet pounding down the short path into the village. Raef, my collie, who slept outside, tried to greet me. But I motioned for quiet and he laid down again. I entered the roundhouse, and with the door open a crack, peered back out.

Laurna had rounded the corner toward her house. Good. She was already hidden from view.

The door to the opposite house opened. They'd finished their search.

I pushed softly, wood creaking on leather hinges, shutting me inside.

Warm air engulfed me, tinged with the smells of wood smoke, pine logs, sweat, and animal hides. This was my *fine*, the home of my father, grandparents, uncles, aunts, and cousins. We were only thirty now, too few for one house. Each winter more and more died of the coughing sickness. The blessings of Crom Cruach, if they were such, were harsh, indeed.

I wove past bodies sprawled across the floor, each in their sleeping furs. I found my bed, pulled off my tunic, untied the thongs of my shoes—but no time for my kilt—and slipped under my fur as the outside door creaked open. I lay there, still breathing hard from the climb, my heart pounding, and my forehead wet with sweat.

Moments later, feet shuffled across the floor. They stopped beside me, didn't move on.

I imagined eyes staring down at me. I tried to breathe slower.

"You've a sweat on you, Taran mac Teague," said Cormag, the words shooting through me like an arrow. "'Tis a chill evening for night sweats." He paused as if considering. "Or has my lad been running?"

My breathing didn't slow but quickened. I rolled away from him, pretending sleep.

He walked two paces and paused again. Then he returned to my bedside and, for some time, was motionless. He stood above me, waiting, watching.

My heart thumped wildly.

Instead of checking the rest of the beds, he left the house.

CHAPTER 2

The Hunt

The next morning, as I met Laurna at the village well, chill blasts blew the scent of yew pine and the shadows of lonely clouds down the slopes into our valley. The shadows mirrored my mood, for I'd made a troubling discovery.

"Taran, 'twas a near thing last night. Sure, and a fool thing. What if they'd caught us?"

I frowned. "They did."

"What!" Her eyes went wide.

I stretched my closed right palm toward her, then opened it to reveal the severed foot of a large crow, reeking of decay. "This was tied to my spear this morning."

"A *curse*. They've called the forest spirits down upon you. They *know*."

"We did what we had to. I don't believe in their curses." But as I said this, the hand holding the crowfoot began to shake.

"You should. There are tales, stories. So what will you do?"

"Today, nothing. But someday . . ."

"Now more than ever, you must say nothing to challenge the druids. Cormag may well try to influence the council. Tonight, whatever he asks, you must do. Or say."

"Why?"

"Taran mac Teague!" She stamped one foot and stared at me, arms akimbo. "The druids could easily keep you off the council. It's happened to others. And Cormag could do you much worse. Donna provoke him."

"Don't worry. I won't. And my father will be there. If Cormag fights the Rí Tuath, he'll lose. But this morning, there's more pressing business." I couldn't help grinning. "A hunt!"

She frowned. "I've heard. Last night, the boars broke through the garden gate and rooted the spring radishes and onions. If this continues, there'll be empty bellies next winter."

"The *flaith* have vowed an oath to hunt and kill them. I'm going, of course."

"So now, on the very morning Cormag calls the forest spirits down on you, you're traipsing off into the forest?"

"What can magic do to me that a boar cannot? I'll trust my spear, sharp and sure, against a boar any day. And Raef will be with me. If I see any boars, their heads are mine." I smiled.

She raised her eyebrows then returned my smile. "But, aye, 'tis a boast well made. I grant 'twas your bow and spear, and na your keen mind, that earned your place among the *flaith*. So is it the poor beastie I should fear for today and na the mighty hunter?"

"My lassie speaks the truth." I beamed. I was young, invulnerable to danger. And tragedy? Well, it was the farthest thing from my mind.

"But when you've actually killed the beast instead of talking it to death, can you bring me back a wee tusk? I'll make a horn for you."

"That I will. But the horn'll be grand, not wee. This hunter kills no wee beasties."

She bowed. "Oh, mighty hunter." She rose and I stared into her eyes, so blue and bright and shining, I feared to lose myself in them.

"As for me, this lowly wench will continue as a slave to needle and thread and finish the tunic I'm making for you. A ceremonial dress it is, fit for one who'll soon sit on the *comhairle*. I'll sew sequins of shells and tiny brass rings on it, with a fishing net and a spear stitched in front. I'll paint designs on all corners."

Smiling, I leaned over and kissed her. But she soon pulled away. "Na now, laddie. Be brave with the hunt, and na with this poor lass. Go and kill me a wee beastie with a tusk." Her smile faded. "But today in the forest, do be careful, Taran."

I nodded and began to turn away, but she grabbed one of my hands and pulled me around to face her.

"And tonight, you'll be remembering what I said? About the council?"

"I'll remember. Just for you."

She searched my eyes, gave me a doubtful smile, and then strode down the path. My heart still leaps at the memory of her. She had the gait, the manners, and the mind of a noblewoman. I remember thinking, with our marriage only a few weeks away, what a fine wife she'd make. A wee bit bossy and feisty at times. But few could match such beauty, intelligence, or fire—when passion moved her. She could hunt and had once even trained for battle though she'd never fought in one. If ever I started my own *fine*, such a lass would surely bless and strengthen it.

Raef bounced from behind a tree and raced toward me. Scarcely older than a pup, his energy was boundless. He stopped at my feet and I knelt to scratch him behind his ears. Eager eyes looked into mine. Then he barked once. He sensed the hunt was on.

The noblemen of our clan, the *flaith*, were already gathering at the edge of the village.

With sharpened spears and eager hearts, twenty of us filed down the path through the forest that sloped toward the sea. Four young men from Gaeadan's *fine* sang a boisterous hunting song, their harmony as rough as the stubble on their chins. Halfway down, more than a beagle's gowl from the village, yew pines lost control to tall oaks and elms. But when fresh boar signs led onto a deer trail, we fell silent, split into groups of two and three, and spread out across the mountain.

I hunted with my father, Teague, my brother, Bohan, and Raef. Today, Father's age showed. His cloudy eyes, unsteady gait, and wandering speech, not to mention a few lapses in memory, often worried me. Now he slowed us considerably. Soon the other groups had left us far behind. How could we ever be first upon the boar like this?

I heard only the honking of geese overhead, the chattering of squirrels, and the squishing of feet into last fall's leaves. The smell of bark, new leaf, and wet loam drifted through the woods. We let Father lead, for it would not do to outpace the Rí Tuath.

Raef followed close behind, nosing the occasional animal hole, his tail wagging.

Bohan came up beside me. I was a full head taller than he, and where my hair was brown, wavy, and stopped at my shoulders, his was red as a puffin's beak and curled to his ears. He spoke softly so Father couldn't hear. "I fear Father willna be Rí Tuath for long. Someone will soon point out he's feeble and weak. Someone will say another might be better to lead us."

"Sure, and it will happen as you say. He'll have to give up being the clan's leader."

"But we canna let that be. Our *fine* will lose its power and influence. We must stop it."

"We can't and we shouldn't. 'Tis the way of the *tuatha*. Everyone must respect it."

"I donna want to. For who then will be king and lead the clan?"

"Someone worthy, as always."

We were silent a while, and then he put a hand on my shoulder. "Perhaps, you could be Rí Tuath? Aye, you're respected, a good hunter, and the son of the king. Why not you, brother?"

"'Twill not be me. You well know my being the Rí Tuath's son carries little weight in these matters. It's decided on election and merit, not kinship."

"But you are smart."

"I'm not. Rather I seek answers to lessen my ignorance."

"Then it's your ignorance makes you smarter than most."

I laughed. "Have it your way, brother."

"But you are skilled in many things. What better reason to make you king?"

"I'm mostly skilled at displeasing my elders with too many questions. And I'm not even on the council yet."

"But tonight—"

Voices raced toward us. I peered through the maze of oaks but saw nothing.

Raef lifted his muzzle toward the distance and froze.

Father looked at us, cupping his hand around his mouth. "Boars. Three of them." He pointed straight across the slope. Only then did I see the approaching beasts.

Somehow the prey had slipped through the line of hunters and doubled back. The lead boar was huge. I myself weighed eighteen stone, but this black monster looked well over three times that. It bolted through the trees, its back rippling with muscle, hooves churning up the leaves behind. Its tusks, as long as a man's forearm, bounced up and down, cutting the air as it ran. Two smaller boars followed.

Ahead of us, Father hid behind a trunk. A dozen paces away, I slipped behind a wide oak, as did Bohan. Raef crouched beside me. I gripped my spear and we waited.

Soon the creature crashed through leaves, breaking branches under its hooves, followed by distant shouting from those in pursuit. My heart pounded in anticipation, my muscles tensing.

Father stepped out first in front of the lead boar. I too left my hiding place. Only then did I see the monster hog bearing down upon my father. But the Rí Tuath, the one-time slayer of dozens in battle, stood his ground. As the beast raced toward him, his spear was ready, poised and high.

At the last moment, as Father thrust down, the boar turned, and the spear glanced off a hide as tough as bark. Its tusks swung an arc, caught him in the chest, and knocked him to the ground.

"No!" Bohan shouted.

I started running. Before I closed the gap, the boar lowered its head. Its tusks ripped back and forth over Father's leg, tearing up dirt and leaves, cutting again and again into flesh. He shouted, but it was unintelligible, almost a scream. My father. Teacher of wisdom and courage. The man who taught me how to hunt and fish. His shout gripped my heart with terrible force.

I was there now. I raised my spear, thrust hard, and broke through a wall of hair and hide. My body became part of the weapon, my entire weight leaning into it, my arm muscles taut and strained. By now, Raef gripped one of the boar's hind legs, growling, his teeth sinking in, holding firm, pulling back. The monster squealed and tried to escape.

Bohan appeared on the other side and thrust his spear deep. We both pushed with and twisted our weapons, pinning the boar between us while Raef's jaws held tight on the leg.

The huge pig squealed and thrashed, its tusks trying, failing, trying again, to gore us. Blood streamed down its flanks. But it couldn't dislodge the spears or Raef.

Then, the tall figure of Eadan mac Gaeadan joined us and a third point punctured its side.

Moments later, the beast went down. It thrashed for a long while, breathed heavily, kicked its legs, and then was still.

I tried to catch my breath and heard shouting. Through the trees, I saw distant shadows running through the oaks after the two smaller hogs. I dropped to my father's side, examined his leg, and cringed. Strands of shredded sinew and muscle. White bone, exposed, mixed with dirt and leaves. Blood soaking the ground. The smell of blood, my father's blood, thick in my nose. His face was white, lips taut as dried leather, eyes wandering from the treetops to his shattered leg, then back to the treetops. He gripped my arm with terrible force, rheumy eyes pleading.

I released his grip, removed the belt from my tunic, and bound it securely above his knee. With a piece of new branch, I twisted the belt to staunch the flow of blood.

"We must get him to the village at once," I said.

"The leg?" questioned Bohan, a hand outstretched.

I shook my head, no. The leg was beyond my ken to heal. From my study with the druids, I knew which wounds healed and which didn't. The leg could not be saved. I winced when I realized—though I did not tell the others—that my father might not survive this.

Others from Eadan's *fine* came now to help. When they saw Father's wound, their faces contorted, their heads shook, and two of the youngest looked away. Then we found two sturdy branches, doffed our tunics to lay over the poles, and made a stretcher.

I gripped one end of the litter, the rough bark cutting into my palm, even as a thought cut into my heart: Was this Cormag's doing? Was it possible he did control the black spirits? I knew the darkness he brought among us when we worshiped Crom Cruach. It was real. I felt the power of the spirit within that crooked stone. It was destroying the clan. Was this disaster, too, part of its spreading evil? Did Cormag's curse somehow enter a dumb beast—to ruin me and my *fine*? Or was this all mere coincidence?

I stumbled. My father would not be at the council tonight to support me. On the most important night of my life, I would have to face the *comhairle*—and Cormag—alone.

CHAPTER 3

The End of a Reign

Late afternoon sun sent shafts of smoky, golden light through the open door of the roundhouse. My father's bed lay in the darker recesses. Beside me stood Laurna. As she looked down at the Rí Tuath's broken figure, tears wet her cheeks.

The smell of cauterized flesh still seared my nostrils. When Doiurchu sawed off his leg, even *popaeg*, the black Roman drug purchased in Ériu for a dear price, couldn't dull the pain. Father still passed out. The rest of the morning and afternoon he had slept fitfully, waking only once. Much to my dismay, Bohan then informed him of the crow's foot tied to my spear—of the druids' spell. At this news, he groaned all the more and, clearly out of his head, shouted curses against them.

Again, I gave him *popaeg* mixed with mead to make him sleep. Had anyone heard? I glanced around, but no one paid attention to his ravings.

"Do you ken?" Laurna wiped her eyes and leaned closer. "Can he be healed?"

"I don't know. I ken only a few survive a wound such as his."

Bohan approached and handed me one of the boar's tusks from the monster's head. "Eadan brought them back for us. I've never seen the like." He turned his sideways. It was as long as a man's forearm. "Still, the trophy gives me no joy."

I nodded agreement.

Father groaned and balled up the fur coverlet with one hand. Yet his eyes remained closed. Even before this accident, I'd seen the wear of years on him. Now the light from the nearby fire and open door showed too well the lines and cracks of weathered skin. His frame, once sturdy and robust, had grown bent and hunched. His hair, once a rich brown covering his ears and neck, like my own, had lately thinned and turned white. And his scalp was now patchy and mottled.

"Certain now," said Bohan, "'tis the end of his reign. Sure now, and our *fine* will lose its status and the honor of bearing the Rí Tuath."

"That it will. I hear Cormag's already appointed Osgar to preside tonight." Osgar was Teague's brother, leader of his own *fine*, and for five years foster father to Bohan and me. As was our custom starting at age ten, each child spent time living with another *fine*.

"Uncle listens too well to the druids. It'll be all the worse for you now."

I shrugged. "'Tis what it is."

"'Tis said both brothers vied for Mother's heart," he said, "yet Father won her over. What was she like, this Hilde who died giving birth to me?"

I looked at Bohan and smiled. "You forget, I too barely knew her. I remember her only as kind and loving. Yet the night she died is clear in my mind, the night my baby brother came into the world." I nudged him with an elbow. "I'll never forget Father's tears. I'd never seen him cry before."

"I remember only Maeve and her long, red hair. And her songs. How I liked her songs."

"Aye, she was the mother we knew." My glance drifted to the closely woven thatch of the walls, hung with the skins of boars, sheep, cows, two bags of herbs, and a trio of spears. Seeing this familiar sight and thinking of her, I sank deeper into the furs, my muscles relaxing. "She sang so quietly to us before we slept. And her voice. How it soothed and comforted. So tender and devoted she was. Yet for Father, she was a disappointment—she bore him no children. Still, he loved her dearly."

"No one should die like she did." Bohan shook his head. "Raving with brain fever. Isolated from everyone in the milk house. I was but a wee lad, and oh, how I cried at the change the fever wrought in her."

"Father was so good to her. Bringing her strong mead to help her sleep. Even sleeping beside her."

"Aye. He tended to her until the end."

"Why did he na take another wife?" asked Laurna.

"He did have a first wife," I said, "but she—Aideen was her name—was frail, also barren, and died young of the coughing sickness. Then came Hilde, who died, then Maeve. After that, the druids told him every woman to lay beside him would also die. Father believed them. He vowed never to take another wife.

Now he will not talk about this. It was hard on him—having no woman by his side all those years. I learned this only from Osgar late one night after he'd drunk too much ale."

As I finished, Father thrashed and mumbled something incoherent. We watched him a while in silence. Suddenly, he ceased tossing, laid his hands beside him atop the furs, and opened his eyes. He caught my gaze, then Bohan's, then Laurna's.

"How do you feel, my lord?" I asked. "You've slept all afternoon."

"My leg. I still feel it. But I ken it's gone ahead of me to the Otherworld?"

I could only nod, my eyes welling with tears. Laurna knelt and offered him a cup of mead.

"*Popaeg*?" he asked.

She shook her head. With difficulty, he sat, took the cup, and drank greedily. Laurna offered him a wooden spoon and a bowl of mutton stew. He ate only a few spoons full then set the bowl aside, wiping his mouth with a sleeve. "The council meeting? Is it canceled?"

"'Tis not. Cormag's appointed Osgar to lead."

He stared at me so long, I thought his mind had drifted off again. Then he shifted. "My sons, I've been a fool. The druids have taken what's na theirs to take—power from the council. And the sacrifices—" He motioned to Laurna for more mead, and she gave him another long drink. "They come too often now. Every two years. 'Tis too soon. We should've said something."

"A powerful sorcerer he is, my lord," said Laurna. "'Twasn't much anyone could've done. Even now, what can anyone do?"

"Thank you, child, for your support, but 'tis the duty of a Rí Tuath to stand against those who threaten the *tuath*. And sure, I ken now that's what they've done. And my inaction, the council's inaction, has led to this." He waved a hand toward his missing leg. "Spells against the son, working instead against the father. A curse to send evil spirits into a beast and the wild creature brings down the very leader of the council."

"We don't know his spells did this." I motioned toward his leg, wrapped in leaves Mungan had dressed with some foul-smelling ointment.

"'Twas so, my son. I've seen it before. Sure now, and the spell was meant for you, na me. But look what's happened. I'll na be there tonight and Osgar's ears—

bless his hairy, difficult head—are easily bewitched by druid talk. Sure, and the end of it 'tis this—it all works against you, Taran." Then he closed his eyes and winced, either from the thought he'd failed us or from the pain. I knew not which. He lay back on his bed and was still so long, I began preparing another mug with *popaeg*. His white pallor, sweating brow, and poor appetite—all signs of a bad healing. Then he opened his eyes and waved away the drink.

"You were the best leader we ever had," said Laurna.

Father smiled. "Sure, and I'm the *only* leader you've ever known, child. But I appreciate your words. Aye, that I do. You'll make a fine wife for Taran. I reckon you'll bear him many sons and daughters. May the gods—and Crom Cruach!— let me live to the wedding."

Now Laurna smiled. "You'll see us wed, my lord. I'll hide offerings this very night in the forest to ask the spirits for healing. But do me well and tell this headstrong son of yours to behave himself tonight. He's whispered foolish ideas of standing up against the druids."

Father caught my glance and frowned. "My son, donna do such a thing. Tonight is na the time for a challenge. First, you must sit on the *comhairle*, become a respected member, a leader of men. Then someday you can lead the others. And they must be led slowly, Taran. Lead them, guide them. And only then, take back the power lost to the druids. But that time, 'tis na tonight."

"But Father, how can we wait any longer? I fear the *tuath* will never recover from this evil."

"Sure, and you're headstrong, impatient, and filled with the energy and certainty of youth, just like your betrothed has said. Listen to me, Taran mac Teague, and do what I ask. Wait. Watch. Later—that's the time to make your move. Na tonight. Not now."

"Thank you, my lord." Laurna leaned down to hug him. "'Tis just what the lad needed to hear."

He smiled but then a spasm shot through him. He winced, closed his eyes, and with sudden force, gripped the pine logs framing the bed. This time, when I offered him *popaeg*, he sat up and drank deeply. He laid back and closed his eyes. Within moments, he was asleep.

Then the elderly Sileas, mother to us all, appeared, bearing three bowls of steaming mutton stew, floating with onions and turnips. "Sure now, and you three have been in here with Teague all afternoon. He'll be sleeping now. Go outside and get some fresh air. I'll na be hearing otherwise." She handed us each a bowl and a wooden spoon, giving us no choice but to obey.

She pointed to my stew. "'Tis the end of last fall's turnips and onions. Saved them for you, Taran, for your special day." She winked.

Outside, away from the entrance, we sat on wooden logs and ate. Above us, a gray cloud, like dirty, unwashed sheep's wool, raced across a barren blue sky, hurrying its dark shadow over the village roundhouses. My gaze followed the shadow as it blackened the path between houses, raced across the field and touched the great fort's plateau. The shade reached the fort's perimeter and its ring of massive log spikes, sunken deep and slanted into the earth. It crossed the drawbridge, the only entrance. Then it dimmed the *tuath's* most feared and prized possession: the gold-covered obelisk of Crom Cruach.

When the shadow passed, the sun burned down and touched The Bent and Bloody One. Even from this distance, his stone of gold, sticking at an angle from the earth, flickered as if alive. Around it in a wide circle, six towering stone slabs stood guard. Beside it lay a stone altar, announcing that *here* death ruled.

As if sensing my thoughts, Bohan turned to me. "Inside, you told Father the druids were doing us evil—evil we'd never recover from. What did you mean?"

I set my empty bowl aside then caught Bohan's and Laurna's gazes. "Cormag and the druids are like that shadow. They darken all they touch."

"You'd better be careful," said Bohan. "No one's ready for that kind of talk. Druids have been casting spells to get their way since the Tuatha Dé Danann came to Ériu and then sailed to Inis Creig. 'Tis the way of our people."

"And a way leading us to ruin. I need to tell you both a tale so you'll understand. Something, I know not what, is warning me to tell it to you. And today. 'Tis the darkest secret of the druids. A secret I was sworn never to reveal."

"Brother, if you've been sworn to silence, then you'd better na tell us."

"Nay, the both of you need to ken where the druids' sacrifices could lead."

Laurna wrapped herself in both arms and frowned. "Tell us then, if you must."

"Cormag himself told me the tale. 'Twas a night like last evening, cold and clear with a full moon. He led me away from the village to a lonely clearing in the pines, and sat me down on a rock. I was his acolyte in training, nearing the end of my time with him. He said it was time I learned the dread secret of the *Oíche dar data Marú*—the Night of the Killing. Have you ever heard of it?"

"I have." Bohan shook his mop of red hair up and down. "Barra, the old one who went senile, mentioned the term once in a moment of clarity. But others quickly silenced him."

"'Tis so. Only a few of the elders remember what their fathers hinted about that time. Either they refuse to believe, or they believe and look on the story with dread."

"Then why tell us now?" asked Laurna. "Aren't some things better left forgotten?"

"Not if we're headed there again."

"Then tell us." She folded her hands again and looked away from me. "You're set on it anyway."

"'Tis the truth, Laurna. We must face it."

"Go ahead then, but be quick."

"'Twas long ago, in our great-grandfather's time. For years, the crops had been bad, the animals infertile, and the people sick—nothing on our island has really changed since then. After many years of this, the druids decided to make an offering to Crom Cruach like nothing ever seen. A sacrifice so big, The Bent and Bloody One would surely have to bless the *tuath* with prosperity and wealth. They waited until after the harvest, until the night of *Samain*, the celebration of Winter's Begin. I'm told it had to occur on one of two nights—*Samain* or *Beltane*—when the spirits of the Otherworld are closest to our world and most active.

"All that day they chopped wood for the fires. They made two great piles on either side of the stone altar. Then the druids went to each roundhouse and took the firstborn child from every mother's arm. Fully one-third of the clan's children.

"On the night he became drunk, I asked Osgar about it. He told me the women wept, pleaded, and fell on their knees, but even this didn't stop the druids from what they were about to do. Cormag never told me about this—how long the women begged or how bitterly they wept."

Bohan's jaw tensed while Laurna's face scrunched into a frown.

"By the setting sun, they gathered the *tuath* at the Circle of Stones like we've done so many times. Then they sacrificed those children, one-by-one, on the altar of Crom Cruach. The druids killed them all. All for The Bent and Bloody One. The men had to tend the fires until morning, just to burn all the bodies. For months afterward, the smell of burnt flesh hung about the spot.

"And this is why, today, someone needs to speak up. And soon. For what happened then could happen again."

"What you say—it canna be." Laurna's voice went soft, her eyes moist. "They'd never have done such a thing."

"If they did," said Bohan, slamming a fist into an open palm, "if so, then sure . . . surely the druids knew what they were doing. Sure then . . . the crops improved and the animals bore healthy young?"

I shook my head, no.

"I canna believe it. You'd best not be spreading this story, Taran. Especially tonight. I donna want to hear more tales like this." Then Bohan leaped up and stalked away.

"Your brother's right, Taran. No matter what happened back then—if 'tis true—nothing like it will ever happen again. But you think and speak of these things now, right before your ceremony as if you're planning something. Even with Cormag and the druids against you. Even with the spell they put on you this morning. Taran, promise me. Will you be silent tonight?"

I looked long at her, then forced out the words. "I . . . I promise."

"Good. The sun's getting low. It's time we head to the fort."

I nodded and we walked the path between houses, across heather to the drawbridge and the Circle of Stones where the clan and druids were already gathering.

But the closer my feet took me to Crom Cruach's stone of evil, the more uneasy I became. About my promise to Laurna. About what Cormag might do. But most of all, about the darkness spreading over my clan.

CHAPTER 4

At the Stone of Crom Cruach

Only too well do I remember the events of the evening I am about to relate. A disc of setting sun hung low and red over the distant sea, so low it cast shadows through the upright stones of the great circle rising from the fort's high plateau. On the opposite horizon, a dim half-moon peeked over the mountain. A beam of sunlight shot through a gap in the stones, touching the bright obelisk and the people gathering around it.

The stone of Crom Cruach, covered with hammered gold, rose gleaming and shimmering from the earth. Carved onto each side were the figures of animals and men, fish and birds, images of the sun and moon, earth and sky. On all of Inis Creig, we valued nothing more than the golden obelisk of Crom Cruach. It had taken decades of trade to gather enough gold to cover it—a dear cost, indeed. As tall as a man, it stuck out of the earth at a sharp angle. The crooked god. The bent one. The bloody one. That was what we called him. Beside it lay wood set for a fire, and a flat altar and a large pedestal, both of rough-hewn stone.

When all were gathered, Cormag rose like a wraith from the crowd. His thin, gaunt frame wore a smooth, goatskin tunic, painted with the figures of red, yellow, and black animals. Animals of the forest and sea, representing their spirits. The likenesses of a tree, a stream, and a mountain—and the gods for each. The garment's colors contrasted sharply with the bleached pallor of his skin and his mane of thin, white hair. He stepped onto the pedestal. In the sun's dying light, his pink eyes appeared almost red. With a hint of disdain, he glanced over the crowd. His forehead, always wet with perspiration, shone in the twilight. He took his staff, raised it high, and spoke.

"We gather before Crom Cruach, the god of the sun, in the time before day gives way to night, in the time before he sleeps, when his terrible anger is weakest. We plead for his blessings and offer sacrifice to avert his wrath. Today also, the *comhairle* must decide whether or na Taran, son of Teague, would be added to their number. We donna make the decision lightly."

Now the sun was setting fast. As he spoke, members of Sionn's *fine* started the log fires just beyond the circle. Soon, blazing light shot through three equidistant gaps between the pillars, meeting at the center, at the gleaming idol of The Bent and Bloody One.

Cormag lowered his staff, the signal for the ceremony to begin. At his nod, the other four druids brought a goat's kid, its firstborn. They lifted the bleating animal onto the long, stone altar. Then the druids Doiurchu and Mungan twisted a rope around its neck, pulled it tight, and with the kid kicking and struggling between them, they strangled it. Pudgy Doiurchu laid the carcass atop the woodpile on the stone table's other side. Yellow-haired Mungan plunged a long, serrated knife into its chest.

"Three deaths, three!" cried Cormag as he lit the fire with a torch. "A rope to kill once! A knife to kill twice! A fire to kill thrice! Three deaths, three!" He pleaded with the sun god to spare us his wrath, to give us good crops and fertility. Then he called for dancing.

While the kid's body burned and the fires raged, the *tuath* danced inside the Circle of Stones. I danced with the rest. With an effort, I kept my mind closed to Crom Cruach's dark allure. I would dance, but unlike the night when Gormal's baby burned on the altar instead of a goat, I wouldn't again give in to his black and terrible spirit, nor let him enter my soul.

When the dancing finished, it was dark beyond the fires at the circle's edge, and my time had come. The crowd gathered again around the platform as Osgar stepped forward. Osgar now counted Cormag a member of his *fine*.

"Taran, son of Teague. Step forward."

I walked out of the crowd and climbed beside him on the stone platform.

28

"It has been voiced that you, Taran, should join the council. You are of age, you are next in line, and your father—may he soon recover—approves. How say you, nephew? Would you join the leaders of the Carraig Beag?"

I glanced at the crowd's faces, flickering and shimmering in the firelight. I swallowed. "I would."

"Then I will ask the questions all must answer if they would join. Will you provide for the common good, protect and serve the Carraig Beag no matter the cost, and seek their welfare at all times?"

"I will."

"Will you hunt with the clan, fish with the clan, and share your kills and plunder with the clan?"

"I will."

"Will you join with others of the *comhairle* when we meet in common council, to carefully consider the clan's welfare, hear the druids' council, decide the clan's future, and then make recommendations to the Rí Tuath?"

"I will."

"Your answers are good and accepted." Osgar then turned to Cormag. "Druid, ask now what you require of a member of our body."

Osgar stepped off the pedestal, and Cormag took his place. A tall man, he glared down at me. His eyes gleamed red in the firelight, fixing my gaze. I didn't look away but held his stare. All I had to do was answer his questions as expected. He'd never mention last night's incident in public. Powerful though he was, even if he came here with plans to keep me off the council because of what I'd seen—if I answered correctly, he couldn't flout custom and tradition. Not before the *comhairle*.

"Taran, son of Teague, will you serve Crom Cruach, the great spirit of the sun? Will you worship him, and if asked, will you sacrifice your firstborn to him? Will you give him the first and finest of your herd? Will you acknowledge him as the giver of life, the one who protects us and who averts his terrible wrath from us?"

He'd spoken the words he was required to speak and no more.

I opened my mouth to reply, but it was as if a gaping hole had opened before me. I felt as though I stood on the edge of a precipice. How I spoke next would decide my fate for the rest of my life. I looked at my people's faces, wavering in the firelit shadows. All were facing me, awaiting my answer. I saw Laurna, her gaze catching mine, desperately seeking, asking, pleading with me to say, "I will."

Truth was the problem. How could I pledge myself to Crom Cruach? I started to speak, but my tongue refused to obey. If I spoke, I imagined I'd step off the abyss into darkness, an awful darkness of the soul. Then who or what would I become? Murmurs rippled through the crowd.

"Taran mac Teague, if you canna say, 'I will,' then what are your questions? Do you have a problem with your duties to Crom Cruach? Or to the *comhairle*? If so, now is the time to ask. Let everyone hear."

"I do have questions." My chest constricted, my brow grew wet and hot. I'd promised Laurna not to speak out. But if I didn't speak now, if I abandoned the truth when it was needed most, what would become of me? Or the *tuath*? The druids' evil could not go unanswered forever. Someday, someone had to stand up to them.

"Then ask. A man's heart should be free of questions at a time like this." Cormag's thin lips turned up in a sneer as if he knew what was in my heart and was hoping I would trap myself. He rubbed his hands together.

I wanted to say, "I will." It was what I'd promised Laurna. How could I break my promise? I tried to speak the words, but my mouth would not release them to my lips, as if they alone, in all the language of the Carraig Beag, were stuck in my throat.

"Speak! A man who would join the *comhairle* must na be a coward." Cormag held his thin smile.

I clenched my fists. "My question is this. If Crom Cruach is our protector, our savior, then why are the Carraig Beag so . . . so . . . cursed?"

Gasps came from those around me, followed by a sudden, unnatural quiet. Beside me was Cormag's heavy breathing. On the perimeter, a log fell into the flames, sending up crackling, popping sparks, as if to emphasize my revolt.

"What do you mean by that?" Cormag's voice rose. Now his eyebrows arched, his lips drew taut. "Explain."

"What I mean is this—what kind of fortune has he brought us? If he's our protector, then why do the berries give out before their season? Why do our oats fall off the stalk before harvest? And why do our goats produce so little milk?" I'd started and now couldn't stop.

"Tell me why, after weeks at sea, do our men return with hardly enough fish for the summer, let alone any to salt for winter? How many times have we faced the winter, hungry, weak, not knowing how many would see the spring? Why does The Bent and Bloody One, if he is our protector, ask us to slaughter our firstborn—mere babies—on his altar every few years? Do we refuse? Nay, we do not. Why does our protector, if he is such, ask so terrible a price?

"If he protects us, then why—after we kill our infants for him—why does he let even more babies die in their beds of the coughing sickness and the oldest among us wither away before the fullness of their years? Why do the boars rage through our gardens and why can't we kill them all? Why are we so cursed with accidents? Today my father was gored. It must have been by Crom Cruach's will, for surely no druid would have cast such a spell against our Rí Tuath. If such a spell were cast, the man who did it would surely be an enemy of the clan, would he not?" I gave a sidelong glance to Cormag.

"So it must have been Crom Cruach's will alone that sent the boar. Just as last year, Crom Cruach willed Ronan to fall off a cliff and die. In the last five years, I could name a dozen more who died by accident. If Crom Cruach truly watches over us, then why, I ask, does he make our fortunes so miserable?"

Cormag stood on the platform, staring at me, his face, pale and white, losing what little blood it possessed. He probably didn't expect such an attack. The chief druid wouldn't admit it, but now everyone in the *tuath* knew that Mungan, his second in command, was the one who'd cast the spell against me. But I'd spoken against Cormag in such a way he couldn't admit what he'd done.

But I'd only begun. I'd already broken my promise to Laurna. With the memory of last night hurtling me on, I rushed down the path I'd started. For no matter what happened here, Cormag might still try to keep his spell intact and consider murder.

"Then there's this: These ceremonies are simply wrong. So many times when we gather to dance and sacrifice, my thoughts fall into a dark and troubled place. Last year, when we sacrificed Gormal's baby, we all danced with abandon and glee at the child's death. You know we did. An evil heart, a wild joy possessed us, and it came from the blood of an innocent child. And later, I knew a dark presence had invaded me. I asked myself, if Crom Cruach is our protector, if he's looking out for our welfare, then why does he do this to us? Why does he cause the death of a child to fill our hearts with evil? Shouldn't he fill us instead with love, comfort, and peace? Shouldn't a protector want life for us instead of death?

"That's why some of us secretly dread these ceremonies. Why we fear even to enter this fort and this Circle of Stones and approach this bent stone of gold. Because we know once we start, his evil presence will worm in and become a part of us. Others have felt it too. When we come to this place, desolation enters our souls. You cannot deny it. At least for some of you—for those whom Crom Cruach does not already own."

A low murmur, a noise like wind across still waters, swept through the crowd, but I went on.

"All this tells me we've been deceived. And it leads me to ask, is Crom Cruach really the god of the sun? What if this one whom we worship is not a god or a protector, but something much, much worse? What if, instead, The Bent and Bloody One is a dark spirit inhabiting this stone beside me? What if he's a being created by evil itself? What if Crom Cruach is really a . . . a . . . *demon*!"

The crowd became like an unsettled sea, whispers bursting into speech, turning into shouts, rippling like a human wave from one end to the other. Heads shook and eyes turned to the ground with frowning faces.

My glance caught Laurna's. Tears wet her eyes. Her head shook slowly back and forth.

Then a voice raised against me, Gormal's. "My baby didn't die in vain!"

Shock coursed through me.

"Sacrilege!"

"Banish him. That's the punishment."

"Heresy!"

"Banish him to the sea!"

It struck me then—what I'd said, what I'd done. I'd uttered words few there could understand. I'd said things many might have whispered to themselves before they went to sleep, but no one would dream of speaking out loud, certainly not at a solemn ceremony of entry into the council. It was the worst sin I could commit, in the worst possible place. I felt the blood draining from my head. What had I done?

A strained smile now turned up the corners of Cormag's pale lips. He clasped his hands together again. "Taran, son of Teague, you have rejected Crom Cruach, the god of the sun, our great protector. In all the time I've lived on Inis Creig, this my home, never have I heard such words of blasphemy against the one to whom we owe our existence. I call the druids and the council to meet, right now, right here, to pass judgment. You will stand and wait for our decision."

Then, he beckoned to Osgar, who, as he gave me a last, sad backward glance, shook his head. The two walked to one of the fires to wait for the druids and the council. They spoke in low whispers. Heads shook back and forth. Foreheads creased. Hands waved. And fingers pointed. Among them was the tall, black-haired figure of Eadan mac Gaeadan. He alone seemed to argue against the rest, especially against the druids, who would be of one mind under Cormag.

I turned my gaze from the white-robed men and the council toward those closest to me, people I'd known all my life. But now as I glanced over them, they appeared strange. Their faces expressed surprise, shock, sadness, disgust, and aye, even hate. How could they turn so quickly? How could a few questions—questions I knew others also asked—cause such turmoil? Sileas, shaking her head, frowning. Bohan, his crinkled forehead and pained, narrowed eyes. He obviously couldn't believe such a thing had happened to one of our *fine*, to me, his elder brother. And Laurna, tears streaming down her cheeks, glancing down, shaking her head, then raising her glance to me with pleading, desperate eyes.

I stood there until Cormag strode through the crowd and mounted the platform. The *tuath* fell silent.

"Taran, son of Teague, you have blasphemed against Crom Cruach. You have insulted and rejected our god and the way of our people. The *comhairle* has met, has heard the judgment of the druids, and has accepted it. At first light, you will go from here, taking a shore *curragh*—but without any sail. Tomorrow, you will leave this land of Inis Creig and the clan of the Carraig Beag, for you are banished forever. You may never return.

"May Manannán mac Lir grant mercy on you, for if you reach Connacht in such a *curragh*—and that's doubtful—it will only be by the sea god's will and na by any skill of yours."

He gave me a final thin leer and left.

I'd always been well-liked, but now the people seemed to stare at me with new, questioning eyes. Faces contorted with disapproval and even pain. Heads shook or turned to whisper to their neighbors. Some gave me furtive glares. As I tried, unsuccessfully, to catch their glances, I felt sick, betrayed. These were people I'd known all my life, and suddenly, they seemed embarrassed even to look at me. Slowly, they began to drift out of the circle.

My legs wouldn't move. I tried to understand. What had just happened? I'd been banished. Would I never see my home again? Would Laurna and I now never marry? Would I never lead a *fine*? *Aye, that's what it meant, Taran mac Teague, and you came round to it powerful slow, indeed.* Tears came to my eyes. Was there nothing I could do? Too late, my father's words, his plea for caution, returned to me. What had I done?

A line of torches led across the dark heath to the village. I sat on the stone's edge and lowered my head into my hands.

"I . . . I am sorry for you, Taran," came the voice of the one I loved, standing now beside me. But in her voice, I heard tears. "Both for you . . . and for us. I canna understand any of this."

She and Raef were all that remained of the crowd. Raef came now to lay his head at my feet. As the night grew cool with dew, the crickets chirped, and Laurna settled beside me.

"Why did you do this, Taran? In another month, we would've been married. We could've been so happy." Her voice choked. "What . . . will happen to us?"

I looked at her face, at the tears shimmering on her cheeks, and my heart felt as if it were crushed by a boulder. I opened my mouth to speak, but could only close my eyes and turn my head. Indeed, what would happen to us? We were about to be torn from each other, and it was my fault. I shook my head, only just beginning to understand.

"'Tis a way . . ." she choked on the words, "a way they'll let you back, you know?"

"What way?"

"The right of *Beart Uasal*." She wiped the tears from her eyes with a vicious swipe, grasping onto her idea as if it could undo what had happened. "If you do some great deed, and the news of it echoes throughout the land, you can return.

But you'll have to make amends for the wrong you did. Only then will they restore you."

"And what would be the amends?"

"You ken what it is. Bow down to Crom Cruach." She held my glance with intense, desperate eyes.

I turned my face away, wiping my eyes. Had Laurna noticed my tears? They'd come on suddenly. "Tomorrow, I must leave. How can I think of such things now?"

Laurna put an arm around me. "I . . . I . . . know." She caught her breath as if stifling a sob. She was silent a moment. When she resumed, her voice took on the tone of a desperate plea. "I can wait for you, Taran. I will never marry. I'll wait for you to do your great deed and return without these thoughts about questioning the ways of our people."

I looked into her eyes, so moist and pleading. I hugged her, then whispered, "You shouldn't wait, Laurna. I may never come back."

"Oh, Taran." Her arms tightened around my shoulders. Her voice was barely a whisper in my ear. "A shore *curragh* is a wee boat. The sea between here and Ériu is so . . . vast. What if there's a storm? What if Manannán mac Lir is angry with you? And why did they allow you na even a sail? Why'd they do that?"

I shrugged. Obviously, Cormag's doing, a way to ensure I'd never reach land.

She pulled away and gripped my shoulders. "Promise me you'll cross the sea and live!"

I tried to force a smile. "I promise."

"You'll na break it as you did tonight?"

"I will no—" But the breath caught in my throat, "I will not break that promise. I will cross the sea. Even in a wee *curragh*."

Laurna smiled through her tears and then pulled me close. But she was right. Again, I'd made a promise I didn't know how to keep. To sail all the way to Ériu, across a vast ocean, in a craft as small as a shore *curragh*, without a sail—ah, that would take a miracle indeed!

Chapter 5

Departure

I woke to find two druids beside my bed—Mungan and Doiurchu. In spring, the day's light stretched ever longer into our sleeping time until the Beltane ceremony, when our nights were cut nearly in half. After all the events of last evening, it seemed too early to rise.

"Gather your things, whatever you need for the journey." Mungan poked at me. "Cormag says you must leave within a pot's boil."

Mungan was quickly becoming second to Cormag. He mimicked everything the pale-skinned leader said or thought, even trying to smile like him, making his lips so taut, they nearly disappeared. Now he hovered at the foot of my bed with Cormag's scowl.

I rubbed my eyes and sat up. I'd slept poorly, tossing, thinking over last night's events. Others in the house were just beginning to wake.

"Can a man prepare for this alone?" I asked. "Without a pair of mother hens clucking and pecking at him?"

"Come on." Doiurchu pulled Mungan by the sleeve of his tunic and led him toward the door.

Mungan hesitated but followed.

I found the large boar's-hide bag I always took on fishing trips. It was thick and waterproof, and I stuffed it with lengths of rope, my long cape, and my knife. I grabbed my sword, bow, quiver, and spear, and then filled the largest water-skin I could find.

Sileas approached me. "Sure, and yesterday I thought you should na have said what you did." Then she lowered her voice to a whisper. "But on second sight,

I've come round to this: 'Tis surely what I've often thought myself, and today I'm glad you said it. But na glad at all you'll be facing the sea alone." Then she kissed my cheek and brought me strips of dried, salted fish, a small wheel of cheese, and a round of rare wheat bread.

I put it in my bag and, in return, kissed her cheek.

Bohan stopped at my bed. "Father is awake. I told him what happened. He wishes to speak with you."

I nodded and finished collecting my belongings.

"I fear today he has the fever."

I winced. A fever. In the next few days, Father would be fighting for his life. And I wouldn't be at his side.

"I donna understand you, brother." Bohan followed me across the roundhouse. "You could've joined the council and become this *fine*'s leader and eventually Rí Tuath. All you had to do was answer Cormag's questions the right way. But you did na such thing. One moment your future was bright. The next . . ." He spread his hands and shook his head. "And now I'll never see you again."

With one hand I gripped his shoulder. "I'm sorry." I hugged him and then released him.

He frowned, avoided my gaze, and waved me off. "Go to him. He's waiting for you." He whirled and headed for the door. I didn't want to quit my brother on these terms but had no time for anything but leaving.

I took my things to my father's bed and sat down.

"I heard what happened." Father grimaced. Thin, gray hair was pasted to a forehead glistening with sweat. "And I'm struck to my soul with disappointment. You could have waited and become the leader of the *comhairle*. If only you'd endured. You were my best hope for our family, my son. You alone, of all the men, could have led our *fine*, even our *tuath*, to a good future, a bright future."

His disappointment cut my heart like a knife. In all the Carraig Beag, I respected my father more than anyone. I realized his hope for the clan's future rested on me alone.

Then his eyes wandered off, seeking something across the room, or on the ceiling—I know not what. His eyes were once like mine, "brown, deep as a forest, and earnest," as Laurna called them. Now they were hazy yellow, dimmed, unfocused. For a moment, I wasn't sure if he was still alert.

His glance returned. "But I'm na surprised at what happened. When you think you're right, you donna compromise. You're na a man to bend or bow to the false ideas of lesser men. And Cormag is certainly such a lesser man."

"Still, I've let you down." I lowered my head and closed my eyes.

"Taran, donna regret what you did. Donna let my words discourage you. For I sense your fate is far stronger and more important than any on this island now ken. 'Tis just a feeling, mind you, but something I sense. You are meant for great deeds, my son."

My heart lifted at these words of encouragement. Then he moved his legs, both good and bad, over the side of the bed. He gasped in obvious pain, closed his eyes, and with an effort of will, waited for it to subside. Then he raised an amulet from around his neck, opened his eyes, and locked my gaze with intensity.

"I give this to you now." A tremor shook his hand as he passed me a circle of dull gray metal, its face carved with the faint image of a tree and a mountain. A leather strap fitted through a small hole at the top so it could hang around the neck. I couldn't remember a time when he had not worn the ornament.

"It's heavy. Is it lead?"

"'Tis that. But only the cover. Beneath is one round disc of solid gold. The Romans use it in commerce—those who conquered the land of Bryton. It's called an *aureus,* to be used for trade. The journey to Connacht will be difficult. You remember how to find the stars of the Hunter?"

"I do."

Suddenly, his eyes seemed brighter, more alert. He gripped one of my hands and squeezed, mustering what strength was left him. "Even leaving early this morning, because you must paddle, you'll na arrive before nightfall, nor even the midday after. At night, you must travel by the Hunter. His stars will show you the way. But you are strong. I ken you'll make it."

"Thank you, Father."

"In Connacht, beware the clans of the coast. Some are without honor, pirates fit only for robbing and killing. And taking slaves. You would trade with them at your peril. But then there are *tuatha* like the one at Foclut. Do you remember the village?"

"I do."

39

"If you can find your way there, they are honorable. They'll na take you a slave."

"I'll find it."

He took several deep breaths, grabbed the bed frame for support, and closed his eyes in pain. Then he forced them open and went on, "If you donna find Foclut and land elsewhere, beware. Use the *aureus* and buy a horse—if 'tis still the going price. But I warn you, my son, travel in Ériu is dangerous. If a traveler is na a poet or druid or emissary of a king, then as soon as he leaves the protection of one kingdom, he's fair game for capture in the next. The deserted lands between *tuatha* are no safer. Take the white druid's robe you possess. Wear it always. Tell all who ask you're a druid. It may protect you."

"But I'm no longer one of them."

"If you donna land in Foclut, it may help you avoid capture."

"Then I'll do as you say."

"Do you remember the right of *Beart Uasal*?"

I almost smiled. "Laurna reminded me of it last night."

"A good lass. Then have hope in that. You may be redeemed yet. Always, you must have hope. I know you'll have courage. Go now, for they're waiting. You've been the best son a man could have. The *fine* and even the *tuath* will be much the worse without you. But I fear the old boar finally knocked me off my perch and I'll na be here to welcome your return."

My eyes were already moist, and now he talked of dying. I took my father's hands, hot to the touch, and leaned over to hug him. But the speech had spent his strength. He collapsed onto the bed and closed his eyes. I picked up my things, returned to my bed, and shoved the white druid's robe into my bag. Then, instead of leaving, I went back to Father's bedside. This was the last time I might see him alive. I watched for a time, hoping he would wake, but he remained fast asleep, his breath coming in short, labored gasps.

We live and then we die. One moment we eat, drink, love, and the next we're as still and cold as winter ice. We labor to build family, accumulate wealth, or create power, prestige, or fame. But in the end, we all—from the lowest *bothach* to the highest *flaith*, and the Rí Tuath who rules—return to dust. In the end, there's only the worm and the grave. On this earth, that is our destiny.

And afterward—well, I believed at the time eternity lay with Manannán mac Lir, god of the sea and the Otherworld. And to that place, under his dim and capricious rule, I greatly feared to go. My father was one of the best men I had ever known. Now I feared for him, this Rí Tuath of the Carraig Beag. I feared soon he would go to that eternal reign where Manannán ruled by whim and wile. For such was the world I lived in then.

I put my lips to his forehead. I took them away and they burned with his fever. I wiped my eyes with the back of one hand and, hurrying, left the house.

Outside, Raef was waiting. He bounded up, put his paws on my chest, and licked my face. I ruffled the collie's fur, distracted and filled with a sadness so deep I cannot describe it.

A large crowd had gathered outside the roundhouse to see me off. Nothing like this had happened on Inis Creig for decades, and it appeared they wanted to watch every detail of the banishment. I knew after my departure I'd become the stuff of stories told round the fires at night: The tale of a man almost appointed to the council, who threw it all away with a fiery speech against Crom Cruach, risking the wrath of The Bent and Bloody One and the druids. Oh, the disgrace! Oh, the blasphemy!

Within the crowd, I saw Laurna, Bohan, Eadan, many others, and of course, Cormag.

The chief druid approached. "You are heavy laden, Taran. Perhaps your *curragh* will sink even before you leave sight of Inis Creig?" A few in the crowd laughed at the jibe. Then he led the procession across the heath to the shore trail.

On the hike down the mountain, I was silent. Laurna walked close beside me, squeezing one hand and never letting go. Raef trotted on the other side, his tail wagging at this unexpected morning adventure. The thought suddenly struck me—this might be the last time I would ever see him, for I could not take him to sea. A pang of grief pierced me like a knife. I'd raised him from a pup. My constant companion, ever happy, ever eager and ready to lick my face and lay his head upon my leg or chest when I sprawled on the hillside to think. My chest constricted and my eyes watered. He could not understand his master would soon leave him, perhaps forever. Was that it? Was this what bothered me so? Would he still be alive if I returned?

I was leaving behind everything and everyone I ever loved.

We left the pine forest and entered the oaks. We negotiated the rock trail down a gorge through the cliffs then stood on a pebbled beach.

"Say your good-byes now," said Cormag. "Be quick about it."

Laurna rushed to me and wrapped her arms tightly around my neck, making me drop my load. "I will wait for you," she said, her eyes wet. She kissed my cheeks and lips, my eyelashes, then again my lips. "No matter how long, I'll never marry another. You *will* come back. I feel it. And when you do, we'll marry."

"Don't wait for me, Laurna. I may not even make it to Connacht. If I do, it may be years before I can return. You'll become an old maid, waiting for a dead man."

"Donna say such things!" Her voice rose. She stamped one foot and pushed away from me, but only for a moment. "You promised."

"I did and I'm sorry. Forget what I said. I'll certainly cross the sea. But do not waste your days waiting for me. And now please do something for me. Take Raef. He has no one else to look after him, to feed him or pull the briars from his hair, or let him into the barn on the bitter days of snow. Will you take my dog for me, Laurna, and look after him as if he were your own?"

She looked at Raef, sitting at my feet. "I will. Whatever you want."

I knelt. Raef lifted a paw. Then he licked my face. For the last time, I hugged the dog, my constant companion. Then I rose, pulled Laurna close and kissed her long.

When we parted, tears tugged again at my eyes and my chest tightened. It was time to end this parting before it tore the heart from me.

Cormag pointed to the *curragh* they allowed me to use. A small boat, only eight feet long, not like the great sixty- and seventy-foot *curraghs* the men took out to sea to fish. A double layer of cowhide, stitched together with thongs and tarred at the seams, stretched over a wickerwork frame. A sturdy craft, sure, but a boat meant for the shoreline, not the vastness of the ocean.

I laid my gear in the bottom, carried the boat halfway into the water, then stepped inside. I grabbed the single paddle and pushed myself off. Small waves rocked the boat as they exhausted themselves on the rock-strewn shore. The smell of rotting kelp—strings of it crept between the stones on the beach—hung in the air.

I looked back. The crowd stared at me from the shore.

Cormag's pink eyes gleamed. He rubbed his hands together. "When Manannán mac Lir towers over you with foam and wave and wind, he'll find your *curragh* a small offering indeed. But maybe your death will serve as a sacrifice to the sea god and bring us good fishing."

"Your prediction will fail, druid." Laurna sent him a glance to freeze a river. "Taran will reach Connacht. I know it."

Cormag's smile was a thin sneer of disdain. "Your faith is misplaced, little maiden. Your future husband will become fish bait before the sun sets. Look at the sky. Even now a storm comes."

Their faces turned north where Cormag pointed. Dark clouds gathered there. Cormag glowered and gave me an upward wave of one hand. "Now away with you. Go and chase yourself off."

Tears rolled down Laurna's face as she snapped her head away from the druid and strode straight into the water up to her knees, wading beside my boat. She leaned over and gave me one last kiss, deep and long, then gazed into my eyes, pleading for something I couldn't give. At last, she released me. "I'll wait for you, Taran. No matter how long it takes."

All I could do was nod. My cheeks were wet as I pushed away from shore and paddled. I needed this departure to end.

I had to get beyond the breakers, crashing forty yards off shore. I paddled in earnest, heading straight into them. The boat rose into the foam of the first breaker, crashed down, then moments later, cleared. I turned around to see the crowd, distant now, watching me from shore. I sat floating for a short time, looking back on the people of my home.

Inis Creig. Everything I'd ever known. My *tuath*, my *fine*, the woman I loved, and Raef—none of whom I might ever see again. All I held dear torn from me. All because I believed Crom Cruach was not a god. I shook my head. How could I have thrown away my life, and Laurna's, on a few feelings, thoughts, and beliefs? Perhaps Bohan was right. Perhaps I just made the biggest mistake of my life.

The boat was drifting sideways, heading back into the breakers. I couldn't think about such things now. Under a darkening sky, I began paddling out of the harbor, toward the open sea.

PART II

In the Land of Ériu, A.D. 432

CHAPTER 6

The Sea

When the sun reached its zenith, noon by my reckoning, my arms already ached. I rested from paddling to eat a bit of bread and cheese and drink some water. I glanced again at the dark clouds gathering to the north. Still distant, they kept piling up and moving east. Maybe they would pass me by.

If only I had a sail, I could make better time. I fished the rope out of my pack and tied everything securely to the boat's wicker frame, especially winding the rope several times around the sheath and handle of my sword. But when my fingers touched the long spear, I had an idea.

I cut four pieces from the rope, pulled out my cape, and fastened a length to each corner. I tied these to the spear and hoisted it upright. The wind caught it and nearly pulled it out of my grasp. I'd made a sail! Though a poor substitute for the real thing, it did catch the wind and now the *curragh* leaped through the seas. But the wind's force wanted to pull me overboard, so I wedged the spear behind the center crossbar. With two ropes, I made guy lines leading from the top of the spear to the crossbar. Even so, I had to hold on to this contraption to keep it upright and in position.

The hours fled from midday and escaped into afternoon, and still the makeshift sail led me on. The storm passed to the north, leaving behind wide, choppy swells. My fingers grew cold, wet, and cramped holding the shaft, so I untied it, laid it down, and paddled for a while. Then I resumed sailing.

My woolen leggings were now soaked. With a free hand, I pulled my tunic closer around my neck. I was beginning to shiver.

Dusk turned into night, and I couldn't find the Hunter. The overcast sky revealed neither moon nor stars. What if I was headed in the wrong direction?

I dismantled the sail, wrapped the cape about myself, and waited for dawn. After eating some fish and bread, I drank, then lay in the bottom of the *curragh* trying unsuccessfully to sleep.

Half the night later, stars poked through the clouds and I rose. I searched the sky. There, the Hunter. With stiff, unresponsive fingers, I struggled to reassemble the sail and raise it into the wind. But after only a short time, clouds again obscured the stars. I pressed on until I became fearful of heading the wrong way. Then I lowered the sail.

Groggy from not having slept, I drifted into the gray light of dawn. I could now only guess the general direction of Ériu, for both sun and moon were hidden. I inspected the horizon. Far to what I believed to be north, dark clouds again gathered. I reassembled the sail and raised it into the wind, heading southeast.

As morning wore on, the skies darkened, the wind picked up, and it rained. The swells became deeper, farther apart. A spray of sea was carried ever on the wind, forcing me to squint. Frequently, I had to lower the cape and bail water from the *curragh*. The wind tore at my homemade sail, and ever so often I retied and strengthened the knots on my cape. Several times, a big gust lifted the spear and cape off the bottom, nearly carrying the whole thing away, but I held on. I hoped I was going in the right direction.

The swells became rolling hills of water. The *curragh* would rise to the top of one hill, then, as the boat fell into the trough, the horizon disappeared beyond a wall of water, appearing again at the peak of the next swell.

A man was never meant to travel alone so far from land, in such a small boat, in the grip of such a mighty sea. A man was meant to stand on solid ground, his feet on green earth, beneath the trees, with his *tuath* around him, and a *fine* and a wife to come home to at day's end. A man was never meant to face, alone, the wrath of Manannán mac Lir.

"Are you there?" I shouted to the sea god. "Answer me. But I think you are not there. I think you are nothing but wind and wave and sea."

I waited for an answer. None came.

"I will not pray to you," I shouted to the wind. "Do you hear me, Manannán mac Lir? You are not my god, and I will not pray to you, even if you do rule the Otherworld."

Again no answer came to my challenge. I sailed on. Perhaps I was mad then. I don't know.

But which way was I going? The wind might have shifted. I hadn't seen the Hunter for so long, I might not know north from south. If only I could determine the sun's position. Yet the sky remained overcast. I searched in all directions, my heart racing. It would be so easy to miss the land.

For a brief time, the rain stopped, the clouds lifted, and the sun warmed my face, raising my spirits. From its position, I reckoned I was heading southwest—away from my destination! The wind must have changed, and I'd spent too much time—half a day?—traveling the wrong way. Using one hand to pull on a guy line, while holding the spear's shaft with the other, I turned my sail to tack against the prevailing wind. Somehow, I had to make up for precious time lost.

Then the wind shifted toward the southeast, toward Ériu, just before the clouds closed in and the rain came again.

The day wore on and the wind's strength increased. The rain came in sheets now, chilling me to the core. The *curragh* began to fill with seawater and I bailed frequently. Needing to rest my arms again, I undid the thongs securing the cape to the crossbar and lowered my makeshift sail toward the bottom of the boat. Just then a gust yanked the spear from my fingers. I stood up, lunged for it, and nearly fell overboard, but the sail was gone.

I watched helplessly as both cape and spear flew away on the wind. They crashed into the foamy sea some distance away. I grabbed my paddle and tried to steer toward it, but the *curragh* was moving too fast. The swells, not my paddling, steered me. There it floated, perhaps twenty yards distant, drifting quickly from sight.

In that wind, I needed to paddle steadily just to keep the boat headed straight into the swells. If I let the craft turn sideways to the wind, it might tip or become swamped when a gust caught it at the top of a wave.

Noon might have come and gone and I would not know. Hungry, I searched my pack, but long ago I'd eaten the last of the cheese and fish. My water was nearly gone. The remaining two mouthfuls of bread were soggy with saltwater. I threw them overboard. Every sailor knew the dangers of ingesting salt water.

Was I now so far from land I might never reach Connacht? How would I know if I'd missed it? The storm, not I, was in control. And what mercy would the sea god show me? If I were off course, I could do nothing about it. I shivered and stared helplessly at the mountains of water, swirling, foaming, tossing my boat with an evil will. A wave broke, sent foam into the *curragh*, and I grasped the crossbar with both hands. Long after it left, I still gripped the bar so hard my knuckles hurt. Would I die now? Was this to be the end of Taran mac Teague?

Then what? What would happen when I died? Was there an Otherworld where we would all live forever, as the druids promised? What would such a land look like if Manannán mac Lir ruled there in semidarkness, as the druids also taught? The sea god might be even worse than Crom Cruach, who himself was certainly a demon. The sea god was ever angry and violent. His realm on earth was dark, deep, filled with mystery and monsters. So why would the Otherworld be any different? How could it ever be a happy place?

No, in death, with the company of such a god, there would be no solace, no rest, only an eternity of—what? Twilight? Emptiness? Subjugation? Fear? I shuddered. Unless something happened quickly to change my fate, I might soon find the answers to my questions.

The moments bled into each other. The ceaseless paddling. Rain. Swells. Constant motion, up and down, over the waves. The wind stinging my eyes with salt. Weariness in my arms. Cramps in my legs. And the ever-present cold—all of it pressed down on me, warned me I was near the end of my strength. I trembled, wrapped my arms around my chest, hugging myself in a vain attempt to get warm.

My efforts against this storm, this sea, this wind, and this cold were useless. I would soon see the Otherworld I so feared. If only before I died, I could have learned something of the God Dughall spoke of—this God, who ruled over all. Did He rule over the demons too? During Dughall's time as a slave to the Romans, he'd learned many new things—this perhaps the greatest of all.

"Oh, great God, who rules over everything, I don't know You. Who are You?" I shouted at the wind. "If You are out there, I beg of You: Please save me from Manannán mac Lir and this terrible sea. I have no one else to turn to. Please help me!"

But no answer came to my request. I didn't know this God. I'd never made sacrifices to Him, or put offerings of food in secret forest places for Him. So why would He answer a stranger? He had no reason to do so. How foolish to call out to a God I didn't know. But I was desperate, perhaps a bit mad.

Much time passed—long or short, I was losing track—and the day began to darken. In the night, I'd be blind. Then I couldn't keep the *curragh* pointed into the swells. Soon it would all be over. I pictured my end. In the dark, the boat would surely rise to the top of a swell, flip over in the wind. Then I'd plunge into the deep. Soon after, the cold would suck the life from me.

For one moment, the rain stopped, the clouds lifted, and at the top of one swell, I saw a dark mass ahead. A great wall of clouds?

On the peak of the next swell, I saw it again. Not clouds, but cliffs! Dark cliffs rising from the sea. And was that the dim light of a fire flickering far to my left?

The rain came again in sheets, blocking everything from view. With energy born of hope, I paddled toward land.

The swells broke into waves, spinning the boat sideways. With every muscle taught and aching, I jerked the paddle through the water to bring the boat around. Another swell spun it again. Between breakers, I tried to bail, but it was useless. Curling, foaming water broke behind me, overtaking and crashing into the stern, flooding the *curragh*.

Chasing the swell came a mammoth, pounding, rushing wave. It lifted me high then flipped the boat. The waling hit my leg. Suddenly, I was in the air, and the boat was below me. I gasped for breath. Salt burned my throat. Was this the end? All happening too fast, I hit the water and went under. Oh, so cold. Cold piercing my flesh to the bone. Still underwater, I fought the urge to suck in air. At last, the surface. I gasped deep lungfuls of air. My eyes squinted against the salt and dark. My gaze jerked side-to-side, sought the *curragh*.

There, only feet away, flipped keel-side up. I reached underneath for a hold on the wicker frame. Another breaker crashed over me, churned me under, broke my grip, pulled me away. I couldn't lose the *curragh*. All my gear was tied to it. I struggled to the surface, sucking short, cold breaths of air and looked around. But in the darkness, I'd already lost it.

A third breaker pummeled me, then a fourth, and for one brief moment, my feet touched something solid on the bottom. I struggled for breath, trying to keep my head above the surface. Briefly, my toes scraped a boulder before my whole body was sucked under. My hands slammed against bottom rocks. I stood up, was knocked down and carried forward, then found myself swaying on a rocky bottom in knee-high surf. From there, I waded through breakers to the shore.

Once on land, I staggered beyond the grasp of the waves and collapsed face down on a pebbled beach. For a long time, I lay there, rolled up into a ball, trying to catch my breath, preserve my warmth, and regain my strength.

Finally, I stood. Shivering violently, I returned to the water's edge and searched for the *curragh*. Fifty yards down the beach, I found half the boat—the stern—smashed to kindling. A few yards farther on was the crumpled, twisted bow. My sword and pack were still tied to it. But I'd lost the water skin, the bow, and quiver. I retrieved what I could.

For a time, I followed the cliff along a narrow beach until coming upon a steep gap where a stream gushed from above. I climbed up beside, and sometimes within, the cold, rushing water. At the cliff top, I stopped to catch my breath. Weak, soaked, cold, trembling from exhaustion, I needed a fire. I scanned the heath in both directions.

Daylight was fading, almost gone. But the wind died down, and for now, the rain stopped.

I needed a warm shelter. An abandoned hut, a cave, a soft patch beneath a tree, anything. I couldn't stop shivering.

Something twinkled through a grove at the cliff edge on the far horizon. A fire? Was that the fire I'd seen from the sea? I squinted. It came again, trees blowing in the wind, the light blinking on, then off, then on again.

I remembered my father's warning. It could be the *fine* of pirates. It might be one of those clans with a dim view of all outsiders. If I went there, I risked being taken a slave. It was getting colder, and in my weakened state, I feared I wouldn't survive the night without shelter.

I started across the moor. Night descended quickly, and in the dark, I stumbled against boulders and fell down small ravines. I tripped over rocks, picking myself up off the moor, falling, rising again. Once I just lay on the heath, shivering and weak, not knowing if I'd be able to stand. Somehow, I found the strength to rise and press on as the rain and wind began again. I kept the light ever in my sight, and as I traveled, the shadowy outline of a structure appeared. Then two. Then many.

Finally, I arrived at the lone grove of trees playing hide-and-seek with the firelight in the wind. Someone had built a single, large fire at cliff's edge, making it visible from the sea. Many roundhouses, a few stone buildings with thatched roofs. These were strong buildings, unlike the mud-and-wattle houses of Inis Creig. This *tuath* was larger than my own.

This was not Foclut, the village with which we traded, for I recognized nothing. Were they pirates? Was their fire to lure ships onto the rocks below? Or were they providing a beacon to warn friendly vessels away in the storm?

Then I heard singing—loud, boisterous song, both men and women—coming from a large, square house at the village center. Between roundhouses and darkened stone buildings, I walked toward it.

The rain returned now in sheets, driven by a biting wind. I was shivering so violently I had trouble walking. Whoever they were, I was at their mercy. As I neared the door, I remembered my father's words to wear the druid's robe always. But I had no strength to change now. I was swaying on my feet. Whatever happened, I needed to get inside, out of the storm. I knocked, but no one heard. Again I knocked. But no answer.

The singing from inside was loud, drunken, and merry. I pushed open the door and entered.

The singing stopped. A large-bellied man, with braided black hair and a ring in one ear, turned from the wooden bench where he sat facing the central fire. As he did so, he spilled the contents of his mug. He stared at me and froze.

Sitting on his leg was a young woman, her lopsided, drunken smile fading, her long red hair tied in colorful braids. She wore a brightly painted tunic cut low in front, nearly exposing her breasts.

On a bench opposite the fire, sat a shorter, thinner man with somber face and cropped red hair and mustache. He set his mug on the bench, turned, and he too stared.

A third man, stocky and quiet, sat on a third bench in the corner, a mug in his hands, a sly smile melting into a frown.

A second young girl, fair of face and skin, sat quietly beside him. Red and yellow braids wrapped her blonde hair, and she wore a full-length tunic, brightly painted.

All were now silent, staring at this interloper from the storm.

53

The large-bellied man set down his mug and spoke in a deep, melodious voice, "Stranger, that's the sword of a warrior at your belt. Are you friend or foe?" Even as the words left his mouth, he pushed the girl off his leg and his hand inched toward the hilt of a knife at his belt.

The other men appeared wary as well, their eyes searching for weapons apparently out of reach.

The room's warmth hit me like a blast. I was light-headed. The benches, the fire, the mud plastered walls—all became distant. I tried to speak, but no words escaped my mouth. My vision blurred, dimmed. The hut began to sway. I was shivering violently. I took a step forward then fell to one knee. I shook my head to clear it, then rose again, unsteadily.

"Friend," I managed to say, dimly remembering the question.

"From whence do you come?"

"From . . . Inis Creig." My words sounded remote as if spoken by another. One of them, I don't know who, gave a low whistle.

"Who came with you?" The red-haired man's brow creased as he looked toward the door.

"I came alone . . . from across the sea . . . my *curragh*," I fumbled for words, "destroyed."

"Look at him, Kilgarren."

Who spoke? I needed to focus. The red-haired woman with alluring eyes and low-cut tunic who was now standing beside the large-bellied man.

"He's all wet and dripping all o'er the floor."

The glance of the large-bellied man, identified now as Kilgarren, wandered over me as if I were a ghost. He took his hand off his knife, sheathed it, and a smile spread across his mouth. "Shush, my lovely. It'll dry." Then he turned to the portly man. "Donnach, this traveler has come far indeed. I'll wager a pitcher of ale he was banished." To the red-haired, somber-faced man, he added, "Coll, I believe we have here a kindred spirit. Maybe a practitioner of unsavory deeds? Or perhaps an unauthorized taker of some fair virgin's purity? Or better yet, a scoundrel given to thievery or drunkenness? Ah, what sweet fate indeed! Mùirne, bring food and drink for the lad, and be quick about it."

As the blonde girl rose to do Kilgarren's bidding, the red-haired man approached me.

The room wavered. I staggered and tried to remain standing.

"Stranger." He was leaning close, whispering so only I could hear. "If you're able, I'd seek shelter anywhere but here. For your own good."

I barely grasped his warning before I collapsed on the floor.

CHAPTER 7

The Man in White

I opened my eyes. It was late and the revelry had stopped. I lay on a mat on the floor beside the fire, under some kind of rough quilt. Beneath the cover, I was naked. I sat up, pulling up on the blanket. All but the quiet, blonde girl were asleep on furs around the room's perimeter. Outside, the wind tore at the hut and lashed it with rain.

The girl saw me, took a wooden ladle to a steaming pot suspended over the fire in the room's center, filled a wooden bowl, then came and sat beside me. "You must eat and regain your strength," she said, her eyes innocent and clear, a weak smile breaking the smooth-skinned beauty of her face. "My name is Mùirne."

I thanked her, pulled the quilt tight around my waist, and my shaking fingers closed over the bowl. The smell of rabbit, long simmered in onions and cabbage, seemed to charge me with energy, even before I took the first bite. It was the best stew I'd ever tasted.

"Where are my clothes?"

"They're drying on the rack." She pointed to a place by the fire. "Everything was wet."

I nodded, my face warming, and not only from the fire. I pulled the blanket closer about my waist, then attacked the bowl again. She brought a mug of cow's milk to set beside me, and I thanked her again.

But when I'd finished both mug and bowl, I could no longer keep my eyes open. I lay back and fell instantly into a deep sleep, my first true rest in days.

I awoke from the dream, my heart racing, my senses alert. A warmth I cannot describe filled my heart with joy and sent my spirits soaring.

Light from the setting sun streamed through the open door as Mùirne, the blonde-haired girl, entered and shut the door behind her. Had I slept through the night and all the next day? The storm had passed, leaving only a brisk wind to rattle the door in its frame.

When she saw me, a look of concern crossed her face. "What's happened to you?"

"What do you mean?"

"Your face—it's glowing. And your eyes. They're . . . bright."

I lifted a hand to my cheeks and felt their warmth. "I guess it was my dream."

"A dream?" Her eyes widened. "I would sore like to hear the tale of such a dream . . . if my lord doesna mind?"

I didn't answer immediately. Something told me I could trust her. But the dream was so powerful, so odd, so . . . holy, I briefly considered keeping it to myself. Yet I felt compelled to tell someone. I smiled at her. "Nay, I don't mind."

"First, let me fetch you some root tea."

While she went to the central fire and poured steaming water from a kettle over some crushed roots, I found my dried clothes, laid out beside me on the quilt, and dressed.

When she was sitting opposite and I was sipping from a mug, I began. "I remember standing on top of a hill in the middle of a forest. But all around me, to the horizon in all directions, everything was dead. Death had touched every leafless branch, every trunk, every scrawny stick poking in the air. It was a forest of scarecrow trunks and stark limbs, without leaves, birds, or animals. My hilltop too was barren. Beside me, I even saw the bleached skeleton of some large animal."

She shuddered. "It sounds terrible."

"Mùirne, it was a forest of death. And my heart grieved for this place because it had once been full of life."

"What did you do?"

"I began to mourn. A feeling of hopelessness and despair gripped me. And I didn't know why. These were only trees. But this vast expanse of death was so profound. And I felt their deaths might be . . . eternal. Then something on the horizon caught my attention. Some of the trees were coming alive. 'Twas then I saw the man in white."

"A druid?"

"That was my first thought. White is the druids' color, of course, but this white was beyond anything I'd ever seen, shining with all the colors of the rainbow. The man in white was walking toward me, and everywhere he passed, dead trees sprouted leaves and the forest became green again. The deer, squirrels, and rabbits also returned. But only some of the trees came alive and only for a little ways into the woods.

"Time passed and soon he was climbing the base of my hill. But when he was close enough I could see his face, my knees weakened and my heart pounded in my chest. I sensed that this man held great power, more power than was possible for any mortal man to hold. And as he approached, what I'd taken for a bright whiteness became a brilliant flame shining from every fiber of his body, mixed with all the colors of the rainbow. It was like looking at a blazing sun, yet somehow I could gaze upon him without squinting.

"Then the man stood before me, and I was overwhelmed. I fell to my knees.

"'Do not be afraid, Taran,' he said, and his eyes were warm and filled with love."

"How did he ken your name?"

"I don't know. But when I looked into his eyes, I saw power. Also great compassion. I felt unworthy to be in his presence. And this is what he said to me: 'Hear now my message and obey. Go to Sabhall at Strangford Loch. Do not delay, but go. Find the foreigner. Listen to him. Then follow me.'

"I opened my mouth to speak, but no words came out. I wanted to ask *why*? Why should I go to such a place? Where was Strangford Loch and Sabhall? Who was the foreigner? What did he have to say to me? And most importantly, Who was he?

"But the man in white only touched my shoulder with one hand. And at that instant, energy coursed through me. My weariness evaporated, replaced by a feeling of incredible joy and happiness. Even now after the dream, it fills me with warmth. I fell to my knees again and simply whispered, 'Thank you.'

"I stood, but he was already heading down the hill toward the dead forest on the opposite side. I wanted to rush after him, to follow him, to be with him. I didn't ever want to be anywhere else but with the man in white. And then I woke."

By now, Mùirne's eyes were wide and she was staring at me. "Surely, Taran of Inis Creig, you have been touched . . . by the gods. To have had such a dream."

"He must be a god, nay?"

"Aye. What are you going to do?"

"I must obey him. I must go to this Strangford Loch, wherever it is, and seek the foreigner, whoever he is."

"I've never heard of such a place. But I've na been anywhere but where Kilgarren has led me."

"Perhaps he will know of it?"

A frown crossed her face. "I would na tell Kilgarren any of this."

"Nay?" Sipping my tea, I looked at the floor. I was not yet familiar with Kilgarren or his ways. But I had barely set down my mug when the door slammed open and the black-haired man himself stepped in.

"Well, look who's awake," said Kilgarren as he entered the hut. "You've slept the night through, right into the day, and now it's almost evening. But I've done the same before. Aye, many times, the same."

I smiled and stood, offering him my hand.

"I am Kilgarren, and I welcome you to our little band. And you won't find merrier company anywhere." His voice was musical, fetching. He took my hand, squeezed it hard, and shook it long. "But we must get you food and drink and begin our revelry. There's no time to waste. And you'll tell us a story. Sure, and you'll tell us more than one." He looked to his hefty companion just entering the hut behind him.

"Donnach, bring the lad food and drink. Then find Coll. And where has my Dearshul gone to? My dear, dear Dearshul. Find them all and let the night begin!"

I had barely left the man in white. A feeling of holiness, awe, and urgent mission still hovered about me, warning me of its importance, telling me to listen. Now, here was Kilgarren, luring me with the promise of food, drink, and an experience of the senses.

Only vaguely recalling the warning from the night before, I entered Kilgarren's world.

CHAPTER 8

Kilgarren

I had barely finished a meal of rabbit stew and cabbage when Kilgarren shoved a mug of ale into my hands. I was so thirsty I took it and drank deeply.

As I ate, the others in Kilgarren's small band gathered in the hut. Dearshul, the girl with the low-cut tunic, painted eyes, and inviting smile, stuck to Kilgarren like a fly to a horse. Thin, red-mustachioed Coll sat apart, always reserved, serious, somber. Stocky, brown-haired Donnach stood guard with a witless smile over a bottomless mug. Mùirne moved obediently to Donnach's side.

"Give us a tune, Coll," roared Kilgarren. "And no long, sad songs, hear me. Only merry ones. And be quick about it."

From a far wall, Coll brought out a strange instrument. Gut strings stretched over a small, rectangular wooden box. Half a forearm's length at one end, a mere finger's length at the other. The strings led over a sound hole, then up a short, flat neck where they wound around pegs.

With one hand, Coll fitted the box to his chin. Another hand gripped a two-foot long bow stretched with more gut, like a saw. He drew his bow, once, over the strings. The air quivered with sound and I gasped. Never had I heard such captivating tones.

Then his bow flew. His fingers pressed the neck strings. Faster and faster Coll played until the air vibrated and shimmered with the sprightly tune of a jig. The lilting, bouncing music filled the whole room. Quick, short, happy notes sliced the air, lifting me with their rhythm. I'd never heard such fetching, magical sounds.

I jumped up and danced the dance of the Carraig Beag for times of joy. An energetic, boisterous dance. I kicked out first one leg, then the other, with an occasional jump thrown in, one arm curved above and held high.

"Now there's a man who knows how to have fun." Kilgarren laughed and raised his mug.

While Donnach sat, stamped one foot, and clapped his hands, Kilgarren jumped up, grabbed one of Dearshul's hands, and the three of us danced and hopped around the room. Then Mùirne joined in. The song—and it was a long one that seemed to have no end—finally played itself out. I plopped down on a bench, gasping for breath. Mùirne sat beside me. Kilgarren and Dearshul sat on an opposite bench, where her fingers grasped one of his arms.

Dancing is sweaty work. I drank deeply from the mug.

"What say you, Coll?" Kilgarren's glance wandered to the red-haired man, sitting on a seat close to the central fire near Donnach. "Can you do more than mind mice at the crossroads? Can you play and dance at the same time, my laddie?"

Coll shook his head, no.

Kilgarren shook his head in imitation of Coll, one brass earring wobbling, black braids flying. "You see, stranger, he doesn't dance. He plays well on his fiddle-thing but doesn't dance. So then, how are you named? We cannot keep calling you 'stranger'."

"I am Taran, son of Teague, son of Rònan, of the *tuath* of the Carraig Beag."

"Pleased to meet you, Taran mac Teague. I am Kilgarren, son of mischief, brother to knaves and friend to wenches, lover of all things merry, wandering poet and bard for the Rí Cóicid of many kingdoms. Hah!" Grinning at his own words, he went for another mug of ale. "But your mug is near empty, lad. You must not let it be so. What say you, Donnach?"

"An empty mug?" Donnach slapped a hand on one knee, then wagged a full head of unkempt, brown hair. "There ought to be a law."

"Donnach, you don't say much. But that was a gem of wisdom."

Despite my objections, Kilgarren filled my mug to overflowing from a wooden keg by the wall and shoved it back into my hands.

Coll laid down his fiddle and picked up a branch from a pile of firewood against the wall. He pulled a knife from the sheath at his belt.

Kilgarren waved a hand at me. "He doesn't know how to have fun, laddie. He's been with me—what? How many years haven't we trekked from here to there, playing and rhyming from this farmstead to that?"

"Twelve, Kilgarren." Coll frowned and shaved a strip of bark off the branch. "But it seems like twenty."

"A dozen, he says. Yet what has my fine student learned? If you don't warn him with grave threats, you'll hear only sadness and infernal wailing from that fiddle of his. Songs to rip the tears from your head. He sits there, morose, without a wench on his lap. He's barely touched his mug. Only his fiddle saves him from total despair. My lad, I've tried to teach him, but he refuses to grab life and *take a hold* of it. What are we to do with him?"

His red mustache drooping, Coll stopped whittling. He gazed at his larger, more boisterous companion. "In the last three days, I've had enough barley ale to last me a month. And it's you who haven't learned the lessons of the past, my friend. Tell me, Kilgarren: Where's the profit we were to make from our time here in Naoú Giall? You were given the silver for the deal—where is it? What if Amalgaid finds us still here?"

Kilgarren waved a hand in dismissal and took a long draught of ale.

Coll pointed his knife at the straw-covered floor. "How much time have you spent in drunken revelry with your slut?"

Dearshul shifted on her seat, frowning.

"You promised the king some kind of grand poem. But since we arrived, I've heard precious little rhyme from you."

"O laddie," Kilgarren shook his head. "I've a poem in me, don't worry. And it'll be verse to etch the king's memory into his subjects' minds for all eternity. A mighty work of words and rhyme."

"So you say." Coll turned a stern gaze to Donnach beside him. "Since we arrived, have you heard anything but doggerel from this one's ale-besotted lips?"

Donnach shook his head, his smile dissipating.

Coll chopped his knife into the branch and dug in. "Watch out, Taran. He's courting trouble. His appetites are insatiable. And his sense has gone up with the smoke of this fire." A vicious slice sent half the branch into the flames.

Kilgarren stared at him, one eyebrow raised. "My, my, what a fine speech. So this is what my benevolence brings? Do you see, Taran? He's all business. No joy in him at all. He ignores today, all for the sake of tomorrow. I ask you: What fun is that?"

Coll reached for a new stick. "There's fun, my friend, and there's business. You're not a merchant to kings; you're a poet. A poet without poetry. You promised the king fine horses, but now where's the silver he gave you to buy them?"

"Oh, my dear Coll, we've enough silver to buy horses in Foclut, I dare say. When I'm done with the deal, those poor farmers will wonder how they gave away such wonderful horseflesh for so little in return. And when the need arises, the poetry will simply fly out of me. You forget—the kings must have their poets. Without my poetry, the memory of their rule will vanish like boots sucked down into a bog. They simply cannot live without me."

"Aye," said Dearshul, giving him a bawdy leer. "And neither can I."

Kilgarren winked at her, took a sip from his mug. Her hand still clutched his arm, and now his fingers gripped one of her legs and squeezed. Then he faced me.

"But Taran, lad, we've done all the talking. Now we must hear about Inis Creig. The rumors of your island have reached us. Is it true about the gold you've laid up for yourselves?"

Involuntarily, my eyes widened. I shook my head. "I'd rather not say."

"Ah, so there *is* gold on the island?"

I said nothing. A glowing log in the fire between us fell into the white-hot coals beneath. A shower of sparks hit Kilgarren's feet. He stamped a coal into the straw, his smile gone.

"He doesn't want to tell you, my lord," Mùirne spoke for the first time, shaking braids wrapped in colored leather. "He's defending his home. And 'tis his right."

"Ah, the quiet one speaks. How she defends you! But tell me the truth, lad. Remember how you lay weak and near death and I sheltered you. How much gold does your island have?"

"Only that which covers a stone of evil—the idol of Crom Cruach. Not enough to make up for the losses my clan would inflict on any who tried to steal it. We men of the Carraig Beag will fight to the death against all who come against us by the sword."

Kilgarren gave an uncharacteristic frown and scratched the back of his head. "I've heard of this Crom Cruach. They worship him in Killycluggin, a few days ride from here. I've no faith in gods, but from what I've heard . . . this is one to fear."

He studied me, his demeanor sobering. "So you're a fighting race, then? I should have known. Well, your gold is safe from me, lad. I'm not much for the thought of having my limbs cut off, even for the sake of profit." Then his smile returned and he slapped a hand on one knee. "But now we must hear the tale of your coming."

Then I told them about my island, my *fine*, my father, and the druids. I spoke of my fall from grace on the day I was to join the council. Of the questions I put to Cormag, and how I rejected Crom Cruach. Of my trip across the sea and my prayer to an unknown God who, it was said, ruled over all. I didn't mention the dream or the man in white.

But as I told of my landing on Ériu, I looked up with a sudden insight. "Now that I think about it, shortly after I prayed to this new God, the land appeared from the sea. I saw Naoú Giall's signal fire and was saved from death. So perhaps this God answered my prayer?" I looked from Kilgarren to Coll to Mùirne.

"I believe He did," said Mùirne. "I can see that this God, whoever He is, must have answered you. You are blessed."

"Mùirne, my child, and my dear misguided Taran." Kilgarren's glance wandered between us. "You're both children in these matters with much to learn. So let me begin with this lesson: I've noticed for some time that after I scratch my rump—" and here he lifted his tunic and scratched his bare buttocks while I looked away in disgust, "— that soon after, my wench here, my precious Dearshul, will come and lie with me in my bed. So let us invent the 'god of rump'. Aye, a fine and fitting name for a god, I think. Next, let us conclude we may all pray to this new god by scratching our respective behinds, and when I in particular do so, he therefore answers my prayers with the favors of my luscious wench. What do you think, Dearshul?"

She looked at Kilgarren, and her tongue touched one corner of her mouth. Then a wicked smile spread across her lips. "Now I think on it—aye, it must be so. Sure, and it's the 'god of rump' calling me to your bed whenever you scratch him so. Why haven't I noticed 'afore now?" She gave me a wink and then burst out in raucous, seemingly endless, laughter.

Kilgarren's gaze wandered back to me. "You see, lad? She confirms it though she laughs too much at the thought."

He stared at Dearshul, still laughing. "Be still now, my lovely. Don't embarrass us with this fuss and be the lummox. The joke wasn't all that funny. If you spend your laughter on so little, then your account will be empty when true humor comes your way."

Dearshul abruptly quit. A frown replaced her grin, shot in Kilgarren's direction. She pulled her fingers off his arm and folded her hands in her lap.

Kilgarren fixed us again with a smile. "Sure, and you must kill these fallacious thoughts, my Mùirne and my lad. Taran's salvation was coincidence, nothing more. You might as well pray to the worms in your bread as to some god floating on the wind. It'll do as much good."

"I respectfully disagree," I said. "Who created the night sky if not some Great Being? Who made the trees of the forest, the birds, the fox, and the bear? Perhaps it was this same God they pray to in Bryton, this God I prayed to. They say He's greater than all the others. Aye, he must have answered my prayer."

"Ah, this is indeed a surprise. Are you a seeker of truth, lad?"

"Who doesn't want to seek the truth?"

Kilgarren laughed. "Beware, Donnach. I once knew a druid like him. Touched in the head, he was. And when he finds his truths, he'll want to impose them on everyone else. Then he'll want to take our drink, my friend. Or our women. If not today, then tomorrow."

Donnach stared at me as if I were a pirate come to rob him.

"Aye, Donnach. The only cure for the truth seeker is to help him make merry."

"Leave him alone, Kilgarren." Coll sheathed his knife. "You've wallowed in your debauchery so long, you've forgotten the meaning of truth and honor and right living."

"Right living!" Kilgarren slapped a hand on one knee then downed his mug in one long gulp. "That's what I think of right living."

Donnach scowled. "All this talk bores me."

"Right you are, my friend. And this is your house, your fine inn. Our talk has been far too sober. We shall seek amends by making merry. And Taran and Coll shall join us. That's the first and most important lesson. Possibly the second and third as well. Coll, give us another tune. And beware it's happy, not sad. I warn you, now."

Coll stared at the black-haired man for a moment, then shrugged. He reached for his fiddle and once more started a lively tune.

I couldn't help but join in the dancing, and this pleased Kilgarren to no end. The music was fetching and fun. But Kilgarren's constant prompting and his eagerness for my participation led me to drink more ale than I ever had in my life. Whenever I emptied my mug, he appeared, winking and smiling, to fill it again with a head spilling over the top.

Despite Kilgarren's dire warnings, Coll's happy songs soon faded into melancholy ballads of unrequited love and lost kingdoms. But Kilgarren soon prodded him toward songs of ribaldry and lechery and adventure, and we all joined in and danced. Thus did the night slip away until the wee hours, when we dropped, drunk and spent and near senseless, into our beds.

I lay on my mat by the fire, watching as the thatched ceiling swam in circles. Then I thought about something Kilgarren had said to me more than once that evening: "You'll join us, lad. Aye, you'll become part of our merry band." And briefly, while lying there, I almost considered it.

But then I remembered the last night's dream and the man in white. For a moment, sobriety returned, and regret shook me like a mother.

The man in white had been pure, holy, powerful. He'd come to me, specifically, with a message for me. And how did I listen? By spending the evening in wild merrymaking. I shook my head, wincing at a pain almost as deep as the regret.

I needed to decide who I was going to follow. But tomorrow, not tonight.

CHAPTER 9

Tardy Decisions

Before any of us awoke, the sun had reached its zenith. With a pounding headache, I rose from the floor. Now I regretted last night's revelry. I'd felt so much better before it had all started.

At the table, Mùirne welcomed me with an innocent smile and a bowl of oat porridge, swimming with milk and butter.

I thanked her, ate, and left the hut for the sunlight where I found Coll sitting on a bench.

"I would return to the shore where my *curragh* broke up," I said to the red-haired young man. "Will you join me?"

He nodded, but as I headed toward the moor, Coll suggested a shorter route. He led me instead to the cliff's edge, where coals from last night's signal fire still glowed red. As I stared at embers, he waved toward the sea. "The fire burns each night to warn ships to stay off shore until daybreak. Too many have foundered on the rocks, especially in storms."

"So the people of this village aren't pirates?"

"Depends what you mean by that. Amalgaid is the High King of the Connachta and when he calls, the men here answer and obey. Just last year, he led them on a foray to the coast of Gaul. But the raid was too far, and the spoils too little. The Gauls of the coast have impoverished themselves fighting the barbarians."

"Would they ever raid Inis Creig?"

"Not Amalgaid. This year the king's obsessed with revenge against Forga mac Dallán, Rí Cóicid of Ulster. Amalgaid plans soon to raid lands north of Ulster. Over some ancient affront, I fear. As long as I can remember, the two have feuded."

"In this country, I see much warfare and discord."

"True enough. The kings of Ériu will have their wars and rivalries and nothing will stop them. 'Twas always so. Makes for difficult trade and profit."

I looked down the cliff at the waves lapping the beach below, then raised my eyes to the western horizon. Somewhere across that vast stretch of ocean was my home. It hit me now—the distance between this land and my own. In travel, but also in its ways. I had entered a new world of strange villages, kings, and wars. Why had destiny brought me here?

"Where is Sabhall on Strangford Loch?" I stared at the horizon.

"Strangford Lough? I know it not. Ask Kilgarren. He's been everywhere. But where'd you hear that name?"

"It's not important. Let's go down." We descended the steep trail on steps carved long ago into the cliff face. At the bottom, we began walking the rocky beach.

"I weary of Kilgarren," said Coll, breaking the silence. "I believe you're an honest man, Taran, so I think you'll understand what I say. Too often lately, I regret joining him. 'Twas his rhyme I was after. He was the *fílidh* and I was the bard. He wrote the poetry and I put it to music.

"There was also the lure of profit. Kilgarren taught me much about how to part a peasant from his pigs, his cabbage, and his cows. And sure, he could talk the teeth out of a saw and steal the honey from your mead. Yet I fear we've done much harm to some folks." He shook his head. "There must be more to life than this constant groveling for some sacks of turnips or a ring or two of silver, only to trade it away for drink, lodging, or in Kilgarren's case, wenches."

"I've never heard of anyone else with a 'fiddle instrument', as you call it. And you play it so well."

"I learned it from a Kilkenny man who moved to Partry, who learned it from the Leinster man who invented it. We were the first fiddlers in all the world, he said. I donna ken if it's true."

"Can you not leave Kilgarren and go out on your own? A bard is honest work."

"Would that I could. I'm known everywhere in Connacht as Kilgarren's bard, the fiddler who shares his profits. He's spoiled my future. 'Tis something I wanted to warn you about. He collects followers like other men do horses or fine blades.

He'll wile and plead with you endlessly until you join him. The more followers he has, the more he can justify how he lives."

I nodded. I hadn't expected this concern for my welfare. But Coll also appeared to be looking for something I couldn't give him. A way out of his predicament.

Then he stopped, gripped my shoulder, and narrowed his eyes. "You should get as far away from here as you can. Today."

I started at the intensity of his warning. "But I've nothing to do with his business."

"Doesn't matter." He released his grip. "Everyone in the village knows you've made your bed at Donnach's. In their minds, you're now with Kilgarren. You should hear what they say about us. Poets and bards should be respected, valued. But not us. I myself have nowhere else to go. If I left, Amalgaid would soon find me. Unless I fled to Ulster or Leinster. But I'm loathe to forsake my country."

"Thank you for the warning. I believe I'll leave at first light tomorrow. I don't know where Strangford Loch is, but aye, 'tis my destination."

For the first time, a smile broke Coll's face. He put his hand on my shoulder. "You're welcome, my friend. Would that I could go with you."

We walked along the shore until I recognized the gap leading up the cliff where I'd climbed during the storm. But after searching the beach, we found nothing more of my gear.

We returned the way we had come, arriving at Donnach's by late afternoon. As we approached the hut, the aroma of roasting pig made my mouth water. Inside, Dearshul hovered by the fire, slowly turning a hog over a spit.

"Tonight, me laddies, we'll have a fine feast indeed." Kilgarren's face broke into a wide smile. "I've been to market and this is what two rings of silver will buy."

"Are you *glipe*, man?" Coll's voice cut through the room like an axe through dry wood. Mùirne dropped a handful of wooden bowls. Dearshul stopped spinning the pig. "When will you stop wasting funds? How much silver is left? Answer me!"

Kilgarren stepped back, his eyes wide. His glance wandered over and around us.

"I'm firm about this, Kilgarren. Either we leave at once on the trade we agreed upon, or . . . or . . . I will—"

Kilgarren raised a hand and spoke in his best melodious, soothing voice. "We have plenty of silver, my friend, plenty for trade in Foclut. Trust me in this. But I see you're far too worried over this matter. So here's my promise. Tonight, let us make merry and drink ale and eat this fine pig. And Coll, I've also bought butter and honey and wine for basting and drinking. And honey cakes. And fresh turnips and cabbage and onions which Dearshul is now boiling in mead and butter. Ah, what a feast we'll have!

> "A pig on the stake,
> A mug in the hand,
> A handful of cake,
> And ale all around!

"See, laddies, I've poetry in me yet. So tonight, let us eat and drink as if there's no tomorrow, for when tomorrow does come, I promise you this: We'll leave. We'll pack and we'll get on our horses—assuming the stableman has kept them healthy, for I haven't yet paid him—and we'll trek to Foclut. You're right, my dear Coll, we've tarried here far too long. Tomorrow it is. But only if you promise to celebrate this evening. All of you. Will you promise me, Coll?"

As Kilgarren spoke, Coll's face changed from anger, to puzzlement, to resigned acceptance. "Aye, Kilgarren. Tonight, we'll feast. But tomorrow, we *must* leave. I hold you to it."

"Agreed, then. But the deal's not final unless our new friend here also joins us. Will you feast with us tonight, my traveler from afar?"

I nodded.

"Ah, my boy, you're a friend, indeed. Here, let us start the ale before the pig is cooked, before the feast ends our fast and our famine. Mùirne! Bring mugs for these fine gentlemen. And one for me. We mustn't tarry. We begin the evening young so we may sleep tonight and rise early for our journey."

Thus did Kilgarren begin another round of merrymaking. But the cooking had started late, and the pig would not be ready for some time, so we simply sat on the benches, drank ale, and talked.

"Tomorrow, I too will leave," said I after a long silence. "But my destination lies elsewhere and I need a horse." I went to my pack, found my knife, and broke the lead from my father's amulet. The gold *aureus* shone by firelight.

"I'm told this will buy a horse. Is that so?"

At sight of the *aureus*, Kilgarren's eyes brightened. When Coll saw it, he shook his head and looked at the floor. In those first few days on Ériu, I was sometimes a bit naïve.

"If you'll accompany us to Foclut—" Kilgarren grinned, "one of those will buy you a wonderful horse, indeed."

"Nay. Tomorrow I would go to Strangford Loch. Can you tell me how to get there?"

"Strangford Loch? My memory is vague. There could well be such a place in northeastern Ulster. Unless I've confused it with Strangfell Lough. But you must have the name wrong, laddie. I remember it dimly. If it's the place I'm thinking of, 'tis a lough of mud and kelp where the ocean washes in. A place of desolation."

"The name's correct. It's my destiny."

"My lad. My dear, dear Taran. We've work to do, I can see. What destiny can there be in such a place? Where'd you get such an idea?"

I shook my head. Kilgarren would only belittle my dream. I would make merry this one night as promised, but then I was done with him. Already, I'd tarried too long.

"As it may be, he doesn't want to tell." He sighed as if to exaggerate his dismay. "Well then, if this be your last night with us, we must give you a good sendoff."

Kilgarren turned to the hut's owner. "Donnach, my lad, give up your wench for good, say good-bye to her, and bring her here to me."

From the bench where he sat, Donnach glanced at Mùirne, then back at Kilgarren. The witless half-smile faded away.

"Give her up, I say!"

Donnach waved her off with one hand and stared at the floor. "Go to him, wench. He's paid for you, na I. And if he chooses now to take you back, it must be so."

Mùirne lifted her glance to Donnach, the corners of her eyes crumpling. Slowly, she left her seat and walked to Kilgarren, her gaze downcast. "Have I displeased you, my lord?"

Kilgarren looked at her and frowned. "No, Mùirne, all you've done is please me. The pleasure you brought—'tis the reason I bought your debts." He took both of her hands and led her across the gap to where I sat. He lifted one of my hands and put hers in mine.

"Taran, my lad, this wench I do give you. She's yours for the night. Do with her what you will. My parting gift for a wayfaring traveler. If she pleases you and you change your mind and stay with us, you may keep her. She's meek and pure—well, she used to be pure. Perfect for you. This is what can happen when your destiny's wrapped with mine. Largesse. Favors. Comely wenches. See what you're giving up, my friend?"

Mùirne caught my glance, her eyes bright and innocent. A smile from the heart spread across her face.

I looked into her eyes and saw the hope there, but shook my head. I did not like where this was going. I held Kilgarren's gaze. "I cannot accept your offer. I'm pledged to another. I cannot take this girl for one night just because you own her. Is she your slave then, a *cumal* you've purchased for debts owed?"

"She is, lad. She's my *cumal*, bought with hard-won silver, paid to her debt-ridden father, dead of the fever soon after the trade, I fear. But you must take her. See how she wants you. She's a fine, beautiful wench and will give you many days and nights of pleasure and service."

I shook my head then saw the tears forming in Mùirne's eyes. "You're a beautiful girl, Mùirne, and I ken you've an honest heart. Were I free to do so, I might consider this offer, but I'm sorry. I love another back on Inis Creig. I cannot betray her."

"Give her up, my boy. You'll never go back. Such false hopes will eat you alive."

I stared at him, my jaw muscles tensing. "It's not for you to say, Kilgarren, or anyone else. There's always hope." My hands clenched into fists at my side. "Tomorrow, I'll buy a horse here in this village, for you and I must part. Your offering me this girl will not change that. I thank you for your hospitality, but you cannot change my mind with clever wiles."

Kilgarren regarded me with narrowed eyes. Outside, I heard the gulls crying to each other. "Then tomorrow it is, my friend. All things seem to be happening tomorrow. I know a seller of horses here in Naoú Giall, though, after a day on your new steed, you'll wish you'd bought one in Foclut. But tonight—" he threw one hand high and swung his mug with the other, "—we must make merry. The pig'll soon be done, and we'll feast."

Kilgarren's promise of a quick meal was a false one. The beast wasn't cooked and the meal not ready until late. By then, much ale had been poured and my disagreement with Kilgarren seemed distant and foggy. When the meal finally arrived, it lived up to expectations, a true feast indeed. Then Coll brought out his fiddle, and again we danced and sang into the night. Despite my resolve not to rejoin Kilgarren's revelry, it was late when I fell into my bed.

The next thing I remember the door slammed open and in burst five men, dressed in leather chest armor, wearing iron helmets, and carrying swords. I woke and blinked in the glare of the midmorning sun as a wash of cold air flooded the room.

"Whatever is the trouble?" Kilgarren fumbled for his tunic and shoes, his glance bouncing from the soldiers to his clothes. "Whatever, my good men, is the problem?"

"Save your words for the king," said a tall man, the apparent leader and the only one wearing chain mail. "He's in a fearsome mood, indeed."

"What have we done?" said Kilgarren.

"I fancy 'tis what you haven't done. The king wants to know, and right quick, where his horses are."

"But I'm not with them," I said to the leader, whom someone addressed as Feachnacht.

"Tell that to the Rí Cóicid."

After I'd dressed, Feachnacht waved his blade and herded me out of the hut. First into the sunlight, I blinked then froze. Surrounding me were more soldiers, swords and axes drawn, faces taut.

Last to come out, Donnach peered nervously up and down the street as if seeking a place to flee to. But the soldiers' bodies and their weapons closed off any hope of escape.

"Off with you, laddies." Feachnacht pointed and we began walking before a cluster of sword points.

From every doorway and side path, the people of Naoú Giall emerged to watch our procession with wide and eager eyes. Heads bent together and whispered. Tongues clucked. Children giggled and started mock sword battles with sticks.

"'Tis what they deserved," shouted one.

"There'll be a grand argy-bargy with the king," said another.

I thought of Coll's repeated warnings to leave, starting with my first night here. And I hadn't listened. Now these men were marching me off with Kilgarren's band as though I were one of them. I reached for the armband Laurna had made for me, still encircling my right arm. What would become of me now?

When we turned a corner and entered the village square, I gasped.

Perhaps a hundred soldiers gathered there. On the perimeter and in the paths between houses stood half the populace of Naoú Giall. But my gaze fixed on one man in the center, wearing a royal tunic over chain mail.

From the way all those nearby bowed and gave him space, he could only be Amalgaid, High King of Connacht.

And his frown settled on us like a dark cloud hovering over an unsettled sea before a storm.

CHAPTER 10

Judgment

"Stand now and face the Rí Cóicid." Feachnacht roared his commands. "I warn you, if you're spoken to, be quick with the truth."

I rose with the others.

Surrounding the king was a throng of swordsmen and axmen, wearing leather chest armor, horned helmets of iron, and bearing tall bronze and iron shields. Lancers held nine-foot spears with sharp, hooked points, rising high. Three archers carried full quivers and unstrung bows. Every soldier's gaze was fixed on us.

The king stood in the center. An empty space opened around him. A large man, black-bearded and muscled, he wore a battle tunic of fine linen, dyed blue, with swirls of royal red. Underneath gleamed a shirt of chain mail. Around his neck hung a torc of twisted gold.

Eyes as black as his beard glared at us. He examined each in our motley band, his forehead crumpling, eyes narrowing. At Kilgarren, he stopped.

"Where are my horses, Kilgarren?" His voice boomed across the square. "I'm told you never left Naoú Giall."

"I regret to say, my liege," Kilgarren shifted his feet and waved his hands, conjuring up his best soothing tone, "the optimum moment for purchase has not yet arrived. I would presume to buy only the best for my lord, only the purest, and only in the proper season. And it's also poetry I've been pondering that's kept me here. Fine words put to rhyme to immortalize your reign for a thousand—"

"Enough! So it's true. You've no horses for me. Then where's the silver I gave you?"

One of the soldiers who had burst in upon our slumber had stayed behind to search Donnach's hut. Now he stepped forward. "I found this, my lord."

In his hand, he offered up Kilgarren's leather pouch.

Amalgaid took it, examined its contents, and passed it to an aide. "Half! You've spent half the silver rings. What compensation can you give me? Besides your life?"

"Oh, my lord, let's not talk of bloodshed. I have collateral. Yes, indeed. I have these two wenches here." He pushed forward Dearshul and Mùirne. Kilgarren's glance flicked between Amalgaid and the women. "Fine wenches, both. They'll make good servants or use them however you desire. The blonde one's quite agreeable, don't you think? As meek and pliable as a lamb, and near as innocent. The red-haired lassie's always quite eager in bed, she is. And aye, my steed and Coll's horse are with the stableman. You may have them also. Fine mounts both. There's a start at finding some immediate horses. You'll also find a gold coin from Bryton hanging around this young man's neck." He pushed me forward. "For he's one of my followers too—aye, he is—so that gold I also offer you."

"It's not yours to give." I glared at Kilgarren.

"If you're part of Kilgarren's band, then what's yours is now mine." The king stuck out his hand, waiting. "Turn it over, lad."

"But I have no part of him. I merely stayed at Donnach's hut for some nights."

"To my mind, this says you've joined him and are party to his dealings."

"But I have not—"

"Enough!" The king's eyebrows rose.

I removed the *aureus* from my neck, hesitated, and then dropped it into his palm.

Amalgaid glared at Kilgarren. "This is na enough. I need horses—and today! You've said many times you were a poet and *flidh* for the King of Meath. So I took you into my lands. But what I've heard from you so far are only words to kill a cow. Tell me why I should na have your larcenous head removed from your body right now, sparing myself and who knows how many others further grief at your hands."

"Oh no, my lord. One cannot weigh the matter of a few horses against a life, no, indeed. I've a store of knowledge, skills to put to your service. I'll create smooth rhymes, memorable words to etch the memory of your reign onto the stones of history. Let's see. Aye, here's a rhyme for the ages:

"Slayer of men, ruler of *tuath*,
His might goes out from Cruachain.
His enemies run, fearing his *flaith*,
The ground's red with the blood of the slain.
His sons stand above, virile and strong,
No equal before them we see.
Of his daughter we sing in joyful song,
No beauty is greater than she.

"It's not finished, but 'tis a poem for the ages, don't you think? But there's one thing more: The young man here speaks of an island called Inis Creig, only a day's sail from here. There you'll find a gold statue of incredible worth. Aye, worth a thousand, no ten thousand, times the loss of a few horses. A valuable piece of information, no?"

I glared at him then, my jaw muscles tensing.

"'Tis well known, Kilgarren. Inis Creig's heavily guarded, and besides, I'd na enrage their god, for I hear he's an angry one, indeed. But there's also this: I require those in my service to be trustworthy and honorable. And that, 'tis sadly apparent, does na describe the likes of you."

"But am I not the epitome of honesty and trustworth—"

"*Stop*. I'm done with your foolery. Feachnacht!" He turned to the man with a large head and thick brown beard, who had earlier broken in on our party of sleepers. "Chain these four while I ponder what to do with them. But take the women to my hut."

Then the king turned and led a procession from the square, for they camped on the village outskirts. Feachnacht bound us with iron ankle bracelets to a ring embedded in a center boulder. Thus did we spend the day under a hot sun.

Night came, and with it a light, cold rain. Occasionally, Coll mumbled reproaches against Kilgarren and sincere apologies to me. Donnach also spoke of regrets for allowing Kilgarren into his inn. Kilgarren, for perhaps the first time in his life, was without words, melodious or otherwise. I simply huddled around my knees with my head down, trying to stay warm, wondering how I could have been so blind.

The man in white had said to go to Strangford Loch without delay. I hadn't obeyed. Now what would become of me?

Late the next morning, the king's men gathered around us. Then Amalgaid appeared and stood with his feet apart, voice booming, dark, bushy eyebrows frowning. "Stand, prisoners, and hear my judgment."

I rose, muscles stiff from huddling through the night's drizzle. I was cold, hungry, and tired. And fearful for the fate of us all.

"You've betrayed my trust, Kilgarren." As he spoke, his hands balled into fists. "You've lied to me and stolen from me. As for poetry—bah! I've heard only drivel. In short, when honesty and fair dealing are on the road, you are always in the field."

"Lie to you I have not, my lord."

"Silence! I've learned the truth from your wenches. The villagers confirmed it. Feachnacht!" The king gestured to the guard.

Then Feachnacht pushed Kilgarren over to a large log, and with one foot, pressed his head down upon it. With Kilgarren squirming and begging for his life, Feachnacht drew his sword and raised it high. In one swift motion, he brought it down with all the force he could muster.

The blade cut through Kilgarren's neck all the way to the log.

I caught a glimpse of his head rolling away, stopping upright in the dirt. His eyes seemed to be fixed on mine. Could he see me? Was it possible? His mouth— caught open in an expression of terminal surprise. An earring askew in its lobe. What thoughts flashed through his mind then, if any? Was he still here, in this world? Or had he already traveled, like an arrow loosed from its bow, to the lair of shadows and Manannán mac Lir?

I looked away and shuddered.

"Donnach." Amalgaid faced him. "Do you have any of the silver Kilgarren paid you?"

Donnach was shaking like a man with terminal fever. "I . . . I have a little left, my lord. I . . . I . . . I buried it. But 'tis all yours."

"Very well. See you deliver what remains. When you let these men enter your house, you chose poorly." He fixed the man with a stern gaze. "But I understand 'twas profit for your inn, na for dishonoring me. So you may live."

"Coll." Amalgaid put his hands on his hips and spread his legs. "Everyone knows you've always been part of Kilgarren's miserable affairs. So your fate should be the same as his. Yet the fame of your fiddle has reached even my ears. And the women said you strenuously objected to Kilgarren's delay, yet he wouldn't listen. So could you perhaps be more trustworthy than your benefactor?"

"I am, my lord. Had I any say in it, I would've treated your lordship's affairs with the gravity they deserved. I'm sorry ever to have been a part of him. I will understand. . . if my . . . my . . . fate is the same. . . as his."

"Well said. But I understand, I think, what's gone on here. Now for the two of you, Donnach and Coll, I offer this judgment: You may keep your lives. But either you will remain here in these chains until summer's end, enduring the elements and the villagers' taunting . . ." His glance wandered between them. "Or you can join my army and fight against Forga mac Dallán. But I'd rather have two fighters now than two starving scarecrows later. What say you?"

Coll swallowed. "Your mercy is great, my lord. I choose to fight for my king."

Amalgaid nodded in approval and looked to the innkeeper.

Donnach scratched his face, glanced at the ground. "I . . . I thanks my lord. You're a generous man. Yet no fighter am I. And sure, I donna have a strong disposition. If I'm chained here in the open, I'll surely die. Surely, says I. So aye, as Lugh wills it, I'll join your fighters."

"Good. Feachnacht, release these men and begin their training. Now, as for this one." Amalgaid's frown fell on me. "Mùirne has told me about you crossing the sea from Inis Creig and why. It was to your great misfortune that you picked the one house in all Naoú Giall that's home to perfidy, dishonor, and thievery. For she tells me this is na who you are. Something about the wench tells me I should believe her, and I can judge character, even a woman's. She tells me you were once a druid. Is this true?"

I nodded.

"I'm powerful impressed by your journey across the sea in a shore *curragh*. I understand you were in a bad way, and Kilgarren's hospitality saved your life, so how can I reproach you for recovering from your journey? I will na have it said the King of Connacht knows nothing of hospitality and honor, so I restore to you now everything that was yours before you entered Kilgarren's den."

Then he handed back to me the gold *aureus*, still on its leather necklace.

"Feachnacht, release this man." The large-headed man took hammer and chisel, and with three quick rings of iron on iron, freed me.

"I thank you for your mercy and wisdom."

"Your gratitude is noted. Now, lad, I ask if you'll consider this offer. I've heard of the fighting skills of the Carraig Beag, so I ask if you'll join my fight against the Ulaid. We could use a man like you. Accept or refuse, I'll respect whatever you decide."

I hesitated, afraid to insult this powerful king whose judgments in one day could range from execution to mercy. "I thank you for the choice, my lord. But I must respectfully refuse. My destiny lies elsewhere. I've seen it in a dream."

"A dream is it? Ah, then you're blessed by the gods. Well, so be it."

"But may I make one request of my lord?" Even as I spoke, I wondered if this was the time for such a thing.

"Sure?" The king's black eyebrows rose. "And what might that be?"

"I have here one Roman *aureus*." I turned it in the sun. "Would it be enough to purchase the wench Mùirne and a sturdy horse?"

The king eyed me sternly. He scratched his thick, black beard. Ever-so-slowly, a smile broke across his face. Then he laughed so hard, most of his men also burst out in laughter.

"Ah, so the lad has eyes for the wench. And a head for business, besides." Amalgaid slapped one hand on his thigh. "One gold *aureus* for a wench and a horse! A fine, bold bargain, indeed, and much to your favor—'tis but half their worth! Well, the girl does have eyes for you, lad. But one *aureus*? Hah!" He slapped his thigh again.

"But sure, what do I care if the request is much in your favor? What brashness before the king! So let it be done. You may have the horse and the wench. I do need horses, yet I'd have all memory of Kilgarren wiped from my sight."

I smiled. "It's not what you think, my liege. My heart lies with another on Inis Creig. Mùirne will simply accompany me on my mission."

The king laughed again and gave me a sly wink. "Sure? Well, we'd better take our fine young man—who's on a quest—at his word. But I do approve the trade and the boldness which brought it forth."

Mùirne came from the crowd, ran up, and hugged me, for she had been present all along.

The gathering broke up. The men went to their camp outside the village. I left with Mùirne to retrieve the rest of my things from Donnach's hut, for it was the king's order to return all my belongings to me.

Two days after the judgment, in late morning, Mùirne and I said good-bye to Naoú Giall. We would follow Amalgaid's army as it headed for Cruachain, where Connacht's kings had kept their palace since anyone could remember.

Of course, it was raining again. A fine day for young ducks.

As the column began to move, Kilgarren's black horse, now mine, neighed and trotted after them. I wore the druid's robe, with my pack slung over my shoulders, Mùirne sitting behind me.

Just outside the village, we passed Kilgarren's head stuck on a pike, staring vacantly, his mouth trapped open in final protest.

"I thank you again, my lord, for purchasing my life from Amalgaid." Mùirne hugged my waist tighter. "Kilgarren nearly got us all killed."

"You're welcome. I freed you because . . . I don't know why. I couldn't stand leaving you in servitude to men you don't know."

She laid her head against my neck. "You're generous and honest, my lord. I'm forever grateful."

"'Twas the only thing I could do."

"How far will we travel to this place that draws you?"

"I don't know. Days, perhaps weeks. We'll cross the whole of Ériu to the shores of the eastern sea. But I fear we should have left days ago."

"I hope your foreigner is a good man. I hope your God is a good god and na a bad one. From what I know of the spirits, they're all tricks and treachery."

"My dream can only have come from a good God. He's different from the gods of our people."

Mùirne again tightened her grip around my waist. "I hope so, my lord."

PART III

In the Kingdom of
Ulster, A.D. 432

Chapter 11

Journey

We followed the army ahead of us, Coll and Donnach among them. Almost from the moment we started, I felt an unease, a gnawing at the back of my mind, telling me our pace was too slow. Something was happening at Strangford Loch, and I needed to be there. I don't know how I knew this, only that it was true.

After three long, interminable days, we arrived at the ancient village of Cruachain on the plain of Rathcroghan. It lay inside a vast circle of sharpened spikes atop an earthen rampart. In the middle sat the circular, two-story palace, at least one hundred twenty feet in diameter. I had never seen such a large building. Massive upright timbers supported the second floor. A gaping portico, columned with giant oak logs, led to the interior. Roundhouses and outbuildings surrounded the palace. Amazing though it was, I was reluctant to stop here, even for one night.

We camped beside the army and moved on with them the following morning. Amalgaid himself led the raiding party, consisting of some two hundred men. We traveled northeast through the rain across the heath. When we came to bogs stretching all the way to the horizon, we crossed them by leading our horses over narrow log roads.

I asked who'd built the roads, but no one could say. Some forgotten people from the distant past, I supposed, and whatever clan lived nearest took up the repairs. Without the log roads, no one could travel across the *sheughs*. For, in places, the bogs might suck both man and horse down to their deaths.

Thus was our travel across the fen and muddy clabber slow and wet until rock outcroppings forced out the bog. Then we entered the forests. Three days out of Cruachain, we encountered no *tuatha*. The farmsteads we passed were small, lonely fortresses. Someone said we had entered the country of Meath, but no warriors rode out to challenge us. Either the size of our band kept them away or the land was simply deserted.

Another day passed under intermittent drizzle. At a fork in the road, the army stopped to rest. The soldiers' route led north. Ours east.

Coll stood on the road, looking up at me on my mount, with Mùirne clutching my waist. "When Amalgaid's campaign is finished," he said, "perhaps we'll meet again."

"I'd like that."

"I hope your mysterious foreigner shows you the destiny you're seeking. I've na yet met any foreigner who wasn't a brigand, thief, or murderer. I must also say, Taran, I've rarely met a man like you, who's good and honest and brave. I take your leave with regret."

"You embarrass me. I'm none of those things."

Coll smiled a rare smile. We shook hands. Then he ran to catch the departing army, filing off to the north. When they turned the bend and disappeared into the trees, I turned my horse and we entered the eastern woodlands at a faster clip than the army's progress allowed.

Eager for haste, I pushed our mount hard.

On our first night alone, we camped late in a forest clearing under dry skies. I made a fire and laid down on one side of the blaze while Mùirne made her bed opposite. I had just pulled my cape over me and closed my eyes, when Mùirne's warm, naked body slid under the covering beside me. I tensed, so surprised I couldn't move.

She began kissing my forehead and cheeks. She was desirable. She wanted me. And we were alone. I let her continue, feeling her wet lips pressing against mine.

She ran her hand down my arm. Then she touched the armband Laurna had made for me.

The armband. Laurna. What was I doing? I sat up and covered her naked breasts with the cloak. I looked, not down, but into her eyes.

"You must . . . not." My voice sounded weak. "We cannot be together like this."

Mùirne rose to a sitting position, hugging the cloak, her bare shoulders shining golden in the firelight. Her eyes widened with disappointment. "Am I na pleasing to you, my lord?"

"I'm sure you'd please any man, Mùirne. You're a beautiful girl. But I didn't purchase your freedom from Amalgaid to bed you whenever I wanted."

"I donna understand."

"You're free to go, to do whatever you want." I knew I was talking nonsense. "You don't have to be . . . a slave. To me or to anyone."

"But where would I go? What would I do? You're my protector and my lord. Without you, the first *tuath* we see will take me a slave. And the next man to own me willna be like you. I've na met anyone like you." Her voice broke. Tears formed at the corners of her eyes.

"I know, Mùirne. I know. I can't explain why I bought you."

"If you donna want me, what am I to do? What's to become of me?"

Indeed, I couldn't free her to roam the countryside alone. In Ériu, slavery was far more a part of their ways than on Inis Creig. Back home, we had no more than a dozen slaves, all *bothach*, debtors whose servitude would end when their debts were paid. Here, anyone wandering outside a local *tuath* was asking for capture—or death. A servant girl would be quickly enslaved. Only druids, poets, and nobility traveled unmolested between the different clans' regions. And, in such wild lands as these, even their fate was uncertain. We were now in Meath, maybe even Ulster. We had left the protection of Connacht and Amalgaid. She was now my responsibility.

"Then you'll be my servant," I said at last. "You'll cook and clean for me. Where I go, you will also. But I cannot bed you. I'm pledged to another."

"As you wish, my lord. But this other—what if you never see her again? What if you stay in Ériu the rest of your life? Would you na want a woman then?"

"I . . . I hope to return someday. It may never happen. But right now my heart lies with Laurna."

She seemed to accept this then went to her side of the fire, dressed, and laid down for the night.

But I couldn't sleep. I ran my fingers over the armband and thought of Laurna. Had she lost status because of me? Would she still remain *flaith*? Would her father want her to marry another? Would she herself wait for me after the years had fled?

I tossed and turned, remembering Laurna's face, the sound of her voice, the touch of her hand, wondering if I'd lost her forever.

The next day, we left the deep forest. But a fear was growing within me. Something—I knew not what—was amiss with my quest. We traveled in haste the next two days, crossing a country of dry heath. Then the land rose up, became rugged hills, climbed ever higher, and descended to a wide river, which we forded naked, tying our clothes to the pommel of the saddle. In the dry country beyond, we made good time.

As evening approached, the trees swallowed the road and grew close and damp on all sides. At a small waterfall, I announced we'd make camp.

"Nay, let's na stop here," Mùirne's voice rose above the sound of crashing waters. "The spirits from the Otherworld might come at us from the falls as we sleep."

"I'm not afraid of them." I glanced at the cascading water, wondering if she were right. "I refuse to bow down to them, whoever or whatever they are."

"But I fear this place." Her voice was trembling. "Taran, I fear something will happen here. Let's move on."

I looked at her askance. "Nay, it's late, and look—the road ahead is already too dark for travel. We've no choice but to stay and move on in the morning. "

Finally, she relented. But her gaze darted back and forth across the woods as if the spirits themselves would at any moment leap out at us. Her unease was so great, I too found myself sending furtive glances into the trees.

The wood we collected was damp and made for a difficult fire. We ate from the dwindling provisions of cheese and dried pork Amalgaid's men had given us. Then we settled down for the night.

After staring once more into the trees and seeing nothing, I sat on my blanket, laid over a makeshift bed of pine needles. I was about to remove my shoes when I heard branches cracking in the shadows. The rustling of leather. The clinking of metal.

I leaped from my bed.

Men burst from the darkness and surrounded us. Too late, I realized my sword lay at my feet.

A short, red-haired man, apparently the leader, eyed me. In his right hand, he brandished a sword. The blade flashed orange in the firelight. "What business have you, druid, with the *tuath* of Rodachan?"

"No business other than to travel through it."

"Sure, and none travels here unless aligned with Sionn and his wretched clan. We'll na put up with his spies in our midst."

"I know nothing of Sionn or his *tuath*. We came from Amalgaid, the Rí Cóicid of Connacht, on the western sea. We travel to the Loch of Strangford in the east."

The red-haired man narrowed his eyes. Slowly, he walked through the camp, regarding my horse, then Mùirne, then my sword, lying on my cape next to the fire.

"What business has you in Strangford Lough? And is you a warrior or druid?"

"You know of the loch? Can you tell me the way to it?"

"I asks the questions here, stranger. What is your business there?"

"A man in shining white told me in a dream to go there and find a foreigner."

Gasps came from the men around him—I counted at least twelve. Even the red-haired leader raised an eyebrow.

A brown-haired man, his large, dark eyes now wide as spoons, spoke to the other, "There *is* a foreigner living there, Gòrdon. And they say he's bewitched the entire village, that they're all acting in strange ways. How does he ken such a thing? What if he's a druid come from the Otherworld? Maybe through the falls?"

The man's words cut into me. The foreigner had *bewitched* the village?

"Do the gods speak to you, stranger?" said the one called Gòrdon, taking a step back. "Does you come from the Otherworld as Osgar says?"

I shook my head. "I come from an island called Inis Creig in the far northern sea."

"What if that island be in the Otherworld, Gòrdon?" Osgar's face was contorted with worry. "What if the spirits sent him, up through the falls itself, to trick us? I fears he's a demon from the waterfall. His wench too. We should leave here."

"Is it so, stranger? Are you a spirit from the Otherworld? But I see your weapon. And I ken spirits do not carry such. So who are you? Spirit or druid or warrior?"

"I'm not a spirit. But I am a warrior. I'm also a druid—that is, I was once a druid, but no longer. We want no trouble here. Only to pass through your lands in peace."

Gòrdon scratched his head. "I think he's na spirit, Osgar. Never has I seen a spirit, mind you, yet I think he has na the look of one." He went to Mùirne, lifted her chin, let his hand trail once through her hair, and then walked around her. All the while she cast her gaze at the ground, only once lifting it to mine.

As Gòrdon did this, my fists clenched and my face grew hot. More than once, I glanced toward the sword at my feet. But there were twelve of them. And only one of me.

"If you're na a spirit or Sionn's spy, but only a man, then what can you pay for passage through me lands? For none travels through the forests of Rodachan, past Gòrdon mac Ninean, without tribute."

With nothing of value to give them, I shrugged my shoulders. My glance shot again to the sword.

"What about the wench, hey?"

"*That* I will not do." In one swift motion, I grabbed the sword and sheath, swung the scabbard free into the dirt, and held the blade before me. "I will never give her up!"

"Ahhhh, so is it the warrior who defends the wench?" Gòrdon inched back.

"Aye." I turned my sword to reflect the firelight, backing up so Mùirne was beside me. "And before you take her, you'll die. Every one of you."

Gòrdon laughed nervously.

Osgar cleared his throat. "He will f–fight, Gòrdon. He *is* a spirit, I fears. He's been lying to us all along. Perhaps he'll change into some terrible creature 'afore we can kill him. Men don't camp beside waterfalls. Nay, they don't. Only spirits. Let's take the horse and leave."

"He . . . he is na spirit," said Gòrdon, but now his voice lost some of its swagger. "Your bravery, I respect it, stranger. Your wench, you may keep her." He circled our fire, keeping a good distance from me. "But we'll take the horse. "

I turned to follow his movements, keeping my sword held high. "Then take it. But tell me—since you rob me like lowly *bothachs* without honor—what's the answer to my question? Where is Strangford Loch? How far?"

Osgar took my saddle. Gòrdon eyed me warily as he took the horse's reins and led it quickly away. When his band entered the darkness of the trees, he stepped back into the light. "Sure, and the lough is two days on foot, northeast over the mountains." Perhaps drawing courage from the gap between us, his voice rose. "And if you still had a horse, you'd be there in one."

"Then away with you." I waved my sword at him. "And I'll tell the tale of Gòrdon's *tuath* and how there is no honor to be found in the forests of Rodachan."

He leered at me, turned, and led Kilgarren's horse into the shadows. We were alone again.

"Did you hear, Mùirne? Strangford Loch is two days' walk. But I fear we should already have been there."

"If we'd camped somewhere other than beside these falls, bewitched though they may be, I'd be a slave now. Or we'd both be dead. The gods themselves must be guiding you."

"We're close. But I'm troubled by what the man Osgar said—that the foreigner had cast a spell over the village."

"Sure, and maybe your God is na as good as you thought? Maybe instead this man you seek is a sorcerer?" Then Mùirne lay down on the opposite side of the fire.

Shifting uncomfortably on my furs, I stared at the fire's dying embers. At least, I knew the dream was true. A foreigner *did* live at Strangford Loch. But he'd done something odd to the people of Sabhall and the news had reached all the way to this remote forest. I shook my head and lay down.

This news had to be wrong. I felt an even more powerful need to hurry our pace. I had to find out what waited for me in Strangford Loch.

CHAPTER 12

The Ridge

Over the next two days, I felt a deep longing, an increasing urge, to find the foreigner. The closer we came to the goal, the stronger became my desire.

At the highest point of the green mountains, we looked over the slopes to the southeast. Tiny flecks danced on the eastern sea, wave tops shimmering in the sun. On the northeastern horizon, mist blanketed the dim outline of a loch. Strangford Loch? Aye, it could be nothing else.

As we started down the other side, we met an old man and woman coaxing their horse and a cart full of barrels up the mountain.

"Hullo, good sir," I addressed the wizened old man. "Have you any news of Sabhall?"

He looked up at me and scrunched his eyebrows. "Aye, lad. The village is bewitched. If I was you, I'd stay away."

His words shot through me like a bolt. "What do you mean—*bewitched*?"

"The druid from Bryton who lives there, he's made them all docile and—" he shook his head and scrunched his face, "—unnaturally . . . kind."

"The Bryton is a druid?" This was distressing news. No good could come from a druid.

"The missus and I think so, aye. He wears a white tunic. But the place may soon return to normal."

"Why?"

"Because the druid's left. Or so they say."

I barely had the sense to thank him as I pondered his words. He'd gone? Was this what I sensed, somehow, that was propelling me to such haste? We continued on our way at an even faster clip, down into a green, wet country.

"My lord," said Mùirne from behind, "I canna keep up this pace."

"We've no choice. We must hurry."

I waited until she'd come alongside then continued at a brisk stride.

By mid-afternoon, we arrived on the banks of a brackish river and smelled the salt sea beyond. We came to a copse of trees some distance from the riverbanks. In its midst lay a farmstead with a large, circular barn.

The odor of manure and fermented fodder met our nostrils as a small herd of cattle scattered when we entered the yard. Herding from behind were two young men. They spied us, drew their swords, and ran through the cattle toward us.

A tawny-haired lad of no more than fifteen years demanded in a cracking voice, "What business, druid, have you in Sabhall?"

My heart raced at mention of the name. "This is Sabhall? We come in peace, lad. I seek a stranger here in your village. I've traveled all the way from the western coast to meet him. Have you seen such a man?"

"You must be speaking of Pátrick, the Roman. But you're too late. He spent nearly six months among us. Just yesterday he left." The men sheathed their swords.

I gasped. "Yesterday?"

"His work here was done, he said."

"But has he . . . bewitched . . . your village?"

He threw his head back and laughed. "Nay, stranger. He's brought us blessings and remarkable teaching. Even Dichu, the Rí Tuath, now follows him. But you should ask my cousin here about him. He listened to the man and believed him. I couldna do it."

He returned to his cattle, leaving us with his young, blond-haired cousin.

"What did he say?" I asked. "Why didn't your cousin believe him? In which direction did he go?"

"You ask too many questions, stranger. He went north to seek the King of Ulster."

"You said the foreigner's a Roman?"

"'Tis so. But he has the heart of the Ériu. He spoke like one of us and lived here long ago as a slave himself."

"Why didn't your cousin believe him?"

"He spoke of the one true God who sent us a Son named Jesu. 'Twas powerful teaching, stranger, and he left us a small church and a young priest named Aurelius from Bryton so we could learn more. One of our own, Latharn, went with him."

My heart pounded inside my chest. *The one true God.* So it was true. That was why the man in white had sent me to meet this Pátrick, this Roman. And the village was *not* bewitched. I leaped forward. Before he could back away, I surprised the young man with a hug.

"You've made this traveler happy beyond words. How can I catch up with him?"

The lad separated himself and smiled. "He took the western hill road. You canna miss it. They're heavy-laden. Still they've got horses, and you're on foot. I donna ken how you can catch them now."

"Has your village any horses to lend?" I had no more gold to offer.

"Nay, stranger."

I thanked the lad, took his leave, and nearly ran up the path toward the hill road, with Mùirne struggling to catch up.

Dusk came and went, and we left the smell of the river and sea far behind. The road climbed over dry, rocky land, then descended into wetter country. We traveled until night forced us to quit, then started out again early the next morning, having eaten the last of our food. All day we walked under a light drizzle, stopping to rest occasionally, only teasing our empty bellies with a few berries from a bush. Late that evening, we topped a steep, rocky ridge. On the dark plain below, within a grove of tall trees, figures moved against firelight. My heart leaped in my chest. Pátrick's group?

But as I started down, Mùirne grabbed my arm. "We canna pick our way through these stones in the dark, my lord. 'Tis na safe."

I looked at the steep, rock-strewn path winding down between boulders, barely visible by starlight and a half-moon, then at the campfire far below. "We are so close. We must go down. Tonight."

"Nay, my lord. I have a bad feeling about this."

I stared into her eyes for some time, then shook my head and started down.

The trail was more like a steep gully strewn with rocks, roots, and the debris of fallen trees. As we descended, the trees on either side closed above us, shutting out the starlight. But we were now so close to the foreigner's camp, I was sure we'd see him tonight.

I slipped on a rock and fell to the right. But I broke my fall with an outstretched hand, sharp rocks cutting my palm in several places. I regained my feet, a bit shaken. I rubbed my palm. Still, I was eager to press ahead.

Behind me, I heard Mùirne's feet sliding over loose scree and a cry of pain.

I stopped and called back. "Are you all right?"

"Aye, 'twas only my shin hitting a boulder."

As I stared at her, all I could make out was the dark outline of her form. I turned back to the trail and hurried on. From the top, I guessed we had no more than a half a mile down the slope and across the field. But who knows how long it would take to descend in this dark?

We trudged down through the rocky gully, skirting boulders, sliding over patches of loose pebbles, climbing over deadfalls. More than once I tripped over a root, only to pick myself up again. Often I had to wait for Mùirne to catch up. I pushed her hard, and she did her best to follow. But I fear my haste to reach the bottom was uncaring and harsh. My only thought was I had to see the foreigner— and tonight.

I don't remember exactly how it happened. One moment I was striding in the dark, stepping briskly through a section of vaguely defined rocks. The next my footing was gone.

Then I fell backward. Something hit my head from behind with powerful force.

I remember no pain, only stunned surprise. I was lying on my back, gasping for breath, staring up at a sliver of starlight through the gap in the trees. Then Mùirne knelt over me, a hand reaching for the back of my head.

"My lord! You're bleeding. What should I do?"

I opened my mouth to speak. And then my world went dark.

CHAPTER 13

Pátrick

When next I opened my eyes, the morning sun glinted on dewy leaves above me. Kneeling over me and wiping my forehead with a wet cloth was a tall man with high, regal cheekbones and a prominent royal nose. He was tawny-haired, with piercing, yet friendly, eyes. When he saw I was awake, he smiled. "You had quite a fall, Taran."

I tried to sit up, but a wave of dizziness sent me back onto my furs.

He laid a hand gently on my shoulder. "Let me see your wound." He looked at the back of my head, removed a small bandage of cloth, stained with blood. "It's much better now. Not bleeding at all."

"Are you . . . Pátrick . . . the Roman?" His tunic was white, but the cloth was sewn and trimmed in a foreign manner.

"I am. They also call me Pádhraig, and my Roman name's Patricius, but most just call me Pátrick." His Gaelic was good, yet carried the hint of a foreign accent.

I looked to the side and saw Mùirne walking across a clearing. "Where am I?"

"Last night, your friend burst in on us, desperate for help. We found you up on the ridge trail and brought you to our camp. We've been worried about you."

I tried again and was able to sit up without the world spinning around me. I felt for the lump in the back of my head where I'd hit the rocks. It hurt, but the injury was not great. It would heal.

Nearby was a smoldering fire and a boiling pot wafting the smell of meat with onions. A portly man, who knelt over the kettle, turned his head to me and smiled.

"I am Latharn." The man by the fire smiled and pointed to the pot. "Would you like some stew, Taran?"

Everyone seemed to know my name. I nodded. Mùirne crossed the clearing, took the wooden bowl, and brought it to me. I thanked them both and eagerly began eating. I'd been two days now with an empty stomach.

When I'd dispatched the first bowl of stew and nearly finished a second, Pátrick smiled. "I think you'll live. Your friend told us you were seeking me, but not much more. May I ask how you heard of me?"

"I must admit you are the object of my quest." I set down the empty bowl. "For nearly two weeks, we've traveled from western Connacht to find you." Then I related the dream and the command from the man in white.

"*Filius Deus!* Was it the Son himself? It seems, stranger, that Providence itself has brought you here. You and your friend are welcome, indeed."

Then Pátrick made introductions, presenting the one called Latharn, a smiling red-haired lad about my age and height and a native of Strangford Loch. But he must have been a grand man for the table, as his girth was twice mine. He'd decided only three months ago to believe the teachings of this Pátrick and to follow him.

Then the third man in their party appeared from behind the horses at the clearing's far end. Pátrick introduced him as Servius Flavius Crispus. The tall, thin Roman with black hair and a round face bowed and said he'd traveled with Pátrick from Bryton. Servius explained he'd studied with Patricius, as he insisted on calling him, in a "town". Apparently a large village, with many people, streets, and stone buildings clustered together where men came from miles around to learn about the "Word of God". Dughall had told of such places. As Servius spoke, he stuttered and stumbled over his words.

Pátrick thanked him, then said, "Perhaps, Servius, you could return to the stream for more water?"

He nodded and disappeared down the trail to the north, laden with water skins.

Feeling much recovered after the stew, I gazed at Pátrick with eager eyes. "Now that I've found you, I have so many questions. The blond-haired lad in Strangford Loch told us you spoke of the one true God. I would learn of Him and all His ways."

A genuine smile broke Pátrick's face. His eyes were alight with energy. "You are blessed indeed to seek God. If only we encountered more like you. First you must know He's the one and only God, and He rules the world. But this mighty ruler also wants us to know Him, for He loves each of us."

What he said was too good to be true. "What about the spirits of forest, stream, and mountain? What about Crom Cruach, The Bent and Bloody One, the angry god of the sun whom my people worship and sacrifice to? What about Manannán mac Lir, the capricious god who rules the angry sea and the Otherworld? What about Danu, the mother of the earth? And Lugh, master of many things? Do they all bow down to this God of yours?"

"My, what a thinker you are! Aye, lad. But also nay, for the ones you mention aren't gods. They're either demons inhabiting idols of stone or wood, or they're false gods, ideas from the Evil One meant to capture men's minds and turn them from the one, true God. The objects you mentioned—the sun, the sea, and the things of the earth—are created things. The one God made everything that exists. He created this world and all that's in it. Even the unseen worlds of the heavens. He's greater than what He created and indeed, rules over everything. He is God Most High and there's none like Him."

As Mùirne came to sit beside me and listen, my heart pounded in my chest. This truth, hidden but somehow known to me, must have been behind my thoughts when I'd spoken out at the stone of Crom Cruach. Now here was the answer to all my questions. The dizziness from a moment ago was now gone, replaced by a breathless surge of energy.

"How do I sacrifice to this God?"

Before Pátrick could answer, Servius burst in from the trail carrying his water skins. Nearly out of breath, he turned to Pátrick. "Th–those soldiers we saw yesterday are b–back."

Pátrick rubbed his chin. "How many?"

"I d–don't know. A large party. They seem to be heading toward us. B–but the road skirts our g–grove. Maybe they'll pass us by?"

Latharn frowned. "Or turn south and ride right into us."

Pátrick frowned. "All right. Keep watch, keep out of sight, and let me know what they do."

Servius nodded and ran down the trail to the north.

Pátrick's glance caught Latharn's. "Perhaps we should start packing?"

Latharn nodded his head, cast a worried glance after Servius, and headed toward the horses.

Pátrick turned back to me. "To answer your question, Taran, our God doesn't require a sacrifice of flesh and blood. He's already made it on our behalf. This God sent His very Son to earth for us."

"This God's Son is here, among us?" I looked around. "Can I speak to him?"

Pátrick laughed gently. "He's here and yet He isn't. You see, Taran, God's Son was once a man who walked the earth. His name was Jesu. He was a carpenter on the far side of the world in a dry and rocky land. He lived a blameless life, and when He spoke, no one had ever heard such teaching since the world began. He urged men to abandon their evil ways and seek God with all their hearts. Lad, this Jesu came to earth to lead us to the Kingdom of Heaven, a place of bliss where God Himself will dwell with us for all eternity. All we have to do is believe in Him. And follow Him."

"*He* was the man in white," I whispered, my heart pounding.

"Surely, he was," added Mùirne, putting a hand on my shoulder.

"So this God is a man?" I wondered.

"Jesu was not just a man, Taran. He *was* God. He was *from* God, yet He was also God's *Son*. While He lived He healed thousands—the lame, the blind, and the sick. People would leave their clans and travel for a hundred miles to be cured and to hear Him. Men who were blind from birth simply touched His robe. Then, for the first time, they saw color and light and the wrinkles on their mothers' faces. We're told of one man possessed by a demon. He'd driven his family away and lived alone among the gravestones, and when the villagers chained him, he broke the iron links with his bare hands—so fiercely did evil grip him. Yet this Jesu healed him in an instant and made him whole again. Then the man proclaimed Jesu was Lord.

"But evil men feared Jesu and became jealous for their own power. They plotted among themselves and killed Him. They nailed Him with spikes through the wrists and ankles and hung Him on a tree to die."

I gasped and looked at Mùirne, who looked at me with widened eyes.

"Aye, he died. And at His death, the entire land shook, tombs opened, and the dead came out of their graves to walk the streets and talk again with their former neighbors and families. Then for three hours at midday, darkness came upon the land."

Pátrick cleared his throat and I spoke into the gap, "But how could He die? This Son who came from God Himself, whose death caused the day to become night and the earth to shake—*How could He die?*" Great sadness filled me. Up until now, it seemed this man must have been God Himself. But if they had killed Him—what a tragedy!

"He died indeed, and His body lay three days locked inside the cold stone walls of a tomb. But then He rose to life and walked the earth again, alive as you and me. More than five hundred witnesses saw Him, talked with Him, and heard His teaching. He even cooked a breakfast of fish on the shores of a loch and ate with the men who followed Him. Then as His disciples watched, God the Father took Him up into the clouds to be with Him in Heaven."

I stared dumbly at Pátrick. Was this the answer to all my seeking? If this God created everything that existed, then He was the highest of all gods, the King above all the Rí Cóicids of the world, the one who truly ruled the earth, sun, moon, seas, and all peoples everywhere. And He had sent us a Son to lead us to Him. My head was spinning. I didn't know what to ask next. For the first time, I'd encountered a God who made sense of the world. Yet some things still didn't make sense.

"I think this God you speak of is a better God than any I've heard of." My eyes welled with tears. "Perhaps He's what I've been looking for . . . all my life. I want to hear more. I've so many questions. Can Mùirne and I join you on your journey? The village lad said your destination was Ulster?"

Pátrick gripped my shoulder, then smiled. "It's good you think on what I've said. Too many readily accept what they don't understand. You may indeed join us. When you're ready, I'll baptize you.

"But you should know, lad, our journey is now toward Emain Macha where the King of Ulster sits in judgment. I'm told Forga mac Dallán is a hard man who does not easily welcome strangers. Our path will be difficult. We bring him a teaching to challenge his ways and the traditions of his fathers. Maybe he'll reject us, or threaten us, or come against us with the sword. It is ever thus, as it was for the great Apostle Paul. We may be martyred for the faith. It's all up to God. But I'm sworn to bring this message of hope and life to all who abide here, to spread the church of Christ across this land which sits at the ends of the earth in the last days. For this is the command of my Lord and I must obey."

I was moved by Pátrick's intensity and resolve. But I feared his bravery would soon be tested. Only druids, poets, or travelers under the authority of a Rí Tuath were safe in the lands between kingdoms. "My lord, may I ask under whose protection you travel?"

"We travel by the protection of Christ, our Lord, and Savior."

"Christ?"

"Aye, another name we give to Jesu the Savior."

"Then I offer you my sword." I stood, pulled my blade from its sheath, and brandished it. "I was a druid once, but I'm also a warrior. If need be, I'll fight and die for you."

Pátrick smiled but waved a dismissing hand. "I thank you, but we've no need of fighting. We don't shed the blood of our foes. We instead throw ourselves on the mercy of our Lord, for only He is our protector. If you stay with us, you'll learn of this teaching. Put away your weapon, lad."

I sheathed my sword. "I'm puzzled at your words, but I respect them. I'd learn of your ways." Still I feared we were headed for trouble. I say "we" for I now counted myself a member of their party.

He patted my shoulder. "Glad we are for you and Mùirne to join us. But now we have a long journey ahead of us." I nodded as Latharn lifted another bundle of goods from the stack on the ground and tied it to one of their five mounts. The Roman did not travel light.

Then Servius Flavius rushed in from the edge of the copse. "A–armed riders. Approaching from the west. Maybe a h–hundred. S–some with chariots. They are headed right for us."

Pátrick looked at his small band, then said in a calm voice, "Pay them no heed. The Lord is our protector." Beneath the deep rumble of many horses' hooves, he added, "But do finish packing with all haste."

CHAPTER 14

Emain Macha

As Latharn and Servius finished packing their goods, the horses' hooves thundered ever closer. Soon, dozens of armed men, each holding a spear, rode into the clearing and surrounded us. Their leader, a hefty, muscled man with a thick black beard, sat astride a white stallion. His bushy eyebrows almost touched the lip of his horned helmet. His chain mail bulged, straining to contain his chest and shoulders. "I am Armadal, in high service to Forga mac Dallán, Rí Cóicid of the Ulaid. I ask you now in his name: Who trespasses on the roads of Ulster? By what authority do you travel here?"

Pátrick stepped out. "I am Pátrick, servant of Jesu, my Lord and Savior, Son of the one true God. These others are with me. Our authority comes not by the orders of men, but from the Kingdom of Heaven."

From behind the soldiers, a man without weapons rode up in a chariot. He was dressed all in white—a druid. As his mare pulled the chariot through, the others drew their horses aside to let him pass. The breeze of his passing blew wispy strands of brown hair across his forehead into his eyes. He was a short man, even when standing and looking down at us from the chariot's platform. Small, dark eyes regarded us intently above a crooked nose and thin lips. "Sure, and I know of no such person, God, or kingdom. You speak oddly, stranger. Though you dress as druids, your clothing is odd. Are you foreign druids then?"

"We are not, my lord." Pátrick gave a short bow. "We are travelers from Sabhall, originally from Bryton, and priests of our God. And it's fortunate, indeed, you should come upon us. We enter your lands to seek an audience with none other than the King of Ulster."

"Has the Rí Cóicid requested this?"

"He has not. But we bring him many gifts. And a message of hope and joy about the one God who rules the heavens and the Son He sent."

The druid narrowed his tiny, dark eyes, frowned, and looked toward the soldiers. "He speaks nonsense, Armadal. There is no such God." Then he turned to us. "I am Ohran, chief druid to Forga mac Dallán, High King of Ulster. You there," he pointed at me, "your dress says you are not of these others. Who are you and where did you study the secret arts?"

"I am Taran mac Teague and, aye, my lord, I was once a druid, but no longer. For three years I studied on Inis Creig, an island in the far northern sea. Nearly three weeks ago, I sailed from there and landed in Naoú Giall on the western coast."

"If you're no longer a druid, then why do you wear the garb of our order? What are you doing here?"

"I . . . I was told it was safer for travel. I'm here because I've joined Pátrick. I've only begun to learn of his God. But I ken what he says is true."

The druid snapped his left hand across his forehead to push wayward locks from his eyes. He lacked a little finger on that hand. Then he addressed Armadal, "They are wayfarers, all. And they all speak the same foolishness. They travel without protection, and I say we kill them and be on our way. That's the price for trespass here. In his current state, the king does not need to—nay, he cannot— deal with this."

The soldier's bushy eyebrows dipped together in a frown. "I'm na so quick for the blood of strangers, Ohran." He faced Pátrick again. "Tell me why I shouldna cut off your heads and take your goods? You come unbidden, without escort, with a foreign manner of dressing and talking. Why should I na follow Ohran's advice to speed us on our way?"

"Take us with you, my lord, and when your king hears what we have to tell him, he will certainly reward you. I promise, he's never heard the likes of the teaching we bring. At least give us the chance to tell your king the great news we bring. Certainly we deserve that much?" With his high cheekbones, long Roman nose, and piercing eyes alight with energy, Pátrick carried an air of authority.

"No good can come of this." Ohran scowled at Armadal. "Right now, this is the last kind of distraction Forga needs. There's no one God who rules the world. They have nothing to bring to the kingdom of Ulster that anyone wants to hear."

Armadal's horse turned in circles, eager to go on. When it spun around again, he said, "I would spare them, yet give them as much rope for a noose as they'd take. Aye, we'll let Forga decide their fate. You may be High Druid, and all the *flaith* quake at your judgments and the threat of your spells. But Forga is still the Rí Cóicid. You forget that at your peril."

He turned to Pátrick. "Your bravery and boldness speak well for you, so I'll do this. We must go ahead now to Emain Macha. But I'll leave a detachment to bring you along behind. Forga mac Dallán will hear your case and decide for himself. But you may regret your boldness, for he's a hard man. At least he was. In days past, he would've brooked no foolish talk about foreign gods. But lately . . . with his grief . . . I donna ken what he'll do."

Then he ordered six men to escort us under guard while the rest thundered up the road to the north.

Apologizing profusely, a pleasant, rough-shaven, rough-hewn man named Sòlas tied us all together. As a fine drizzle fell, our stocky, muscled captor led us through rain and mist over a wooden road spanning a bog pungent with mold, then under the canopy of a dank forest.

Our march lasted only until noon. As the rain quit and the sun coaxed mist from the earth, we approached Emain Macha. From the wet, green forest rose a wide hill topped by an earthen fortress. Sòlas led us across a drawbridge, over a deep ditch sprouting heavy log spikes. We crossed through high earthworks, emerging onto a hilltop village. Oddly, inside the fort, another ditch hugged the earthen ring. At regular intervals, narrow log bridges crossed the gap.

"Why another ditch?" I asked our guard.

Sòlas stopped and narrowed his glance at me. "If we lose the high mounds, and our enemy finds himself up there—" He pointed at the earthworks. "We'll pull the bridges away and meet him in battle as he tries to climb from the second ditch." He looked both ways, then winked. "But you didna hear old Sòlas say it."

Then he led us up a lane between a dozen roundhouses, with half as many stone houses. We stopped at the edge of a wide yard of trampled grass. Beyond were two great structures. The first was an enormous conical building, faced with thatch laid over increasingly smaller concentric wooden circles, rising to a point—a druid temple. The second was a great round edifice some two hundred feet in diameter, built of sturdy pine logs chinked with pitch and covered by a thatch roof—the palace of the King of Ulster.

At the yard's edge opposite these great buildings, Sòlas led us into a dank hut. On the dirt floor, coiled lengths of chain were fixed to a central post. He picked up one leg iron, looked at Pátrick, and his face fell. "I'm sorry, my lords, but 'tis my duty." Then he bound us.

"As our captor, Sòlas, you've been so kind," said Pátrick. "May I ask where you've taken our goods?"

"Your horses will have feed and water. As for your goods, no one will bother them. At least until the Rí Cóicid decides what to do to you."

"What is the grief Armadal spoke of that grips the king?"

Sòlas scratched the stubble on his chin. Then he peered out the doorway into the yard as if to determine whether anyone was listening. He shut the door and shook a mop of reddish-brown hair that fell to his shoulders.

"If anyone has been ill-used by the gods, 'tis Forga mac Dallán. First his wife were taken from him, dead of the fever in a single week. Happened only last *Samain*, before the first snow. Then his eldest son and greatest pride fell off his horse, and broke his neck, killed. Was there myself. Sharp, like a twig snapping, were the sound. The best swordsman in Emain Macha he were, and his father's eyes were sore red at his passing. And that only two full moons past.

"Then, as everyone were still mourning his son—if this weren't enough sadness and misery heaped atop one man's head—his daughter Eivhir up and took fever only three weeks ago. Sure, and the fever broke, but then she fell straight away into a death sleep. Just lies in her bed, they say, barely drawing breath. Na dead. But na living, neither."

"But this is terrible." Pátrick's face showed pain. "Can nothing be done for her?"

"The druids have tried everything—potions, salves, herbs, incense, and killing all manner of critters beside her bed to appease the spirits. But the gods must be terrible angry, for nothing has changed. Nothing but the king. After a spell of their critter-killing, he flew into a rage and threw the lot of them out and away from her bedside. Even threw out Ohran, the high sorcerer himself. Threatened to behead them all if they ever stepped beside Eivhir's bed again. To this day, she willna open her eyes nor flinch if pricked with a pin. Least, that's what they say.

And now Beahak, her maid, says she can barely get a sip of broth or milk between her teeth."

Pátrick shook his head. "What a burden for the king to bear."

"Worse it couldna be. All of this has put the king, not to mention Ohran, in a fine state, indeed. Now everyone's been acting the goat." He squinted at Pátrick, his brow furrowing. "Stranger, we have a palace full of goats here. The king's no longer fit for reasoning, nor even for clever tales from his bard. He's no longer the wise and hard man he was just a few months ago. I fear 'twill be the undoing of everyone."

Servius sent Pátrick a worried glance, but Pátrick's face showed only concern.

"And that, fine sirs, is what has ailed the king and all Emain Macha. If I was you, I wouldna be speaking foolish talk about foreign gods to Forga mac Dallán just now. And you didna hear any of this from me. If you have any heart for my welfare, that is."

"Thank you, Sòlas." Pátrick smiled. "We'll keep your secret safe."

Sòlas nodded. A flicker of a smile crossed his lips, and he bowed. Then he left us alone.

Servius looked at Pátrick, frowning. "H–how can we b–bring the Gospel message to the king, wh–when he's plagued with such grief?"

For myself, I feared what would become of me. I wondered where, in all this affair, was any place for a warrior and his sword? I could think of nothing I, or anyone, could do to get us out of this. Indeed, after Sòlas's speech, I was sure we would all soon come to a bad end.

But Pátrick just smiled, and then he began to pray. And I'd never heard such prayers as he said that afternoon. He gave himself completely to his God, trusting that whatever happened would work out for the best. He prayed for wisdom, courage, a good outcome for the mission, and an opportunity to bring the king his message. He asked for something called the "Holy Spirit" to descend on us and give us guidance. And he prayed for the health of Forga's daughter. Then he asked his God to show Mùirne and me the truth of his Jesu and to spare our lives until our names could be written in something called the Book of Life.

When his prayer ended, I felt strangely comforted. I almost believed his God might come to our rescue. Then I said, "My lord, Pátrick, I am overwhelmed by your concern for us. No one has ever spoken to a god on my behalf like you did."

"You and Mùirne only just joined us. You haven't had time to become Christians yet."

"What is this Book of Life you speak of? How do we get our names written in it?"

Before he could answer, Sòlas reentered the room, accompanied by a skinny youth in guard's dress. "The king would see you now. Remember, you didna hear about his condition from me." Then he released us from the post and chained us together. He led us across the clearing toward the palace of Emain Macha.

But, as we crossed the field under the stares of village bystanders, the druid Ohran approached Pátrick, his tiny eyes glaring. His next words sent a chill rippling across my neck. "Say nothing of this God of yours to the Rí Cóicid. Or I promise—none of you will see the dawn."

CHAPTER 15

Forga mac Dallán

Sòlas and three others led us into the palace of Emain Macha, through a high doorway framed with timbers and nailed up with iron shields. Ohran trailed behind. We walked down a short, dark hallway over uneven flagstones. Torches burned at intervals, lighting our way, and revealing dark side rooms. Then the passage opened into a great hall, where wall torches lit an enormous inner chamber.

Surely, the room was greater than any interior space I'd ever seen, at least fifty feet on a side. A furred creature was chained in a prominent alcove to one side. As we entered, it hopped up and down with strange chattering noises. Two dark eyes stared out of a hairy face and two large holes broke a flat, shiny nose. It grinned at us. Hairy arms reached up, and a black-fingered hand grabbed a metal hook protruding from the wall. Then it flipped itself upside down and landed on its feet. Were a man to become cursed as a demon, it might well end up as such a creature.

Sòlas leaned toward us, his thick russet hair falling over his eyes. "'Tis a Barbary ape they say, whatever that may be. Brought from the coast at a dear price. Romans captured it, they did. But pay it no mind. 'Tis only a dumb beast."

With an effort, I ignored the creature's chattering and antics. At the room's center, an open fire burned on the floor. A smoke plume curled toward a thatched ceiling. A murky cloud filtered through a wide hole under a cone of thatch, blocking not only the rain, but the light.

A man well past middle age, of lean build and disheveled state, sat on a tripod stool before the fire. He stared at the blaze, head down, one temple resting on a fist, the other hand absently poking a blackened sword at the embers. His long blond hair curled down to his shoulders. He was many days unshaven, and he wore a flimsy night cloak, the kind only the wealthiest *flaith* can afford. The cloak was smooth as skin, marred in places by the stains of charcoal and spilt mead.

Ohran stood to one side and stared at us.

Sòlas led us to the fire's opposite side. The guards accompanying us backed away to a corner and stood at attention.

Armadal arched his heavy eyebrows. "You stand in the presence of Forga mac Dallán, Rí Cóicid of the Ulaid, king over all the lands of Emain Macha and Ulster." Then he turned to the king. "My lord, these strangers we found this morning, crossing our lands by their own authority. Their leader said they traveled here to petition you for an audience. So I thought it best to offer them temporary protection until you decided what to do with them."

As if nothing had been said, the man called Forga still leaned forward, resting his head on one hand, while the other poked the fire.

"They await your consideration, my lord." Armadal cleared his throat. "These strangers here now. Standing before you."

The sword halted its prodding and rested for a moment on a log, its tip cherry red.

Armadal shifted his feet while Sòlas looked up at the ceiling. Pátrick stood straight, watching the king. The ape used the moment to flip upside down in its cage.

Armadal opened his mouth to speak, closed it, and then frowned.

The king's gaze remained lost in the fire.

"'Tis as I told you." Ohran snapped a three-fingered hand across his face to free his eyes of wispy brown locks. "We should've disposed of them in the wood. Let's take them now to the yard and teach them with the blade of an axe what 'trespass' means in the Kingdom of Ulster. The king shouldn't be bothered with—"

"Who are you?" The king slapped his sword on the log, interrupting Ohran, but did not lift his gaze. "And what do you want of me?"

"I am Pátrick, son of Calpornius, a Roman by birth." Pátrick spoke now in a low, measured tone. "Twenty years ago, I was a slave, living in Foclut, far to the west. The one God who rules the heavens and earth spoke to me and gave me a mission to return to Bryton and the great southern continent, where I learned about Him. Now I've come back to this blessed Isle of Ériu to preach the wonderful news He gave me. I bring this news to Ulster and its king, whose wisdom and leadership the *tuath* of this region have proclaimed well and loud all the way to Strangford Loch, where I lived these last six months. To prove our goodwill, we've brought many gifts for you among our belongings. But more than this, I bring news of joy and hope. This news will change your life and the lives of everyone in your kingdom."

The king looked up from his poking. His eyes were black as night. "What news?"

"That God has sent His Son to earth to rescue us from our miserable condition and finally reveal Himself to us. He is the one true God, the only God, and He created the sun, moon, stars, earth, and everything in it. And the seas, forests, mountains, and even the land of Ériu."

"What has this to do with me?"

"Why, my lord, it has everything to do with you. For this God has also sent us His Son who lived as a man four hundred years ago in a far distant country. This Son performed miracles and taught as no one ever taught. Yet He was destined to die, killed by evil men, all so He could rise from the grave and walk the earth again. Many witnesses saw Him alive again, eating and talking, like you and me. My lord, God sent His Son, and if we believe in Him, we will have eternal life in a blessed, happy place—the Kingdom of Heaven—where God will bathe us with eternal love. This promise is for all eternity. Yes, my lord, He's not like the gods of the Tuatha Dé Danann, who descended into the earth, who leave us to fend for ourselves, for He loves us. He'll not trick us with wiles and deceit. And all we have to do to find this peace is believe in His Son."

The king gazed at the fire and resumed poking. "Would that I could believe you. Or go right now to such a place as your God offers and leave this cursed life. If only your God were real. For, I admit, you tell a fetching yarn. But such promises are all too easy to make. Oh, but what I really desire is for fate to take my life right now and end this misery!"

Pátrick frowned. "I've heard of your grief, good king. And I will pray to the God of all that is true and right and ask Him for Princess Eivhir's recovery."

At mention of his daughter's name, the king's eyes moistened. He looked up and stared at Pátrick. Then for the first time, he seemed to notice Mùirne, me, and the others.

"What is a man without those who love him?" said the Rí Cóicid. "When wife and son and daughter have been taken from him without reason or warning? Battle didn't kill them, or old age, but cruel fate—the wiles of the gods, curse them all! If your God is as you say, ask Him to undo what the gods of Ohran have done, for they're all evil and conniving. And sure, they've made merry havoc with the life of this king, for here I am, ruined and alone. I'm sinking into a bog, stranger, and so I fear is my kingdom. I'm undone by the fickle hands of Danu and Lugh and by the ghosts of the Tuatha Dé Danann."

Armadal shot a worried glance toward Sòlas, who looked at the floor, shuffled his feet, and shook his head.

"I've good news for you, my lord," said Pátrick. "Those you mention are either false gods or myths. A few may be evil spirits, and if so, they must bow to the one true God, the Lord in heaven, whose power is limitless. Only He can undo the evil done to you."

"Evil! 'Tis a true word, stranger. Evil gods have run amuck over my lands and pulled Eivhir into the Otherworld. Yet the gods are witless lummoxes, for they forgot to take her body. They've left it behind by mistake. My lass has one foot in the Otherworld and the other in Emain Macha, and I'll wager she's adrift between the two, conscious in neither. Only a demon of evil could do such a thing. Can you undo this terrible thing 'afore my daughter falls off the perch of life into oblivion?"

"I can pray, my lord. 'Tis all I can promise. I can ask my God and, if it is His will, perhaps your daughter will wake and live again. My Lord Jesu said whatever we ask of Him, He will give us. So I'll ask, and if God sees fit to give us grace, then your daughter will live."

"Others have tried, stranger—Pátrick, is it? My druid, Ohran—he's the chief of all my druids, for what it's worth—has worried long over her, cast spells, and shed the blood of beasts at her bedside. His power is spent, or he never had it, or his demon spirits no longer listen to him. After all his ministrations, she's only the worse for it. I fear my Eivhir . . . my beautiful daughter . . . my last and only ray of light . . . I fear she'll die.

"What is a palace, Pátrick, when emptiness stalks the halls? And lately, whenever I try to sleep, death herself crowds close around me. She kisses my cheeks with lips of ice. Touches my forehead with her clammy caress. And when the dawn comes with a damp chill, she pulls the warm fur from my grasp and I awake from my stupor, shivering and alarmed. This is what I've become, Pátrick—through every moment, awake or asleep, a man haunted by the specter of death."

Armadal shook his head back and forth. His eyebrows dipped together. Then he glanced at Sòlas, at Pátrick, and back at the king.

"But she's also a temptress, I say, for her wiles fall strongly upon me. Sure, and I've been thinking lately of a tale from the days of the Fir Bolg, if that's where it arose from. Would you hear this tale, stranger?" Forga glanced at Pátrick with moist, defeated eyes.

"Tell me the story, my lord." Pátrick bowed.

"You say this just to humor me, I ken. But it doesna matter. They all ken, all here in the palace, that I'm losing my mind. What do you ken, Sòlas? Does the king flirt with madness?"

Sòlas looked up and his square jaw dropped. "I . . . I doesna think any such thing, my lord. 'Tis grief, I say. Grief has a hold of you."

"Aye, Sòlas." Forga stared again into the fire. "And my tale is one of grief, dark and deep, so I'll tell it. 'Twas once a young warrior who loved a maid with all his breath and life. But she fell into bad dealings and made bad blood with a druid. The sorcerer's revenge was to poison her gruel, and so the druid did murder her. Then this warrior, renowned in battle, was filled with such anger, he went to the druid's house at midnight and slew him in his bed with a dagger through the heart."

Here, Ohran's glance rose to the king and a frown distorted his features. He opened his mouth as if about to speak, but Armadal took one step toward him and shook his head. Ohran closed his mouth and stepped back.

The king saw none of this and went on. "Afterward, a terrible grief laid upon the warrior's heart. He rode his horse to the edge of a cliff above the western sea. There, he sat in the dark. He looked down at the sea crashing on the boulders and pondered his loss. His grief grew and grew. Then he thought he heard his fair maiden, singing below among the rocks, calling him to join her in the Otherworld. As he listened and waited, looking down the cliff-face by moonlight, he came to a grim decision. When dawn broke, he backed his mount, then ran at full gallop toward the edge and went over, horse and all." Here the king lifted his gaze to each of us as if to let his words sink in.

"I've heard the tale, my lord." Armadal spoke into the silence. "They say 'tis the reason the wind so howls through the cliffs and whines around the rocks at cliff's edge in places by the western sea. For 'tis the sound of two lovers, parted before their time."

"Just so. Now spirits on the wind, haunting the cliffs into eternity. A fitting end for such grief as his, don't you ken?"

"But sure, my lord, 'tis only a tale. You donna believe this?"

"A tale, aye. But perhaps a true one? And I've been thinking on it lately, and I ask: Is not my love for my wife and son and daughter greater than that warrior's love for a woman he hadn't yet married? And the answer is—aye! My love is greater by far. So what am I to do with this, hey? Shouldna my fate be the same as his? Wouldna such an end do great honor to my loss and my family? 'Tis what I think about should Eivhir die. For though my heart screams otherwise, my mind sees no outcome but that death will take her. And I long for a high cliff in the land of Ulster."

"Nay, my lord." Armadal stepped forward, his heavy brows closing together. "Nay, you must na let such dark thoughts take hold of you. You are the Rí Cóicid. The strength and hope of Emain Macha. The warrior-king who leads us. Where is the hero of the Battle of Farney? The one who repulsed the forces of Meath and left a field strewn with swords, banners, and the bodies of the fallen? You are that leader, my lord. You rallied the men of Emain Macha to victory. I long for that king, my king, to return. Where is he, my lord?"

"He's gone, Armadal. I thank you for your devotion, but the man you remember is gone, touched in the soul by the specter of death." He turned suddenly to Pátrick. "Can you help me, stranger? Can you give me back my daughter?"

"I'll try, my lord. But nothing I do will bring her back. Only God's will can accomplish such a feat."

"But you will try. And if you—and your God—don't give me back my daughter . . ." He resumed poking his sword into the embers. "If I canna have her . . . then . . . then . . . aye, then blood will flow."

He stood and faced Ohran, then Armadal, Pátrick, and the rest of us. For the first time, I saw how tall and lean a man he was. "If I canna have my daughter, alive and standing by my side, then blood will flow in Emain Macha. You, Ohran, will be first. You, Pátrick, and *all* your followers, next. All the gods must pay. And all who proclaim them. If they'll not return my daughter, then damn the fiends. Damn them all! I will strike down all who come to me in their names."

"But, my lord," objected Ohran, "it's not I who comes to you today with promises of a mythical, impossible God. Why threaten me if this one," he waved a hand at Pátrick, "fails to call upon his God to do the things he's promised?"

"Enough!" The king, slammed his sword upon the burning log. This raised a shower of red sparks and embers so high it rained over all of us and sent the ape in the corner jumping and chattering with glee. Forga faced Ohran and brought the point of his sword, red and glowing, to within an inch of the druid's crooked nose.

"This afternoon, for the first time—just now, actually—I know my mind on this. I'll have my will here and 'tis this: All the gods will pay. If I canna strike them to their faces, I'll take the lives of whoever comes to me in their names, starting with you. Especially you. You've wearied my patience with your casting of spells and your sacrificing of goats and pigs and chickens. My daughter's room reeks yet of spilled blood, and what good did it do? Did they listen, these spirits of yours? Nay, they mocked me! You and your gods are one, druid. Yes, Ohran, my revenge on them—damn them all!—starts with you."

As the king lowered his sword, the blood seemed to drain from Ohran's cheeks. Then Forga whirled to Pátrick, his face taut, his black eyes narrowing.

Pátrick bowed. "As you wish, my lord. If my God does not heed my prayers and cure your daughter, you may take my life. I only ask that you spare the lives of these others, especially these two," he waved at me and Mùirne, "for they've joined us only this morning. Only Servius and Latharn serve my God."

"Bah! You're all together. If my daughter dies, so do you all."

After he spoke, the king's gaze seemed to lose focus. Then he sat with a thud on his stool. Soon, his sword again poked the fire. His hand again propped up a drooping head, and the coals again transfixed his gaze. "Save her, stranger," came a much weakened voice. "Bring her feet back from the Otherworld. If your God is what you say He is, He'll cure her. Aye, if He brings my daughter back from the grave, then I'll follow Him. I'll denounce the gods of the Tuatha Dé Danann and the Fir Bolg, for surely they've fled down into the earth, as the tales go. Now I say they've abandoned us all. And I admit, the pleasant fantasy you've spun appeals to me, so we'll see if it's true. I leave it up to you and your God. Let Him show me what He is, if He can."

He looked up from the fire and narrowed his eyes. He raised the sword from the log and pointed it at us. "But if she dies, then blood will flow. The five of you. And the druids. All will die. That's my decision and my solemn promise, my word as Rí Cóicid."

Behind the king's back, Ohran took two paces forward.

Quickly, Armadal stepped in front, glaring at him. His eyebrows dipped dangerously close together, and he shook his head.

Ohran frowned and was still.

"Armadal." The king set the blade back on the log and watched it. "Take them to her bedside. At sunrise tomorrow, if they fail, when they fail, take them out to the yard, Ohran included, and do what I've ordered. I'll see it done. You'll do it or your head will be among those rolling on the ground tomorrow morning. Now begone. All of you."

Before we left, Armadal held a quick, whispered conference with Sòlas. Then our guard led us from the great room, past the ape, now jumping and chattering, and down a different torch-lit corridor.

As we left the great room, my muscles were tense and my heart skipped beats. How had my fate become so tied with Pátrick's? For tonight, he would either cure the king's daughter. Or in the morning we'd all die.

CHAPTER 16

Sòlas

"You've up and done it now, my lords," said Sòlas as he dragged us through the hallway by our chains. "You've scheduled your own execution for dawn, and 'tis yours truly, your friend Sòlas here, who's charged to do the deed, as always. 'Scuse me, fine sirs, at my lack of faith in your God, but when 'tis apparent you canna raise the dying Eivhir from her death sleep, 'twill be me suffers most from this affair. Much to my surprise, I've come to like the lot of you. I beg your pardon in advance, my lords, but 'tis my duty and I'm sworn to it."

As Sòlas spoke, we traversed a narrow and smoke-stained corridor paneled with yew. A few metal sconces held flickering torches. Our steps echoed over flagstones.

"Once, I saw the thing done wrong, and 'twas a terrible sight indeed. 'Twere a young and inexperienced hand who was up for it that day. And he piled up the mistakes, one after the other. For starters, his blade were too small, barely half the width of a man's neck. For another, I couldna see a bit of glint on the edge, an edge plain filled with nicks aplenty and shoulda been retired long ago. And the man had no strength in him. Were a sickly weakling, I say, and in the wrong profession. He couldna hit a hole in a ladder. 'Twas na a pretty sight, what with him having to hack and hack and hack again. And the blood squirting from all manner of places, what with his poor aim, and the victim screaming and squirming, legs kicking. All of this worked the crowd into a fine state, indeed. Then the bleating fool finally did the deed and cut the top of the man loose from the bottom. A terrible disgrace to the profession, that horrible sight."

"Aye, Sòlas." A young guard in his teens called out in a high voice from behind us. He was so thin, I thought he had consumption. "I saw the same sight. A fool axman who couldna cut the limb off a tree. And he was swinging at a man."

"How many rooms does the palace have?" I asked, trying to change the subject.

Sòlas went on. "I promise you, lads. Tomorrow won't be like that. My axe is as wide as a man's forearm and sharp as a razor. My swing is as sure and strong as a woodcutter's. Your heads will fall off quick and easy, so's you won't even know what or when or how it happened. 'Tis the least I can do for you."

"Thank you, Sòlas." Pátrick looked back at me with a wry smile. "Your concern is touching."

"Donna mention it, my lord." He scratched the stubble on his chin. "And there's one other thing needs mentioning. After I've got you safe to Eivhir's bedside, I'm to go to Ohran and the other druids. Tonight no less. And as to Armadal's orders, I'm to take the druids at sword-point and lock them in chains until morning, to wait in the very same hut you spent time in today. Armadal's afraid Ohran might flee, and Armadal's a stickler to carry out Forga's will when so ordered."

"That be so." The young, emaciated guard piped up again. "There's the time I didna put the horses in the barn 'til late, and for it Armadal had me marching round the square to no purpose from dawn 'til dusk."

"Earc, them horses needed tending. Watering, currying, fresh hay. You deserved it."

"I guess. Still, Armadal's a hard one."

"Hard but just. Now I ask you, my friends: What will the druids do after I carry out these orders? Will the short one give me his blessings and go before the forest spirits on my behalf, do you ken? Nay, he'll give me the evil eye. Or he'll conjure up spirits to haunt me the rest of my days."

"He might change you into a crow." The young Earc gave a high-pitched laugh.

"Funny 'tis not. But it would be his style. Turn me into a blasted crow. Trap me in a small, dirty cage. Give me to some bowsey *bashtoon* with orders to poke me and pull my feathers, and taunt me with little food and water."

Earc giggled uncontrollably.

Abruptly, Sòlas stopped our procession and looked back. "You'd best be respecting your elders, lad."

I turned around to see Earc put a hand over his mouth. Under Sòlas's withering gaze, the boy's laughter died.

Sòlas faced us. "Then there's the tale of how Ohran lost the little finger from his left hand. Chopped it off himself, 'tis said. All to use in a spell of dark magic to increase his powers. But this tale involves his daughter and methinks we donna have time for it. This is her room." He pointed to the door beside us.

"A daughter?" said Pátrick. "Ohran has a daughter? You must tell us about her. It could explain much about him."

"If you want." He gave a slight smile and a nod of his head. We stood in a group before him. "Now, hard knowledge as it might be today, he once had a daughter. It were hanky-panky in the wee hours between himself and one of the king's kitchen maids that brought forth the child—against all the druids' codes and rules, of course. And 'tis told how such a beautiful creature as would melt a heart none have seen since. All the womenfolk were agog over her. At the time, says they, Ohran were a different man. Na so bad as now. 'Tis hard to picture, I ken, but his heart were terrible soft on the child—perhaps even toward the mother, once."

"I canna picture it," said Earc. "He's cold as iron. Always been so."

"Nay, lad. He's changed. Ohran doted on the mother and his daughter for two years. Then he was called north on druid business. But news reached him that the child lay dying in her maid's bed. For three whole days, the coughing sickness which were going around had gripped her. The druid rode back, then went to her in a terrible state, trying all manner of tricks, but none of his potions did a thing."

"Just like now." Earc shook his head back and forth. "Nothing he's done has helped Eivhir."

"The same, lad. And that's when Ohran comes up with a desperate scheme to increase his powers. A dark ceremony, it was, one he'd discovered long ago but feared to perform. He cut off his own finger and sold his soul, so they say, to the spirits. All so's to cure her. But the deed didna work. She died anyways—his daughter did. Now this were early on when he were young. If you can imagine such a thing. And I donna ken if the spell has done him any good since 'cept to make him bitter and mean."

"Cold as iron," Earc joined in.

"Hard as nails. Now if you'll also observe, he's obsessed and annoyed with that hand—the one it did him no good to lop off the finger. And when he uses it, he's sometimes irritated with it as if it reminds him of his failure. Or his dead daughter. Or perhaps the dark magic itself makes him do that."

"But what happened to the child's mother?" asked Pátrick. "Where is she now?"

"Here's where we come to outright murder, we does. During a month of mourning, Ohran's soul grew black as night, they say. Late one evening, he up and goes to the maid and accuses her of na bringing the sick child to him sooner. Said his potions should've worked and puts the blame for the child's dying squarely on the maid. For hours out in the dark, 'twas arguing and shouting everyone heard. And after that, dead quiet. And the next morning, what do you ken, but they finds her stabbed to death, bloodied behind some bushes? But no one says a thing. She were only a lowly scullery servant in the king's kitchen. And he were a powerful druid."

"'Tis different from what I heard." Earc's voice squeaked. "Didna he kill two maids? The one he poked and another who went out in the dark to see what all the fuss were about?"

"There's na any truth in that story. We needna magnify Ohran's crimes beyond their original sad state."

Sòlas faced Pátrick. "But the point for you, my lords, in your situation, is some now swears, because of that, his spells can well kill a man, if not maim him. Now I donna ken what's the truth. Still, I'd be fearing his spells and curses, I would.

"This is her door and 'tis time we entered. More's the pity, as from here on, there's na joy or hope, only the prospect of the morrow and the blade. And I do apologize for having to swing the axe on you tomorrow."

"Apology accepted," said Pátrick.

"And now we'll have to run the gauntlet of Beahak, her maid, bless her soul."

With this warning, we entered the bedchamber of Eivhir, the princess of Ulster.

CHAPTER 17

Eivhir

The princess's room hugged the palace's outside wall. A drape of heavy wool, once colorful plaids now darkened by smoke and age, hung over a small window and shut out most of the light. A small fire burned in the floor's center. Its smoke rose to a hole in the ceiling, gathered there in a cloud, and filtered through an opening. The fire kept the room uncomfortably warm and smoky.

Beside a low bed covered with soft furs and pillows sat a pert woman with her back to us. Black leather strips bound her bright red hair, tight and neat, behind her head. She perched erect on a stool close at the princess's side.

Eivhir rested amid the furs, her face gaunt and pale, her arms thin and motionless, laid carefully atop the bedcovers. Even from this distance, I sensed the presence of death.

The woman, Beahak, swiveled on her stool, fire in her eyes. A sturdy figure, with short, stocky legs and arms built from carrying heavy loads. "Sure, Sòlas, and you'll be bringing more druids, foreign ones at that, to torture my mistress against the will of the Rí Cóicid. Well, there'll be na more of it." She stood and took two steps toward us. "And I'm thinking you'll be turning around right now and marching back the way you came, the lot of you. Be quick about it now, or I'll call the guards and have your heads, I will!"

For a moment, we stood there. I was stunned by this onslaught. Then Sòlas stepped forward, and with a tone a child might use after being scolded for some mischief, said, "If you'll please to remember, Beahak, it's me who's the chief guard in these parts. Now calm down and listen for a mite, 'cause I'll be explaining the reason for these gentlemen. We come to the princess's bedchamber on the orders of the king himself. 'Tis because this man here," he pointed to Pátrick, "says he'll pray to his God. And 'tis a new one in the world, I'm thinking, the way he describes Him. Because of this praying, says he, Eivhir will get better. And if this doesna happen—and I'm thinking to myself, sadly, it's *when* this doesna happen, not if—well, then tomorrow at dawn, they'll be losing their heads over the matter. And sadly again, it'll be yours truly must do the deed."

Beahak regarded us for a while with a scowl. "Harrumph. If 'tis the king's will, then I'll be letting you come to her bedside. But I warn you, there better be na more killing of critters in this room or filling the air with foul vapors. Or I'll be shooing the lot of you out and going straight to the king himself, regardless of what he said, and putting a quick end to more druid nonsense."

Pátrick stepped forward. "My dear Beahak, I am Pátrick, and I respect your devotion to protect your mistress, which is plain for all to see. Be assured we're here only to pray for Eivhir's recovery. We're not druids. We'll sacrifice no animals and burn no incense. Our God, who is the one and only true God in all the world, requires nothing of the sort, having given us His Son as a final sacrifice to end all sacrifices. We'll be as respectful and quiet as we can. Our purpose is simply to ask for the grace of God to fall upon your unfortunate mistress and bring her back to health and a quick recovery."

By the time Pátrick finished speaking, a steady, intense gaze replaced Beahak's scowl. "Perhaps your intentions are pure, and maybe your heart as well. Though it's a bit early to judge any of that. She's near death, Pátrick." Her voice broke. "If the king's . . . willing to give you a chance . . . then I must give you leave to do your praying. But I fear she's in her final hours and beyond what anyone can do for her."

Pátrick thanked her and bowed, even as she turned away from us. Then Sòlas released our chains with a request not to attempt an escape, or he *would* chase after us. With Beahak's permission, we approached Eivhir's side.

Pátrick laid a palm on the girl's forehead, touched her cheek, then held one of her hands. "The room's warm, yet she's cold as ice." Still holding her hand, he raised his glance to the ceiling. "O Lord Jesu, reach down from heaven to this girl and cure her affliction. Make her well again, O Lord of life. Breathe on her and give her again life, health, and strength. O Lord Jesu, You've said if we ask such things in Your name, then You will honor our requests. We ask You now to return to this woman the life fleeing all too quickly from her. Do this not only because we ask, but also because it will show Your power and love to the people of this land."

Once started, they repeated this prayer in various forms. After a time, Pátrick fell quiet and Servius joined the refrain. Oddly, when Servius prayed, he ceased to stutter. When I asked him later about this, he said it was God's mouth speaking through him. Latharn prayed, but his prayers were shorter. Then long moments of silence passed until one or the other picked up the thread again.

A powerful connection existed between these men—especially Pátrick—and this God and Jesu of theirs. They spoke as if they knew their God personally and were confident He would hear their petitions. They praised Him. They asked Him to forgive the sins of the household of Forga mac Dallán and their own, though what this had to do with Eivhir's recovery, I did not then know.

While this occurred, Mùirne and I sat at the far end of the room in silence. To my shame, as afternoon dimmed into evening, and evening darkened into night, I could not keep my eyes open and frequently slept. When I awoke, I saw Mùirne sleeping also, and Sòlas, who never left the room, and found a spot on the opposite wall.

Often, I moved to Eivhir's bedside, hoping for some change. But each time I did so, I saw no difference in the gaunt pallor of her face, the shallowness of her breath. I saw only a young woman who was once beautiful. Long, red hair fell in curls over her shoulders, in need of washing and combing. A few freckles, hinting of a former playfulness, touched fair skin on each check. All was now overshadowed by a deathly pallor, a face sunken and emaciated by long illness.

As Beahak listened to these prayers, her demeanor gradually changed. New hope—even respect—entered her eyes. She dropped her stance of angry defense and became solicitous, even helpful. Toward midnight, she brought us each a bowl of thick mutton stew with wheat bread and a mug of mead.

I accepted, thanked her, and ate and drank, thinking it might be the last meal I would ever eat. But Pátrick refused all sustenance, asking only for water. He explained that while he went before the Lord on such a grave matter, he must fast. Servius and Latharn followed his lead, eating and drinking nothing, though Latharn looked long at the stew before refusing it. I believe this greatly increased Beahak's respect for Pátrick. But to my shame, I partook with relish. Mùirne and

Sòlas, of course, took Beahak's offer, with Sòlas even asking for a second portion. Beahak brought it to him. Sólas finished it, and then he asked for thirds. But at this request, she simply stood over him with her hands on her hips, scowled down at him as if he were a child, and chided him for flirting with gluttony. Thus scolded, he took back his request and, with head down, turned in his bowl and mug.

The night wore on. The prayers continued. Eivhir's condition showed no change. Then Beahak grew restless. Locks of her previously neat red hair now flew free and unkempt. After an early glimmer of hope, she paced the back of the room, her forehead wrinkled, eyes narrowed.

Then we all turned our heads as Eivhir's father, the Rí Cóicid, entered the chamber. Forga gave our group a quick glance and shuffled to Eivhir's side. He sat on a stool and slowly reached out a hand to hers. For long moments, he stared, caressing her pale fingers and slightly shaking his head back and forth. His glance fell to the blankets and his whole body seemed to heave. Then he rose and dragged his feet from the room, never having said a word. Several times that night, he repeated this scene.

Late in the night, Sòlas went to the window, pulled back the curtain, and examined the sky. After one of these trips, he turned to us and scrunched his face. "Willna be long now. The sky's showing a bit of light, so I'll be going and sharpening my axe, leaving you for a bit. I'm sorry, my lords, but seems I told you it'd come to this. But don't get no ideas about 'scaping, as there's guards outside the room." Then he left.

Pátrick and his band had been praying most of the previous afternoon, through the evening, and all the night. And what was the result? I walked again to Eivhir's bedside. Same death pallor. Same shallow breathing. At the back of the room, I looked at Beahak and shook my head. Her eyes glistened with tears, which she brushed away. Hope was fleeing each of us. Eivhir, it appeared, would die, and before she left this life, those of us who followed Pátrick would precede her to the Otherworld.

Soon a glint of light brightened the curtains. Sòlas entered, axe in hand, accompanied by soldiers with spears.

"I'll be doing my duty now, my lords. You'll be forgiving me if I do it, 'cause it's na one I care to do today, 'specially to you. But you'll be standing now and coming with me, the lot of you."

Pátrick was still praying. He finished with, "In the name of Jesu, the Son of God Most High, I pray for this sickness to leave and health to return to Eivhir, daughter of Forga mac Dallán."

"Come now, my lord." Sòlas's angular forehead and square chin were even more imposing when his large hands held an axe. "You've been at it all the night and 'tis na working. Donna make me come for you."

Pátrick nodded and stood stiffly. He left her bedside.

Sòlas gathered us in a line, chained us, and marched us through the palace halls and into the yard. He led us some distance across the battered grass to a spot where waited a single thick log. Around us now gathered a crowd of men, women, and children. Among them were soldiers of Forga's army. Apparently, news of our execution had spread through Emain Macha.

But Sòlas gazed toward the palace, saying we must wait for the druids to be brought.

In the following silence, Sòlas looked at each of us, frowned, and shook his head. Pátrick just stared at the ground, his lips moving slightly. Was he praying? Mùirne gave me worried glances, then glanced toward Pátrick, Sòlas, and me again as if expecting one of us to stop this nightmare.

As for me, I cannot describe the thoughts running through my mind. The previous day, when I'd discovered the one true God, I soared to heights of joy. He was the answer to my quest for truth. The night began with great hope as Pátrick prayed like I'd never heard anyone pray. For most of the evening, I thought his God would really raise Eivhir from her death sleep. But in the end, my hope was crushed.

Even now as I write this, my hand shakes to remember my state of mind that morning. All was lost. I would not find the hope I'd sought in Pátrick's God. I felt the fool to follow Him, to believe the man in white—only a stupid dream! And what returned to me with terrible force was my old dread of the Otherworld. My fear of that eternal land where Manannán mac Lir ruled in dim light—he, the god of fickleness and deceit and anger.

There is nothing so terrible in life as the death of hope.

Six guards led a string of chained men to stand beside us—Ohran, his lips now tight, his eyes dark and narrowed, and the four druids of Emain Macha.

Behind the druids walked Forga. Twenty paces distant, he stopped, his face pale and without emotion. His glance fixed on the ground, looking up only occasionally. His soiled nightdress dragged in the dirt. His hand still clutched the blackened sword.

Sòlas glanced once around to ensure everyone was present, then looked over each of us, his gaze settling on Servius.

"You'll be the first, I 'spect. I'm sorry, again, my lords, but 'tis time to get on with the deed."

Sòlas undid Servius's chains and pointed to the log. Servius's lips still muttered prayers. His hands shaking, he lay his head against the wood.

"There's a good lad. It'll be good and quick, I promise."

With large hands, Sòlas gripped his axe and moved to a position beside the log. For a moment, he held the blade motionless over Servius's neck, sizing up his target. And as he bent over, thick locks of russet hair fell across his cheeks. True to his word, it was a large blade, enough to span a man's neck and more, gleaming sharp and polished in the morning sun.

Then shouting and a disturbance arose from the direction of the palace.

Oblivious, Sòlas cocked the axe high over his head, ready to swing down with all the muscled force he could bear. But the shouting grew louder, closer, finally upsetting his concentration. He lowered his axe, cast a quick glance around, but apparently saw nothing. Again, he lifted the weapon back over his head and focused, the muscles in his neck tightening, his forehead creasing in concentration.

I looked toward the palace. What was happening?

Beahak was running toward us, screaming, her voice growing louder. "Stop! Halt this accursed killing. Halt, I say."

Sòlas focused only on the log and Servius's neck. He raised the axe farther, his muscles tense and sprung, ready to strike.

Then Beahak shouted with a set of lungs no one could ignore. "Drop your axe, Sòlas! Are you daft as well as dumb, man? Sòlas, you lummox, stop. Eivhir is *awake*."

Sòlas paused, turned toward Beahak, and then lowered his axe. He stared at her without expression, seemingly looking through her. He scratched his chin and squinted his eyes as if puzzled, confused.

"She's awake, I say." Beahak stopped before us and panted, gripping her side. A wide smile spread across her lips to her eyes. "Sure, and she's sitting up and asking for her father."

I looked to the others, stunned. Had Pátrick's prayers worked?

Then Pátrick and the others gazed toward heaven and spoke praises to their God.

Forga rushed to us, his eyes bright with tears. "Your God is as real and powerful as you said. Sure, and He listens to you, 'tis plain. Your God has done this thing, and no man can speak against the deed. But now I must see her. Give me a moment, then follow me to her chambers, for she must see this very day the men who did this."

The events of that morning once again twisted my head and turned my emotions. The hope I thought had died was resurrected, returned to sudden life. Not only did Eivhir live, but Pátrick's God was proven real. He had done the deed. My heart soared. I looked at the sky and whispered, "Thank you."

Within moments, we gathered at her bedside where her father held her hand, wetting it with tears of joy. When we arrived, she was sitting up. Already her cheeks had regained some color.

"Are these my saviors?" Her voice was weak, but gaining strength. For the first time, I saw eyes of auburn, the hint of a half-smile crossing her face.

"They are indeed, my lady." Beahak beamed, taking the empty mug Eivhir handed her. She refilled it from a pot. "They prayed to their God over you all the night. Aye, we've them to thank for this."

"Thank you, my lords," said Eivhir.

"You are welcome." Pátrick bowed. "But 'tis not we who did the deed, but God on High, through His Son Jesu. We are merely His servants."

"I must learn of this God and pay homage to Him, to thank Him properly."

Then Forga spoke with a strong, eager tone I hadn't yet heard from him. "This is an occasion of great joy and calls for a celebration. Six weeks from now, at midsummer's eve, I declare a *óenach*, a great fair in honor of Eivhir's recovery and to thank this God who brings the daughters of kings back from the dead. All of Ulster will join us. Everyone must rejoice and celebrate this miracle of deliverance."

"Father, a fair! This is wonderful news." She clapped her hands. Then a frown played with her smile. "But sure, now that I haven't popped my clogs, everyone's just standing around jabbering, and here I am, near starving to death. If you'll all excuse me—Beahak, does our kitchen still have any food? I could eat a horse."

Then Beahak shooed all of us from the room—all but the king—as she sent for food.

When we emerged again in the yard, it seemed the heavens themselves were opening, pouring joy and happiness on the *tuath* of Emain Macha. The news had spread quickly. People ran through the village streets, shouting, ringing bells, hitting pots with wooden spoons. Swords banged on shields and everyone sang—in tune and out.

This joy and commotion was but a foretaste of the great celebration the *óenach* would soon bring.

PART IV

At the Great fair,
A.D. 432

CHAPTER 18

A Druid's Ploy

While Eivhir recovered, the king gave us beds in the large roundhouse of a *fine* that held his kin, a far more comfortable abode than our prison hut. How good it felt to be back inside a *fine* and part of a *tuath,* even if not my own. I stood on the threshold, sensing and listening to the place. Mothers sang softly to their babies. Men argued over who was the better hunter. Lads teased and chased the lasses until their mothers chided them. And the scents: stew, smoke, skins, bodies huddled close. Then, with night, came the familiar sounds of everyone sleeping— the snoring, coughing, breathing, and even of husbands being with their wives.

An old woman of the *fine*, Borgach, quickly adopted me. She cleaned and mended the old tunic I again wore since my masquerade as druid was over. At night, she brought me an extra fur, even when I protested I didn't need it. She reminded me of Sileas in my *fine* back home.

The next day, Pátrick requested an audience in the great room of the palace. Standing before us was a vastly different king than on the day before. He had abandoned the soiled nightdress for a brightly colored tunic of plaid. Around his neck hung a torc of hammered gold. Someone had trimmed his hair. It now fell blond, neat, and curling to just above his neck. He was also clean shaven. Perhaps his new demeanor removed my blinders and allowed me to notice, for the first time, the face of the King of Ulster. High cheekbones. Dark brown eyebrows. Black, shining eyes.

When he saw the presents we bore, the king smiled broadly and motioned toward the deep rugs on the floor beside the room's central fire. We piled our load before Pátrick's seat. Then we sat cross-legged in a semicircle facing the king's large, embroidered pillow. Forga took his seat last, his gaze fixed on Pátrick's pile, his eyes shining.

"We honor the Rí Cóicid with gifts from Bryton." Pátrick rose to a kneeling position and handed over a small, leather bag, obviously heavy. "Roman *aureii*. Coins of gold." Then he transferred one, two, five more heavy bags to a stack before Forga. "And these are silver. My lord, we use coins in Bryton in place of barter."

Forga grinned, opened one bag, pulled out a gold coin, and turned it over. "I've heard of these. Used instead of barter, you say?"

Pátrick nodded. "Like gold and silver rings." Then he carefully unfolded a long, red cape, woven from the finest silk and hemmed with gold fringe. He placed the cloak in Forga's hands.

The king ran his fingers over the cloth. "'Tis smoother than anything on Ériu. Fine workmanship, this. And so red. Truly a king's mantle."

Pátrick smiled. "And every king should have a scepter, my lord." He passed him a heavy silver baton, carved with designs and tiny figures. On one end was a crown of metal leaves.

Forga hefted it as if testing its weight. He laid it beside him. "Thank you. I've never had such before." He looked from the scepter to the last item in the pile. He squinted as if the next gift held even greater interest.

Pátrick presented a gleaming iron sword as long as a man's arm. The polished blade revealed swirling, intricate designs. Its hilt and handle were gilded with gold. Every inch of the handle was etched with so many curls and swirls, it was a work of art.

The guards standing in the corner of the room gasped and took a step forward, craning their necks to get a better look.

"Never have I seen the like." The king beamed and accepted the blade. The metal shone and glimmered by firelight. "Such an elegant handle. What a sharp edge. Truly fine metalwork. But 'tis so artful, do I dare use it? My friends," his gaze caught each of us in turn. "Aye, friends. What you did for my daughter, and now these gifts—truly, I now call you friends of the king."

Pátrick smiled and nodded in return. "Thank you, my lord."

Yes, we'd made a friend of the king. But as I learned the next day, we were soon to make fierce enemies.

On the second day of our stay, after Eivhir began her remarkable recovery, Ohran appeared before me as I was leaving the roundhouse.

"How are you, my lad, this fine morning?" Ohran was full of fawning smiles and sweetness. But when I caught his gaze, his eyes were lifeless.

"I'm well." If I'd been a fortress watching the approach of riders, I would have drawn up my bridge.

"Come with me, lad. I've a proposition that may interest you."

I didn't move, trying to think of some excuse to be elsewhere.

"What else must my lad do on such a day? When the chief druid calls, most obey."

"As you wish, my lord." I bowed, then followed him across the yard to the druid temple, that enormous conical building. The morning sun cast its long shadow over the eastern yard. We approached its base, a ring of heavy logs about one hundred feet in diameter, topped by smaller rings fixed with beams to the circle beneath. More ascending rings contracted to a point at the top. A mat of thin poles filled the gaps and was faced on the outside with layers of thatch.

I followed him through a yawning doorway. On the floor in the center, directly under the high cone, was a flat stone altar, similar to Crom Cruach's. Before the platform stood perhaps a dozen shrines, their stone pedestals holding various figures of clay, metal, and wood, representing the many gods of forest, river, and bog. We stopped before the row of idols. The stench of old altar blood and dried entrails hovered about the place, turning my stomach.

"I ken you were once a druid, lad?" Sweetness and honey dripped from his thin lips.

I nodded, my heart pounding in my chest. I was keen to leave this place.

"Then you're familiar with our secret ways, the powers we control? You know the spirits of the rocks, the trees, and the haunted, lonely places where only the initiated fear to tread? And the trickery of Lugh, he who answers our call? You ken how to make the forest your friend or your nightmare enemy? And you fear the spells we can cast on a man who goes dead against us?"

"I learned their ways. But our druids worshiped Crom Cruach."

At this, he blinked and stared up at me. I was always looking down on him, for he was indeed a wee man. I sometimes wonder if men of small stature often overcompensate for their size through excessive will, ambition, and fierce resolve.

"I'm impressed. Sure, and a powerful but demanding god he is."

"Why did you bring me here?"

"I was getting to that. You seem an intelligent young man. I've an offer should interest you, one to ensure you a position and a bright future here in Emain Macha."

"What?"

"Why, Taran—it is Taran, is it not?"

"It is."

"Why then, Taran, it's to ask you to join us—we druids of Emain Macha— and be lifted to a high position among us solely for accepting our offer."

"And what'd be the offer?"

"Why, to do a small thing, really. 'Tis simply to renounce this God of Pátrick's, this ridiculous and false idea that there's one God who rules over everything. Surely, you cannot be serious about this—you who once studied the true arts, the spirits of the forest, and felt their lure and power? Renounce Him, join us, and we'll give you riches and position like you've never experienced in your young life. Of this I promise."

I had expected something like this. But I was appalled at the treachery of his words, at the perfidy implicit in his drawing me here, alone among his idols. When I entered the temple, I had only looked for a way to flee. Now my heart raced, my forehead became hot, and I wanted to strike him.

"And if I decline?"

Until that point his face had been the picture of sweetness, but with my question, his lips tightened and a scowl briefly distorted his usually straight eyebrows. He whisked his left hand across his forehead to knock thin strands of reedy, brown hair from one eye. The thin smile returned.

"You've no reason not to accept. We wish you no harm. Only great good fortune. Believe me, this Pátrick will come to no good here. He's turned the king's head and confused his mind. This accident of Eivhir's recovery is not of his doing. You don't want to share Pátrick's fate. You'll not refuse us, will you, my friend? Imagine the power, wealth, and prestige we can give you. Wouldn't this be sufficient compensation for abandoning what's false and unprofitable?"

"What benefit do you seek from me? Why do you care if I join your cabal?"

"I'll tell you straight, my friend, as we've high hopes for you. If you'll join us, if you'll publicly abandon Pátrick, deny Pátrick's God and all he believes in, and if you proclaim your allegiance again to the druids and the ancient spirits—well, then, it's our hope this will plunge a dagger of doubt deep into the king's thoughts. He'll then be forced to reexamine his whole relationship with Pátrick. If one of Pátrick's closest followers abandons him publicly—and we'll provide the venue for all to hear your denunciation, loud and clear—it can have no outcome but this. Pátrick's hold over the king will be severed. His influence will wither.

"That, my friend, is the benefit to us. 'Tis why we offer such largesse to you if you come to us. You dare not refuse."

I looked straight into his tiny, dark eyes. "So you'd have me betray Pátrick and my new friends? I should embrace treason and dishonor? And abandon the one true God I'm already coming to know? I should return to following idols?"

Ohran's lips tightened. "I wouldn't put it like that. 'Tis not treason or betrayal or dishonesty to do what's best for oneself, to provide for one's future. What we offer should be sufficient compensation to overcome any qualms you have. The gods we serve, whose powers we employ, are not idols, but true spirits. As you should know, if your studies were proper. We only ask you to return to what you once knew. You cannot come to know a God who doesn't exist."

I stood in silence for some moments, trying to calm my thoughts, my anger. Then I spoke slowly, so he would understand the depth of my passion. "I will *never* abandon Pátrick's God or return to the path of the druids. For that way, your way, is the road to darkness. This new God, and His Son, are the true course, the path of light. 'Tis what Pátrick teaches and what I ken from my time wasted in learning the dark arts. Your way is the same as Crom Cruach's, the way of death and deceit. Of finding the worst in a man and feeding it. Of letting it build in him until wildness and abandon fill his soul so he'd kill his own children for the sake of a worthless stone of gold. Your altar reeks of blood, Ohran, the blood and the insides of animals cut open for your false gods. You consort with demons and devils, and you don't even realize it. Your clever wiles are wasted on me, for I'll never join the likes of you, your cabal, or the demons you worship."

As Ohran listened to my speech, his small dark eyes narrowed, bored into mine, and became black, burning coals. His eyebrows arched. His lips, then his entire face, tightened while his fists clenched at his sides. I thought he might strike me then and there.

"Be the stupid lummox then. Sure, and now you'll go down with them. For on this very night, I will prepare a curse against you. And when you wake sweating, clutching your breast, with your heart pounding, and wonder if your next breath will be your last—well, you were warned!"

I turned abruptly and strode through the archway into the light, leaving him under the temple's dome.

I looked back once. In the dim interior, Ohran's tiny eyes, burning black with anger, were still fixed on me. His lips pulled taut. I shook myself, as though I had emerged from a nest of cobwebs, and hurried away.

Later that afternoon, I warned Pátrick of this encounter, but he didn't seem surprised. "We are in a spiritual battle," he said, holding my gaze, "and the forces of darkness are gathering against us."

I nodded. "And Ohran, is leading the dark side of the fight."

CHAPTER 19

Children of God

After Eivhir's recovery, we fell into a routine. Pátrick began to teach Mùirne and me about Jesu and God. Since Forga now offered us protection instead of execution, Pátrick suggested we postpone my baptism so he could teach me about living as a Christian. He also spoke of one grand event where others could join me. Each morning, the three of us, and sometimes Latharn or Servius, would gather in the shelter of a large oak tree outside the village. There he would tell us of the birth, travels, miracles, followers, teachings, and trials of this most amazing, loving, and powerful Son of God.

The first time Mùirne and I met him at the oak, Pátrick stood waiting for us. He carried a thick, rectangular block, heavy, faced with smooth leather and etched with colorful designs. It was over a foot tall and not quite as wide.

"What do you bear with such reverence?" Mùirne craned her neck to get a better look.

"'Tis called a book, but a special one, indeed." He beckoned, and we stood close at his shoulder. He put his thumbs in the middle of the block and then it *opened*.

I peered at its contents. Two sheets of vellum—thin white parchments of calfskin—lay exposed before me. Covering its surface were hundreds of tiny symbols, each clearly made with painstaking craftsmanship.

Then he looked into the vellum and spoke words, obviously not his own. "The poor in spirit are blessed, for the kingdom of heaven is theirs. Those who mourn are blessed, for they will be comforted. The gentle are blessed—"

"What magic is this?" I reached out my hand. Pátrick allowed me to touch its surface. "It speaks to you?"

"Aye, it does. This book carries the words of God, Himself."

"We have no magic like this on Inis Creig."

"Nor on Ériu," added Mùirne. "Only some symbols carved on stone to mark boundaries. But they don't speak to us, as do these."

"How did this come to be? This book?" I looked into Pátrick's eyes, marveling at this new development.

He smiled, closed the pages and beckoned us to sit.

"Over a hundred calves went into the making, their hides—"

"I mean the writing of it."

"Ah, yes. 'Tis true history, wisdom, and teaching, recorded long ago by men whom God chose for the task. They were prophets and Apostles, followers of Jesu. A man named Jerome recently translated it from foreign tongues into Latin, the language of my people."

"And those figures record your speech?" Mùirne pointed a finger.

"They do. And Taran," he put a hand on my shoulder, "I will teach you and Latharn how to read and write it."

My blood surged with anticipation.

To this day, the wonders of the pen still seem to me like high magic. Even now, decades later, my quill scratches out the story of my life in the Latin Pátrick taught me. And as my pile of parchments builds here on the table by firelight, I look with amazement at this ability Pátrick brought us, this wonderful art of writing.

But I stray from my story. And I have forgotten to mention what happened to Servius. After Sòlas's axe nearly took his life, he ceased entirely to stutter. When next I heard him, he spoke the clearest, most perfect Gaelic. Servius's explanation was this, "When God answered our prayers to spare Eivhir, He also answered mine. For as my head lay on the block, I asked the Lord that if I ever got out of this alive, could He also allow me to speak henceforth without hesitation." In the months to come, we saw many more answers to prayer like this.

During the first week of Pátrick's teaching, while Ohran plotted and tried to turn me to his cause, Eivhir recovered rapidly. By the second week, she had left her bed and was walking—nay, bustling—about the palace and village. One afternoon, I encountered her outside our *fine*.

"Good morning, your grace. It's good to see you up and about." I bowed, noticing how slender she was, and nearly as tall as me.

"Greetings, Taran. And glad I am to leave my bed. But enough of me. How's my handsome young rescuer?"

"I'm well. But it wasn't I who did the rescuing. I simply watched as Pátrick prayed to his God, who's now my God."

"Still, you're part of his company and deserve my thanks. But a thing has puzzled me about you." A playful smile crossed her face below her freckles.

"What's that?"

"I consider you a friend if I may be so bold as to call you that."

"Why thank you, your grace." I bowed again.

"If friend, then please address me by name. I care na for formality. And any savior of mine need na bow. I ken you are *flaith*, nay?"

"'Tis so . . . Eivhir." I stood erect, resisting the urge to bow, and smiled.

"Thank you. I really have two questions, and the first is this: You're too striking and desirable a lad to be unmarried, perhaps the kind a lass like myself might be seeking, were I in the search—na that I am, mind you. So have you a woman somewhere whom you bed?"

I blanched. Surely, she was direct, and more than a bit playful. For as she said this, she smiled broadly, her eyes bright, as she watched me squirm.

"I do, Eivhir. She's my Laurna, whom I love dearly. But she's a virgin, for we have not yet been joined in wedlock. She lives on Inis Creig, my island home, but I may never see her or my home again."

"Ah, 'tis sad, indeed. A lad already spoken for, and worse, a lad separated from his lass and his home. And a handsome, tall lad at that, with such a fine head of wavy brown hair to grace a lassie's pillow. Such a loss! But if you're na yet wed, are you sure I canna tempt you to give up your Laurna for the daughter of a king?" She winked.

I shifted my weight between my feet and smiled. "Only she has my heart. But should I ever consider abandoning her, a beautiful young lass like yourself, and the daughter of the king, no less, would make a formidable substitute."

"Sure, and a 'formidable substitute' I am now." She gave me a mock frown, yet her eyes sparkled. "Well, I see there's no hope for the two of us, as your mind and your heart seem made up. But this leads me to my second question: You are of the Ériu, 'tis plain, but Pátrick is a Roman, and I wonder how you came to serve him?"

So I told her of Laurna and my home on Inis Creig. Of my falling out with the druids and my sea voyage. I spoke of my vision of the man in white. And of all the events leading me to Emain Macha.

When I was finished, she'd grown serious. "You must be blessed by the gods, Taran, to have survived such a sea journey and to receive such a vision."

"Pátrick teaches there's only one God."

"And sure, I must learn about Him. I've already placed a dozen offerings of bread, cheese, and mead in clay cups in secret forest places. But I donna ken where He lives and if these sacrifices are enough to appease His wrath. Can you tell me if this God would welcome my offerings? I donna wish to fall out of favor with Him."

"I'm learning He doesn't require or desire gifts such as we're accustomed to making. And He's not evil, like the forest spirits, who need always to be appeased. He wants only our worship and our belief in His Son, whom He once sent as a man to a distant land ruled by the Romans. He doesn't live in any one place, but in all places, and in an eternal place called Heaven, where we'll all end up—if we follow this Son." I peered in the direction of the wood where Patrick had been teaching me, pondering. I lowered my voice. "'Tis so different from what we learned."

She raised her glance to mine, her eyes glistening, searching. In that glance, I saw eagerness. And hope.

"But one thing's certain: This God is not capricious, spiteful, or cruel, and He will not toy with His people like our gods are wont to do. He's a God who loves and that's something new, indeed. But of all this, I'm just learning. Pátrick's been teaching Mùirne and me."

"I should like to join this teaching, if Pátrick approves, and hear about this God, who brought me back from the Otherworld."

"I'm sure he'd like that. If you behave."

She smiled and promised she would. Then a frown crossed her face, and she lowered her voice. "But before we part, I must warn you about Ohran."

"What about him?"

"He's become your sworn enemy. I've heard him say as much to Boodan, another of his druids, when I passed the temple yesterday. Father has not sent for Ohran since I recovered, and when he attempted to enter the palace last week, Father simply dismissed him. Father used to consult him on nearly everything. In matters small and big, the king would always go to his chief sorcerer. Ohran would cast sticks on the ground or splay open a rabbit to read the entrails, seeking the future by the will of the spirits. But now Ohran has fallen far in my father's estimation, and this, I fear, has made the druid bitter. He's now Pátrick's sworn enemy, and for some reason, yours as well. He mentioned you by name."

"I'm not surprised. Thanks for the warning. I'll tell Pátrick."

"It's the least I could do for a lad as handsome as you. And my savior as well. Will you also ask him when I can join your lessons about his God?"

I promised I would, and the next day, Eivhir and Beahak joined our little circle of acolytes under the oak tree. With Eivhir's recovery, Beahak's original attitude toward us had melted away, and now we were helpless to fend off her attempts to mother us, feed us, and mend our clothes—even correcting Borgach's sewing. She would even scold us if we did something she thought was against our best interests. No one could resist this red-haired, fiery-eyed lady, not even Pátrick. Indeed, both women in Forga's palace—Beahak and Eivhir—were formidable in their own way.

After a week of Pátrick's teaching, Eivhir, Beahak, and even Mùirne said they would become followers of Christ.

One day, Eivhir came to our class under the oak bearing a sly smile. "I've a secret to tell you, one you're going to like."

Pátrick smiled. "Will the lass make us guess? Or remove the agony of our anticipation and tell us straightaway?"

"This lass has been teaching her father all she's learned." She caught each of our glances as if waiting for us to prompt her for more.

"And?" I finally asked.

"And he's ready to accept it all. Pátrick, he wants to acknowledge your God and Jesu, His Son. The news of your God and what He's done has made him very happy."

Pátrick beamed. "'Tis wonderful news, Eivhir." He patted everyone on the back and huddled us into a circle to pray. Then he suggested we hold a grand event of baptism without delay.

The next morning, with frosty breath, a large assembly trekked into the forest: Pátrick and his two priests, the king and half his court, a scattering of villagers, some of the army, along with Beahak, Eivhir, Mùirne, and myself. We stopped at a pool made by a swiftly flowing stream before it rushed down, gurgling and bubbling, over the rocks below. The sunlight played through the leaves as the grassy banks crowded with onlookers. Then Pátrick and Servius, tall men both, waded into cold water up to their waists. When they found their footing on the rocky bottom, they turned to face us.

Since I had been the first to believe, Pátrick suggested I go first. Yet he asked Forga's permission. When Forga nodded, I undressed and, as is always the custom, waded naked into the water. For the old man must shed everything of his former self before the new man reemerges.

"Do you believe in God the Father Almighty?" said Pátrick.

"I believe," said I.

"Christ Jesu was born of a virgin called Mary. He was murdered by Pontius Pilate, the ruler of Palestine. He died, was buried, and on the third day rose again, alive from the dead. Then he ascended into heaven where He sits even now at the right hand of God the Father. Some day He will come again to judge those who are alive and those who are dead. Do you, Taran, believe all this?"

"I believe."

"And do you believe Christ Jesu is the Son of God?"

"I believe."

"Do you believe in the Holy Spirit, in the church of all believers, and in the resurrection of the body?"

"I believe."

"Then I baptize you in the name of the Father, the Son, and the Holy Spirit."

Pátrick put one hand at my chest's center and another on the small of my back while I held shut my nostrils. Then Servius and he dunked me backward into the cold stream until my head went under.

When I emerged, sputtering and shivering, such a surge of joy and energy rushed through me, I knew this God was now living inside me. His Spirit was within me! And this feeling—though it ebbs and flows and only rarely has been as strong as on that blessed day—has never left me.

After I returned to the bank and dressed, the others followed. One by one they undressed and went where I had gone into the stream until all were baptized. Then Pátrick pronounced we had entered the family of God and could now be called children of God. Those were his very words—we were now children of God. Many from Forga's court, from the army and the village, watched their king be baptized that day. Because they'd seen, their hearts were moved. And in the weeks afterward, so many joined the church, we held baptisms nearly every week. In the months to follow, many more confessed Christ.

Evening came and Forga invited everyone who had witnessed the baptism to a special celebration in the palace. There we feasted on partridges, deer, fish, turnips, rare black bread with honey butter, sweet cakes, and mead. After Eivhir's recovery, the king had called his bard back and we heard poetry, including a new poem composed on the spot about Forga's baptism. Until late, we sang and ate and drank. But Pátrick and Servius politely refused the mead and instead drank water. When asked, they said abstaining from mead was not a requirement of being a Christian, that it was up to each conscience to do as the Holy Spirit directed. Yet they did urge restraint in our merrymaking. My only regret was that Coll and his fiddle were absent, for I had heard nothing like his music since our parting.

The only dark cloud over the affair was while Forga was being baptized, I had glimpsed Ohran hiding at some distance among the trees, glaring at us with tiny, dark eyes, his lips taut. That night at the feast, I wondered what mischief he was plotting. Pátrick simply shrugged, saying God would protect us. Still, I was concerned what the druid might do.

But in the last few weeks, a change had been occurring in me, and it greatly diminished my fear of Ohran. The next morning, with my baptism, I realized the change was complete. I no longer feared death! My dread of Manannán mac Lir and the Otherworld was gone. Compared to the God Most High, the ruler of the universe who had sent His Holy Spirit to live inside me, Manannán was but the whisper of a ghost—if he existed at all. Now I knew the truth about the afterlife: The Otherworld did not exist. For those who knew Christ, there was instead a heaven, a place where the God of light and truth ruled with love and justice, where Jesu welcomed with open arms all who were called the children of God.

I experienced a sense of true joy. I was right with God. He was now a part of me. There had been a hole in my being, in who I was, which He now filled. This was completely unexpected. For the first time in my life, I was complete. Christ was the missing piece, the thing I lacked. I nearly *glowed* with joy.

My outlook on everything changed. I cared little for my own life, this temporary container of flesh, for when I took my last breath, I was destined for an eternity in a new body with a God who loved me.

I still felt fear. I had not entirely banished that emotion. But the emotion itself changed. Or perhaps I do not understand it anymore—this thing called fear, what it once was.

My fears became centered on whether I would make of my life all God wanted for me. Whether I would use my days wisely, in worship and service to the Christ I loved. For He deserved all of my time on earth, all of this, my life. I feared for the people I knew and what might happen to them. I was suddenly concerned for the welfare of others, and especially for Laurna and the people of Inis Creig, who knew not this God and His Son.

As I thought about Ohran and his threats, his brooding presence in the woods that morning, I feared also for the damage he could do to Pátrick's mission. For Pátrick's goals were now my goals.

My concern was not in vain. Only a few weeks later, as preparations for the *óenach* began in earnest, Ohran brought us a challenge laden with evil intent.

Chapter 20

The Challenge

In the weeks before the *óenach*, all Emain Macha seemed alive with preparations. On Inis Creig we'd had celebrations to be sure, but nothing like the great fairs on Ériu. The heart of the fair, as anyone would tell you, was the horse racing. There were short races at full gallop across the field. Long races through the forest to far destinations. Chariot races circling round and round the field for a mile or so. And mock battles on horses with wooden, yet still dangerous, weapons.

One morning, Pátrick was teaching some of us in the palace's great room, with the king and many others present, when Ohran and Boodan rudely pushed past the lone guard at the entrance, interrupting the session.

"The druids do not believe," said Ohran to Pátrick, with a sideways glance at the king, "that your God has cured Eivhir."

"How can you deny it?" Forga rose from his seat on the rugs, and we followed. He stood, arms akimbo, and faced Ohran. Boodan was a head taller than Ohran, and with the king facing him, he turned his eyes away. "We all witnessed it. 'Twas only when Pátrick prayed that she recovered. Plain as day."

"I say it was coincidence." Ohran shook his head, freeing a few dangling brown threads of hair from his face.

"Sure, and it'll be coincidence if I lop off Boodan's arm with my sword and he bleeds all over the floor, hey?" This brought a rousing laugh from everyone.

"I say he cannot do it again. I say it was an accident, and I'll prove it with a challenge."

"What challenge?" Pátrick rose.

"Let us devise a test for whose powers and whose gods are the greater. Let us pit our gods against themselves, mine versus yours, with a race. You, Pátrick, will pick your best rider and we'll pick ours. The race will be four miles through the Forest of Mists, to the Standing Rock and back. You'll pray to your God for victory, and we'll call upon the spirits of the Otherworld. Whoever has the greater power, the greater skill and cunning on their side, that group shall be given their rightful place before the Rí Cóicid of Ulster."

"I'll not test my Lord like this," said Pátrick. "We're not to test him as Gideon once did."

"Then you willingly forfeit the race before it's begun?"

"'Tis a race I choose not to enter."

Chasing a tuft of hair from his eyes with a three-fingered hand, Ohran turned to the Rí Cóicid. "What say you, king of Ulster? Is na my challenge valid and binding? If a warrior can challenge a Rí Tuath in combat for a clan's leadership, should na a druid be allowed to challenge another 'man of the spirit' for the right to minister at your side, using the contest of his choice? Can I na demand such a challenge from this interloper and bind him to the contract?"

Forga frowned, looking first at Ohran, then Pátrick. "Where's Armadal? I need his counsel."

Someone said he was out in the field, overseeing ground preparations for the fair. We waited in an awkward silence while the king sent a runner to get him. When Armadal arrived, the two huddled in a far corner, in long conference with much waving of hands and heated discussion. Then Forga returned to the group, his eyes downcast. "'Tis as Ohran says. By Ulaid tradition, the challenge is valid and binding. Pátrick's group must participate in the race, and the victor will take his place as my spiritual counselor. If one party doesn't participate, they forfeit."

Pátrick frowned, looked at the floor in silence, and then raised his glance. "Very well, my lord. If that's your ruling, then we'll race and leave the result to God."

Ohran was grinning now, his lips tight. "You must choose a rider from the party you came here with. From the five of you, including the maid. But know that Boodan will be our rider, and he's never lost a race through the Forest of

Mists. For once you enter those green walls, the spirits of the trees—and even your rider, whoever he is—will answer to my spells."

Pátrick glanced at him. "Cast your spells, Ohran. They'll have no effect on us." He turned to Forga. "But my lord, we've no suitable horse. Ours are but pack animals."

The king said, "You may race with Gaoth Bán, my personal mount."

Pátrick bowed low in thanks.

In Gaelic the name meant "white wind" and I'd heard of him.

"A difficult beast, my lord." Sòlas leaned down to whisper in my ear. He'd followed the druids into the room as Pátrick spoke and now stood behind me. "A will of his own, with a mind to throw a rider. But he's a fast one, he is. One to endure over a long race."

I looked back. "Thank you, Sòlas."

Ohran added, "Gaoth Bán is a fine beast, to be sure, but he'll be up against Spiorad, a horse that's never lost, even against Gaoth Bán."

The name meant "spirit".

"'Tis true, Ohran," said Forga. "Your mount has never been beaten in the forest. But perhaps there's a first time, hey?"

Ohran grinned through tightened lips, then left.

Later that afternoon, Pátrick gathered Servius, Latharn, Mùirne, and me at the secluded oak down from the hilltop village to discuss the race. With Pátrick's permission, Eivhir stood with us to listen.

"Who has ever ridden a horse in a race?" asked Pátrick. "For surely, 'tis not I."

No one spoke. Reluctantly, I said I had.

"Then you, Taran, will be our rider."

"But I've only raced for the short distance on Inis Creig that crosses the high heath, the only flat space on our island."

"You'll have time to practice. 'Tis weeks until the race. Eivhir has volunteered to train our rider. She'll show you the route."

Eivhir stepped forward. "I must tell you, Taran, the druids have always won this course. The main route follows the stream for half the distance, then splits in three. Sure, and I've often run it myself and found only one good path from the split, on the far north. Every other rider in every other race has also chosen that route. The other two paths are shorter, but take them and down goes your beast and your hopes for victory. The middle trail crosses a bog over three rough and ill-maintained log bridges where a rider must dismount to cross safely. That loses much time. And some of the bog is uncovered; go that way and you'll get stuck in the mire.

"The southernmost trail is the one the druids take. But it holds a long, straight stretch that's a nasty morass of roots and rocks and ravines the likes of which I've never seen. It canna be raced without ruining an animal. I've been unable to cross it without dismounting and walking, which in the end makes it by far the slower route. Yet somehow the druids always make it safely over the path and always win. 'Tis their spells they say, that guide their beasts and claim the forest, *sheugh*, and rocks as their own.

"Mind they'll put curses on you, Taran. Or use potions to confuse you, slow you down, or give Gaoth Bán the willies and throw you. I've seen it done. I believe in their magic. It's na happened to me, but I've seen others undone by their spells."

"There's no magic but from the Adversary," said Pátrick. "Druid magic from Satan himself will have no effect on one who's given his heart to Christ. Put your faith no longer in such things, Eivhir and Taran, for they're works of the Devil, and in the presence of Christ, the Evil One trembles."

But the crumpled smile Eivhir gave when she was worried did not change. And though I nodded at Pátrick's words, I wished I had faith such as his and could dismiss my fears so easily.

Early the next day, Eivhir led me to the pens where I learned to control Gaoth Bán, a horse whose legs and body were sleek and light, with a coat and mane of purest white. I expected a beast of sinew and muscle, but Eivhir told me Gaoth Bán and horses like him were meant for distance. He was built for the fast trot and the canter, and only at the end, for the gallop.

Eivhir climbed onto a mottled mare and led us on a slow trot through the northern trail, beneath a thick forest canopy heavy with mist. Dark and green, it smelled of leaf and loam. We stopped at the Standing Rock. I must admit, Gaoth Bán lived up to his reputation, for twice he threw me on my first ride. But only twice, and never thereafter.

I was unused to the trot, but the technique Eivhir taught me, of standing in the saddle as the horse's back rose to meet my rump—a rising post she called it—quickly became second nature. Without this, I'd have been bouncing up and down on my horse's spine, wearing out both him and me.

"'Tis a hard route to follow," I said when we reached the landmark, "with rocks and roots and too many side trails to lure one from victory. I fear to remember how we got here." I noted how dark it was at the Rock, even in full daylight. The trees hugged the perimeter, and a ceiling of ferns and vines hung from the rocks, making it almost as dim as the forest ride itself.

"We'll run the route many times. You'll master the trail, Taran, and the horse. Of that, I'm certain."

I thanked her. Then with Eivhir's urging, I tried to lead the way back. Several times, I took us down side trails before she corrected me. We returned to Emain Macha without me being thrown. There we let the horses rest, for they could only handle one such hard ride in a day.

Through the next several weeks, Gaoth Bán and I became old friends. I learned the course and felt confident I could ride it as fast as any man. Once, Eivhir and I even took the far southern route the druids favored. It was much like the northern path until we came to a root and rock and boulder strewn tunnel that bored straight into the forest for a hundred yards.

We dismounted and Eivhir led the mare into a stretch of trail choked by nests of roots sticking two feet above the ground. I followed behind with Gaoth Bán, looking back often to check his progress. Soon, a thick tangle of creepers joined the roots, and our pace slowed to a crawl. Then my horse stopped. I knelt to free vines from his legs and led him on. Now heavy grass fought with tall thistles and obscured my view of the roots. Gaoth Bán stumbled, knocking me to the ground. Standing again, I examined his legs. He seemed unhurt. We continued until a field of loose scree, mixed with small boulders, overtook the roots and thistles.

Here our every step sank into the earth, scattering pebbles, rocks, and dust. Gaoth Bán whinnied in protest and tried to rear. I let him rest, then tugged on his reins and we trudged on. A deep gully dropped before me. I led him gingerly to the bottom, then up the far side into another stretch of tangled roots.

Finally, we reached the end and turned to look back the way we'd come. Oddly, we could see the whole of the devilish route from beginning to end, even the place where we'd entered.

"It's worse than the last time I tried it," Eivhir said. "They surely canna be riding their steeds over this. They must be walking. But walking they'd lose far too much time. This trail isn't *that* much shorter. They tell us 'tis their spells makes them win. And sure, only a horse floating on spells of air, with a rider on top, could cross this mess at any speed. I'm sorely puzzled."

I shook my head. It didn't make sense. "But Pátrick says their spells are useless."

"Still, they always win."

"Where does that lead?" I asked, pointing to a side trail at the end of the rough stretch.

Eivhir looked down the path. For a long while, her chestnut eyes gazed into the trees.

"That trail," I said again, thinking she hadn't heard. "Where does it go?"

"The orchard trail?" She finally looked at me. "It ends at Emain Macha. It's quite passable. But 'tis merely a side trail. It dumps into an orchard a hundred yards south of the village. Nay, nothing here makes sense."

She stared down the orchard trail, her eyes distant. Gaoth Bán reached down to munch on a patch of grass.

Finally, she looked at me. "This puzzle bothers me fierce."

I nodded, and we rode to the Standing Rock, where we took the main trail home, not wishing again, anytime soon, to wend the way of rock and root.

For many weeks, I practiced the race with Gaoth Bán through the Forest of Mists, until the day before the *óenach,* three days before the race. As people arrived and the excitement built, I decided to give both the horse and myself a well-deserved rest.

I would simply enjoy the Great Fair.

CHAPTER 21

The Óenach

The *óenach* would last a full week and, even before it began, clans from all over Ulster arrived and set up shelters on the outskirts of a field where much of the activity would take place. By the morning of the event, more people had gathered in the valley than anyone could count, with more coming all the time.

The first morning of the *óenach*—pronounced "way-nock" —Forga mac Dallán stood upon a log platform and looked out over the great throng with shining eyes.

"Greetings, clans of the Ulaid." His voice echoed loud and strong. "We of Emain Macha welcome you to this *óenach*, this grand celebration of life and spirit with all the *tuatha* of our people!"

A thundering cheer went up from the crowd.

Forga raised both hands until the roar died down. "There are wares and arts for sale, bards and music to listen to. Mead and ale and food for all to partake. We'll have races and sports to test your skill and wagers to empty your purse. 'Tis all for your pleasure."

More cheering, boisterous agreement, and laughing at the reference to wagering.

Forga stretched out his hands. "But you must ken the reason for this *óenach*, which reason is like no other that's ever gathered us together."

A strange silence spread through the crowd. Everyone had heard the news of the king's lost kin and Eivhir's illness, and now the Rí Cóicid was about to tell them what, until now, had been for most only rumor.

"Who among us can understand what it is to lose those he loves best? What's left a man once the demon spirits have snatched the wife of his youth to the Otherworld, quick as you can snap your fingers, without warning or reason? How can anyone know the depths to which a man's heart will sink when death has stolen the best of his seed, his only son? Aye, the grim lady nearly snatched my only daughter, the light of my life. Death made her to lie sickly and motionless, caught between two worlds, but alive in neither. When such happens, where is the bottom of terror? Surely, it threatened to destroy this king and all he touched."

Quiet attention now lay upon the thousands of upturned faces—faces only a moment ago filled with cheering and boisterous merriment.

Forga's voice echoed out over the crowd like thunder. "When Eivhir fell into her death sleep, the druids did all they could, but their gods abandoned them." He paused, casting his gaze upon his audience as if to give weight to his accusation. "Aye, she was only hours away from leaving this life for that place where Manannán mac Lir rules in dim light with a fickle will. And I was prepared to follow her, I was. Such was my despair.

"But then came a savior whose name was Pátrick. He spoke of a new God in the world. 'Tis a God who's been here all along and we didn't know it. The God who created all that lives and breathes and who rules over all. And in the late afternoon of Eivhir's death sleep, this Pátrick, and the ones who came with him, prayed to the Son of this God. By morning's light, even as I thought he had failed and I was ordering their beheading, Eivhir awakened and asked for me.

"This is why I've called this *óenach*—to give thanks for my daughter's recovery and to thank the God Most High who smiled on this king and the people of the Ulaid when all the other gods looked away. Now the king's heart sings with joy and his happiness must overflow to everyone around him. And because Eivhir and your Rí Cóicid are saved, so too are you, my people of the Ulaid, saved. Aye, Pátrick's God has saved us all. So go and listen to him, to this Pátrick, this holy one, under the lone oak at the far end of the field. Give thanks to this God of his, and follow Him, for that's the real reason for this fair.

"Now let the music play. Let the mead and ale be poured. Start the games and sports. I declare this *óenach* started and begun!"

A deafening cheer rose from the crowd. Men threw their caps in the air, clapped each other on the back, and whooped. This continued for long moments. When the roar finally died and groups drifted toward the booths, I began my exploration.

How can I describe the sights and sounds of the *óenach* through the eyes of yesteryear, through the senses of one seeing such things for the first time? Back then, the world was much smaller, and the great fairs of Forga mac Dallán were the grandest events the land of Ériu had ever seen. Every *tuath* of Ulster would send people to Emain Macha until many villages were nearly empty. Each farmstead volunteered someone. And all came dressed in their best. Every tunic was painted and dyed, boasting artful designs, colorful plaids, or stripes of red, yellow, green, and blue. Around their necks, they wore brass and silver torcs. On their hands and fingers, gold bracelets and rings. Everyone came in their finest clothes.

People waited years for a *óenach*. When it arrived, no one wanted to miss it. Pity the poor herdsman's son or daughter who was chosen to stay behind and tend the sheep or look after the cattle. Since his death, the likes of Forga's *óenacha* have never been repeated. I've now been to a *óenach* in Connacht, and they say the *óenacha* in Leinster are grand, but for my opinion, none were greater than those of Ulster under Forga mac Dallán.

The fair filled a large field next to the forest below the fortified hilltop. Tents rose everywhere. At one end, log structures topped with hide served as shelters from the frequent drizzle. Here, the vendors slept and sold their wares. Sweet-smelling wine from Gaul. Forge-hammered swords and daggers cast by expert metalworkers—iron for business, silver and bronze for show. Fruit pies, sweet breads, and honey cakes, filling the aisles with enticing aromas. Capes and tunics of newly tanned leather, smooth silk, or white wool—painted or dyed, decorated with shells, brass, or animal teeth, or woven with plaids and stripes. Hats of fur, silk, or skin. Saddles and bridles—aye, the finest hard leather all. And the musical instruments—harps, bagpipes, bone whistles, and *bodhrán* drums.

Early in my exploration, I chanced to meet Mùirne.

"Never have I seen such a sight." Her eyes were wide with excitement. "Kilgarren never let me see anything. And before him, I traveled na but five miles beyond our *tuath*."

"So you like the fair?"

"Like it?" She looked at me and smiled broadly. "Sure, and I like it just fine."

We decided to walk the aisles together. A man wearing a leather apron, his face scarred by years of sparks, beat a hammer on white-hot iron. Children's eyes grew round at the sight of swords and sickles coming straight from his furnace. He pounded, bent, and shaped them on anvils before our eyes. Another smelter worked only in gold and silver. That day he was fashioning a torc, a wide, circular neck ornament of silver, on which he made intricate designs.

Further on, an old woman made furs and blankets, her loom set up to weave, rods clicking back and forth. Her fingers quivered as she flipped the wooden poles, the different colored threads lining up and falling into the cloth exactly where they belonged.

"Bright plaids, lassie." She winked at Mùirne as her fingers flew. "Na but bright and cheerful plaids from my loom."

A potter turned a wheel with clay-greasy fingers, shaping a tall pitcher, nearly ready for a handle. We ran our fingers over a finished jug, admiring a painted forest scene, with its greens, blues, and yellows. Behind him, a woman used a long wooden paddle to pull jars from a small kiln. Even where I stood, the fire's red heat warmed my face.

"Would you take this knife for a leather saddle?" At the next booth, a tall red-haired man bargained with a tanner working a hide. "'Tis hard metal from Iberia, smelted for strength."

The tanner took the knife, turned it, and gave it back. "Throw in two jugs of Gallic Roman wine and 'tis done."

"I donna have such wine, but I'll have two bags of shells to give you by fair's end. Will you trade?"

"Agreed. And this work'll be done end of the week. Aye, and a fine piece of leather I'll have for you."

They shook hands, clapped each other's shoulders, and parted.

And so it surrounded us. Barters on the spot. Promises of future exchanges. Sometimes deliveries stretched beyond the fair, requiring a journey between *tuatha*.

Children ran beside us, up and down the aisles, laughing and playing tag.

Besides the trading, there was, of course, the mead. The Ériu could never do without that intoxicating beverage. From shortly after the noon meal, it flowed like a river from the mead tents.

Forga maintained rows of hives, spread out over five fields, with men to tend the bees. The honey was stored and chilled in caves, kept for the promise of a *óenach*. From this, he prepared vats of the drink, enough to drown a thousand men, he said. Maids dispensed it freely from four makeshift tents. Forga liked his mead drier, rather than sweeter, and even allowed a limited amount with nutmeg. Everyone brought their own mugs. Forga also provided plenty of barley ale at these tents, but he prided himself on his mead. All partook and walked the ground with mugs in hand—all except Pátrick and Servius. Indeed, after Pátrick observed some of the excesses of this drink, he later gave a message on the subject.

As we walked, Mùirne abstained, but I did not.

Each *tuath* sent their bards, and we stopped long before each poet to hear their rhyme and verse. Epics of ancient warriors fallen in battle. Sad accounts of maidens and lost loves. Sly ones of maids tricking druids and the terrible consequences. The Tale of the Taín. Traditional stories of the ancient *Fir Bolg* and of the *Tuatha Dé Danann*, the great rulers of old who left this world and went down under the earth. Or ribald tales full of innuendo, double meanings, and puns. Some bards began long, involved boasts with endless bragging, piling absurdity upon absurdity until their brag was so outrageous it had everyone laughing and clapping.

Clowns roamed the field and aisles at will, men acting the goat, playing the fool, their faces painted in scary reds and blacks and yellows. Some would throw mocking, piercing jests at every passerby. Others told bawdy jokes and had their audiences laughing, holding their sides, and spilling their mugs. These I tried to avoid.

"I donna like the clowns." Mùirne frowned. "They're funny, but also . . . mean."

"Aye, they're wicked. At any other time, some of these jests would end in dead clowns."

Mùirne laughed. "I dare say you're right."

We entered the side of the field reserved for sport and games of strength and skill. Men heaved round boulders, weighing at least three or four stone, and the one who threw it the farthest was the victor. There were contests of spear chucking and axe throwing for distance and accuracy. Mock swordplay. Arm wrestling. Foot races. Wrestling. The men competed nearly naked, dressed only in loincloths.

These events always attracted large, sweaty, boisterous crowds, with much spilt mead and ale, wagering, and the threat of fights among the onlookers, always over bets lost and the amount the loser must pay. But most controlled themselves. Fighting at the *óenach* was taboo.

Smells hovered thick on the air. Sizzling meat. Bubbling stewpots. Mouth-watering pastries. Newly tanned leather. Horses' urine and the straw to soak it up. Sweating bodies. Smoking fires and torches. Wet grass and mud. Pine logs newly cut and the furs they held overhead. And occasionally, the odor from the privies at the field's southern end.

The music filled the field, forest, village, and every corner of Emain Macha, from the beginning of the *óenach* to the end. It began at Forga's call and never quit until the last shelter was torn down and all the *tuatha* departed. Of course, when the mead and ale started to flow, nothing could stop the men's boisterous and hearty songs from bursting forth. The women, too, would break out in song.

And the musicians! Their music floated over the crowds from dozens of players, each ensconced in their own quarters. Eerie music of the pipe to put your hair on end and your skin aquiver. Drums and cymbals syncopated to the drummer's inner beat. Tunes from the bone whistle and bagpipe to send your heart aflutter. Harps to accompany the singers' ballads and fill your soul with grief or joy. Each musician chose his territory, and before them, the dancers would gather. The livelier the music, the more dancers they attracted.

"On Inis Creig we had no instruments but the *bodhrán* and the bone whistle. Nothing like the fiddle. But I've not seen even one of those here. They must be rare, indeed."

"And I'm thinking you like the fiddle?"

"Very much so. I miss Coll's playing."

"Kilgarren didna appreciate him enough. His playing was magical."

"'Tis true. But look at these dancers. I never saw so many men doing the jig or the reel with such skill and energy."

"I'm thinking the mead and ale do half the work."

I winked at her. "But the other half is skill."

Mùirne joined a crowd of women, laughing and applauding. As she clapped, I joined the dancers, spinning round and round with one arm over my head, jumping and kicking out with one leg, then the other.

"'Tis the mead I think," said Mùirne, smiling, as I handed her my mug.

"Nay," I responded, "'tis skill." I smiled and spun back into the dancers.

The first day, Mùirne and I parted late, weary yet energized by the feast the *óenach* offered our senses.

Alone on the second day, I discovered a new booth someone had set up the night before. There, I heard the most beautiful, fetching fiddle music. At last, here was someone who could play this magical new instrument. Again, I thought of Coll and how much he would have liked this particular song. The sound floated over the booths and drew me toward it. When I arrived at the fiddler's tent, such a crowd of listeners had gathered, I could scarcely approach. Soon the music finished, and a voice announced the fiddler would take a break. As the crowd broke up, I wormed my way closer to congratulate the player's performance.

As I neared the front, the short, thin musician turned around and there, with red mustache drooping, was my old friend Coll! We hugged and pounded each other's backs as if we'd been separated for years, though it had been less than three months.

"Are you well?" I asked. "What brings you to Emain Macha? And where's Donnach?"

"Alas, Donnach is dead. Killed in the raid. 'Twas a terrible fight, Taran, with two dozen slain, another dozen taken captive. Their chariot attack was . . . devastating. Amalgaid and the rest of his men fled for their lives to Cruachain. I'm a slave now, captured in that raid."

"But then—how do you come to be here?"

"We were several days north of here, going from farmstead to farmstead, stealing—'taxing,' Amalgaid called it—cattle from every farm until we'd assembled a large herd. As we drove them toward Connacht, the army of the Ulaid surprised us. In the fight, they took me prisoner.

"After Amalgaid's fighters fled, the Ulster men retraced our path and returned the cattle we'd stolen to each *tuath*. At each farmstead, they left one of us as a slave. They gave me to a man named Ceallach, Rí Tuath of a tiny clan and a hard man. He spent the first week beating me and tying me at night in the mud under the open sky, away from the rest of the *tuath*. Punishment for the raid, I guess. I like to have died in the chill rain. My side still aches.

"Ceallach thought to make me a sheep herder, with only sheep and a dog for company for days on end. But when he finally decided to let me play my fiddle, everything changed."

"So it wasn't lost in battle?"

"'Twas not. My captors gave it to Ceallach. Even they held respect for such an unusual instrument and the one who could play it. The night the Rí Tuath heard my music, he brought me into the roundhouse, gave me light duties, and began to treat me with more respect. I started playing with his bard, and as with Kilgarren, he provided the poetry, I, the music. I played for the Rí Tuath nearly every evening.

"Then last week, when most of the farmstead journeyed here, Ceallach brought me along. He said I'd bring great honor and glory to his clan, for none offered more fetching music than I. His very words."

"What's your honor price?"

"More than anyone could pay. Ceallach's now convinced I'm worth two dozen cows, for he fancies my fiddle playing even more than his bard's poetry."

"Sure, and a steep price it is."

"But what happened to you, Taran? Did you find the man you sought?"

"I did indeed." Then I told Coll what happened since we'd parted, how I'd joined Pátrick and ended up in Emain Macha. But we could only talk for a few moments as Machar, Ceallach's brother, appeared and herded my friend back to the stage.

"Let's meet for supper at the eastern mead tent," I said as Coll was leaving. "For we have much to talk about."

"I'll try. But as you can see, I have a constant companion."

Thus we parted. I moved to the edge of the crowd and listened for some time as Coll again coaxed magical notes, both sad and happy, piercing and lilting, from his fiddle.

To serve so many mouths, Forga had scattered seven supper tents across the field. A pot's boil before dusk, the maids of Emain Macha stood under each shelter, ladling out tasty portions of mutton and beef stew, brimming with onions and turnips. The smell had teased us all day. In the morning, they'd serve porridge with goats' milk. Each clan brought oats or barley, a few cattle or lambs, and some honey so Emain Macha's resources would not be overly strained by Forga's generosity.

That evening, as arranged, I waited at the tent until dark. My friend never arrived.

Though the stars came out, the fair went on. For, as on the night before, no one wanted to quit. Torches lit the aisles between shelters, but at night the action moved toward the music, the dancing, and the mead. As the moon rose higher, the reverie wore itself out. Women pulled their men, if they could find them, to their beds under makeshift tents. Or the men simply left exhausted, without wifely prodding. Finally, the sleep of spent merrymaking stole over the field.

Back inside the roundhouse, I lay in my bed. Coll's bondage distressed me, but I could do nothing for him. I thought instead about tomorrow and the race—a race upon which rested the fate of Pátrick's mission to Ulster, perhaps the fate of Ériu itself.

And following Pátrick's teaching, I prayed to God for victory.

CHAPTER 22

The Race

I awoke, wishing this heavy responsibility were taken from me.

As I left the roundhouse, I wore only a loincloth, for our custom was to ride nearly naked. I'd already spiked my hair with mud, dried so it stood out at all angles.

Eivhir caught up with me and looked me up and down. "I say again, 'tis a shame such a handsome lad as yourself has been spoken for." She grinned. "Even with your fearsome hair."

I felt my face flushing.

"But you must forgive me, Taran, for I willna be at the start to see you off. I must attend an errand that'll take me out of Emain Macha. It may also make me late to catch the end of your ride, so please forgive me. But 'tis important. And does concern the race. I canna say more than that."

I frowned. "I thank you, Eivhir, for whatever you're doing. I'll try to remember your training."

"You'll do fine. Remember, your job is to preserve your mount, keep a steady pace until the end, and then finish strong."

I nodded.

"But before I leave, we must paint you, as no one should ride barefaced off the starting line."

She sat me on a log and produced jars of green, red, and yellow colored grease from her bag. With her forefinger, she drew stripes and swirls across my forehead, around my eyes, chin, and even down my neck, arms, and chest.

"Fearsome, indeed." She stepped back to examine her work. "That should strike terror into the heart of any opponent." She paused, one side of her mouth curving in a half-smile, wrinkling her freckled cheeks. "Or else he'll fall off his horse in a fit of laughter."

Just what had she done? I walked over to an abandoned bucket of water by the roundhouse entrance and looked down. The image was murky and wavered with ripples. "Sure, and what if it scares my horse to death and I lose the race for lack of a beast?"

Eivhir laughed. "Gaoth Bán is a strong animal. He should withstand the look of you."

Shaking my head, I thanked her for her efforts. Then she climbed onto her spotted mare and rode off to the south on her mysterious mission. I was glad she had my best interests at heart.

Ours was the fair's second race, to start at midmorning, and everyone was talking about it. All day yesterday, they ran short sprints at full gallop. Today, we were the first distance race, and the only one through the forest. The stakes in our matchup were so high, all manner of wagers were placed. The odds against me were enormous.

The time for the race approached, so I went to the pens to pick up Gaoth Bán.

As I entered the barn, I passed Boodan leading Spiorad into the yard. He too, wore only a thin loincloth. But his face and chest were painted with so much grease, not a speck of skin showed above his waist. Even his legs were colored. When he saw me, he gave a barely perceptible nod. Then the corners of his wide mouth turned up in a ghost of a smile, grotesque through the gaudy paint. But he turned away without catching my gaze.

I found Gaoth Bán in his stall, and for some moments, just petted his muzzle and whispered to him. This was more to calm my quivering stomach than anything else.

I arrived at the starting line to a crowd of rowdy onlookers and a waiting Boodan.

A bearded man raised a handful of gold and shouted to the crowd. "Six gold earrings to your one the lad loses to the druid."

"Six, you say?" said a short man, stepping forward. He looked down at the pieces in his hand. "Sure, and I'll take the wager."

"Are you glipe, Sèitheach?" someone shouted.

"Don't be the lummox." A portly man beside Sèitheach hit him on the arm. "You'll lose it all."

Sèithach looked at the rings in his hand, raised his glance, and caught mine. He looked again at the jewelry he held. "Nay, you're right." He raised his hand high and shouted. "I'll take eight to one against the lad. Who'll risk it?"

Beahak approached me on stocky legs. "Sure, and I've wagered ten silver bracelets in your favor, Taran, on behalf of my mistress, so you'd better be winning this morning." She gave me a smile and a wink.

The start of the race began at the field's far edge near the sporting events, and there waited Forga mac Dallán, Ohran, Sòlas, Pátrick, and many others. Both Boodan and I stood beside our horses. I was tense, my heart thumping. I said a short prayer for victory.

Low-hanging clouds dropped a fine mist and wet my forearms. The gray sky allowed only a dim light on the field.

When the time came, the king rose and stepped onto a log pedestal. "The race for who shall counsel and minister to the king will now begin. A course of distance runs through the Forest of Mists, to the Standing Rock. There, two men chosen by myself wait even now with batons. At the Rock, each rider must take a baton. The first to cross the finish line with his baton wins. Riders, are you ready?"

We both shouted, "We are!"

"Mount your beasts!"

I slipped one foot into a stirrup and leaped onto Gaoth Bán's back. He had raced often and knew what was happening. Beneath me, he was a bent sapling, ready to spring. He pawed the ground with one hoof, threw his head up, and shook it.

Forga drew his sword and raised it high.

"Riders take your reins!"

I glanced sideways at the fearsome visage of Boodan, who caught my gaze before quickly turning away. We both faced the course.

In one swift motion, the king lowered his sword. The crowd roared. Even before I kicked my beast, Gaoth Bán leaped from the starting line into a fast gallop across the field.

Boodan was right beside me. As we crossed the field's quarter-mile distance, the crowd's shouts, cheers, and encouragements receded. Then we entered the forest's dark trail and dropped to a canter. Horses could not last such a distance at a gallop.

I was in the lead, with Spiorad holding back. The course immediately began its familiar winding and twisting, plunging into the wood's heavy darkness, worsened by the drizzle and the overcast day. Spiorad's hooves clopped on the path behind.

We passed something unusual—a leather sack hanging from a branch beside the trail. After Gaoth Bán and I passed, I looked behind. Boodan had taken it and now threw the pack over one shoulder.

About a mile in, the trail opened up for a short distance, and suddenly, Spiorad was close behind.

"Move over," cried Boodan above the clopping of hooves, "and let me pass."

"Take the lead if you want," I shouted back. "You'll kill your beast."

"'Tis my worry."

We were already going at a canter. We could not keep such a pace, so I let the druid pass. Eivhir had warned me not to push too hard in the race's early going. At the end, we'd have time for a sustained canter and a short gallop, but not yet. This all assumed, of course, that the druids would not somehow use their magic to gain advantage in the tortuous stretch of rock, root, and ravine.

As Boodan came even with me, he pulled something out of the pack—a length of rope. Tied at one end was a stone and something wrapped in a bag made of husks. He twirled the rope and circled it over his head, making a sound like a hive of angry bees. Then he released it.

Too late I realized what he was doing. I tried, unsuccessfully, to duck.

The rock and the bag struck the left side of my face and the husks broke. At once the air around me filled with white powder.

Before I could react, I'd breathed it in. Instantly, a bitter taste was on my lips. My mouth, my throat, and my eyes burned. I blinked. With one hand, I brushed at my cheeks to clean them of the acrid substance. My hand came back covered in colored grease.

I tried to let Boodan get ahead of me, but he slowed Spiorad to keep even. He dropped his rope onto the trail and from the pack brought out a second, this one fixed to a heavy rock on one end.

"So this," I yelled over the clopping of hooves, "is how the druids win? Through trickery and foul play?"

Avoiding my stare, Boodan twirled his new weapon. It hit Gaoth Bán's neck a hard, bruising blow and spooked him. The horse slowed, stopped, and then reared in a circle.

I clung to his neck with both hands, fearful of falling off, trying to bring him back under control.

Boodan and Spiorad surged ahead. When my steed calmed, I kicked his sides, and we started at a fast canter. Now Boodan was far ahead.

Suddenly, my lips and throat were burning. Sweat dripped from my brow. My vision dulled, and on either side of the trail, fog appeared. I still smelled the acrid white residue, so I slowed Gaoth Bán. I rubbed my face with my hand, smearing it with paint, trying to clean away the powder so I could focus on the race.

Within the next mile, I was again behind my opponent, for it seemed Gaoth Bán was naturally faster. But I still remained about ten lengths to the rear, fearful of another attack.

Several times, Boodan gave me a backward glance, but I was far enough back, he didn't slow his mount. We rode this way until the fork. Boodan, of course, took the far southern route while I went the northern path I'd practiced so often.

Safe from attack, I tried to find the gait Eivhir told me to keep. Without a rival, it was harder to keep the pace. Fortunately, Gaoth Bán was untouched by the powder and knew his duty well.

Then the drug began its work, and the forest closed in. Suddenly, an endless dark tunnel surrounded me. In some devilish manner, I had entered a different path than the one in practice. Had I taken a wrong turn? Nothing around me was familiar. This trail would not lead to the Rock, but to some vague oblivion! A mist hung in the air, a thick fog hitting my bare chest and legs and forearms, drenching my arms, fingers, and legs with cold rain. I went from burning up to shivering.

The day was dim already, but now the shadows lengthened like living, growing things. Between the trees arose a brooding, swirling darkness, a blackness so deep and thick and menacing, there seemed no end to it. The canopy of leaf and branch seemed composed of fingers and claws, live grasping things, all reaching toward me. Surely, the trees themselves wanted my death. I believed they were capable of wrapping me in their limbs—and of murder itself. I wanted to flee, but where to? I'd entered a strange, new world of shadow, swirling color, and terror behind every tree.

My rump slammed into the saddle to meet Gaoth Bán's rising body. I was surprised, confused. What was happening? I crashed into the saddle again, hard. Then again. And again. My horse slowed. I felt sore where the saddle hit. The saddle came up to hit me again on my buttocks.

I shook my head, trying to focus. The drug. The thoughts and visions weren't mine. I was there to win a race, to keep a proper pace, to finish strong. I tried to concentrate, to drive away those phantom fears and turns of mind the druids' drug brought. Remember what Eivhir taught. I had stopped posting my body upright in the saddle. The drug distracted, confused me, and I was no longer riding well. The druids' trick, trying to drug their opponent, was shameless, without honor. I *must* not let them win by deceit.

"Please, God, guide me," I said out loud. "Take these fears from me. Clear my mind and lead me through this forest. Don't let me lose this race. Everything depends on it."

Then I kicked my horse to continue the trot, concentrating on my posture and on a fast gait. The prayer helped. My fears lessened. The darkness lightened. The trees seemed less menacing. I rose in the saddle when I was supposed to and stopped hindering my horse. Gaoth Bán broke into a fast canter. Soon we were making up for lost ground.

The distance to the Standing Rock over the last section lengthened as I fought to keep the darkness, the dread, and the fear from clouding my mind. I rounded the last turn and entered the final stretch of tunnel.

Then I burst into the dark clearing under overhanging ferns, leaves, and vines. One of the king's men held my baton. Boodan's man had already given his away.

"Been here and gone," said my man. "Has 'bout a quarter mile on you."

I nodded, then with baton in hand, I whirled Gaoth Bán and reentered the northern trail at a fast trot. A quarter of a mile. Too much time to catch up. If he gained more distance on the return leg, I had no chance of winning. I shook my head again and tried to control my shivering. But the wet and cold kept my mind focused and helped fight the drug's effects that were slowly dissipating. I said another prayer.

The forest held fewer fears on the return journey. I kept a steady gait—faster, I think, than anything I'd ever done in practice. We cantered, then trotted, then cantered again. Before long, we passed the fork where the southern two trails joined the northern route. Gaoth Bán did not seem winded, so I increased the pace. By now the drug had mostly worn off, replaced by a headache.

When we passed a series of twists and turns, the trail straightened out, and I had a glimpse of Boodan ahead of me. He'd dropped the pack somewhere. Now I was only two hundred feet behind him, and he didn't realize I'd caught up. Somehow, improbably, I gained a lot of distance on my return trip.

Still, it was two hundred feet. I increased the pace to a canter and Gaoth Bán, seeing his adversary now, fairly leapt through the forest. I gained, but also recognized the trail's end. We were on the final stretch before the field. This was my last chance to take the lead.

The trail opened up into the fair and a course lined with spectators. When I entered the field at full gallop, the crowd erupted in a deafening roar. Boodan was now only sixty feet ahead and Spiorad still trotted at an easy pace. Neither man nor mount realized we threatened their victory. Only now, with the crowd's thundering announcement, did Boodan turn in the saddle. He saw me then kicked his mount to a full gallop.

But with every stride, Gaoth Bán gained a foot on Spiorad. He was truly the better horse. The crowd cheered and their noise only spurred my steed to greater efforts. The race was closer, apparently, than anyone expected. We were in a true battle, not the foregone conclusion many assumed.

But the finish line was fast approaching. The distance from forest to finish was too short, only about four hundred yards. Now I was six lengths behind and closing. At a hundred yards from the finish, we were four lengths distant. At a hundred feet, only three lengths.

In the final stretch, when I was a horse's length in his rear, Boodan turned to see me, his forehead creasing in surprise.

I pulled side-by-side with him. The finish was only twenty feet away. Tall wooden stakes and a painted white line marked the end. I needed one more stride, a single lunge, and Gaoth Bán would cross to win.

But the finish was already upon us and Spiorad took Boodan over first. The crowd's roar died quickly. The conclusion was indeed foregone. For a time, it had seemed like a close race, and the crowd appreciated this, but once again, the druids prevailed.

A heaviness constricted my chest, and I briefly closed my eyes. I let Pátrick down. I lost the race. I made a good showing at the final stretch but still lost. Everything Pátrick hoped for in Emain Macha lay in shambles.

Gaoth Bán's sides heaved and foam hung from his mouth. I dismounted and led him in circles, trying to cool him down.

But Boodan stayed atop his mount, raising his baton high, his wide mouth grinning. As he passed me, he averted his eyes. Then he rode to the Rí Cóicid. The king ignored the druid and stared at me with obvious disappointment. Without waiting for an acknowledgment of his victory, Boodan pulled Spiorad away from the king's entourage. He began a slow, easy ride, with baton held high, back to the fair's center, heading down each aisle to proclaim his victory.

Ohran and the druids joined him. In a loud drone, they repeated to all how Boodan had won, how the druids prevailed over Pátrick and his God. Then their victory announcement became a chant. A few people cheered. Others remained silent, their glances downcast. Before that day, word of Pátrick's God had spread, and it appeared I let down many of these new believers. Around us, the bets were sorting themselves out, with the losers paying and regretting their trust in this new God and me.

I wanted to run to a far corner of the orchard and hide from everyone.

Pátrick appeared beside me. "Do not blame yourself, Taran. You did well. You rode a respectable race. It was close, very close, and I thank you for your efforts. I don't understand it, but—apparently it was not God's will that you win for us today."

"They tried to poison me, Pátrick. But I was able to resist the drug's effects."

He frowned and shook his head. "Then you did the best you could."

I nodded but avoided his gaze. More than anything, I wanted to be alone then.

I caught a glance from the king. His fallen face showed plainly his disappointment. Not only had I let down Pátrick, but Ohran's plan to discredit this new God seemed to be working. I myself again doubted His power—for my faith then had barely taken root.

"What will you do now?" I asked Pátrick.

"There are other provinces. We will move on."

I nodded, unable to meet the eyes of this man who'd put such trust in me, whom I'd failed so badly. Then I thought: What if I left tonight with a bag, some food, and a weapon? After this, how could I continue to face Pátrick, the king, or anyone else in Emain Macha?

But at that moment, Eivhir returned from her mysterious mission, riding through the crowd, causing a stir, and upsetting everything that had happened until then.

CHAPTER 23

The Burning

Eivhir rode straight through the milling throng, calling loudly to make way, until she stopped before the king and dismounted. Foam hung from her mare's mouth, and its sides heaved while Eivhir held a hurried and earnest conference with Armadal and Forga mac Dallán. As the conversation progressed, the king's eyes narrowed, his face grew red, and Armadal's black brows sloped toward a dangerous frown. Then Forga ordered a group of men away on a mission.

When her conference was over, Eivhir searched the crowd, found me, and approached. "You must come now before the king. Bring your baton. This race isn't over yet." She gave me a quick half-smile.

What had happened?

We waited in grim silence, as neither the king, Armadal, or Eivhir would say what this was about. What did they anticipate? I was puzzled, for the king's face painted a picture of deep anger.

Within a short while, ten armed men led Boodan, Ohran, and three other druids of Emain Macha before the king. Only one druid was missing. Ohran stepped before us with a thin smile. "What is it my king? Why do you call us from our victory celebration?"

With black, intense eyes the king stared at Boodan, then at Ohran, then back at Boodan. "In all my days as leader of the clans of the Ulaid, I have never encountered such perfidy, treachery, and foul play as I've seen today."

Ohran snapped a three-fingered hand across his face to bat the hair from his eyes. But did the hand shake? I thought it might have. "My king, why do you say this? About the race? It was won, as always, through magic, through the skill of my rider and the power of the forest spirits. Was Boodan not first to cross the finish?"

Forga's face was tight. His glance bored into the druid. He turned to Eivhir. "Speak, daughter! Tell them what you told me."

Eivhir put her hands on her hips and stared directly at the druids. "You won the race by fraud, Boodan. It appears you druids have won every race you ever ran through the forest by deceit, fraud, and foul play. And today is the last time it will ever happen."

Ohran's glance flicked back and forth between us. "Eivhir, my lass, you're mistaken. You're the king's daughter, and I respect your opinion, but these charges are baseless, without—"

"Silence!" interrupted the king. "Let her speak."

Ohran must have sensed, as did I, the danger in his tone, for he fell silent.

Eivhir began anew. "I've always been curious how you druids won every race through the forest, by taking the far southern route over a stretch of ground so mired in rocks, roots, ravines, and boulders. So today I decided to find out. Long before the race began, I rode my mare up the orchard trail south of Emain Macha. I led her to the place where that path joins the southern race route, just beyond where the rocky, rooted stretch ends. There, I found a hiding place in the forest, where I could see but not be seen. I arrived early and waited. And what do you think I saw?"

Ohran shifted from one foot to the other, never finding a comfortable stance. Boodan's glance searched from Forga, to the crowd, then to the booths beyond, looking for something, not finding it.

"I saw Boodan come after me—from behind me!—from the orchard trail and riding Spiorad. Mind you, this was long before the race began. And this Boodan, or what appeared to be Boodan, stopped and waited at the end of the rocky route, sitting atop his horse. But there was something different about him, something I couldn't identify at first. The same with his horse. The Spiorad he was riding certainly looked like Spiorad, but below the knees the legs were slick as if covered with grease.

"Then a curious thing happened. After a time, another Boodan appeared at the far end of the impassable section and gave a signal. At that sign, my Boodan—and I'll reveal his real name in a moment—started at a gallop toward the Standing Rock."

"'Tis a fine story you're spinning, Eivhir," Ohran broke in. "But forgive me, my king, if I question her motives. I know she's your daughter, but she's also become an acolyte of this, this Pátrick, and perhaps she's making up a tale to steal the rightful winner of the race from—"

"Silence!" Forga's black eyes narrowed, grew dark with warning. "You willna say another word. You will listen to the tale of your perfidy, or," he drew his sword and pointed it at his chief druid, "this very morning I will have your heads."

Ohran's thin lips formed a narrow slit and fell silent. Boodan's glance flicked between the ground at his feet and the crowd.

"At this point," resumed Eivhir, "I knew the Spiorad nearest me was a different beast. And I remembered a stud belonging to one of the druids that was all black, but with white fore and hind legs below the knees. So I figured the slick spots I'd seen were black grease paint. And the face I'd seen on the Boodan at my end was so covered with paint, underneath he could have been anyone. Yet I thought perhaps his mouth was a bit small that morning. And he'd gained a little weight. Now I didn't want the real Boodan, waiting at the far end of the root tunnel, to know what I was up to. So I crept through the dense undergrowth beside the trail to a point where it rounded the corner. Just off the main trail, I hid and waited. When the Boodan lookalike came galloping back from the Standing Rock with baton in hand and turned the corner, I moved my mount in front of him. You should've seen his face. Startled is not the word.

"His horse stopped and reared before me. I asked him who he was and what trick he was playing. Even then, he pleaded with me to let him pass. But the moment he spoke, I recognized him as Cesan, one of the druids. And when I revealed his ruse to him, his eyes went wide, for he was sore filled with fear. Even so, he tried to get around me. For a time, I prevented him. And that, my lords, is why the race was so close today. Eventually, in the scuffle, he knocked me off my horse and slipped away.

"Think of it! He knocked the Rí Cóicid's daughter off her horse.

"By the time I remounted and chased him down the path, he'd already signaled to the real Boodan—the one here before us—telling him to ride off and finish the race. For the real Boodan knew nothing of my discovery. I retraced my route down the orchard trail, never seeing Cesan or his mount again. I expect he's hiding somewhere in the southern forest, as the last look he gave me was the one a child would give to a wolf he met alone in the forest.

"So that, my lords, is how the druids have always won the forest race."

Forga's eyebrows dipped into a permanent frown. Now his glance narrowed and bored into Boodan. "Give me your baton."

Boodan looked at the wand he still held, then up at the king, then back at his baton. He dropped the baton to the ground and broke into a run, heading toward the congestion around the booths.

"Stop him!" cried the king.

As the words left his mouth, two guards on the far side, hidden by the crowd, ran out and gave chase. Within ten paces they'd tackled him. He went down, landing face first in the grass and mud. When he was back, standing dirty and disheveled before the king, blades of grass stuck out of his stiff, tan hair and from the greasepaint on his face.

The king pressed the point of his sword, still drawn, into the druid's chest.

For a moment, the king held the tip there, pressing hard, as though he might pierce him then and there.

Boodan's forehead crumpled and his eyes widened. He backed up a pace.

But instead of skewering him, Forga withdrew his sword. "Were I not a temperate man, I would have your life. And have it right now."

Then a guard gave Boodan's baton to the king. Forga sheathed his sword and studied the stick, turning it end over end. The race batons were cut from a sapling, about an inch in diameter, and painted white. Three rings of red, yellow, and blue were drawn around each end. Forga handed the wand to Eivhir. She examined it then said, "Taran, may I see your baton?"

I gave her mine. She inspected it. "Last night, I still didn't know how they did this trick of winning every race through the morass, but I knew in every contest we always used the same batons. Race after race, we never changed the batons. So last night, as a test, I put three notches in the end of each. Taran's baton is notched. Boodan's is not. There, Father, is absolute proof of the fraud. They must've hidden a replica at Boodan's end of the path so when he saw the signal, he could pick it up and continue his ride."

The king's face was strained, his eyes dark and fixed on his druids. He looked at each of them. "You've forfeited the race. You've also forfeited any claim of belonging to the clans of the Ulaid." He faced Armadal. "Put them in irons—all the druids—until I decide their fate."

"But my—" One look from Forga stopped Ohran in mid-sentence.

On Armadal's orders, men with swords led the druids away.

Moments later, after he'd calmed down, Forga announced all the bets should be reversed. A huge groan rose from the crowd, yet they complied. Beahak, an intense gleam in her eyes, walked with short, businesslike strides, searching for her wagering partner to reverse the bet a short while ago she thought she'd lost.

I caught Pátrick's glance. He smiled broadly and nodded his head.

Like rainwater gushing down a clear mountain stream, hope returned to me. Our prayers were answered though not in the way we expected. I had won the race. If the race had been fair, there would be no question Gaoth Bán outpaced Spiorad.

Soon after the druids were taken away, Forga mac Dallán approached me. His black, shining eyes looked into mine.

"I owe you a great debt, Taran mac Teague. You've helped expose the druids' deceit and turn Ohran's poisonous counsel out of my court. You've also allowed me to keep this new faith Pátrick teaches, that fills my heart with such joy and hope. I don't know what I'd have done if the druid's win went unchallenged. What can I do to repay you for finishing your ride with such courage?"

I opened my hands and shook my head. "Nothing, my lord. I rode for Pátrick and his God."

The king laid a hand on my shoulder and smiled. "If you think of something, I will grant it—anything within reason."

Thus did the fair's third eventful day conclude, with the king's gratitude, the druids in chains, my victory declared, and Pátrick's place secured. I'd ridden bravely against impossible odds, and everyone agreed that in a fair race, I'd have won. And so the fragile faith of the new believers Pátrick had gathered was not damaged, but strengthened.

The fair went on, with more races, sports, selling, buying, eating, drinking, music, poetry, ribaldry, boasting, and endless merrymaking.

Several times during the *óenach*, I wandered to the lone oak where Pátrick preached to the masses. There were always women at these events, but sometimes a few men. He spoke of the same things he had to Mùirne, Eivhir, Beahak, and me in our daily gatherings. Of how God had sent His Son to earth, of His undying love for us, and of what we must do to enter His glorious Kingdom. And whenever I listened, my heart would soar.

Each day I found time to go to Coll's tent and hear his marvelous music. We had little opportunity to talk, only enough for me to speak of Pátrick's God—now also my God—and the great things He had done for us.

On the *óenach's* sixth day, I finally decided what to ask from the Rí Cóicid and I went to him. That very afternoon Forga accompanied me to Coll's tent to hear his fiddle. After Coll had played for a while, and as Ceallach's brother, Machar, began to lead Coll away, Forga stopped him. He asked the man to take us to Ceallach. When we stood before Coll's master, Forga said, "Ceallach, I've listened to your fiddler and this magical, new instrument is grand, indeed."

"I thank you, my lord." Ceallach bowed. "It is indeed grand. Fine compensation for the damage Amalgaid's men did to my *tuath*."

"'Tis about that subject I wish to speak. I'd like to purchase the fiddler's freedom."

Ceallach's expression dropped. "Is there something else my lord wishes to buy? A pair of fine *cumal* perhaps? This fiddle player is dear to me."

"Bought wenches don't interest me. I wish to purchase Coll's freedom and no other. What price do you ask?"

They entered negotiations, settling on a price of fifteen cows, a great honor price, indeed, for a mere musician, but less than Ceallach wanted. Thus did Coll leave the service of Ceallach and once again become a free man.

"How can I ever thank you, Taran?" he asked as we stood before the mead tent after supper.

"You don't have to thank me. I could think of nothing else to ask the king and your capture and slavery weighed heavily on me."

"Still, from this day forward, I pledge you my service. Wherever you go, there I'll be. Whatever difficulties you encounter, I will share them with you, as your servant and your friend, now and forever. I take this oath on my life."

I was stunned. I fumbled for words, couldn't find them. I wiped a hand at my eyes, suddenly moist. "Thank you," I said, my voice barely above a whisper. "From the bottom of my heart. But I didn't ask your freedom only for you to become my servant. I release you, right now, from your pledge. You've your own life to lead."

"And I'll lead it as I please. In your service."

He would not be dissuaded. I hugged him and said, "So be it!"

We sat on a log together, talking. Later, he pulled out his fiddle and played. Quickly, a large group gathered around us. But with no one to guide him, the notes grew long, sad, and lonely, as was ever Coll's way. Music to wrench the heart, move the spirit, and bring tears to the eye. He played until midnight while many sat around him, drinking, eating, and listening quietly.

The next day was the seventh and last day of the *óenach*, and Forga mac Dallán had still not ruled on what to do with the druids. I heard him discussing it often with Armadal. The king was inclined to lop off their heads and display them on poles for a month. But Armadal feared making enemies. Attending the fair, of course, were a number of druids who serviced the Ulaid's different *tuatha*. Instead of a public beheading, Armadal preferred simple banishment. Yet that was too weak a punishment, said the king, for the perfidy they had carried out. The discussion went back and forth to no conclusion. But after Eivhir presented an idea secretly to her father, Forga ended the discussion.

It was late in the evening on the fair's last day. Everyone had drunk their fill of mead or ale and made as merry as they could before their departure the next morning. Then Forga mac Dallán sent men through all the aisles. They closed down the music and gathered everyone in the wide clearing on the hilltop fortress before the druid temple. So many crowded within the village, they overflowed the streets beside the roundhouses. The king had scattered men with torches throughout the yard and lanes, and their dim light spread flickering shadows over the crowd, now a rippling mass. Then the king's men passed out more torches.

Thousands of eyes turned toward the temple, before which the Rí Cóicid mounted a high pedestal.

He was already tall. When he stood there with his high cheekbones, dark eyebrows, and shining eyes, he made an imposing figure. Forga raised his hands, and a man beat on a *bodhrán* for silence. The king's men brought in the six prisoners, kept in chains the last few days. Only the day before, Cesan had been captured sneaking back for food.

"Hear me, people of the Ulaid! These men," the king pointed at the druids, "are the perpetrators of deceit and treachery. These are the men who defrauded us of fair play in every race they've ever run."

The crowd booed. Those nearest threw the bones of the chickens and pigs they'd been eating at the druids. The drum beat again for silence.

"I have decided on their punishment. From henceforth, they are banished for life from Ulster and from all the lands of the Ulaid. The banishment will begin this very evening. They'll na sleep another night under the protection of this king. If you catch them inside our borders, I decree their deaths by whatever *tuath* comes upon them."

Cheers rose. The *bodhrán* beat again for quiet.

"But there's the matter of this temple." He arched his eyebrows. "For me it has become a sign of abomination and disgust. What am I to do with such an affront—this monstrous cone towering over my palace and all Emain Macha? Should I let it stand? Should it forever look down on me and my kin? Or should I destroy it? That's what I've pondered lately and why you are assembled here tonight on this, the fair's last day."

Again, for apparently no reason, the crowd cheered. The drum beat and the voices quieted.

"So after much thought and, I might add, not a little mead—"

The crowd, as if anything said, especially in reference to mead, was worthy of applause, interrupted and roared its approval.

The *bodhrán* beat and silence again fell.

"So after much consideration, my thought is tonight, this last night of the *óenach*, before the eyes of the druids who built this detestable structure, we should—*burn it!*"

Now the crowd erupted in a deafening roar. Without prompting, those holding torches nearest the temple ran at the structure. I don't know if the king had planned for this, but within moments flames climbed all sides of the massive conical building. More torches touched its base.

Soon the night was ablaze with its light, and even from where I stood, some distance away, heat radiated. The flames grew, leaping up the sides, jumping from log to log, from mat to mat. It tore off the covering of thatch until a sheet of red, yellow, and white fire crackled in a great cylinder of heat. The blaze quickly reached the top and engulfed the temple's highest point in an angry display of heat, light, and color.

Night became day. The cool, moist air of evening burned away in a hot blast. The fire roared now, becoming a great noise that drowned out even the crowd's cheering.

In the face of this tremendous destruction, the crowd fell silent. The roar was angry, as if God himself were destroying the druids' false gods. The logs around the perimeter turned yellow, then red, dropping sparks and coals, breaking into pieces, and falling through to the floor of the temple. I caught a glimpse of idols being crushed, melting and breaking under logs and flames.

Everyone stood, watching a blaze such as none had ever seen—a great fire licking, crumbling, tearing the thatch from the walls, sending up showers of sparks and burning debris. The whole structure began to collapse in upon itself and fall into the center. The heat nearest the temple became so great, the crowds backed away to a distance well over a hundred feet. For a time, I worried about the king's palace, but it never caught fire.

A fitting finale for the fair, it also marked an end of the druids' reign in Emain Macha, and later in most of Ulster. Their days had come and, with the burning of the temple, were gone. The days of Pátrick and his God had arrived.

I caught a glimpse of the druids that night, as they watched the fire destroy their temple, their influence, and their power. Ohran's tiny eyes were dark, angry, his lips pulled taut. But the king also noticed this and, at that moment, gave a word to his men. Even as the last temple logs collapsed upon themselves in a shower of sparks, coals, and flame, the king's men marched the druids from the fortress into the night, banished forever from Ulster.

At the time, I hoped never again to face the cult of the druids on Ériu. But the druids were like wolves. You can drive a few from the local forest. But how do you stop the pack that returns in force from afar?

PART V

In Northern Leinster, A.D. 432 - 444

CHAPTER 24

The Way of the Faith

In the months following the fair, I became a true disciple of Christ, Son of the God Most High. Our daily learning under the lone oak continued, expanding to include more than a dozen others. At the fair, many had heard Pátrick's preaching and realized that the druids' ways, the forest spirits, and the old gods were false.

A few druids even converted to the new religion. They had seen Ohran's fall from honor and position, the perfidy and deceit of his followers. They became disillusioned with the ways of the spirits and demon gods and the need always to appease them, tired of the ever-present fear, for this was the constant druid message. The people were ready to abandon the old and leave behind all magic.

Other druids, it's true, heard and rejected the teachings of Christ. These returned to their *tuatha*, confused, badly chastened, and angry. Pátrick's God challenged the basis for their way of life, and they couldn't abandon all they'd known.

And after the clans returned home, many of the people lost respect for the sorcerers' teachings. It was the beginning of the end for the ways of old.

Each Sunday, Pátrick held a simple service under the lone oak. He had begun these even before the fair. Our numbers in the early days were less than sixty. But after the *óenach*, more came, until on some Sundays, upward of three hundred people sat on the dewy grass. We had many visitors from nearby *tuatha*, traveling the day before and staying the night for our Sunday meetings. If the king was not away leading an army to defend his clans from Connachta raiders, he also attended, and this brought respect and acceptance to these events.

Down in the valley a short distance from the lone oak, Forga began building a church for the savior of Emain Macha and the God of Everything. He'd heard Pátrick tell of the great basilica which Melchiade, the Bishop of Rome, had built over a century ago. So the king erected a building to rival his own palace. A log structure fifty feet wide by one hundred deep with a floor of paving stones. A peaked, thatched roof, log benches, and a fine altar in front, hewn from a great oak specifically for the Sacrament of the Eucharist.

Samain came and went, and for the first time in memory, no one celebrated that pagan holiday to lure the dark spirits of the Otherworld closer to this world.

The workers finished the church only a month later, in time to escape the cold rains and occasional snows of winter. At the front, Pátrick placed an iron cross he'd brought from Bryton, an expertly crafted piece of art with images of angels, cherubim, and other fantastic designs etched into the metal on each side. Its top and crossbars each ended in a triangular point.

In every service, Pátrick read from the ponderous Bible he carried, translating from Latin to Gaelic as he spoke, and if it was a Psalm, we repeated the verses to him. Many were greatly impressed at this feat of reading, for as I've said, before Pátrick brought them, books were unknown on Ériu. Then he or Servius, and later even Latharn or myself, would pray. We'd ask for recovery from the illnesses afflicting the members of our congregation. We'd pray that our friends and loved ones would hear the message of Jesu and believe. And we'd pray for the prosperity, health, and success of the clans of the Ulaid.

Often we sang hymns, and sometimes Coll invented a fiddle tune to go along, so the finest of music accompanied our singing. The services always left us looking to heaven, knowing God loved us, and expecting the day when we would leave the troubles of this earth behind. They also proclaimed how Christ wanted us to live on this earth.

And here I must relate, from Pátrick's time forward, the *tuath* of Emain Macha was blessed abundantly in children, crops, livestock, joy, and love.

Through all this, I devoted myself to study and to learning how to live as Jesu did. Pátrick began teaching the mysteries of Latin to me and Latharn—how to read and write the language of the Bible. Within a year, I was reading in the service from one of Pátrick's books.

In one message, no doubt suggested by some excesses observed at the *óenach*, Pátrick preached on the evils of mead and ale. Neither he nor Servius drank fermented drink, except the wine of the Eucharist. Unlike most of his messages, the group sitting under the oak tree did not receive this one well. Afterward, I heard a bit of grumbling.

But it did cause many to think upon the sin of drunkenness. I myself realized on too many occasions I had let others lead me to drink too much. My time with Kilgarren's band came first to mind. But the way of our people was ever to make merry, to celebrate with energy and abandon, and telling folks to give up their mead—or at least to drink less—was asking for a great change. Still, I learned after this to be moderate and avoid extremes. Later, I learned others had decided on the same course.

We spread the news of Jesu, made converts, and built our church. I became one of Pátrick's most trusted aides. And God filled me with the knowledge this was what He wanted me to do.

Yet throughout, my thoughts turned, again and again, to Laurna and my people. Someday, I would return. But not until Pátrick released me.

Winter melted into spring, then warmed into summer, and somehow a year passed.

Then one cloudy day, late the following summer, Pátrick and I were fishing for trout in a calm part of the stream, near where we held our baptisms. We stood in knee-deep water, holding long, narrow spears with barbed points made for spearing fish. The stream flowed cold around my bare shins.

"You've got four to my one, Taran." He smiled, his eyes alight with humor. "I don't know if I'll ever get the knack of stabbing fish."

"Remember, your water vision is bent," I responded. "You've got to aim lower."

"Aye, but even then, I don't believe I could hit a hole in a ladder."

I laughed then returned to my stance with spear ready, watching for movement in the shallows.

"You know, lad, that my bishop's authority confers on me the power to select and ordain priests?" But the words barely left his mouth when he suddenly released his spear. It stuck between the rocks before the current knocked it over. "Glory be! Another miss!" He retrieved his weapon and aimed again at the shadows in the rocks. "What I am saying, Taran, is that I'm greatly pleased by your ability to learn Latin and your strong and growing faith."

"Thank you. It seems I've searched for this truth all my life."

He nodded. "I wish you could but see the vision I've seen that drives me onward and fills me with such hope—men and women from the lowliest swineherd to the highest *flaith*, hearing the news of the Light, their eyes aflame with joy, eager and rushing forward to join God's holy family. Someday, Taran, there will be a church in every village, a bishop in every province, and the news of God's Son will spread like heather fire from one county to another. And all it needs is a few willing men to see it through.

"Aye, lad, I'm looking for a few men to become priests to spread the faith and found new churches. And Taran, I'd like to make you the first."

I do not think my immediate reaction was what he expected. I rested the point of my spear on the bottom and leaned against it. "I've often thought about the good I could do for God if someday I became a priest. But I don't know. I've no wish . . . to become like I was with the druids, sworn to celibacy . . . to face a life without hope of a mate, without sons or daughters."

As I'd often done lately, I ran my fingers over the leather armband I still wore, feeling its design. Laurna's fingers had carved those indentations. "I haven't said much, but my thoughts seem drawn lately to my island home, to Inis Creig, and Laurna. Someday—and I don't know if this is a foolish hope—but someday, I think of returning and making her my bride. For she holds a place in my heart I can never give up. Perhaps this is a great failing in my faith—that she and Christ are equal in my heart—but I can't help it. I still love her. Though I often despair of going back, someday, if God wills it, I think of returning. And when I do, if I do, I don't want to find myself bound to a pledge I couldn't keep. If I became celibate—well, I couldn't even think of returning. So I must decline. A priest I can never be."

Unsaid in all this were other fears. So much had occurred since I came to this land. I was changing in so many ways, growing in my faith, taking on new responsibilities. Had Laurna also changed? If we met again, would we still love each other? Had she waited, as she promised? What if she'd taken a mate? Life without a husband would be difficult. But if something I did now prevented me from ever again holding her in my arms or becoming her husband—this I could not accept.

The wind rippled the pool beyond the current, driving a dozen leaf rafts toward us. The reflection from the treetops wavered in the stream.

"You misunderstand the Apostle Paul's teachings on celibacy," said my mentor, friend, and teacher. "The believer's goal, surely, is to devote oneself wholly to Christ, to spiritual matters. Thus for a few, it's better to give up attachments to the world, especially sexual attachments. Paul himself wished celibacy for his followers. But he never required it. For most it's far better to marry, to join together as husband and wife, and thus remove sexual temptation. For the Evil One is always trying to lure men and women into illicit affairs, to make them think there's nothing wrong with wanton sexual liaisons, and stray from God's will for their lives. Paul plainly taught celibacy is not for everyone.

"Now the church's rulings are different. The Bishop of Rome teaches celibacy. But this is not the teaching of the Apostles. And in practice, this instruction is universally disregarded. Most priests of the church are indeed married. I wish it were otherwise.

"I myself have chosen the path of continence, but like the Apostle Paul, I realize it's not for everyone. Taran, you can still become a priest and someday marry your Laurna. For I see now your love for her is deep and lasting. It would not do to keep the two of you apart forever."

As he spoke my heart soared, lifted by hope. "Ah, 'tis a good answer, indeed. If I can be a priest and still keep alive the prospect of going home and marrying Laurna, I think that—aye, a priest I will become."

Pátrick beamed. "I'm pleased. More than pleased. You'll make a fine priest. And with your help we'll turn this land of Ériu from the darkness to the light."

"Thank you," I said, though I was unsure what it all meant.

Suddenly, he was all attention, focused on a large shadow under the water. I saw it even from my position a few yards away. He threw his spear. It struck, and the water boiled with the flopping of a fish tail. "It's a big one!" he exclaimed with the enthusiasm of a child, stepping forward, reaching down to raise the long shaft.

He lifted a trout the length of my forearm from the water, stuck through the side, flapping onto the grass.

"But there's another reason I must return to Inis Creig." My shadow fell over him as his long fingers pulled the spear point through the fish. He added the catch to our string. "If you remember my tale, the druids on Inis Creig have a power over my people even greater than Ohran had. Cormag, the chief druid, leads the Carraig Beag to worship the worst of the druid gods—Crom Cruach. Pure evil, he is. For his sake, we've abandoned everything good. This demon spirit leads us into the darkest parts of ourselves, filling us with wildness and hate. Every few years, we take a child, place it on the altar, and sacrifice his or her life for this god of darkness. The druids promise it will bring good crops, fishing, and hunting. But rather than blessings, Crom Cruach repays us evil for evil. Far more than any other, our land and people are cursed."

Silent, he rose and stared at me. A frown spread over his mouth as he shook his head. "This is terrible. We must prepare you to fight this. Someday, when you're ready, you must return to your homeland and lead your people from this idol. Aye, making you a priest is the perfect preparation. It will gird you for battle. And Taran, understand this is a spiritual battle—of light versus dark, good versus evil."

Pátrick's words elated me. Before that conversation, my return was something I'd only longed for but didn't know how it would happen. Now, with Pátrick's support, I had a plan. I would become a priest. I would return to Inis Creig and find a way to fight the druids. And maybe, when I arrived, Laurna would still be waiting for me. Suddenly, I had new hope and a new goal for my life.

We caught twelve trout that day, enough to feed twelve men. Though we spent much time preaching and teaching others, we occasionally also served the *tuath* of Emain Macha in more mundane duties. We were not all books and learning. We helped the clan by working in the fields, herding cows, and even hunting. Fishing was one of the more pleasant tasks.

After our conversation, Pátrick gave a number of messages on celibacy, to present the option for those who sought it, but also to encourage the rest to marry. This cleared up many misconceptions. Some who heard this teaching accepted wholeheartedly the idea of a great sacrifice by denying themselves the pleasures of sexual liaison. Indeed, it was in the nature of our people to be attracted to such grand, sacrificial gestures. A few women even saw it as a way to free themselves from the servitude in which many found themselves. Under the leadership of one called Una, independent-minded women banded together and moved to a new roundhouse on the edge of the hilltop.

A few weeks later on a rainy afternoon, Mùirne, who had attended every service Pátrick ever held, approached me in the shelter of the newly-built church. I was sitting on a log bench before a table, memorizing Latin verbs.

"Taran, thank you so much for what you've done for me, for saving me from a life of slavery." She stood beside the fire, smiling, hands together in front of her.

I waved a hand and she sat beside me on the bench, folding one leg under her.

"I could not stand to see you used in such a way. I had to do something."

"Still, you bought my freedom. You've the right to own me. You're my rightful master, yet you've never claimed me. Instead, you've said you donna own me."

"I don't own you. Please understand that. You're free to go and do what you will with your life."

She looked at me with wide, innocent eyes. "I think I understand. Pátrick's teaching has helped me in this. 'In Christ, there's na slave or free, Jew or Greek, male or female.'"

I smiled. "You've listened well. Words of Paul the Apostle."

"We have different stations in life, but we're all equal. 'Tis a hard idea to hold in my head, but perhaps I ken it now."

"And sure, 'tis truth well taken for all Christians."

The log fire crackled and spit sparks onto the flagstones. With the edge of my shoe, I kicked them back toward the coals.

"Long have I been thinking about this." She frowned as if the idea was difficult. "And I'd like to make a big change in my life. I'd like to join Una in the women's lodge." She caught my gaze as if searching for some sign of approval. I smiled and she went on. "They've pledged themselves to be women of Christ, to serve and worship God, and never again to lie in bed with a man. Some are virgins. I am na such. But even so, among them I can purify myself of my past sins. I can be a woman devoted to God. I want very much to join them. But before I do, I must receive your blessing. I know you say you donna own me. Still, I ask for your blessing. And your release."

This was unexpected. But it was perhaps the best thing ever to happen to her. Though I was pleased, I realized she still did not fully understand some things.

"I'm happy for you. I give you my blessing. And sure, as Christ is my witness, I release you. But you understand, do you not, you cannot 'purify' yourself of past sins, as you put it? Only Christ's death can do that, and He's already done it, through His death on the cross."

"I understand. But I want to forget I was ever Kilgarren's paid wench, and Donnach's—that I was anybody's cow. It was their right, of course, but I realize now it was a sinful thing to be a part of. I want to be pure and holy for Christ."

I smiled. "Mùirne, I give you my wholehearted blessing. Go and live with Una's women and be happy. I'm glad for you."

She beamed and threw her arms around my neck. Much to my surprise, she kissed me on the lips. As she left, I feared she would struggle with a life of chastity.

Not only did Mùirne take a vow of celibacy, so did Coll.

And here I must say a word about him. For Coll took Pátrick's teaching to heart. Shortly after the fair, when he first heard the message about Christ, we held another baptism for him and dozens of others. A few weeks later, Pátrick was also teaching him Latin. Coll was soon learning everything I was. Then a month after I'd told Pátrick I would be a priest, he determined to make Coll one also.

As for his promise to me, Coll was true to his word. Wherever I went, he went also. I did not view his presence as a burdensome thing but as the company of a true friend—the most loyal comrade and companion one could ever hope for.

With the second fall came another *Samain*, the pagan festival before winter. The year before we'd simply ignored it. But that year we turned the old pagan rituals on their heads and held a service in the new church Forga had built. Then came another winter, and I continued learning the ways of this faith that filled me with such hope, joy, and meaning.

Often, as I lay under my furs at night, I tried to recall the sound of Laurna's voice, the touch of her fingers on my face, and the look of her half-smile. There in Ulster, I was building a new life. And Pátrick relied on me more and more. But part of my heart was always with her.

The following spring, Pátrick made forays into the Ulster countryside to distant *tuatha*, where he preached the Word, made converts, and found new acolytes. Some of these men he brought back to Emain Macha to teach, with the goal of sending them out again as fully trained priests.

By that point, much of the populace of Emain Macha was Christian, and Pátrick spent even more weeks away from the village. Often Coll, Latharn, and I accompanied him. At times, we became semipermanent travelers, living on the road between Emain Macha and somewhere else.

By the end of the second year, I was proficient in Latin, and Pátrick was ready to ordain me. One Sunday, with everyone present at the regular service, he took me to the front of our new church. There he prayed for me. He laid his hands on me, asked me a few questions I answered in a clear voice, and then pronounced me a priest of Christ. A few months later, he repeated the ceremony for Coll. This allowed Pátrick to take the gospel to other parts of Ulster for months at a time, leaving Coll and me behind to lead services in the church.

Thus did five years pass, serving my Lord by helping Pátrick in Emain Macha. Many times, I made up my mind to confront him with my desire to return to Inis Creig. But during those years, he might have lived in the village but nine months, total. So I waited. He'd promised I'd go home when I was ready, and I couldn't leave without his blessing. But there was also this: I felt far, oh, so far, from being ready to confront Cormag and his druids.

Then one sunny morning in early spring, Pátrick returned from Ulster's northern coast, and we walked together through the orchard south of the village. The buds on the apple trees had partially opened. Newly awakened from their winter slumber, yellow-banded bees buzzed and landed on the white flowers. The previous night's rain made slick the grass and clover, and it wet the soft leather of my shoe all the way through. The scent of awakening life filled my nostrils. How much I'd come to enjoy living and working in Emain Macha with Pátrick, despite my longing to return home.

"My lad, 'tis time we leave here and take the gospel to a new country." He glanced at me, letting his words sink in.

My eyes widened as I tried to understand the changes this would bring.

"Aye, Taran, we've spread the Word far and wide through the Ulaid. Everywhere in the Kingdom of Ulster, we now find believers, priests, and churches. But to the south, in Leinster, they've never heard the Good News. So I'm pondering a mission to Tara, where Lóeghaire rules in Leinster's north. And I'd like you, Coll, and Latharn to join me. Servius has agreed to stay behind and continue our work here."

I did not expect such a move. But Pátrick's vision included the entirety of Ériu.

"I understand. But have you forgotten your promise to send me back to Inis Creig? Thoughts of Laurna and my people come to me almost nightly."

Pátrick smiled and laid a hand on my shoulder. "I've not forgotten, my friend." His voice was slow, gentle. "But this missions to Tara is . . . important. And I believe you are vital to its success. So I'm asking you to put aside your personal wishes for now. I know it's a lot to ask."

For some time, I stared into his eyes. He was asking a hard thing, indeed. If I agreed, would I have to give up all hope of ever seeing Laurna again? Would I be able to endure more long years away, not knowing what was happening to her or my clan?

He smiled. "Remember how Christ gave up his divine privileges and humbled himself to the point of death on the cross, all to obey his Father in heaven? For you today, I believe it's that kind of decision."

"But I'm torn, Pátrick."

"I understand."

I looked at the way ahead. I was faced now with perhaps the hardest decision of my life. I could reject his request, abandon my mentor, and return to Inis Creig tomorrow. He'd be disappointed, but I knew he'd support me. Or I could give his mission a few more years of my life. But that meant more years away from Laurna and my home.

I turned to face him. My jaw muscles tensed. Slowly, I nodded my head.

I thought I saw tears in his eyes then, so great was his appreciation for my sacrifice. He squeezed my shoulder, nodded his head, and looked away.

"How long will we be gone?" Before the words left my mouth, I knew the answer.

"Two or three years. Perhaps longer."

"When do we leave?"

"The day after tomorrow."

We prepared to depart for the palace of Tara in the south.

CHAPTER 25

Pátrick's Story

It was good to travel again, but we didn't know if the people we sought would welcome us with song and mead or meet us with drawn swords. I had grown used to the welcoming hearts and minds of the Ulaid.

Our party consisted of Pátrick, Coll, Latharn, me, and two men whom Forga would send that morning for our protection. At the moment of our departure, I was pleasantly surprised to find Sòlas was one of these. The other was called Finnean, and true to his name, not a hair on his head was other than white.

"Sure, and we're here for your protection," said Sòlas, as he rode up on a black stallion. "For the country 'tween Emain Macha and Tara is full of thieves, ne'er do wells, and bandits. They'd as soon strip you of all you have as throw you a glance. And did I mention the wolves?"

On our first night out, the clover became stiff with a rare frost and we feared for the apple blossoms back home. For some time the next morning, we broke through frozen puddles while the ice coating the tree limbs melted, dripping onto our traveling party from above.

As I've said, Latharn was a portly man, and he did not travel well. His saddle seemed always a bit wee for his frame, even though he rode the largest steed. He slowed the pace, but we were in no hurry and gave our red-haired companion as much time as he needed. Our days of riding began slowly.

We traveled south, climbing rocky hills, crossing a bog over a log road, fording rivers naked and shivering with our belongings tied to the pommels of our horses' saddles. We traversed a confusing country of drumlins, low hills and bogs, where no path ran true, and often feared to lose our way.

On the fifth night away, the air was crisp and quiet with frost. We huddled in the space between two fires, still savoring the rabbits we'd stuck with sapling spits and roasted. The logs on either side sparked and glowed. Blue flames sent wisps of smoke heavenward, curling first one way, then the other. On a chill night in spring after supper, it was always pleasant by the fire.

"Pátrick." Latharn shifted his large frame as though seeking a more comfortable position. "You've been gone so much you haven't fulfilled your promise to tell us about you coming to Ériu and your mission from God."

"Aye, and I must make amends. Tonight is as good as any for a tale.

"My family home was in Bryton near the town of Bannaventa Berniae. My father was Calpornius, a Roman patrician, and a deacon in the town church. He inherited the deaconship from his father, and it gave him respect and business contacts. I was baptized as an infant and learned the stories of the Bible, but I confess I did not know my Lord and Savior. As a member of the Roman elite, I was a privileged, spoiled child. Of course, I studied Virgil, Homer, Cicero, and Aristotle, but always I struggled with Latin and had barely begun my study of public speaking. I lacked for nothing, except knowledge of what was most important. To the gospel and its truth, I was indifferent. Inwardly, I rebelled against my parents' faith.

"Then the raiders came. In a single night, everything changed.

"They were slave traders from across the sea, from the land we called Hibernia. My parents and my sister had gone to visit relatives to the north, leaving me alone with the slaves and hired freedmen. The pirates appeared out of the night, in the middle of our farmstead. They captured the younger servants and slaves. Killed outright the older men and women, said they were too feeble for travel and wouldn't bring a good price on Hibernia, our name for Ériu."

"Despicable business, that," Sòlas interrupted. "The pirates of the coast have no honor. Slaves are to be won in battle, or made out of debtors, na taken from a man's house and home in the dead of night."

"Truly they are without honor, Sòlas. They stole me from my home in the dead of night. They chained us together—the younger, stronger ones—then took us to the beach. We sailed in their seventy-foot *curragh*, to the coast of Hibernia. Through a series of bargains, I ended up in Foclut, on the northwestern coast, with a farmer named Miliucc. His business was sheep and his farmstead was miles from his *tuath*. His farmstead was inside a small, stone ring fort that some ancient peoples had built and abandoned. But from clan and kin, he was isolated. On his farm, I became the lowest *bothach*. A sheepherder, sent into the high, rainy fields to watch over his flocks, far from the warm cottages where the others slept."

"Pardon, sirs," Sòlas interrupted again. "But did you hear that?"

We listened, but I heard nothing. While we waited, Sòlas stood from his seat by the fire, walked to the camp's edge, peered into darkness, checked our horses, and then returned.

"Sorry, lads." He jerked his head, throwing thick locks from his forehead. "Thought I heard something. The horses are a bit unsettled, thinks I. Go on, Pátrick. Pay me no mind."

Pátrick continued. "So there I was, a lad of only fifteen, roughly torn from home and family, a lad who'd barely learned his Latin. For days on end, I was alone in the hills with the sheep, seeing nobody, talking to no one, half-naked as my clothing wore to tatters, and usually with little to eat. Sometimes at night, wolves came and stalked the sheep. I fended them off with my staff. Always it seemed I was hungry. Whenever Miliucc called me back to the farm, I stole scraps of bread and cheese and hid them under my tunic to augment my meager rations at the pasture. Miliucc did not believe in 'spoiling' a *bothach* with too much in the way of food.

"Bit by bit, I learned Gaelic and the ways of the Ériu, for I had sparse companionship. But Gaelic is similar to the Brytish tongue many spoke back home. I learned it well.

"Thus did I live for six years. Outcast, isolated, torn from all I'd known, living a cold, lonely, hungry existence. My companions? Only the sheep. The rain. The wolves. And the howling of the wind.

"Early on, I remembered the Bible stories and the priest's teachings in my church. Then I prayed. I drew comfort from my prayers, from talking to God. And it became God who sustained me through those long years of trial. I prayed out loud, and even when, on occasion, Miliucc called me back to the farmstead, I prayed. Even there I rose before sunrise and prayed long. And every night before sleep, I prayed again. They called me 'holy boy' and made fun of my piety. Still, I prayed.

"My prayers brought me closer to the God I had earlier rejected and abandoned. I began to obey my master as if his will were from God Himself. I didn't know why God put me in the predicament I was in, but I made the best of it. I embraced my hunger and fasting. Then one night, six years after my capture, God spoke.

"In a dream, I heard a voice saying, 'I've seen your fasting and heard your prayers, Patricius, and soon you'll be going home.' I awoke, startled, realizing—without question—it had been the voice of God, but wondering even still, how I could ever leave this island. It was a vast place, I knew it not, and the only ships leaving for Bryton or Gaul sailed from the eastern or southern coast. Far, oh so far, from Foclut.

"The next night, I dreamed and heard the voice again. It said, 'Behold, your ship is ready.' And the voice told me where to find a ship on the southeastern coast. I knew it as a command, as my mission, and I dared not disobey. I must escape my prison farmstead and flee to this ship God Himself prepared for me. But how?

"Two days later, under cover of darkness, I left my flock and started south. I had only a vague idea of where I was going, trusting God to guide me. I traveled by night to avoid detection, traversing the boggy lands, making only five or ten miles a day across log roads and fields of heather until I came to a great river. Unable to ford, I followed its banks for many nights. Finally, I came to a shallow place and waded across with my clothing tied in a bundle and the current up to my chest.

"I scrounged what little I could from the fields on the edge of farmsteads, killing a few rabbits or hens with a homemade spear, but eating them raw, for fear of making a fire. Over a period of a month, I traveled nearly two hundred miles until I reached the port I had seen in my dream.

"Up until then, I was fairly safe from detection. But as I sat hidden in an abandoned hut, looking down at the harbor and the ship my dream had revealed, I knew I would have to go out into the open. But I was an escaped slave, an *élúdach*, a fugitive who would bring a good price for anyone turning me in to a local Rí Tuath. In the morning, as the ship made ready to depart, I knew I had to move. I screwed up my courage, left my hiding place, and headed straight down the village path to the wharf. I crossed the dock, walked up the gangplank, and stepped onto the deck.

"The captain was giving last-minute orders for departure. They were loading Irish hounds the Romans prized for hunting. I must have looked a sight with my torn clothes and my face smudged with dirt from bog and forest. I was also lean from near starvation, yet strong and sturdy after years of herding. The sailors were Irish and spoke Gaelic, but the captain spoke Latin to a man I assumed was first mate. I approached the captain and said in Latin, 'I would like to join your crew.'

"He stopped what he was doing and squinted at me. Right then, I believe he knew me for an *elúdach*. He might even have calculated the profit from turning me in. But he was leaving straightaway and too busy for anything but departure. He said, 'Forget about it, lad. As sure as the day is long, you canna come with us.' Then he turned back to his cargo and crew.

"With my head bowed, I walked down the plank to the dock. I had put all my hopes on this one moment. God Himself had directed me to this harbor, this ship, and now I seemed confounded in my mission. Indeed, I was in a worse position than before. Surely, someone in this small port village would see me for who I was and turn me in for a reward.

"But as I reached wharf's end, someone touched my shoulder and I whirled. One of the sailors said, 'Come quickly, lad. Come back and talk with us a bit.' My hopes rose as I returned up the gangplank.

"'You may join the crew,' said the captain, 'as I've decided to take you on trust. We're departing at once.'

"Eagerly, I agreed, and no sooner had I spoken, than the ship cast off and was away! For six days, we sailed under heavy weather until we reached a foreign shore. In vain did we search for a port until finally the captain disembarked on a deserted beach. Looking back on this, I don't think the captain knew where to land. We were to have met a certain purchaser for our cargo of hounds, but it appeared the captain simply couldn't locate the town where they waited. In any event, we unloaded the hounds and made our way on foot to the interior of a barren land. It was winter. I believe we landed in Germania, not Gaul.

"As we walked, we found the country deserted, without a living soul, with farms abandoned and fields stripped. What villages we passed through were ransacked, with signs soldiers had marched before us. Nowhere did we find food.

Snow and ice encased the ground. We trudged over a white, snowy desert, stripped of inhabitants and sustenance. For twenty-eight days, we wandered thus, until we and our hounds were starving.

"Then the captain came to me and said, 'Well, Christian, what will you do? You tell us your God is great and powerful, so why don't you pray for us? Unless we find food soon, we will die of starvation—all of us. In this barren land, I fear we'll never see another living soul again.'

"I looked at him and the others. And I tell you this: I was filled with a conviction that the God of Hosts would surely provide. I said, 'I will pray for us, but first everyone must turn to the Lord God with all your hearts. Nothing is impossible for God. Yet He wants our hearts and our souls. If we turn to Him and ask in that way, I know He will send us food for our journey. We will eat until we are full.'

"The sailors heard me and were moved. They were starving and weak, yet my little speech must have touched them. As I prayed for our deliverance, they too bowed their heads.

"I had barely finished when we heard a noise like many hooves clattering over icy ground. As we looked up, what do you think we saw? A herd of pigs was racing toward us! We caught most of them, butchered and roasted several, then ate our fill. I told the sailors God would provide, and that day He surely did."

Sòlas stood. "Pardon, sirs. 'Tis quite a tale, and surely your God listens and answers you as if He was walking next to you all the time. I ken 'tis more than I've heard from any of the druids' fearsome spirits. But 'tis an unsettled night, thinks I, with some kind of mischief afoot. Animal or human, I knows not."

He went again to check on the horses' shuffling and neighing beyond the circle of firelight. He walked into the darkness, his footsteps rustling leaves, breaking branches. He returned to sit between the fires, shaking his head.

"Pardon again, sirs. Seems tonight old Sòlas is hearing ghosts." Then he withdrew his sword from his sheath, laid it on his lap, and was quiet.

We exchanged worried glances as Pátrick went on.

"I must tell you of one other incident with the men. One day, they found some wild honey and offered me a share. As I was about to eat of it, one of them said they had dedicated it as a sacrifice to the gods. When I heard this, I refused to have anything to do with the honey.

"Later that very night, I came under attack by Satan himself. As I lay sleeping, something dark and heavy, like an invisible rock, fell on me so quick and hard, I couldn't move my arms or legs. For hours I lay like that—in pain, paralyzed, and afraid—until just before sunrise. From somewhere, a voice told me to call upon the prophet Elijah. But I was so frightened, I may have misunderstood. Then I shouted with all my strength, 'Elijah! Elijah!' And when the rays of morning sun touched my body, the heavy weight lifted in an instant. The Evil One had fled. I now believe it was Christ himself who called me.

"Eventually, the captain found the town and we delivered our hounds. I left my shipmates and wandered from port to port, trying to find a willing captain to take me to Bryton. For months on end, I interrupted my search to work for food and lodging. Nearly two more years passed before I returned to my home in Bryton.

"How can I relate the joys I experienced when I walked again through the door of my parents' villa? They'd given me up as lost forever, or dead. There I was, a young man of twenty-one, standing alive and well beside the fountain bubbling in my parents' atrium. We hugged and we cried.

"The next day, my father threw a feast for everyone in town who could come, for those who knew me before, and for all the slaves and freedmen who worked at Bannaventa Berniae. But these new slaves were strangers to me. On the night of my capture, the raiders had killed or taken away everyone I'd loved, all who'd ever held me and fed me as a child. Week after week, my father called more feasts as relatives from distant farmsteads and towns journeyed to welcome me home. Everyone wanted to hear my story—how I was captured, lived as a slave, and then escaped.

"My parents begged me never again to leave. My father scheduled make-up lessons and tutors, so I could continue the education I'd missed. He made plans for me: I would take over the farm's business, managing the harvest, storing the crops, repairing the villa, and supervising the slaves.

"But there in my home, I felt like a foreigner. I was unsettled, out-of-place. Calpornius was ever concerned about the Roman troops that Stilicho, the general then in charge of Bryton, had stripped from the land and sent to defend the continent. The legions were gone or departing. 'How,' my father asked, 'can we defend ourselves?' He wanted me to join in the debates concerning this issue with the Decurions, but I declined.

"I'd become different from them. Focused on God. The Decurions' discussions didn't interest me. That well-ordered villa and way of life became as foreign to me as the woods of Foclut once were.

"Then one night as I lay sleeping, I dreamt a man came to me from Ériu. In his hands, he carried a stack of letters. His name was Victoricus, and I'd known him in Foclut as a fellow slave. He too had been stolen from his home in Bryton, and when I came in from the rainy hills, we sometimes talked about life back home. But now he was grown, standing at the foot of my bed. He dumped his load of letters on the covers. From the pile, he chose a single parchment and broke the wax seal. He unrolled the scroll and handed it to me. The heading on the letter said, 'The Voice of the Ériu.' Then a great chorus of voices broke out in song, but the sound appeared to come as if from inside the scroll itself.

"They sang, 'Holy boy! Holy boy! Come here and walk among us!'

"I awoke, sitting straight up in bed, feeling as if my heart had been stabbed with a dagger of sorrow for the people of Ériu. They did not know the Savior. They had no one to tell them the good news of Christ's coming. An entire country, the whole of Ériu, was living in spiritual darkness. If nothing changed, they would go to their eternal doom. And the letter and the voices were asking me—this young man called Patricius—to be the one to go back and bring them the gospel.

"For months, I walked around with that vision preying on my mind, undecided, unsettled, trying to formulate some plan, any plan. I had just escaped from that savage place and a life of slavery. How could I go back?

"Then I had another vision. I heard a voice, beautiful and heavenly beyond description, reciting the words of a prayer. But I didn't understand anything the voice said. I listened intently, transfixed by the celestial words, yet it made no sense. Later, when I awoke, I tried to determine if the words came from within me or from somewhere beyond me. For weeks, I agonized over the question. What was this message telling me? Where did it come from? Was it a plea from the Ériu? From God? Something my sleeping mind created? It mattered greatly where this message came from. But I knew not from where.

"Then God sent me a final dream. In this vision, a man's voice spoke to me in a strange tongue, pronouncing divine words, profound words, words beyond all human understanding. I knew his message was important but could understand none of it. Then the last thing he said became clear: 'He who gave His life for you, who gave you your Spirit—it is He who speaks within you.' I awoke, filled with joy. For now I knew the voice came from the Spirit of Christ within me. And I knew my mission. All indecision vanished. My course of action was clear. I must return to Ériu.

"My parents, of course, were not happy with this. They begged me to reconsider, but I could not, would not. My goal was to become first a priest, then a bishop. For only as a bishop could I ordain priests and plant new churches. That was the only way to change Ériu into a Christian nation—through the spread of churches with priests to run them. Dismayed, but giving in to my resolve, my father started the long process, arranging for me to start as a deacon in the church of Bannaventa Berniae.

"For the next few years, I assisted our local priest by overseeing charity to widows and orphans, burying the dead, balancing the church books, and playing messenger to parishioners. With his glowing recommendation and my father's connections, I petitioned to become a priest. But I needed to train with a bishop, someone who himself could eventually ordain me to the bishopric. For this, I traveled to an island in the Tyrrhenian Sea, off the southern coast of Gaul, to the great monastery of Lérins. There, the sun drenched the rocks, the breezes blew warm, and gulls called to each other from sunrise to sunset. I studied and learned what I could. Finally, at thirty years of age, I was ordained a priest. I preached, taught, baptized, and administered the sacraments. I fulfilled all the requirements they laid in front of me.

"More long years passed, and still the Ériu called to me. Ever was my heart filled with sadness for their plight. I begged my bishop for a commission to go back. For that to happen, I would have to be called bishop, and for that, *my* bishop said I was too young. For everyone on the continent, Ériu was a country of barbarians and wild men, a place that stole Roman children from their beds in the dead of night. It was a land where naked warriors painted themselves with blue and red paint, dyed their hair with lye, and ran screaming in a mad frenzy, swords in hand, at our legions. But I persisted, annoying my bishop with constant requests and petitions.

"Then one day, I learned a man named Palladius had instead been chosen Bishop of Hibernia, that he'd already left on a journey to convert the pagans. The news crushed me. This was a failing of mine, I admit, this deep jealousy that came over me after learning another had received the task meant for me. But within a year, we heard reports of his dismal failure and of a quick withdrawal from Hibernia. My sin of jealousy departed.

"So at last, with Palladius's failure, my bishop relented. Within the month, finding no one else willing or qualified, he ordained me with the charge of converting the land of Ériu and saving its people from spiritual death. There's little more to tell. I returned to Bryton, where Servius and Aurelius joined me. As you know, Aurelius we left in Sabhall. I said good-bye to my parents and, laden with gifts from the church and my parents, we set sail for Ériu. You know the rest."

We all sat in silence, digesting his story, listening to the crackling of the fires.

"You are indeed a holy man." Latharn shifted again, searching for a more comfortable seat on the hard ground. "Who among us will ever become so holy and pious?"

Pátrick shook his head. "You must not compare yourselves to me. For each is given his own gifts and mission in life. My early lot was a hard one, and I would wish it on no other."

"Thank you, Pátrick," I said, "for giving us the whole story of your life. Now I better understand your mission and your passion for the plight of the Ériu."

"It was born of hardship and a deep sadness for the spiritual fate of others. I know—"

A twig snapped. Loud, unmistakable, and followed by a rustling of leaves as if from hidden watchers. The horses reared against their ropes. Sòlas and Finnean were on their feet, swords in hand, racing toward the noise. The rest of us stood, fearing an attack.

As the two soldiers left the fire circle, the shadows of two figures stepped from the darkness.

"What have we here?" Sòlas demanded.

The two intruders walked cautiously into the circle of firelight. Two women—*flaith* by the look of their dress—stopped before us, meek and dirty. Both looked like they'd been wandering in the bogs for weeks.

"Have mercy, lords," cried one of the women, her hair as red as flame. "We seek only shelter and food by your fire."

Before the first had finished, the other woman, her face beautiful beyond words, said, "Have mercy, lords, we are lost and without guardians."

Pátrick looked at the two, thought a moment, and smiled. "Then mercy it is. Come and warm yourselves by our fire."

CHAPTER 26

Tara

Unimpressed by the women's pleas for mercy, Sòlas stood his ground. "What mischief, lassies, brings you sneaking round the edge of our camp in the dead of night?"

Both the women were the same height, slightly shorter than me. Their tunics, once bright with color and covered with designs and brass rings, now were torn and smudged. They looked like sisters.

"No mischief, sir, only great need," said the first lass, fiery red hair falling in curls to her shoulders, spoiled only by bits of leaf sticking out. A streak of dirt also graced her forehead. She briefly touched the back of her head and gave us a weak smile that crinkled the freckles on both cheeks.

The one I believed to be her sister echoed, "Need and great hunger. For we haven't eaten decent food in a week." This one had high, regal cheekbones, smooth skin, beautiful, blue eyes, and long, blonde hair, now disheveled and dirty. As she spoke, a smile also turned up the corners of a small, sensitive mouth.

"So if you've anything at all to eat, kind sirs, we would surely—" began the redhead.

The other cut her off, "We'd surely be grateful."

Sòlas narrowed his eyes and rubbed his chin. "And how is it you come to be wandering in the woods and bogs with no protection? Is anyone else out there sneaking around? Thieves or bandits, perhaps?"

The red-haired one put her hands on her hips, frowned. "And sure, fine sir, do we look like the kind of women to consort with bandits, thieves, and ruffians? We are the daughters of—"

"Fedelm!" interrupted the fair-faced lass. She bent her lips to her sister's ear to whisper something.

The red-haired lass identified as Fedelm turned back to Sòlas with a smile. She went on, in a slower, calmer tone. "Please, sirs, my sister Eithne is concerned you don't know we are *flaith*. But I ken you already know this, and I'm unafraid to tell you so to your faces. Sure, and we are daughters of true noble blood. We'd be pleased to tell you how we came to this depraved and unworthy condition."

"We started out with an escort of four men, including a servant," continued the fair one, called Eithne. "They were armed for our protection, but one night bandits attacked our camp. While we ran into the woods and escaped across a stream, our warriors fought them off."

"We ran and ran," said Fedelm, "across the stream, into the forest, and up a hill until we came to a cave."

"And we climbed down into the clammy dark," said Eithne.

"And hid there until dawn. When we came out, we tried to find our men and horses—"

"But they were gone. We saw blood on the leaves. Then we found our servant, killed by the sword. We buried him. 'Twas a ghastly thing."

"We scraped a grave with sticks and buried him. Ghastly, it surely was. But the others had gone. We waited a day and a night, but no one came back."

"We surmise they were captured and taken away," said Eithne. "So we tried to find the route back home, but true and sure, I fear that on foot and without guide or horses, we're lost."

"We're lost, true and certain," finished her sister.

Pátrick stepped forward. "Sòlas, these women are no threat and deserve our help. Latharn, we still have two rabbits, do we not? Cook them now and give them a meal, for it's hospitality and mercy they need, not fierce questions."

"Thank you, kind sir." Eithne smiled, bending a knee and giving a slight bow.

Latharn gave them bread and cheese while they waited for rabbits to be roasted. They ravaged the food.

After they'd eaten their fill, Fedelm faced Pátrick, for she obviously understood who was in charge. "If I may presume to ask, fine sir, what is your destination?"

"We journey to Tara of Leinster."

Eithne shot a quick glance at Fedelm. "That, sir, is where we live. Our father is a . . . a nobleman . . . of Tara, and we long to return there."

"Pardon my boldness in asking," said Sòlas. "What business have two frail lassies, mere babes in the woods so to speak, to be wandering 'round the lands 'tween kingdoms? Even with such a grand escort as you once had?"

"A good question, fine sir," said Eithne. "I will let my sister answer."

Fedelm shook her red hair and a bit of leaf fell out. She took up the challenge. "We have just returned from a visit to our cousin in Cruachain, a hard journey of ten days' ride. She married high and we hadn't seen her for many years."

"So you was coming back from this journey when you was attacked? That's your tale?"

"That is so, fine sir. We were returning to Tara."

Pátrick spoke again. "How fortunate for you we go the same way. You may travel with us tomorrow under our protection."

"We give you our profound gratitude, holy man." Fedelm smiled.

Eithne gave another delicate bow of her head. "We thank you and accept your offer."

Sòlas scrunched his face as if thinking hard. "This is all fine and dandy, but still I wonder if you're having us on, me lassies. Tell me this: How long was you standing out there in the dark? How do you ken our Pátrick, here, is a holy man? What was you up to, sneaking 'round like that?"

Fedelm notched her chin a little higher. "We were afraid of who you might be. I wanted to approach, but Eithne thought we should wait and listen until we knew if *you* were bandits, thieves, or ruffians."

"But when we heard his story," Eithne looked at Pátrick, "I kenned he was a holy man, true and certain."

"He seemed the same to me," added Fedelm. "For I ken he is not like the druids of our country. I knew from his tale he was a good and kindhearted man, and that's why I stepped out of my hiding place into—"

"It was I who stepped out, sister. My feet advanced first."

"Nay, Eithne. 'Twas I. I knew the man's story was true and he was holy, so I led us out of the dark."

"'Tis not so. I stepped out."

"Nay, not true! You're always claiming the better spirit, the higher motives, the first impulse, always over me."

"I dare say, no, Eithne. 'Tis *you* who's being described."

"Lassies!" Pátrick interrupted, smiling. "Perhaps we should grant both of you came to your conclusions at the same time, and both of you, perhaps, stepped from your hiding places at the same instant?"

Eithne looked at Fedelm, then back at Pátrick.

"You're right, holy man." Fedelm touched the back of her red head. "We often think alike, I fear—my sister and I. And this leads to arguments over who was first, and who said what, and when, and, of course, why. I ken we are too much alike."

"My sister is right. Please forgive us."

Pátrick chuckled. "You are forgiven."

"But I—we?" Fedelm shot a questioning look at her sister. "We would like to know more about this God of yours who talks to you in dreams and visions, who has given you such a great mission to Ériu, you've spent your life pursuing it."

"I, as well," said Eithne. "I too want to know more of your God."

Pátrick smiled, and then we all settled around the fire as he told them the story of the carpenter from Nazareth, the Son whom God sent to save every people on earth from eternal death.

When he finished, Fedelm said to Eithne, "I believe I like this Jesu and His ways. True and certain, I believe we should accept this story that He is the Son of a single God who rules over everything. It makes more sense than the druids' teachings."

"I ken you are right, sister. He is the Son of a single God, true and sure. It takes a bit to wrap my head around it, but I ken it makes a great deal of sense. His tale fills my heart with joy. I would follow Him, that I would."

"I as well. But what would Father say?"

"It matters not. We are right."

"Right you are, Eithne. For we can think for ourselves, can we not?"

"That we can. But I fear sleep is upon me."

"I as well. Thank you, everyone, for taking us in tonight. The rabbit and cheese and bread were delicious. Perhaps Father will reward you when we arrive in Tara. Perhaps, he will hear about this God of yours as well?"

"Not likely, sister." Eithne yawned. "He's a bull in these matters. He'll probably never be turned." But her eyes were half-closed, as were Fedelm's.

Sòlas threw a few more logs on both fires. We laid our heads on our saddles then pulled the blankets over our heads to spend another night in the open.

The next morning, we took turns giving up our mounts for the two women. When it was my turn and Sòlas's, we walked beside each other. "Don't it seem to you as if they're keeping something from us, Taran, me lad?"

"It's possible, but whatever it is, I think they mean us no harm."

Sòlas looked at me with a questioning frown.

Since Fedelm and Eithne had accepted the message of Christ with such ready enthusiasm, when we arrived that afternoon at a swiftly flowing stream with a deep pool, Pátrick suggested we baptize both of them. They agreed, and we gathered in solemn ceremony at water's edge while they undressed and waded into the cold stream. Pátrick dunked them under as pagans who worshiped forest spirits, but brought them up as children of the God Most High. When they had dried and dressed, both women beamed and clapped, their joy at joining the family of Christ plain to all of us. The rest of the day, I treasured their delight, forgetting Sòlas's concerns.

That night was the last we spent on the road. On the day after, we entered familiar trails where the sisters directed our journey. When we passed a few outlying farmsteads, men and women ran out to meet us. They called greetings to "Eithne, the Fair" and "Fedelm, the Red" in such a manner I wondered, indeed, what kind of *flaith* they really were.

We entered a deep wood, and then our trail turned and broke into the open. There before us, as Eithne explained, was the hill of *Rath na Ríogh*. The Fort of the Kings of Tara, enclosing the village above. A long ramp of dirt crowded the hill's edge and was topped by thick logs, sharpened and sunk into the earth. We climbed the hill, crossed a drawbridge on top, and then walked a path between roundhouses and small stone huts. We passed a small mound tomb.

Then Eithne stopped and pointed at a tall, round obelisk sticking out of the earth, surrounded by a circle of flat stones radiating outward. "This is the *Lia Fáil*, the Stone of Destiny. 'Tis said it came from the Otherworld in ancient times. It gives power to . . . to the kings of Tara."

Pátrick stared at it and frowned.

"Since time began," Fedelm continued where her sister left off, "when the true king of Tara strikes it, the stone rings like a bell. For those not so chosen, it remains silent."

Sòlas looked at us, then strode up to the stone and kicked it. Nothing happened.

"Best leave it alone, Sòlas." Pátrick shook his head. "For surely 'tis a thing of evil, gaining its power from demons."

"How can that be, my lord?" Fedelm's forehead creased in a puzzled look.

"We will speak of these things later when your lessons begin."

Fedelm looked to Eithne, who nodded. Then the sisters led us to a wide yard before which stood the *Forradh*, the palace of the Rí Cóicid. It was circular, at least a hundred fifty feet in diameter, and great columns of oak ringed its base and supported a sloping, thatched roof. Beside it stood another building, an enormous conical structure that appeared to be a replica of the druid temple at Emain Macha before it burned to the ground. I shuddered at the sight.

Fedelm advised us to go first to pay respects to the king. As this was the object of our mission, we approached the *Forradh*. The palace door yawned open, its heavy oak studded with iron buttons and hung on wide iron hinges. In the opening, a man stood guard. He saw us, disappeared inside, and moments later, returned with an assembly of high *flaith*.

At once, I recognized the man who must be Lóeghaire, the Rí Cóicid of northern Leinster. He was of medium build, with strong, muscled arms, a chiseled jaw, black eyes that brooked no dispute, and blond, wiry hair flowing down to his ears. His tunic was brightly painted. Around his neck hung a heavy gold torc. A sword swung from his leather belt. He called out, "Daughters! You have returned to me. When Artagan came back sore wounded, bringing a tale of attack and defeat, I despaired of ever seeing you again."

Sòlas, standing beside me, elbowed my ribs.

"Father." Eithne bowed, smiling broadly. "We too despaired, for we've been wandering in the forests and bogs for nigh over a week—"

"Through the clabber, mud, and bogs. Hungry and tired—"

"And if it were not for these men, we would still be—"

"Wandering," Fedelm concluded. "Sure, and they took us in and fed us and brought us home safely."

"And they deserve our respect, honor, and gratitude," said Eithne.

"They deserve the respect of no one!" cried a new voice, a familiar voice, one I hadn't heard in many years, and one I'd hoped never to hear again. Before we could react, Ohran stepped from behind the king's entourage. "They deserve only death. All of them!"

Lóeghaire faced him, dark brown eyebrows arched in a question. Ohran wore the druid's white robe and moved to the king's right side, the place of honor. Once again, he was the chief druid of a kingdom. Behind him in the royal crowd stood Boodan, with his mane of stiff, tan hair. "Explain yourself, druid," said the king. "My daughters say these men rescued them."

"These are the very ones from Emain Macha who turned Forga mac Dallán from good tradition and made him burn the druids' grand temple to the ground. With their talk of a single God, they desire only to destroy your kingdom. Their teachings will strip your rule of its authority and turn your power over to myth and fable. This one here," he stabbed a shaking, three-fingered hand at Pátrick, "is the one about whom I wrote the verse of warning:

"From across the sea will come Adze-head,
crazed in the head,
his cloak with hole for the head,
his stick bent in the head.
He will chant impieties from a table in the front of his house;
and all his people will answer, 'So be it, so be it.'"

"This is the one?" exclaimed Lóeghaire, looking at Pátrick in a different manner now. "This is the interloper predicted to destroy us?"

"The very one. And I warn you: Put them to death now before it's too late. Or your kingdom will fall." He jerked his head, throwing thin brown locks away from his eyes.

"Father," said Fedelm. "True and certain, this is no way to repay generosity—"

"And kindness," added Eithne. "They saved us from starving—"

"And from wandering in the forest—"

"They brought us home, true and sure."

"My daughters are right, Ohran. Whatever ill tidings they bring, for now I must give these men my protection and gratitude, or sully my reputation of generosity in all the kingdom."

"We bear no ill tidings, my lord." Pátrick bowed low. "Only the news of the one true God who rules over all, who Himself created the forests, seas, rivers, and mountains. He is above the spirits of all those places. He is not capricious, or hateful, or mischievous like so many of the gods of this land, who are evil and selfish. Instead, He comes to us in love. Indeed, He has sent us His Son to save us from ourselves."

"Stop!" said Ohran, his small, dark eyes contracting. "You will speak no evil against the spirits of forest, river, and bog. We druids will na stand by while you again poison a king with falsehoods, delusions, and witchery."

"Ohran, it is you who practice witchcraft." As Pátrick spoke, I beheld a strong impression of Roman *flaith*, with his high royal cheekbones, long Roman nose, and piercing dark eyes. "It is you who cavort with spirits of evil, calling upon demons to harm others with your curses. You bring your followers into a ring of darkness that blinds their minds to the truth. I bring instead the light of Christ, the lamp of eternal life. You bring darkness, death, and the Evil One."

"Enough!" said Lóeghaire, who listened to Pátrick's speech with arms crossed and a rumpled brow. "You will na speak against my druids or their ways. Years ago, your coming was foretold. I was warned of your mission, and now I hear it for myself from your own mouth. You have my gratitude for rescuing my daughters—certainly—and for that I grant you lodging, food, and free passage in Tara. For how long, I donna ken. But within the boundaries of Tara, you will na speak against the traditions of our fathers or the ways of the spirits. They are our ways and we will na give them up. I will never convert to your religion. I, the son of Niall, am to be buried in the earthworks of Tara, face to face with the son of Dúnlaing in Mullaghmast. That is my decision, for that is my destiny, decreed from long ago, and I will hear no words against it. I have spoken."

"But Father," said Fedelm, frowning, "Eithne and I have heard the story of this Pátrick's God, and both of us are convinced of its truth. We have become followers of this Christ. Both of us. Eithne and I are now Christians. We were even baptized in a stream."

Lóeghaire turned his head of wiry, blond hair and stared at Fedelm, then at Eithne, then Pátrick. His eyes narrowed and his brow crinkled. "What else should I expect from two such willful creatures as these daughters of mine? You traipse to Cruachain on a visit without my permission, are almost killed by bandits, then meet a strange holy man—warped in the head as Ohran says. And you take on his strange ideas without a moment's thought. You abandon the ways of the Laigin, our ways since time began. If you were na of my own blood, this very day I would have you beaten and chained to stones in the square." He turned his back and stalked into the palace.

Ohran stared at us, his lips taut and tiny eyes narrowing. "You have been given the run of Tara. For now. But do na think it will prevent you from disaster, here where my druids rule. By his generosity, the Rí Cóicid shows weakness, but this druid will not. I will bring a curse against all of you. You would be wise to leave Tara right now before nightfall. Now away, and chase yourselves off!"

Ohran snapped a three-fingered left hand across his eyes to free them from their enemy—the errant strands of wispy brown hair. Then he whirled and went inside, leaving us to ponder our welcome in this land.

"I'm sorry." Eithne faced us. "I apologize for Ohran's rage and father's stubbornness. I don't understand it." She gave a beautiful smile, looking at us with such deep blue eyes, I could nearly forgive them.

"But you do." Fedelm shook her head. "For even you said earlier, Father was a bull in these matters. And when the druid Ohran speaks, the king seems to have ears for no other."

"I said as much, did I not?" said Eithne. "Now the druid's voice has grown so strong, it is he who seems to rule Tara. And Father cannot even see it."

"You must beware," said Fedelm. "Ohran's threats are real. He will put curses on you. With my own eyes, I've seen men die by them."

"We are unafraid of Ohran's magic." Pátrick frowned. "His power comes from the Evil One, and no mere spirit of darkness can prevail over Christ, and those who abide in him."

"Still, my lord." Sòlas shifted uneasily between both feet. "I've a fair experience with Ohran's wiles, and we're in sore danger, thinks I. If na from his spells, then from an outright attack by his druids."

"I understand, and your concern is noted. But we're not leaving. For our mission is to bring the gospel to Tara and the Laigin and to all the clans of the Kingdom of Leinster. Tonight we will pray. God will protect us."

"Come." Fedelm pointed to a small building across the field. "We'll put you up in the hut reserved for visiting Romans during the *óenach*. It is one of two for guests, with new straw on the floor. I will bring you food, drink, and comfortable furs."

Eithne nodded. "You can decide what to do in the morning."

We thanked them, followed Fedelm to the house, then settled down for the night. But Ohran's threats gathered in my mind like storm clouds darkening a wind-whipped sea.

CHAPTER 27

A Bold Plan

Despite our fears, the night passed without incident. We woke the next morning, our first in Tara, as Eithne and Fedelm brought us a breakfast of oat porridge and goats' milk with honey. Afterward, Pátrick gathered us together and read from one of the great books he had brought:

Psalm 3

O Lord, I cannot number my foes. They gather their spears against me.

Among themselves they say, "God will not deliver him."

But you, O Lord, are a great shield that surrounds me.

You, who lift me and sustain me, your glory fills me.

When I cried out to God, he answered me from his holy mountain.

Though I lay down to sleep in the shadow of the wicked, I wake in safety,

For the Lord, my God, watches over me.

Though the blades of ten thousand enemies surround me, I will not fear.

Arise, O Lord! Deliver me, my God!

Humble my enemies and bring them to their knees.

Attack the wicked and shatter their teeth!

Only you, my Lord, can bring victory.

May you bless the ones you call your own.

"By this prayer from the Psalms," said Pátrick, "we ask for the Lord's protection in this land that opposes us. In Jesu's name, Amen."

Then he proposed we preach the message outside the boundaries of Tara to those of the Laigin who wished to hear. This would honor Lóeghaire's restriction. Eithne and Fedelm eagerly agreed. To find an audience, I accompanied Eithne as Coll went with Fedelm. All morning, we walked the paths between roundhouses, through fields just outside the fortress, down the village byways, approaching all we could find, asking them to join us that day on a hill outside Tara's domain.

Eithne led us far from Tara to the Hill of Slane. No farmsteads were near it, she said, and Lóeghaire would not consider it within Tara's boundaries. It was so far away, our visitors came only on horseback. Its crown was grassy, strewn with occasional boulders, barren of trees. In the distance, we saw the faint outline of the *Rath na Ríogh,* the Fort of Tara's kings.

We gathered at mid-afternoon, about sixty of us, to hear Pátrick preach. In the face of opposition from the druids, his message held unusual fire and energy. After he finished, nearly half the audience proclaimed their willingness to believe his teaching and become Christians. We thanked God for His blessings upon us. Already we had enough to start a small church.

Pátrick, Coll, Latharn, and I were the last to leave the hilltop. After we put out our fire, Pátrick gathered us and spoke. "Long ago, I had a vision of this hill. Until tonight, I never knew what it meant. Yet I realized as I was preaching, this was the dream's location. Something will happen here. Conflict. Danger. It will happen at night. But fear not, for I know what we must do. This hill is my destiny. We will face the danger together, and by the grace of God, we will prevail."

None of us knew what to say. He'd been cryptic and said no more about it.

We arrived back in Tara just before sunset and penned our horses. We heard nothing from Ohran or Lóeghaire. Though Lóeghaire made no further efforts at hospitality, neither did he prevent our coming or going. Thus we lay down, thinking the storm had passed, and we might be out of danger.

But long after dark, when silence like a blanket smothered the Hill of Tara, we awoke in a chill hut to the prodding of Pátrick's hand. I heard urgency in his voice.

"Get up, everyone," he said. "We must leave at once."

I yawned and rubbed my eyes, trying to force the sleep from my head. "What's wrong?"

"I had a dream. We must leave this hut *now*. Quickly. We are in great danger."

Instantly, everyone was awake and ready to do anything Pátrick asked. We gathered our furs and meager belongings and then crept under the wooden archway, into the yard. Crickets chirped and stars shone, bright and clear in the crisp spring air.

Once outside, Pátrick closed the door and, with a sliver of kindling, wedged it shut at the bottom so it appeared locked from the inside. Then we stole across the yard to the second hut reserved for visitors. We entered, laid our furs on the hard ground and, before shutting the door, examined our new quarters by moonlight. The straw was trampled and stale. We'd also left our water skin in the other building, but when Coll offered to go back, Pátrick warned against it.

"I had a vision, a dire warning. In my dream, I awoke and saw all of us standing in the middle of the room, unable to move. I watched, paralyzed, as the roof's timbers fell upon us. Then the walls collapsed inward. I could neither move, nor cry out, nor escape. So tonight, had we stayed there, we would be in great danger. We'll be safe here until morning."

After we heard this, we looked at each other, stunned, saying nothing, but simply grateful his vision had led us here. I tried to go back to sleep but couldn't. I kept changing position, wondering what danger we might have escaped.

Much later, shouting erupted outside. People gathered in the dark. There was talking, yelling, running. Then another sound, a familiar noise—a crackling, roaring sound.

We burst out of our hut into a yard alight with a raging inferno. The building we had just abandoned was in flames. Fire tore at each side, waving, whirling up the walls, curling high into the night until the heat became intense even where we stood. The roof of burning logs was already falling in and timbers smashing onto the very place where we had slept. Up against the hut door, a cart jammed tightly and, burning, was propped in place with poles stuck in the ground.

"'Twas Ohran," said Sòlas, his voice low. "'Twas the druids."

"Surely it was." Pátrick nodded. "But God warned me in time, and now we're safe. For as the Psalm says: 'Though I lay down to sleep in the shadow of the wicked, I wake in safety.' When we put our trust in God, He sustains and protects us."

"I . . . I am coming to believe . . . in your God," said Sòlas. "That I am. 'Tis na my nature, and sure, I know 'tis not. But I'm thinking, despite myself, that—I'm thinking that . . . sure . . . I should be baptized."

I looked toward him in wonder. He'd been a hard case, never saying much about Pátrick's talks, listening to many messages, but never acknowledging or responding even after others recognized the truth and believed.

"That's wonderful news, Sòlas!" said Pátrick. "The next time we have a baptism, you'll be first in the water."

Then we clapped Sòlas on the back and congratulated him. A rare smile broke out on Sòlas's face—and that smile warmed my heart.

Our night was short, as we watched until nearly sunrise while the building burned to a pile of glowing coals. For a time, Ohran stood across the yard, also watching the fire, a satisfied smile curving his thin lips. Then Boodan approached him and whispered in his ear. His gaze fell on each corner of the yard until he found us. Starting with his lips, the whole of his face tightened, his eyes contracted to angry black dots, and he left.

"We're no longer safe here," said Pátrick. "We cannot sleep another night on the Hill of Tara."

By noon of the next day, we had set up camp on the field atop the Hill of Slane. There, Pátrick began daily meetings to preach the message about Christ. He also charged me and Latharn with teaching the new converts, and so daily the two of us met under the shelter of some large boulders to give short talks on the Christian way. Eithne and Fedelm made it their business to invite the villagers. Those with horses gave rides to others to overcome the barrier of distance. Each Sunday afternoon, we held services on the hilltop. By the fourth such event, we could count about two hundred converts.

As the days passed, the festival of Beltane drew closer. The druids taught that the spirits of the Otherworld were most active two times a year. One was Samain, the day of Winter's Begin. We learned that on Samain morning, the druids of Tara led the entire *tuath* to the nearby hill of Brú na Bóinne and its great mound tomb. From the outside, Eithne said it appeared as a massive, grassy hill, set atop walls of gleaming white quartz. Yet with no one to maintain it, much of the hillside had collapsed and covered the quartz walls. No one knew what ancient people had built it. All year, darkness wreathed the single, open passage that led to the tomb's interior, guarded on all sides by massive stones covered with interlocking swirls. But on Samain morning, the entire clan gathered outside while druids entered within. Then the rising sun would send a single shaft of light shooting along the floor, lighting three chambers deep at the tomb's center where the druids waited in darkness. This event, said the druids, opened the door to the Otherworld for the whole day.

The other time when the spirits were closest was Beltane, the night of Summer's Begin.

"I fear both days," said Eithne, when I mentioned them. "Old feuds break into fights. Children begin crying for no reason. And formerly contented husbands take other men's wives down into the valley and have their way with them. Everything becomes unsettled."

I nodded, for well did I know those observances and the personal darkness they brought my *tuath* on Inis Creig. On those days especially, the bonfire burned bright on the hill and the druids brought forth all their incantations, spells, and sorcery. Then demons and spirits would leave their idols, or abandon their forest haunts, and find homes in the hearts of my people.

In Emain Macha, we had changed these celebrations to honor Christ.

When Beltane was but two days distant, I warned Pátrick what was coming. He nodded, and then looked at the ground as if thinking.

Fedelm also heard and stepped forward. "But I think you are unaware of our tradition and the great taboo here in Tara. Since time itself, every hilltop fortress has burned a great fire to welcome the spirits. But the druids have preached that on the night of Beltane, the king of Tara must be first to light his bonfire, and he must light it only on the Hill of Tara. And before his flame is lit, in all the land no other such fire must be kindled. The druids say that if ever this taboo is broken, the kingdom will fall, true and certain."

Pátrick frowned. "I think it more likely the druids' reign would end, not the king's. For it's the druids keeping the people in slavery to the spirits of evil."

"I ken you are right," said Fedelm. "But no one has ever questioned this taboo or sought to break it. The druids hold powerful sway over the people."

For a time, Pátrick was silent. Then he said, "We are close to Easter. It may even be past, for I've lost track of the days. Perhaps, just perhaps, we should celebrate Easter—the resurrection of our Lord—on the very night of Beltane, opposite this pagan practice? Perhaps on that night we should light our own fire, right here on the Hill of Slane, in full view of the druids' ceremony, but light a great blaze in remembrance of Christ, and do it well before theirs?"

Bold was this plan to celebrate the resurrection of our Lord, supplant a ceremony honoring pagan spirits, *and* challenge the druids' power. Latharn, Coll, and I agreed. Fedelm hesitated, smiled, and then said it was a good idea. But Eithne remained silent. For the first time, I sensed a serious disagreement between the sisters.

"The druids will never let it stand," she said. "They'll view it as a dire threat. They'll convince Father to prevent it and do so that very night. What will you do if the king sends men here to stop you?"

Pátrick gazed at her. "'Tis time I tell everyone something. The conflict Eithne describes is the very one my dream warned me about so long ago. But fear not. We'll pray. We'll put our trust in the Lord. I know what we must do. We'll not bow to a pagan practice on a night when the druids hope to raise demon spirits from the earth."

Eithne looked worried. "What if it ends Father's rule, like they say? What will happen to him?"

"Child, you must put your trust in Christ, not in the ways of men. Lóeghaire seems to have made up his mind about our message. He's unwilling to listen. If he changes his ways, he may survive. I understand your love for your father, but do not put your spiritual future in doubt over this. This is an opportunity to confront the darkness these druids have brought your people and show them a different way. Sometimes we must confront evil plainly, without flinching or turning aside."

Eithne looked at the ground, silent for a time. Then she left us.

Later that day, she returned, frowning. "I've thought about this, and I bow to your wisdom, Pátrick. Let my father decide as he will. If he aligns himself with the druids, then God help him, for true and sure, I am aligned with Christ and the one God who rules over all."

I was glad she'd made the right choice.

Pátrick smiled, laid a hand on her shoulder, and prayed for her, for Lóeghaire, and the bold plan we would undertake the night after.

But as unholy Beltane approached, I paced and couldn't be still. For we faced a battle between good and evil that would decide the very fate of Tara, and perhaps, of Ériu itself.

CHAPTER 28

The Bonfires of Beltane

On the day of Beltane, the rain stopped. White clouds dotted the sky like bundles of sheep's wool, washed clean, fluffed up, and floating silently. It was late afternoon, and all the believers in Christ gathered on the Hill of Slane, nearly two hundred souls chosen by God from the ranks of Tara. Our numbers were less than on a Sunday morning. Still, it was a large group.

We prepared food, and after praying, ate a meal of roast beef and fermented cabbage. Afterward, we dowsed our cooking fires. As we waited for darkness, Pátrick picked a large shamrock and climbed atop a log pedestal. Then he explained how the shamrock could explain God's nature. Its three leaves could represent the Father, Son, and Holy Spirit, yet all were still part of the same plant. He talked about this for a while then passed out the wine and bread of the Eucharist and read a few passages from the large New Testament he carried.

Beside him lay a great mountain of logs set atop kindling, for we had spent the morning chopping trees and building the enormous pile. We also cut wood for torches for everyone, wrapping them with old cloth, tying each with cord. The torches stacked in rows beside the logs.

The slanting rays of the dying sun lit both the horizon and the woolen clouds, tingeing their edges with dark shades of blues, reds, and yellows. We could barely see the *Rath na Ríogh* and the druid temple in the distance. Around us stretched a deep forest, a green landscape darkening with the dying light until all the land, from our hill to the horizon, turned black. Only the western sky held a sliver of dying blue light and a bubble of red sun. That too dimmed.

Pátrick gave the word, and torches touched the base of the woodpile. Soon, a great bonfire raged. We looked toward the Hill of Tara. It was dark. Our crackling flame had gone first into the sky, preceding the fire of the High King of Tara. In the Kingdom of Leinster, the taboo was broken.

We tended the fire and waited, glancing now and then across the dark space between our hill and theirs. The taboo was an idea in the people's minds, not some kind of magic we had broken. The druids taught it was a great spell of power, but we rejected that notion as pagan nonsense, a symptom of spiritual darkness. When we lit the fire, we were saying, "Here is Christ. He has come to Tara and the land of Leinster. The old ways of the spirits are dead. Christ is alive and resurrected!"

It was a long ride from Tara. We were unsure what to expect, or how long we might have to wait. To warn us when they came, if they came, we'd posted a watcher along the trail from the village.

I was nearly ready for sleep when our lookout galloped down the trail, dismounted, and left his horse at the bottom. He ran, walked, and then ran up the hill. He stopped before us, breathing heavily.

"Many men on horseback. Torches. Weapons." He leaned forward, put his hands on his knees, and tried to catch his breath.

"How far away?" Pátrick's eyes narrowed.

"Almost here." He turned to look back down the hill.

Where the trail bent through the trees, we saw a glint of light and shadows, flickering, bouncing, moving.

Instantly, a feeling like that before a lightning storm swept through our group. I felt fear, but also exhilaration.

Pátrick gathered us together and gave orders to pass torches to everyone, but we were to keep them dark. Then he climbed on a pedestal and began to pray.

"Almighty God, You have chosen in Your providence to bring those among us out of darkness and error into Your true light and knowledge. Grant us to walk in Your light, that we may come at last to the light of everlasting life. Lord, protect us now, on this night, from the enemies of your Word and from those who wish to harm Your people. Do not let the followers of demons and spirits undo Your work here. We are Your servants, Lord."

As he prayed, I felt like a man emerging from a stagnant tunnel into a fresh, ocean breeze, energized with hope.

He added this: "We ask all this through Jesu, Christ our Lord, who lives and reigns with You and the Holy Spirit, one God, now and forever. Amen."

Below, they dismounted and continued on foot. Their torches bobbed. Voices echoed along the trail. Their path led straight to the base of our hill. To reach us would be an easy climb. We carried no weapons, not a one. Pátrick had given strict instructions we should not bring as much as a dagger. Only knives for cooking and eating, but these were no match for the weapons approaching below by torchlight.

Marching toward us was a makeshift army of perhaps three hundred men. Spears, swords, and axes waved in their hands. Angry shouts rushed the hill. It would take only moments for them to be upon us.

Pátrick motioned for us to look away from the advancing throng. He dropped to his knees and prayed silently. Others did the same, including me. We gave ourselves to God's mercy. Then Pátrick called for the torches to be lit, and everyone to huddle in the center and be still. And we obeyed.

On his signal, we ran to the edge of the hilltop, where it began to slope, and stood in a great half-circle, looking down. We raised our torches high in the air, all two hundred of us. Then we waited. From all sides came the faithful's mumbled prayers.

Pátrick gave us a second signal, and we let loose with a cry of, "Halleluiah! Gloria Deo Christus!" Seven times we shouted this, then ceased.

When we had retreated to light the torches, our enemy advanced rapidly toward the base. But when we returned, made our semicircle, and began shouting, the swarm of torches, weapons, and men—some of whom had already started up the hill—paused.

Suddenly, individual figures began rushing back through the crowd, running *away* from us. More broke in twos and threes, racing headlong down the hill or across the field toward the forest. Then entire groups began breaking away, one after another, fleeing and dropping swords, spears, axes, and even torches in a mad scramble. The horses reared, ran this way and that, and then rushed back along the trail. What had happened?

I turned to the others on the hilltop. Everyone watched the scene below. Enough torches had fallen so we could see the outline of the darkened trail to the bend where the forest hid the path.

Coll was beside me. His eyes widened.

"We are delivered!" said someone.

A cheer rose from our gathering, for the enemy had fled. We didn't know how or why, but they were gone. At Pátrick's urging, we said prayers of thanksgiving. Until sunrise, we kept the fire alight and the air charged with hymns. Only then did we break up.

The next day, believers who had remained in Tara told us what happened. Nothing like it had ever been seen in Tara. Everyone who'd been part of it was compelled to tell their brother who then told anyone who would listen about the night's strange events.

When Ohran saw the fire on the Hill of Slane, he said that what he'd warned against had happened. The taboo was broken. While others listened, he approached Lóeghaire and nearly shouted at his king. "That fire must be put out this very night. If that blaze continues to burn, its flames will rise above all others to seduce the people of your kingdom. Aye, all your kingdom, my lord. Unless you put it out, it will surely be the end of your reign, the end of our ways."

Lóeghaire then ordered every able-bodied man and all the druids to find horses and weapons, ride to the Hill of Slane, and kill every last man, woman, and child, sparing only his daughters. Yet, a moment later, some heard him bemoan that, in the confusion, he feared he'd just ordered their deaths. He retreated to his palace. Back in his chambers, he drank so much mead, he fell into a stupor.

The mob followed the darkened trail by torchlight. Rage consumed them and drove them on, for Ohran had given a speech against us filled with hate and lies. But as the men rounded the turn, dismounted, and approached the foot of the Hill of Slane, a few saw a fearsome sight. Instead of two hundred believers holding torches, their eyes beheld a terrifying vision. And fear of it infected the entire crowd. Standing on the upper slopes in the very spot where we waited, they beheld an army of heavenly warriors, vast and alight with a celestial glow.

Maybe one out of ten attackers stopped their advance. These few who saw simply stared, shaking with fear. Then the army of light blew horns, thousands of horns, and the sound—it was said for those who heard it—echoed from hilltop to hilltop and rang in their ears like thunder. Those who heard turned and ran. For nothing could have prepared them for such sights and sounds. Soon they didn't care if they dropped their weapons or their torches. All they wanted was escape.

The larger group didn't see or hear anything different. They looked up the hill, saw two hundred torches, heard the shouts of two hundred voices, and were puzzled by their fleeing comrades. But when more and more around are fleeing in sheer panic, doubt takes hold. Then fear becomes tangible, something to touch and taste and feel. Soon the fright of those who ran spread like a plague. It traveled to the horses, spooked them, and they stampeded down the trail. In the end, all were infected and the crowd disintegrated.

In the end, the night belonged to God.

When we entered Tara the next day, we were met with sideways glances and downcast eyes. Many who had come to kill us the night before hurried into their huts, fearful of us and what they'd seen. Perhaps they thought somehow, in broad daylight, our mere presence might revive the night's fearsome visions.

In the following days, the druids could no more incite the crowds against us than against their own mothers. As the weeks passed, word of the miracle spread throughout the land and increased the reputation of our God and Pátrick who led us. Within the month, our numbers at Sunday services doubled.

One noon, as we ate a meal of porridge, Eithne approached with a message from her father. "The king wants to meet with Pátrick, Coll, Latharn, and Taran to discuss an accommodation. He requests the four of you, plus Ohran and Boodan, the two leading druids, to assemble for a private dinner at the palace tomorrow night."

We looked at each other with questioning glances.

"Is it a trap?" asked Coll.

"I don't think so," answered Eithne. "The events of Beltane shook Father badly, and he's frightened. He believes the druid prophecies and thinks his reign is threatened. He will always support the druids. But Father values honor above all else. If he's personally invited you to the palace, he'd never make plans to do you harm."

"What about Ohran?" I asked.

Eithne opened her hands in a question.

"Tomorrow we will dine with the king," said Pátrick. "But we put our trust only in the Lord."

The next morning when Pátrick and the rest of us met as usual for prayers, he seemed unusually distracted. I worried he was ill. After a breakfast of oat porridge, he gathered us together. "I've had another vision."

He had everyone's complete attention now. Too well had we learned the import of Pátrick's visions.

"Seven figures were sitting around a table, eating. Among them, Lóeghaire, Ohran, Boodan, and the four of us. A dim light shone from only three—Lóeghaire and the two druids. A bright light surrounded the other four—us. As I watched, my light faded then went completely black. One dim figure stood over me, looked down, and poked. Then the other three bright lights dimmed and also went black."

He frowned, looked at each of us, and then said, "At this dinner, I sense great danger. We must be on our guard."

"Should we still go?" I asked.

Pátrick frowned and, for a moment, stared at the ground. "Whatever danger we face, we'll not give up an opportunity to present the news of God's Son to Lóeghaire and turn a kingdom to God."

CHAPTER 29

The End of the Old

Until the night of the dinner, none of us had been inside *Forradh,* the palace of Tara's kings. At the entrance, two men with spears waited. They led us down a dark hallway to a chamber and then stood at attention by a far wall.

The chamber was smaller than the great room at Emain Macha, but still thirty feet by thirty. A fire burned in the open near one wall, its smoke curling to the ceiling, filtering out through a covered hole above. Wolf and deer heads, crossed spears, and burnished swords decorated walls darkened by smoke. The room smelled of wood smoke, spilt mead, and musty animal heads.

Upon news of our arrival, Ohran and Boodan, followed by Lóeghaire and three servants, entered. We bowed politely and the servants directed us to sit on straw-stuffed cushions at one end of a long low plank that served as a table while Lóeghaire and his druids took the opposite side. Boodan looked only at the oak planks while Ohran, a head shorter, stared at us with narrowed, tiny eyes. Lóeghaire sat stiff and straight. His muscled arms on the tabletop. His jaw jutting out. A man in control. His large black eyes searched first us, then his druids, seeking something between us. Five feet of empty oak separated us. Not a good beginning.

"I hope, tonight, over a fine meal, we can discuss our differences in a civil manner." Lóeghaire gave the druids a long, sideways glance. "After the events of . . . Beltane . . . the kingdom is perhaps . . . in jeopardy. Yesterday, I went to the *Lia Fáil,* the ancient Stone of Destiny, and struck it. For the first time since I took this throne it was . . . silent. Silent, and my druids cannot explain it. But I tell you, holy man—" he stared straight at Pátrick, "—I fear this omen. For if I am no longer king here, then who is?"

Ohran and Boodan exchanged worried glances.

After an awkward pause, Lóeghaire motioned to his servants. They exited through a side door, appearing a moment later with pitchers of mead. They filled mugs set before us. First for the Rí Cóicid, then for us, then the druids. When Pátrick refused mead, they brought him water.

Lóeghaire frowned. "Can I not interest you in some mead, holy man? When earnest men come together to talk through their differences, a mug of mead or two often smooths the way."

"I do not drink the wine of intoxication, my lord. Only the wine of the Eucharist."

"I have no such wine, or I would offer it tonight."

"It's only for celebrating our risen Lord, not for feasting."

Lóeghaire opened his hands in a question. Then his forearms thumped back onto the table's edge. "I'm sorry for that."

Pátrick raised the glass of water to his lips and paused. He looked at the mugs before the rest of us, at his mug, and then set his water down.

Ohran's small eyes watched his every move. Even Boodan raised his glance from the tabletop.

"Perhaps, tonight—yes, tonight only—I will take mead and not water."

I nearly dropped my mug. This was not like him.

Lóeghaire smiled, motioned to his servants. They removed his water and replaced it with a mug of mead, poured from the common jug.

"To friendship and understanding," said the king, raising his cup. Everyone raised their mugs and drank.

Next, the servants brought a tray of cheese and wheat bread, customarily serving the king first, then us, finally the druids.

"When you arrived, we did not begin on good terms." Lóeghaire faced Pátrick. "But let us strive to begin again. I have many questions, now that certain . . . events have played out. I do not understand these affairs, but I ken you do. My druids," he pointed with a bit of cheese, "seem to have no answers. They spout admonitions and remind me of old traditions. But their words are empty, for they cannot make the *Lia Fáil* sing again. I'm sick of their warnings. I want answers and, perhaps—reconciliation, if I may call it that." He munched on the cheese then blurted out, "Holy man, is my kingdom in trouble?"

Pátrick cleared his throat and hesitated. The king held his gaze as Pátrick spoke. "Any kingdom founded on the gods of this world and not on the Lord of All, not based on Christ, is built upon sand, not rock. 'Tis true both for spiritual kingdoms," he gave a short nod to the druids, "and for the reign of kings. The first flood that comes along will wash away all that's not well grounded."

Apparently, it was not the answer Lóeghaire wanted. His brow creasing, he stared at Pátrick, trying, but failing, to find words for a response. "Is your answer then, I must convert to this God of yours before I can have peace, before I can know my rule will not be overthrown by the breaking of some ancient druids' taboo?"

Pátrick remained expressionless. "The taboo is your belief, not mine. But if you claim Christ as your Lord, whatever curse exists will have no power over you."

Lóeghaire narrowed his eyes and rumpled his brow. "I'm trying to find an accommodation here. You must understand, I cannot convert to your God. I am the son of Niall of the Nine Hostages. I am to be buried in the earthworks of Tara, lying face to face with the son of Dúnlaing in Mullaghmast. I must die upholding all my ancestors held dear, with honor. 'Tis my fate, decreed from long ago. 'Tis an honorable thing—tradition. Is not tradition important to you, holy man?"

Pátrick nodded. "Tradition is certainly important when it doesn't lead one into spiritual darkness. But sometimes when we encounter new information, we need to circle our thoughts around it and reexamine our lives. That's what the message of my Lord and Savior, Jesu, does for us—makes us reevaluate and reorder our lives."

Lóeghaire cupped his mug with both hands, then looked up. "Good. We're talking. I do not know about this Jesu. I only know I can never abandon the old ways. But at least, we're talking. Perhaps we should eat, then talk some more. Maybe we can find a way around this curse you have brought upon me. Maybe we'll get further in our talking—you and me—on a full belly." He motioned to the servants, who brought in a large platter of fermented, spiced cabbage. With his knife, the king pulled a goodly amount onto his trencher of bread. We were served, then the druids.

When we had eaten the cabbage, the servants brought in the venison. The meat was served on two metal platters, one for the king and the druids, and a second for us. Enough was piled on each plate to feed ten men. Ours was dripping with juice, so much so it slopped to one side of the container as the servant set it down.

Latharn grabbed our serving dish, pulled it carefully toward him and began carving a large, juicy slice.

Pátrick stared at the platter, at the plate at the table's far end, then back at ours. He dropped his hand onto Latharn's and squeezed, stopping his knife mid slice. "Why two platters, my lord?"

Lóeghaire set down his mug and looked up. A servant had already knelt to cut him a large piece of meat, now laid carefully atop his bread. The king glanced at the serving tray in front of him, then at ours. The servant was at his side. "Why two platters, Blàr? Did we not discuss just one?"

Blàr, a small man dressed in a plain white tunic, arched his eyebrows. "I donna ken, my lord. I found two trays when I returned to the kitchen. I'd ordered but one. I assumed Lulach prepared it."

Lóeghaire lifted his face to Pátrick. "'Tis a wee thing, is it not? Does it matter to you, holy man?"

"It matters. Call it a mere preference, but I would prefer to eat off the same platter as my lord. If it pleases you?"

Lóeghaire's chiseled jaw tightened, and his large, black eyes narrowed. He glared, and as the silence lengthened, his cheeks grew red. "What do you imply? I am the Rí Cóicid, the High King of Tara. I asked you here in good faith, backed by the good name of my honor and generosity, all for the hope of reconciliation. Do you imply I might now try to, to—poison you?"

"I'm not implying that at all, my lord. But now you've said it, would you allay any suspicions and care to sample, yourself, some meat from this platter at our end? It does appear different from the one by you, does it not? Methinks ours slops with too much juice."

Lóeghaire's eyebrows bent and his forehead scrunched. "Blàr! Bring me a slice of meat from their platter. At once."

The diminutive Blàr hastened to obey. He removed our serving dish and carried it with shaking hands to the king's side. He bent down, trying not to spill the juice. As he stabbed the middle with one knife and sliced into the meat with a second, Ohran began to fidget and shake his head. Blàr finished his cutting and slipped one blade under the piece.

Ohran's head shook back and forth, waving thin brown locks.

Blàr lifted the meat off the plate and rose.

Suddenly, Ohran rose from his cushion and stood. "You must not, my lord. Do not eat of it! Take it back to the kitchen. It appears to me to be—spoiled."

Blàr stopped, holding the meat in midair, balanced between his two knives. Lóeghaire stared at the druid, his eyes bulging. Stony-faced, Ohran returned the king's gaze. But Boodan's attention fixed as if frozen on the tabletop.

"What nonsense is this?" asked the king. "Why should you say my meat is spoiled? My kitchen does not serve spoilt meat. I killed this animal myself only yesterday. Lulach butchered and stored it in my cellar overnight. He tastes everything that comes into this room. Why, Ohran, should I not eat this meat?"

"I do not know, my lord. It's only a feeling, an instinct." Ohran shot his three-fingered hand across his forehead.

"Instinct, is it? Feeling, is it? Blàr, go and bring Lulach here at once!"

The king's voice had grown louder and must have drawn Lulach to listen at the door, for he pushed it open without being summoned. His apron was stained with cooking. His hair was disheveled. His hands shook.

"Lulach, explain to me this second platter of meat. Did we not discuss just one?"

"We did, my lord."

"Then why are there two?"

"Because, my lord—because Ohran, here, said he was providing the second one, and it was by your orders, and I should by no means question it. He claimed it had already been tasted, and I should not eat of it. Who am I to question the chief druid?"

Lóeghaire's eyes narrowed, his jaw tight and jutting out. He fixed his druids with a withering gaze.

"Is Ohran now providing meat for the king's table? Is he now the host instead of the Rí Cóicid? Has he by his own authority set the king's orders aside and put his generosity on display in place of mine? Well then, perhaps Ohran should taste what he's brought us? Blàr, take a slice of this to Ohran's trencher. We'll watch as the druid eats it all."

"Nay, my lord," said Ohran, his face blanching. "I've lost my appetite. Nay, I would rather not eat." He stood as did Boodan. "The meat is spoiled."

"What do you mean—spoiled? Who spoiled it?"

Ohran just shook his head. Boodan's face went white and his glance bounced wildly from Ohran to the king, then back to Ohran.

"Blàr! Take the meat to Ohran."

Blàr was shaking so much he dropped the slice onto the tabletop, spraying the king's tunic and his own. It began a quick slide toward the edge where Blàr had to stab it twice with a knife to halt its progress. He slid the knife under the meat and pried it off the plank's edge. With small, careful steps, he sidled over to the druid's seat, dripping all the way while Ohran stepped back and watched, transfixed by its journey across the room. Blàr plopped it onto Ohran's trencher of bread, spraying the plank around it.

Lóeghaire stood up from the table, stalked to the wall, and tore a sword from its display. Metal hooks ripped from the wall, fell to the floor, plinked across the stonework.

"Sit and eat, druid, or I will have your head!" He rested the tip of the blade on Ohran's chest. "The choice is yours. Eat the meat or lose your head. Tonight, I'll have it no other way. My generosity and good name will not be besmirched in my own palace against my will and behind my back."

Ohran stared at the king, at the sword, then at the meat, its juice quickly soaking the container of bread, spilling onto the table. He took one hesitant step, then lowered himself to his cushion and sat. With shaking hands, he raised his knife, cut a small piece, and then, with shaking fingers, raised it to his lips. But there it stopped.

"I did it to stop adze-head and his infernal spouting off about his God. I did it for the—"

"Silence, druid! Chew it and eat!" It was like a hideous parody of an angry father forcing a defiant child to eat his supper.

Ohran put the piece into his mouth, chewed, and swallowed.

"Again, druid!"

He took another bite. Lóeghaire prodded. Again he ate. Meanwhile, Boodan's eyes were so wild I thought he might bolt. But the guards at the room's far end sensed what was needed, sat him down again, and hovered on each side of him with their spears.

Prodded by continuous threats from Lóeghaire's sword, Ohran ate half the portion. Between bites, his lips became thin lines of pale, blue flesh and his eyes grew wider than I'd ever seen them.

Then his knife dropped to the table, clattering. With uncharacteristic slowness, his three-fingered left hand drew across his eyes to free them, once more, from their enemy, the errant, wispy locks—but nothing was there. Slowly, carefully, he pushed back from the table. His tiny eyes looked across the room, seeking something. He must have found it, for there they stopped, fixed on a single spot on the wall. Then he stared.

What did he see? A wraith? A vision of the next life? I don't know.

His small eyes grew wider yet. His hands clutched his chest. He tried to stand, but instead fell back to the floor. He began writhing, gagging, kicking his legs under the planks. I looked away. For long, agonizing moments, I heard this struggle with a death meant for us. Then he was silent.

As Ohran kicked his last, Lóeghaire's anger switched to Boodan. He moved behind him. Backhanded, he gripped his blade, drew it up and back, and thrust it straight through Boodan's back. The sword tip popped out beneath the druid's breast.

Boodan looked down, open-mouthed and surprised, for two inches of sword point poked out through the front of his tunic. He took a short, burbling gasp then coughed.

Putting one foot on the man's back, Lóeghaire gave a mighty yank and pulled the sword free, knocking Boodan onto the table in front.

The four of us stood, averted our eyes from the carnage and backed to the wall.

Lóeghaire rocked on his feet, staring for a moment at the scene and the sword dripping red at his side, a vacant look in his wide, black eyes. He mumbled something incoherent, turned, and then shuffled from the room.

We fled the chamber and that palace of death. When we gained our refuge at the Hill of Slane, we thanked God for the salvation He'd granted us that night.

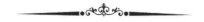

Lóeghaire was never the same. He let Pátrick and us alone. With Ohran and Boodan gone, the other druids never regained the influence they once had. The false ways were fast disappearing, replaced by truth. Within a year, the news of God's Son spread throughout the region around Tara. Many became Christians. But through all our time in that land, Lóeghaire remained fixed on the dying pagan ways. He became, in his own country, an outsider.

The years passed. Throughout, I looked forward to finishing our mission in Tara and returning to Inis Creig and Laurna. Then the day finally came when we had established churches and believers throughout much of northern Leinster, and Pátrick declared our work in this country was finished. We returned to Emain Macha.

We'd been only a week back in Ulster when Pátrick took me to a bench in the apple orchard and we sat. "I have one more favor to ask of you, Taran. Perhaps the greatest yet. I know we'd planned to return you to your island home. But God has given me a new mission. In a few weeks, I must go to Connacht and preach at the palace in Cruachain. I believe this task is just as important as the one we finished in Tara. But I cannot go unless I leave someone here I can trust. Someone to minister to the church and train new priests. So I'm asking if you will stay in Emain Macha, you and Coll, while I'm gone? Servius is going with me."

I closed my eyes tightly. I felt as if I were falling. More long years away from Laurna. More time not knowing what the druids were doing to my *tuath*. If possible, this was even worse than when we'd left for Tara, three long years ago. But how could I refuse this great man whose obedience to God was bringing the Ériu out of spiritual darkness? Slowly, I opened my eyes. I caught Pátrick's gaze, and I'm sure he saw the pain in my eyes. "I . . . I will stay. But only once more, my lord. After this mission . . ."

Again, tears glistened in his eyes, and he laid a hand on my shoulder. "Aye, Taran. This is the last time I'll ask you."

Only days later, Pátrick led me to a site at Ard Macha, a hill only three miles distant from Emain Macha, and told me his great vision for the future. He talked with gleaming eyes of building a town and a university, with great buildings on wide, cobbled streets. The first town in Ériu, it would be, far bigger than any village. All the priests of the land would go there to be trained, he said, and from there, they'd take the news of God's Son to the world. His model was the great universities on the continent. One day, said Pátrick, he would ask Forga to grant him the land. But he was not yet ready for the project. He had his mission to Connacht. And after that, he talked about carrying the message of Christ west and south, to the Kingdoms of Meath and Unster, where Palladius once tried and failed to establish churches.

A month later, Pátrick departed for the west with Servius, leaving Coll and me behind.

The years passed in Ulster. I began to see the changes we had wrought, with God's guiding hand, upon Land of Ériu. Before Pátrick came, the people worshiped demon spirits and the darkness. Now they were children of God, worshiping the Light.

The slave trade dried up. Occasionally, we heard of a few Irish raids against Bryton or Gaul, but now the raids were for plunder, not slaves. Only the *tuatha* we hadn't reached still sailed the seas as pirates and slavers. There were fewer murders and blood feuds. The ancient wars between Leinster and Meath, between Connacht and Ulster, decreased in frequency and violence. The old ways were slowly ending.

Time also brought changes to the people I knew.

Soon after arriving in Ulster, Latharn returned to the environs around Tara, becoming a priest in a large *tuath*. He continued our work there, and we always heard good reports of his ministry. And, of course, his table served the best that Leinster offered.

Eivhir married a handsome nobleman from a *tuath* to the north, and there they moved and settled with his clan. A priest I had trained myself accompanied them. News arrived that their worship drew many from the countryside, and in their *tuath*, God was honored and held in high esteem.

Sòlas married Beahak, and the two made a feisty pair, with fights aplenty. Both attended services regularly each Sunday, and as long as I knew them, they proclaimed Christ as their king.

Forga mac Dallán became an old man but with great energy. Shortly before we left for Tara, he'd married a young bride, and by the time we returned, he had a son and an heir, Muiredach, later nicknamed Muinderg, he of the red neck. During Forga's reign, he'd seen his kingdom change from pagan idolatry to one serving Christ. Under his leadership, the people of the Ulaid thrived.

To see everything we had worked for coming to pass should have made me happy and content. But as the years fled and I watched the changes we'd wrought, my thoughts returned again and again to Inis Creig. I compared the improved state of the Ériu to my people's sad plight.

My love for Laurna, I never abandoned. Always I clung to a hope she still held the same love for me. Instead of fading, memories of home and Laurna appeared to me ever more often. They came as I walked in the fields, prayed, bathed in the cold streams, and even as I gave out the bread and wine of the Eucharist or taught a lesson from the Holy Book.

Only a few days later, Pátrick and I went alone into the church Forga mac Dallán had built so long ago. The afternoon was cold and rainy, and we sat on log benches before a fire of pine logs.

"We've changed the Land of Ériu, have we not?" I said, listening to the crackling flames, smelling the pine smoke drifting to the ceiling.

"With God's guiding hand, we did."

"Have I been faithful to your mission, Pátrick? Have I done all you've asked of me? Can you find any fault in me these last years?"

He looked at me, smiled, and laid a hand on my shoulder. "You've been the most faithful priest and servant any bishop could hope for. You've not flinched from any mission, no matter how mundane, difficult, or dangerous."

I smiled. I was not looking for praise, only for confirmation my work was pleasing to God. And Pátrick was the only person I could ask. "I've been thinking much lately about my home on Inis Creig."

He was silent for a time. "I've not forgotten my promise. All these years, you've allowed me to spread the Good News and plant churches everywhere. And I've appreciated it."

"Nearly every day now, I think about Laurna."

"And our plan was to send you home when I returned from Connacht?"

"And now you are back."

Pátrick smiled. "Forgive me, Taran. Without you, I don't know how we would have done what we did. But now 'tis time I fulfilled my promise to return you to this island you love so much, for as I remember your telling, they're in sore need of the gospel. Aye, you'll go at once. As your bishop, I hereby release you—this very day—from your duties in Ulster."

Tears formed at the corners of my eyes. I was going home. I would see my Laurna again. "Thank you," I said, then surprised him with a hug.

That afternoon, I went through the village of Emain Macha, finding the people I had grown to love, and began saying good-bye. I planned my departure for Inis Creig.

PART VI

In a far Northern Sea,
A.D. 444 - 445

Chapter 30

The Journey Home

When Coll learned of my plans, he came to me in a sorry state. "We've shared everything, Taran. You're like a brother to me. You canna leave."

"I feel the same way. But my destiny lies with my people. I must bring them the same news I received, give them the same chance for eternal life. And my heart is ever with Laurna."

"After all this time, how do you know she still loves you?"

"I don't. I can only hope."

"Will you ever return to Ériu?"

I smiled. "I don't know."

Coll was silent a long while, then said, "I'm going with you."

My eyes filled with tears. He had been with me these last twelve years, going everywhere I'd gone, always at my side, even paralleling my career. Coll was a priest in his own right and a good scholar.

My voice might have choked a bit as I responded, "Your place is here, Coll, with your ministry. You don't know my island. When I return, the druids may oppose me fiercely. They are worse than those on Ériu. Their spiritual darkness, if possible, is even greater."

"Then you need my company all the more. Long ago I pledged to you my companionship, loyalty, and friendship. That pledge—I will not break it. I'm going with you. You canna change my mind."

For a long time, I just looked at him. Argument was useless. I smiled, and then we hugged. I had a companion for the journey, a true and faithful friend no one could turn aside.

On the morning of our departure, a small crowd gathered to see us off. Coll arrived with a new triangular box he'd made for his fiddle, lined inside with sheep's wool to cradle the instrument.

The king brought us horses and four soldiers, one of whom was Sòlas. Beahak was there to see us off.

"Taran," said the king, "these men will escort you safely to the coast."

I thanked him.

"You should disembark from the northern shores, as they bow to me there. But they're a wild bunch. Some of those who go their own way are pirates. Sure, and they've always been rogue. Avoid them. At the coast, you'll need something to barter with, something to charter a ship to make a fall voyage over stormy waters." He handed me a small leather sack. "In this bag are some Roman coins—*aureus* they are called. Or *aureii*?—their tongue befuddles me. In any event, there should be gold enough for the task."

"My lord, I'm overwhelmed by your generosity. Truly overwhelmed."

"You've done much for my kingdom and its people. 'Tis the least I can do. Your absence will be keenly felt."

I bowed and thanked him again.

"But, lad, there's more." He fumbled with a cord around his neck then lifted a large golden disc from inside his tunic. The symbol of his reign emblazoned the surface—a sword laid atop wavy lines, surrounded by a square. The images of three eyes cut into the top and bottom. On either side of the sword, two large green emeralds embedded in the metal.

"'Tis the Talisman of Ulster," said the king. "And though I ken it no longer carries magical powers—for only the Devil owns such—'tis a symbol well known to all who bow to this Rí Cóicid. It's useless to me, now that I am in Christ, and I give it to you. Use it on your journey. Not for magic, but to identify you are under the protection of Forga mac Dallán, High King of the Ulaid, and to announce that any who oppose you will answer to me with their lives."

I took the disc, bowed, then fell to my knees. "You are truly a worthy king of the Ulaid. Your generosity is beyond words."

Next it was Pátrick's turn to say good-bye. "I will pray, Taran, for a successful mission against the druids. And for your reuniting with Laurna. She is blessed to have one such as you as a suitor. But if she has not waited, if after all these long years, she has found another—and, Taran, it's been twelve long years—consider her plight and have grace. Do not hold it against her."

I hesitated then responded, "I've thought often of this. I've prayed she waited. But I cannot expect such a thing of her, and if she's already betrothed to another, I . . . I will accept it. I must. What other choice do I have? But I pray otherwise."

Pátrick smiled, grabbed my shoulders with both hands, and then pulled me close in a hug. When we parted, his eyes were moist. "I could not have had a better friend than you."

"Nor I, you. You've been more than a mentor. You've been a true friend."

"But I too have some parting gifts."

He motioned to one of our young acolytes, who brought forth the cross that always stood in the front of the church. It was two and a half feet of forged steel, expertly hammered and shaped with swirls, cherubim and angels.

"Pátrick, I cannot accept this. It belongs to the church of Emain Macha. It's too much."

"Use it to plant a new church. I'll have our Gaelic forgers here make another."

I thanked him, tears in my eyes.

But he wasn't done. He motioned, and Dàn, our latest young acolyte, brought forth a large rectangular object wrapped in cloth. "You cannot start a church without this."

I took the package and opened it. Inside, nestled a Bible, newly copied onto sheep's hide under an ornate leather cover. "On my instructions, young Dàn has been copying it for one of our new churches. 'Tis a New Testament but also contains the Psalms and Proverbs. Over a hundred calf skins in this book. He's been at it for nearly a year."

I had no words to thank him. My eyes brimmed with tears.

Then Pátrick said good-bye to Coll, with hugs, more wet eyes, and the gift of a silver goblet for the Eucharist.

Pátrick took one of my hands and one of Coll's, holding on tight. "May God go with you both!"

Then the six of us mounted our horses and headed north toward the bogs and forests of Northern Ulster.

I need not tell of our trip to the coast or the events on the way. Ériu was already becoming more civilized, and our adventures were few. We left in late autumn, and our mornings arrived with frozen grass and frosty breath. In the evenings, we fortified ourselves against the chill with a blazing fire.

Forga suggested we embark from Coleraine, and within the week we arrived at that remote *tuath* on the River Bann. Not a mile north of the village, we found three large *curraghs* pulled up and anchored on the river banks, heavy with the smell of mud and salt. Each ship was over sixty feet long, built for fishing the open sea.

I haggled with the Rí Tuath there over the rent of one of these and the lending of a crew. But he would not trade, he said, for a bag of gold. He knew not its worth. He wanted cattle or pigs. And besides, he said, it was late in the year, too late for an extended sea voyage. With difficulty, I gave a long, painful explanation that such sums of gold could be exchanged for goods—a foreign concept to most on Ériu. I also reminded him Forga mac Dallán himself had sent me. I told him Sòlas would take word of his help back to Emain Macha, and it would raise his personal reputation with the king. In the end, he agreed.

Two days later, our eleven-man crew, Coll, and I shoved off from the banks into the deep channel and set sail downstream. Sòlas and his men waved from shore. By midmorning, we were riding the swells of the northern sea, under full sail, heading northwest.

After so many years, I was happy to be again on the open ocean. I rejoiced at the salt wind in my face, the ship's hide squeaking against the timbers, the rigging singing in the wind, the rise and the fall of the deck as the hull broke the waves. I smiled at the seagulls crying out to each other, following in our wake, and racing beside us as the land disappeared behind. But how can I describe the anxiety and the anticipation I felt on that voyage? I was finally going home. I knew not what I would find. I was torn between hope, great expectations, and a fear that in my long absence, I might have lost everything I held dear.

We sailed under dark clouds, through heavy seas, for it was late in the year. The storms of winter could come at any time. Having never been at sea, Coll did not fare well. He ate hardly anything and lost much over the side. I must admit that at first I, too, was a bit queasy. But I soon regained my sea legs.

On the fourth morning, I awoke, went to the bow, and peered toward the west. Had we still not arrived?

I found the captain by the tiller. "Sir, I fear we've missed our destination."

"Laddie, we have not. I ken the way to your lonely isle, I do. Used it often to guide me to a fishing shoal north of there."

"How soon then?"

"Midday, I reckon. Maybe a bit later."

As predicted, around noon a craggy stretch of blue mountain broke through the clouds on the horizon. Inis Creig.

At my direction, we sailed to the side of the island where lay the beach and the trail leading up to my *tuath*. As we rounded the point and the familiar beach came into view, we saw the clan's two *curraghs* pulled up on the beach. Two foreign *curraghs* lay beside them.

"Pirates!" said the captain, shaking his head. "And by the look of the demon carved on their prow, I'd wager they're from Inis Rathlin. A nasty bunch of ruffians that ever you'd care to meet. Sure, and they've left a guard. Laddies, I canna land here."

The raiders had camped on shore, with at least three men sitting around a smoking fire. When they sighted our ship, they rose from their seats and walked down to the water's edge to eye us.

"Sail round to the north and put ashore where they can't see us," I said. "We can find our way back from there."

"Are you sure, laddie? I'm thinking it's too late for them in your *tuath*, for I'd bet my mother's tunic they've come to plunder the gold everyone knows lies hidden in the fort of the Carraig Beag. And when they're done with their looting and plundering and raping, they'll kill every last man, woman, and child up on that mountain—excluding them that's now slaves."

He knew of the gold of Crom Cruach? Had news of it spread so far and wide as even the northern coast of Ulster? To my ears, his grim prophecy rang true.

I caught Coll's worried glance. "You didn't bargain for this, Coll. You can return with the ship if you like, and I'll think none the worse of you."

He shook his head. "I go where you go."

"We'll go on," I said to the captain. "Sail beyond the next point and put us ashore there."

"Have it your way. It'll be your wakes, lads, na mine."

So we sailed parallel to the breakers, near the spot where so many years ago I'd pushed off from the beach in a shore *curragh* and entered a new life. When we passed the next point of land and were hidden from view, the captain put us ashore in water up to our chests. We waded to the beach, carrying above our heads our clothes, my cross, two spears for hunting, Coll's fiddle box, and our packs with some food and the rest of our belongings.

On shore we dressed and waved good-bye as the ship sailed away to the north. The captain promised to circumnavigate the island, tricking the pirates into thinking his business was with fish and not men.

I stood at last on the shores of Inis Creig. My glance climbed the slopes, to the forests above. What would I find up there? Only one thing was sure: My homecoming would be nothing like what I had envisioned.

We hiked south along the pebbly beach for a mile or so until we found a faintly remembered trail leading to the village.

"It's an hour's climb," I said. "At the top, this trail converges with the main one the pirates would take. Before the paths join, we must veer off into the undergrowth and hide."

Coll stared up the mountain and frowned. "Then what will we do?"

"Find out what's going on, I expect. After that, I don't know."

I threw the pack over my shoulders, grabbed the cross and spear, and we began our ascent. We climbed through the forest of oak, then of pine, heavy with the smell of juniper. I remembered it all. Once, we heard voices and ducked behind a low spreading yew, breathing quietly. The voices moved on, heading down the mountain.

When the slope lessened and we entered thick heather, I knew we had reached the top. Beyond the hedge would be the high meadow and home.

We left the trail and plunged through the undergrowth on the valley's western edge. Roundhouse tops occasionally poked into view. We climbed until the brush thinned and below us lay all the roundhouses and the valley of the Carraig Beag.

The clan had retreated to the fort, and the pirates of Rathlin surrounded it with four encampments. Each group had built upright log barriers to protect themselves from the fort's archers. I counted at least twenty-five men in each cluster, and by the look of their camp, I guessed they'd been there for some time. The fort's ring of sharpened poles, bound together with iron and leaning out at an angle, had prevented a direct attack. Several charred logs showed where the Rathlin had tried to set fire to them, but to no effect. Our archers would have made any such attack difficult.

On the plateau stood the dread idol—and the hope of riches that brought the pirates. I shuddered as I saw that ring of upright stones and the gold obelisk in the center, bright and harsh in the sun. It stuck out crookedly from the earth. The Bent and Bloody One. The stone of Crom Cruach. Even from this distance, even after all this time, I sensed its evil presence.

Inside the fort, men and women moved about. The women tended but a single cooking fire. Its smoke drifted lazily on the breeze. On the fort's perimeter, opposite the encamped pirates, the men of my clan lounged beside log shelters, keeping watch with swords and spears at the ready. Behind them stood the archers, staring down at their enemy. Not many clans were so used to the bow as the Carraig Beag. It made us a formidable foe. Deeper in were two horses, but no cows, goats, or sheep. They must already have been eaten. Farther toward the center, women huddled in quiet groups.

"How long do you think they've been here?" asked Coll.

"Hard to tell. The Carraig Beag have prepared long for such an attack. They can hold out for months. But not forever."

"Now we're stuck on the outside, and there's no way in. If we tried to cross the village and stand before that drawbridge, no one inside would look twice or lower it for us. The men of Rathlin would spot us. Then sure, we'd both be grain for the sickle."

"I know a way to get inside, a secret entrance."

Coll stared at me. "How's that possible?"

"Long ago when they built the fort, they started digging a well. But they broke through the ceiling of a cave. A tunnel leads under the mountain for over a mile until it opens onto the northwest slope. The entrance is covered in brush and hard to find. Even among our people, few know about it. I do because my father was Rí Tuath. It provides the fort with a hidden supply of water, game, and wood. If I can still find the opening, we can be inside the fort before nightfall."

Coll's eyes widened. "Good, I'm sore knackered from all this climbing."

We started back through the heather to the northwest, heading for the cave.

253

CHAPTER 31

The Wild Woman of Inis Creig

Until we left the heather for the pine forest, travel across the slope was difficult. But as we entered the shadows of the yews and junipers, the undergrowth thinned. We found a deer trail crossing the slope to the north. It had been years since I'd seen the cave entrance, and I remembered it dimly. As we neared the cave's vicinity, the mid-afternoon sun already cast thick shadows through the pines.

Between the evergreens ahead, we spied two men dragging a buck.

"Hide!" I whispered to Coll. "They could be Rathlin."

I slipped behind a yew's sprawling trunk, trying to recognize their dress. At once, I saw the familiar colors of our people's tunics, and the designs of forest, stream, and mountain our people were fond of. I began walking toward them.

Coll followed.

"Good day, men of the Carraig Beag. We are friends. We come in peace."

I guessed the pair was no more than sixteen and seventeen years. At my approach, they dropped their kill, took bows, and aimed their arrows at us. Just beyond, brush blocked the cave entrance.

"Stay, strangers!" said the tallest lad with brown hair and the beginnings of a mustache. "How do we know you're friends?"

"Long ago, I lived with the Carraig Beag. Tell me your names and I may be able tell you something about yourself."

The first one looked at his companion, a diminutive lad with red hair and a fidgeting, busy manner about him.

"Angus mac Dughall," said the first, his bow shaking a bit. "This is my brother Guaire. If you come any closer, we'll shoot you through."

"Your father isn't the Dughall who was once a slave in Bryton, who returned with tales from the wide world beyond? Not the same?"

"The very same." He looked at me, his eyes wide, and then at his brother.

"I knew him well. We had many a long talk."

"How do we know you're na with the Rathlin and just happen to know a name or two from our visits to Foclut? How came you here?"

"We came from Ulster by way of Coleraine. The ship we chartered dropped us off this very afternoon. It's been many years since I've walked this land, but I'm back. Inis Creig is my home."

"You wear the dress of druids. How do we know you're na druids of Rathlin, full of trickery?"

"We're not druids. We're priests of the one God who rules over all the earth."

"I know of no such God," said Angus.

The red-haired lad identified as Guaire shook his head and said in a squeaky voice, "Why should we believe you? No one sails to Inis Creig, 'cept they're lost. This land is cursed."

"Believe me because it's true. But tell me, who is Rí Tuath now?"

"Gahran mac Madadh."

I was afraid of that. Before I left, the talk had favored him. Gahran was conniving, self-centered, often averse to telling the truth. He always thought more of himself than of those around him and told everyone only what they wanted to hear. He had the worst qualities one could ask for in a leader. Yet the druids favored him.

"Is he as headstrong and full of himself as ever?"

"So you know him?" said Angus. "Then tell me your name. I remember no one who left Inis Creig."

"My name is not important. Besides, you wouldn't have known me. You would've been only five years old at the time. But were you the tiny lad from Eadan's *fine* who used to chase the goats inside their pen until Dolidh would come out with a stick and shoo you away? And you'd come right back and do it again?"

He stared at me and put down his bow. "So you *are* from our *tuath*?"

"I am. But there's something I must know, lads, for I've been away too long. How is the woman called Laurna? Is she well? Is she betrothed?"

Guaire, who had by now also lowered his bow, giggled. "Betrothed? No one would ever want to marry *that* woman."

"Why not?"

"Because she's cursed," said Angus, leaving his deer, both now walking closer to us. "She roams the island alone and throws rocks or shoots arrows at anyone who comes near her. But if you've been gone, you wouldn't know that, would you? We call her the wild woman of Inis Creig."

The words sank into my heart like a knife. I couldn't think. The wild woman of Inis Creig? Roaming the island alone? How could this be? What happened to her? Something was wrong here. She was not like that. Nothing could have made her like that. The only thought in my head now was that I must see her. I forgot about Jesu, my people, the rest of the *tuath*. All I wanted to do was see her. Nothing else mattered.

"Where is she? How can I find her? Tell me!"

They started at the sudden ferocity of my voice.

"She lives on the slopes about two miles north of here," said Angus, petting the beginnings of a mustache. "Between the mountain and the beach. She's found a cave among the rocks. But don't go there. She'll kill you."

I shook my head. She wouldn't shoot me. Would she? How could this have happened to her? I turned to go, walked a few paces, hesitated, and then came back.

"I'm going to her now. But tomorrow afternoon, I'll return and meet you by the entrance to the cave. I want you to bring Bohan with you. He's still alive, isn't he? Bohan? And his father, Teague?"

"Bohan is doing well though the *fine* he leads is struggling."

"He leads the *fine*?"

"He does. But 'tis down to twenty. Too much death. Too much illness."

"And sacrifice," added Guaire, frowning.

I didn't understand what he meant but didn't have time to ask. "What about Teague?"

"Stranger, sure it is, you've been gone a long while. Teague died so long ago we never knew him. Died of the fever, gored by a boar's tusk."

I should have expected as much. Even a younger man might have been overcome by the fever gripping him on the day I left. Yet the news hit me hard. He was my father. For long moments, I looked away, trying to control my grief. My silence even caused Angus and Guaire to exchange glances.

"But will you do as I ask? Will you meet me tomorrow afternoon with Bohan?"

"We'll do as you ask," said Angus. "But what should I say if Bohan questions me? Who should I say is asking him to come?"

I thought a moment. "Tell him, I'm the one who helped him kill the largest boar he'd ever seen. And lads, one more thing—"

But before I could finish, Angus blurted, "You canna be Taran mac Teague? The same of legend? He who was banished to the sea? Sure, and you loved Laurna and your brother was Bohan!"

I glared at them both with as fierce a glance as I could muster.

"You don't know who I am. If you have any love for your *tuath*, tell no one what you just said. Keep the secret of my meeting with Bohan tomorrow. 'Tis for the good of the clan. Trust me in this. Even after all these years, there are those who would do me harm. I came to help my people—to help *you*—and if I'm stopped, I cannot do that. You will understand eventually, and then you'll be glad you were quiet about this. Tell Bohan everything I told you. Will you do that for me?"

Angus's eyebrows turned up, and he gave me a weak smile. He bowed low, and so did his brother. They were looking at me with new eyes now.

"I really should think on it, but aye," said Angus. "I'll tell Bohan and bring him here."

"Please trust me. The Carraig Beag have been in my thoughts for twelve long years. I would do nothing to harm them."

Then Coll interrupted, saying, "Believe him, lads, as I've known Taran mac Teague for all of those last twelve years. He's as honest a man as ever you'll find. You can trust him."

Thus we parted, they to their buck and the cave, and we to find the place where lived the wild woman of Inis Creig.

We were losing the light, racing the dying sun. We'd traipsed back and forth over the ground Angus had indicated, but found no cave, nothing to hint she'd ever been here. Soon it would be dark, and I feared we'd lose our way. We had returned to the beach, close to the place where we arrived earlier that afternoon, trying to find some trail, any trail, to lead us to her. At last, we found an old deer path ascending the mountain from the shore's edge and there began to climb.

This was our third ascent of the day. My legs ached, and the heavy pack bit into my shoulders.

The trail climbed sideways under oak and elm and ash, their leaves already turning red and yellow, some beginning to fall. When the path entered the pines, it simply vanished. Again, our search seemed thwarted. But higher up the slope, the mountain itself pushed a pile of boulders and jagged stone to the surface, rock outcroppings battling with yews and juniper for territory. On a hunch, I led Coll in that direction.

We entered a maze of shadowy crevices and tunnels between high rock walls. Soon we'd have to make camp for the night. That meant one more day without seeing Laurna. I'd waited so long. Could I wait another day? We followed a dim path between two rocky crags until it forked. We chose one path, then clambered over slanting stone faces and plunged into a dark tunnel, only a sliver of fading daylight guiding us above.

To our rear, came a low growling.

I whirled. In the shadows crouched some kind of animal. It snarled then crept forward.

We backed up. We had our spears for protection, and I raised mine high, ready to thrust.

As it inched forward into a patch of fading light, I saw it was aged and limping. Its hair was nearly black. Underneath, I detected a tawny mane, mixed with white.

It was a dog. It limped closer, sniffed, and then stopped growling. It rose from its crouch, cocked its head, and whined. It started plodding toward us, slowly, painfully. Coll raised his spear to strike, but I shouted, "No, Coll! Don't!"

I dropped my spear and sat on my haunches. "Raef! Come here, boy."

He whined, limped up to me, licked my face, and then gave a short bark.

"How've you been, boy? Where's your mistress? It's been so long."

259

I hugged the dog, not expecting to find him alive. He must've been fourteen, near the end of his life.

"This was your dog?"

"I raised him from a pup. On the day I left, I asked Laurna to keep him."

"Then she must be close."

I couldn't part from him. I petted his thick mane while he whined, slobbered me with affection, and wagged his tail.

Finally, I stood and we strode on between the high rock walls, but now when we came to a turn, Raef became our guide. Eventually, he led us off the trail, up a slanting rock face to an opening under an overhanging ledge. There, the rocks yawned, the earth opened, and we found ourselves staring into a small, dead-end cave.

Empty, except for a firepit with the morning's coals still banked to one side and glowing.

Coll added wood and a fire soon lit up the interior.

Inside was a bed of pine needles, some dirty sheepskin blankets, a few spears, half a dozen clay jars stoppered with rounds of pine. One item in particular caught my attention. In the corner was a garment, folded neatly, clean and out of place. I unwrapped it—a ceremonial tunic. Sequins of shells and tiny brass rings lined the front, surrounded by a fishing net and a spear, outlined in thread and dyed. Curving, colorfully painted designs decorated each corner.

I sucked in breath. I was staring into the past, across more than a decade. This was the very tunic Laurna had been making for me when I left, my tunic to wear after I'd joined the council. I ran trembling fingers along the sequins. How often had she unwrapped it, looked at it, and thought of me? She hadn't forgotten me, that was plain. I folded the garment and returned it.

We sat at the entrance and waited, Raef beside me, occasionally licking my hands and face, shoving his muzzle into my neck. My mind kept returning to the tunic. Whatever else had happened, she'd kept the tunic—that promise of a life together, the one we never had.

Then Raef rose and padded down the rocks, leaving us alone.

Soon afterward, footsteps treaded the rocks below. I froze. What did the wild woman of Inis Creig look like? Would she still be my Laurna? The sun was almost gone. Heavy shadows claimed the rock warren. The footsteps stopped. Something moved in the darkness, then ducked back in and disappeared. I took one of the torches from the corner and lit it.

"Laurna!" I raised the torch high. "Come back."

An arrow whizzed past my head and clattered off the rocks above.

"It's me," I said again.

I ducked as another arrow flew by, missing me by several feet.

"Who are you?" came the voice I'd longed to hear. But it croaked as if ill-used to speech.

I stood. "Taran. It's Taran. Stop shooting."

"Your tricks won't work here. Away and chase yourself off!"

For one brief moment by torchlight, I had a glimpse of unkempt hair. A tunic, torn and dirty. Eyes, wild as a hunted animal's. She ran, crouched forward along the rocks below, clutching a bow, quiver, and pair of rabbits.

Then she disappeared into the shadows.

CHAPTER 32

A Bitter Homecoming

She was gone, and I raced down the rock slope after her with the torch. "Laurna! Come back. It's me—Taran!"

I ran along the narrow path until it split in two. I stood at the fork, undecided. Where had she gone? There. Movement in the shadows to the right. Raef. He limped toward me, slowly.

"Raef," whispered a hoarse voice in the dark. "Come back."

But Raef whined, padded up to me, and sat at my feet. When I knelt and petted him, he licked my face and wagged his tail.

From the shadows came a watchful silence. A figure stepped cautiously forward, and I gasped. I saw the face I had longed to see for so many years.

"Taran? Can it really be you?"

"I'm as alive as you."

Dropping her bow, quiver, and the rabbits she carried, she took a few steps, hesitated, then walked slowly toward me. She stopped, her eyes moist. She looked into my eyes, touched my face. She traced the outline of my cheeks, my forehead, my nose, as if to determine whether I were real or to remember what I looked like. Her tunic, ripped and torn, was smudged with what looked like dirt. A dark streak crossed one cheek. Her hair was wild and unkempt and a haunted look leapt between her eyes.

With my free hand, I reached and pulled a twig from her hair. Gone were the colorful braids and decorations. Gone was the playfulness, the ready smile, leaving behind only wariness, watchfulness. No wonder they called her a wild woman.

"Taran, your eyes . . . still brown and deep as a forest, but . . . serious. Your eyes are serious."

"'Tis the years, I expect."

"I've . . . waited." Her voice broke. From emotion? Disuse? "I didna marry. I had suitors, but didna marry. I knew you'd come back, hoped you'd come back. But I almost lost hope. And now you're . . . here. Am I dreaming?"

"No," was all I could say. I dropped the torch, went to her, and looked into her eyes. I drew my fingers over her cheek in a caress. Her hand shook as she took mine and pressed it lightly, hesitantly to her lips. Then I pulled her close.

When we finally parted, I asked, "Why are you living like this? What happened?"

She gazed at me, and the hint of a smile flickered across her face. But it was as if she'd grown so unused to the feeling, it was now foreign to her. Then that expression I remembered, that always filled me with such joy, grew and spread across her face, a smile that brightened even her eyes. This was the Laurna I'd remembered from so long ago. Yet at the corners of her eyes, I saw tears.

"I canna . . . canna talk now." Her voice choked, her eyes brimming. "Let's go to the cave."

I grabbed the torch, and we retraced our steps, clambered up the slope to where Coll waited. I introduced him as my most trusted friend and companion.

When Laurna saw us both in the firelight, she took a step back and a flicker of a frown crossed her face. "You wear the robes of druids. Are you druids then? Say you're na a druid, Taran."

"We're not druids. We're priests, but not bound to celibacy. On Ériu I found the one true God, Laurna, and I will tell you all about Him. He's sent a Son to earth that will save our people."

"You're really here. You really came back."

"I'm really here."

We hugged again. When we pulled apart, the tears came once more, and she looked into my eyes.

"I waited so long. I . . . I almost gave up hope." She paused as if searching for words. "You were becoming a . . . a ghost to me, a memory I struggled to hold onto. Sometimes, the memory . . . fled from me. More on some days than others. But you were all I had. The others—they abandoned me. It was only you. I kept going. But I feared someday, I would forget . . . even your face, the color of your eyes, the way you looked at me. Now you're here."

She hugged me close, clinging, her hands caressing my back. Then we kissed, and the feeling of her lips on mine, almost forgotten, returned. Their moist warmth filled me, warmed me, made me want to cry out. I'd found her at last. Slowly, she pulled away and laid a cheek beside mine. Tears wetting my skin. A whisper so soft, I barely heard it. "Oh, Taran."

When we finally parted, she wiped her tears and motioned for us to sit on the rock ledge.

I grabbed one of her hands and held it. "But how did you come to be in this state? Tell us the length and breadth of it."

"The sacrifices. The crops were failing. Always failing. The animals were dying. So the clan sacrificed. And I disagreed."

"Children?"

She nodded. "Given to Crom Cruach. The druids. 'Twas their doing."

Reluctantly, I let the warmth of Laurna's kiss, still lingering, depart. I balled one hand into a fist, pressing it slowly into the other. "How often? How many children?"

"Two each year. I've talked with so few in—maybe—two years. It's good to talk again."

"Is that how long you've been here? Two years? Alone? How did this happen?"

"Oh, Taran. I've longed to see you, to be with you. You were right. The druids have led us into darkness and death. 'Tis even worse than when you left. Crom Cruach does na bring blessings, only curses. Now nothing goes right for the Carraig Beag, and the only thing the druids can do is ask for more sacrifices."

It was as if the clouds opened after a long drought and her words poured out in a torrent. "Five years ago, they began yearly sacrifices. One child every year. And I was silent. Two years ago at the Lughnasa festival, in the twilight at the Circle of Stones, we gathered to sacrifice a goat. Then Cormag told us we must begin killing one child on the altar at Beltane and another at Samain. I walked right up to him and told him it was wrong, that Crom Cruach was evil. I told him straight to his face we should end the murder of innocent babies and instead throw The Bent and Bloody One, himself, over a cliff.

"I did the same as you, Taran. I couldn't abide their killing any longer. I spoke out in front of Cormag with all the *tuath* watching and hearing. But before they could meet to banish me to the sea, I grabbed a few things and fled here. When I did, the druid put a curse on me. Ever since, they've warned everyone away from me."

I looked at her, and my chest tightened. I squeezed her hand and brought it up to my lips. While I'd been comfortable, with companionship and plenty to eat and drink, she'd lived the last two years in isolation, scared and alone, an outcast for speaking the truth and standing up to the druids.

"Are you well, Laurna? I mean, after all that time alone?"

She looked at me and smiled. "I was lonely, oh so lonely. Terribly so. I thought I'd forgotten you, but I haven't. Now you're here. You're the cure for all my loneliness. I'll be fine now. I'm na crazy if that's what you mean. The others sometimes came to taunt me. They called me crazy, but I learned to harden myself against that.

"Once a man even surprised me here in my cave and tried to rape me—Doiurchu the druid, the pudgy wretch. But he got a knee, full in the groin, and Raef took a bite or two from one leg as he fled under a hail of rocks. After that, I let no man approach me without a warning shot or two. After word of Doiurchu's fate spread, no one else has come against me. If they had, they would have gotten worse."

It was all in self-defense. And, of course, the druids used that to make her into some kind of monster.

"Your brother did come to me on several occasions, bearing food. One other stood by me. He, among them all, still comes to me regularly with encouragement."

"Who?"

"Eadan mac Gaeadan. On occasion, he's brought a bit of news, a word of kindness, a loaf of bread. Once, he gave me an old tunic some woman cast off though I fear I've worn even that to tatters. He said his thoughts about Crom Cruach had changed, and he was inclined to agree with me. But he didna think he could ever approach the *comhairle* about it, na while Gahran was Rí Tuath. Gahran is like clay in the druids' hands."

"Eadan was always fair-minded. He thought the druids' influence too great."

"But you must be hungry, you and Coll. I've only two rabbits, but we can share."

"We have some bread and quite a bit of cheese."

"I haven't eaten bread or cheese in a year. I'll stoke the fire for a feast."

We built up the fire again, cooked and ate her rabbits, while Laurna had her fill of bread and cheese. But just as the darkness became complete and Coll was throwing another log on the flames, we heard the clatter of pebbles on the rocks below.

Laurna drew back from the fire and grabbed her bow. "No one ever comes here this late. I canna imagine who it might be. The Rathlin?"

Raef growled and fell into a crouch, ready to attack.

I reached for my spear.

"Who sneaks here in the dead of night?" Laurna raised her bow and aimed into the darkness below. "Speak, or I'll shoot you through."

"Don't shoot. It's Eadan mac Gaeadan."

Laurna lowered her bow.

I took the torch and clambered down the slope to meet him.

"Taran mac Teague." Eadan rushed toward me. "We thought you dead."

We hugged, beat each other on the back, then I held him at arm's length. He was as tall as I'd remembered, his black hair still touched his shoulders, and his brown eyes still bored into me. "I've had my share of adventures since leaving, but somehow, I never fell off the perch. It's good to see an old friend again."

We climbed back to the cave, where Eadan ducked to get his tall frame under the entrance. In his hands he carried a new tunic which he passed to Laurna. Then we sat by the fire and I introduced Coll.

"But you wear the robes of druids," said Eadan. "Is that what you are now?"

"We are not. We're priests of the one true God and His Son. But tell us how the siege is going. Are the Carraig Beag able to hold out?"

"A good question, that. Our supplies run low, for we canna bring enough game in through the cave, though we have a party out each day. But right now, we've a greater concern. Our *tuath* is on the eve of the worst disaster it's ever faced—and it'll come from our own druids."

"What do you mean?"

"As you know—or maybe you don't?—tomorrow night is Samain."

A shudder went through me. I feared instantly what he would say.

"These last few years the crops've been poor. Our cattle, goats, and sheep—all are sickly. The fishing parties return with empty holds. We've had so much sickness among the people, we're down to five *fines*."

Five *fines*! The *tuath* had lost an entire roundhouse since I'd left. The clan was shrinking, dying.

"As if that's na enough, raiders from the clan of Rathlin landed on our shores, and for the last two months they've besieged us. So we couldna harvest the fields. The Rathlin say they want only our gold, but their tongues lie. They want slaves—our young boys and women. Then they'll kill whoever's left. When they're done, nothing will remain of the clan of the Carraig Beag. Inis Creig'll be but a stretch of craggy rock in a lonely sea. And how, lad, do you think the druids have responded?"

I shook my head.

"They've put their hopes in appeasing Crom Cruach. The reason for our calamities, says they, is we have na given him enough sacrifice. The solution, says they, is more killing. So tomorrow night, when the spirits of the Otherworld are nearest, they've announced another *Oíche dar dáta Marú*."

I gasped. My mouth fell open.

Laurna whispered, "No!"

Coll looked at us, at our shock, at Eadan's grim face. "What is meant by 'The Night of the Killing'?"

In a low, steady voice, Eadan explained, "They plan to take one-third of the children—fifteen of our little ones!—and sacrifice them on the altar of Crom Cruach. Only that, says they, will appease the anger of the sun god, drive the raiders from Inis Creig, and restore us to prosperity. It happened once before, in my great-grandfather's time. Now the druids will do it again."

We were silent. It was inconceivable. The druids were about to bring down on the clan a disaster as bad as or worse than the Rathlin's invasion.

"Who have they chosen?" asked Laurna in a whisper.

"Five babes and ten older children. Bohan's daughter is one. And," Eadan's voice broke. "And . . . my son . . . Cailean."

It was a calamity beyond words. For a time we sat in the dark, unable to speak.

"What can anyone do?" whispered Laurna.

"I donna ken." Eadan's gaze held mine. "But when I heard from Bohan that you'd returned, I came here as quickly as I could."

"So Angus and Guaire delivered my message?"

"They did and when I, too, asked them to keep quiet about it, they did so. They're in awe of you, my lad. For them, you're a legend come to life. You should hear some of the stories they tell of your leaving, na all of them bad. Especially with the druids' killing of little ones these last years. When Bohan heard of your return, he wanted to come here right away, but felt it was too risky. He sends his greetings and his love. He's sorry for na believing you when you left. He couldna leave tonight. I, myself—I shouldna be here. The risk of someone discovering I'd gone out . . ."

"How does he feel about the druids now?"

"Last week, they told him his daughter Seàrlaid, a lass barely ten years old, will be sacrificed tomorrow. Since then, he's been sullen, brooding. I think he opposes them. But na publicly. Na yet. Before then he was already upset they'd taken so many children from his *fine*."

"Ten years old!" I exclaimed. "That's beyond anything ever asked of us before. The clan has only offered babies to The Bent and Bloody One."

"Everything's changed. Last year, they took a baby girl on Beltane, and a seven-year-old boy on Samain. My lad, a terrible cloud hangs over us. No one knows which child the druids will take next. They're killing the clan's future—our little ones! My son's but eleven."

"Eleven! I'm distressed for you, Eadan. And for the *tuath*."

"What can we do?" He raised his hands in despair. "They hold Gahran in their power. Sure it is, they've put a spell on him. And the inner circle, bewitched as well, goes along with Cormag. Among them, there's na one with backbone."

I thought a moment. "I must confront them."

They all turned to me with questioning glances.

"Perhaps that's why God has sent me here. Aye, tomorrow, on the night of Samain, I will confront them. Everyone will be present. All will hear me. The surprise will work in my favor. But in this, I must rely on God. Only on Him."

For a time, silence again descended over our group. By their looks, I knew they thought I was out of my head. Coll, who had witnessed God's provision, just appeared surprised.

Eadan said, "Of which god do you speak?"

Then I told them the story of the one true God and the Son He sent to earth as the final sacrifice to make us right with Him, and how Christ will lead those who believe to an eternity of peace and joy. When I'd finished, both Laurna and Eadan exclaimed they believed and wanted to follow this God and His Son. For they saw at once the truth, the peace, the joy, and the happiness the story promised. I'd witnessed the same response so many times on Ériu. Compared to the dread promises, the forbidding tales, and the demands of the druids' dark spirits, the God of Christ—this God of love, peace, and joy—was an easy choice.

"But how will this help you against the druids?" asked Eadan.

"Because it is the truth. Truth will win out over lies. It must. How? By God's hands alone, not mine. Whatever happens, I know this: I must confront them."

Laurna moved close against me by the fire, wrapping her arms around me, leaning her head against my shoulder. "I'm worried for you, Taran. You've just returned, and now I fear they'll take you away again."

"What else can we do?"

"Here's the worst of it." Eadan narrowed his eyes. "Even if you convince the druids to stop the sacrifices, we still have the Rathlin."

"Aye. It seems I've come home to a disaster beyond words. And the only thing left is to put our trust in God."

"He's right." Coll caught Eadan's glance. "Pátrick, our teacher, has done great miracles through his trust in God. This God is powerful beyond imagining."

"We've heard rumors of this man Pátrick," said Eadan. "And the tales leave us in awe. He was your teacher?"

"He was," said Coll. "For nearly twelve years, Taran and I followed him."

"You've given me hope. But I canna tarry here. Soon, they'll be changing the guard at the tunnel entrance inside the fort. I should return before the men of my *fine* give up the watch."

"But tomorrow, Eadan." I grasped his arm to stall him. "How can I enter the fort without being seen?"

"Come late in the afternoon when everyone's busy with preparations for Samain. Follow the cave to the ladder and go up the chute. It'll take you inside a hut. I or someone else'll be waiting there for you."

I nodded. We hugged and gripped each other's shoulders at arm's length. Eadan took a torch and walked off into the night.

CHAPTER 33

The Dread Night of Samain

The next day in the cave, I found time to sit alone and pray, but also to talk with Laurna. I cleaned her hair, and she put on the new tunic Eadan had given her the night before. After this, she looked less like the wild woman and more like my lass Laurna. Only then did I see the passage of time in her and was confronted by this reality: The girl I'd remembered was gone. I'd left her a youth and returned to find a young woman ill-used by the years. I must admit, seeing her mortality moved me to melancholy.

In late afternoon, we left Laurna's cave, but something—a feeling, a thought, I'm not sure what—told me to return and get the heavy crucifix. With the cross over my shoulder, we finally quit the rock warren. Laurna led us across the slope, and soon we stood at the entrance to the cave leading to the fort. All of us, Laurna included, stepped inside the clammy dark.

"No matter what happens tonight," she said to me, "I must go with you."

Inside the cave's mouth, we started a fire from the ashes still banked and smoldering, then took torches from a pile on the floor and lit them. A dark tunnel beckoned, twisting deep into the mountain. I'd never followed the cave path and found the way difficult. We clambered around numerous mounds, spikes and daggers of wet rock reaching from the ceiling and growing from the floor, sometimes meeting to form shiny, bulbous columns. Once we passed a roaring stream that crashed down from a high dark crevice, roiled into a small lake, then disappeared into the mountain depths. From this, the fort could draw an endless supply of water.

At last, we met a rough log ladder reaching from a square opening above. I climbed up inside a crude chute lined with pine logs, using one hand to hold the ladder and the other to hang onto the heavy cross. On top, the chute opened into a small hut, where I threw my cross onto the rocky floor, then pulled myself up.

The noise of iron clattering on rock surprised a portly, red-haired man, sitting in the corner with a sword across his lap.

"Bohan!" I said, as the others emerged behind me.

He stood, ran to me, and we hugged, beating each other on the back.

"I never expected to see you again, brother. Last night Eadan told me everything."

"You're looking well, Bohan. A grand man for the pan, perhaps, yet looking well. I hear you're head of the *fine* now, with responsibilities. How is the *fine?*"

"In grave trouble. But I'm glad to see you. Powerful glad indeed. Especially on today of all days. You seem more dignified than when you left. Perhaps more . . . serious?"

I laughed. "If I appear more serious, I expect 'tis the years of hard travel and even harder study that's done it. Now tell me about tonight."

"I heard about your plan—some vague idea of standing up to them, alone. If you call that a plan, I donna ken what to say. It's flying mad. But somebody must do something. Tonight they'll sacrifice my daughter Seàrlaid, for—aye, they chose her! If you can do anything to stop this, I'm with you. Others will be too. Some of us have been talking these last years—quietly, secretly—and the words you left us with still ring in our ears. You donna ken how much your words have grown here. Taran, my brother, a terrible darkness *has* settled on us. I fear what it's done. No one's willing to stand up to the druids. Their power . . . grows."

The weight, the grief, in his voice, overwhelmed me. I felt inadequate and unprepared for what lay ahead—whatever it was—for I really didn't know. I gripped his shoulder, silently praying to God for help.

Bohan hugged Laurna, glad to see her in a better condition than the last time they'd met. I introduced Coll.

"But the sun is low, and you must come quickly," he said. "We'll hide you in a wood cart under blankets and place it near the standing stones. Two men of my *fine* are charged with feeding the perimeter fires. I trust them for they, too, will lose children tonight. They know the plan. You'll be able to hear everything that's said, and when you think it's time to do—whatever you have in mind—you can leave your hiding place. But I think you've gone daft, my brother. 'Tis a brave and noble thing, but quite mad. Flying mad."

"My trust now lies in God alone. Whatever happens tonight, happens according to His will."

"I donna understand that."

I put a hand on his shoulder. "I'll explain later. Perhaps we should go to the Circle now?"

Bohan nodded. He peered outside the hut to check for passers-by, then herded us into a wood cart. He threw a rough blanket over us, heavy with the smell of smoke, and we settled to wait among the logs.

After a time, someone climbed into the wagon's seat, reins slapped, and horse's hooves clomped. Our cart jerked forward, jiggling and swaying as it crossed the fort's rocky ground. The wagon bed tilted while it climbed the plateau to the Circle of Stones, and then stopped.

Above us, a man's rough voice whispered, "Be still now and wait. You're just outside the Circle." Then we heard his voice no more.

Long moments later came the shuffling and slapping of many feet passing by. The *tuath* was gathering in the center around the idol of Crom Cruach, their voices low and somber. Inside our cart the sunlight dimmed, then went dark. Yards away, someone lit the fires, and their glow cast flickering shadows through the blanket's coarse weave.

Then Cormag, the chief druid, called from a distance, ordering silence. The sound of his voice awakened memories of dread ceremonies from long ago. Remembering again the feeling of darkness that touched my soul at such times, I shuddered.

I lifted the blanket and peered through slats at the top of the cart. We were unattended. To either side of us stood two of the six pillars. I had a clear view of Cormag climbing to his position on the center rock pedestal. He seemed thinner, if that was possible, but I could never have forgotten his pale forehead, always glistening with sweat. Those lifeless, pink eyes. That dead expression. And that tall, gaunt frame, a bit more hunched by the years.

273

I shuddered again, feeling as if I'd left only yesterday. Beside Cormag lay a great pile of timbers—perhaps ten times larger than normal—stacked and ready for burning, with more wood piled alongside. The heap was so great they had to build it beside, not on top of, the altar.

Cormag lifted one hand and scanned the assembly. "We gather before Crom Cruach, the spirit of the sun, on this night of Samain, when the spirit portal is open. We come in the time before day gives way to night, in the time before he sleeps, when his terrible anger is weakest, to plead for his blessings upon us and to turn aside his wrath with living blood.

"I call upon you, Crom Cruach, great god of the sun! On this night of Samain we bring you the greatest sacrifice we have ever brought. By this offering, we beg you to avert your anger. Give us instead your blessing—deliverance from the siege, health for our people, abundance from our crops, and fertility for our animals.

"Now bring the offerings!" Cormag rubbed his hands together.

Fat, black-haired Doiurchu and another druid led in the string of ten older children, bound together with ropes at the waists, their hands tied in front. When I saw their faces, my chest tightened. Most were crying. They'd lived all their short lives putting their trust in the clan. Now this clan, their family, had turned against them. They'd become—not children of the *tuath*, not the progeny who carried our future—but offerings to be slain and burned before a terrible demon.

Doiurchu stopped beside the altar. The other three druids—yellow-haired Mungan among them—came carrying the five babies in their arms. These small lives they set upon the ground near the others. Atop the long rectangular altar was an ornate-handled dagger, its blade-edge glistening in the firelight. Two of the babies wailed.

"To you, Crom Cruach, dread god of the sun, do we dedicate these lives tonight. And now—we dance!"

The assembly began to move around the center. They circled, slowly at first, around Cormag and his druids. Around the gold obelisk of Crom Cruach, glimmering in the firelight, leaning crookedly from the ground. Around the mammoth pile of logs laid for the fire. Around the babies on the ground. Around the children huddled close and frightened. Around the long stone altar holding its gleaming dagger.

Outside the Circle, opposite our position, someone beat on a *bodhrán*, and the drumbeat increased the pace. The moving bodies circled faster. They writhed and stomped and waved their hands. I remembered the old pull of Crom Cruach's demon allure. The flirtation with madness. Losing oneself in wildness. The lust, not for a lover, but for the sight of blood. The desire for death—anybody's death—rising up like bile.

I felt Crom Cruach's evil almost as a physical presence, hovering over the Circle of Stones. I looked away, said a prayer, and then turned back. The prayer released me, strengthened me against it.

The dancing went on, and the people of my *tuath* circled, giving themselves up to their darkest inner selves. A few who danced appeared to do so half-heartedly, perhaps out of duty, not conviction. Among these, the figures of tall Eadan, portly Bohan, and white-haired Dughall.

Finally, Cormag called for the dancing to stop. Again, he slid his thin frame up to the pedestal.

"It's time for the first sacrifice. Bring the child Cailean."

Eadan's head snapped around and looked in our direction, his forehead lined with worry.

I swallowed, threw the blanket aside, grabbed the crucifix, and jumped to the ground.

Coll followed.

"Put him on the altar," ordered Cormag.

I began walking between the outer stones toward the crowd at the Circle's edge. I held the cross before me in both hands. Coll was there beside me. My heart was pounding in my chest so hard I thought it might burst through.

The two druids forced Eadan's son onto the stone table. Cailean was tall and thin like his father. His face was pale, and glistening wet streaks ran down each cheek. His eyes were wide, and his glance bounced between his father, the druids who held him prisoner, and back to his father. As he caught Eadan's gaze, his brow wrinkled in a final, desperate question.

Coll and I entered the crowd's outer edge. My friend went before me, touching shoulders, making way.

People turned, saw me, and then shrank from us, their eyes wide. A path opened.

Mungan and Doiurchu tied Cailean flat on his back to iron rungs embedded in the four corners of the altar.

"Three deaths, three!" called out Cormag. "A hammer to kill once. A knife to kill twice. A fire to kill thrice! Three deaths, three!"

Doiurchu bent, grasped the long handle of an iron sledge, and lifted it off the ground. One end carried a pointed wedge of heavy iron, meant to smash rocks, now used for the heads of children.

Mungan tied Cailean's forehead to the altar with a leather thong. Under the strap, the boy twisted his head toward Eadan, his young cheeks pale and drained, lips open, eyes wide, his glance flicking between Eadan and the druids.

Doiurchu raised the sledge over his head.

"Stop!" I shouted, walking ever closer. "Stop this travesty."

Now everyone turned. All saw us. We must have appeared like ghostly apparitions—two strange holy men, walking with dignity, carrying a large symbol no one had ever before seen, its ornate metal flashing golden in the firelight. Some in the crowd cringed and backed away. Others stared, their eyes wide. One old woman fell on her knees and bowed to us.

Doiurchu dropped the sledge. Cormag took one step off the pedestal and stumbled. He stared at us, his mouth open.

"There will be no killing of children here tonight!" I shouted into the silence. "I come to challenge the right and the power of these druids—by the one true God of the World, the Maker of all things, the One who brings life, not death."

"Who . . . ? Who . . . are you?" Cormag's voice came barely audible through thin, tight lips. His eyes widened, glowing pink by firelight. From fear? Surprise?

"I am Taran son of Teague, and I come tonight to stop the Carraig Beag from a ceremony of evil that will destroy the *tuath*."

Fingers pointed and heads leaned together. People whispered to each other, no doubt recalling my banishment years ago. The crowd became like a forest where the wind blows suddenly on a still, clear night and the leaves rustle against one another, a forest of frightened, surprised, desperate whisperers.

Cormag stared, perhaps not believing his eyes, for I must have seemed to him like an apparition from the dead. But when he spoke, his voice had grown a wee bit stronger. "By what right do you come here—you, an outcast banished to the sea?"

Twelve long years ago, before I left, both Laurna and my father had reminded me of the right of *Beart Uasal*—that if I did some great deed, and the news of it echoed throughout the land, I might be forgiven the druids' judgment. I now invoked that privilege.

"By the right of *Beart Uasal* and by the power of the God Most High whom I worship, He who rules over all things. Crom Cruach is a fraud, a false god, a demon. And I can prove it."

Gasps echoed around me.

"Crom Cruach is a false god!" I shouted, louder. "Because of him, you've given yourselves over to evil. Stop and think what you're doing! You are killing your own children. You're destroying your future. And what do you receive in return? A dim prospect without descendants, an empty household where the children don't play and the babies don't cry. And after you sacrifice your young ones to The Bent and Bloody One, do your crops improve? Do your animals produce more milk? Is the harvest, the hunting, or the fishing any better? Nay, it never is.

"Has the Bent One prevented the Rathlin from invading and laying siege to you? Nay, he has not. Crom Cruach deceives you. Have you ever wondered why the sun does nothing but rise in the morning and set in the evening? Has he ever once changed his path? Has he ever once made a different choice? He has not! For it's a dumb, created thing. Nothing but a ball of light in the sky that comes up and goes down. And this gold-covered stone before us—this abomination representing the sun—it's a *demon*!"

The crowd murmured and gasped.

"So I come today to bring you news of the true God, of the One who created everything that is. He created the sea, the mountains, the land, and, aye, even the sun. He created all that lives and breathes. And this one true God does not require sacrifices like Crom Cruach because my God has already made a single, final sacrifice on our behalf—and it was *His* very Son that He offered up for us some four hundred years ago.

"This Son walked the earth as a man, then was killed for us and put in a tomb. But three days later, He rose from the dead. His name was Jesu. And everyone who believes in Him will see an eternity of peace. My God brings the end of sacrifices. He doesn't require the deaths of children. He brings instead joy and peace, a better way to live, and the promise of eternal bliss. *That* is the news I bring to my *tuath*, my clan of Inis Creig, my home. This is the God I now worship. Your god, Cormag, is a fraud. He's not a god at all. He's a *demon*!"

"You canna prove any of this." Cormag looked at one person in the crowd, then another, his eyes pleading. "Crom Cruach is greater than these myths you spout. There's na such God as you claim. I say He has na such power. I spit on your God." He stepped toward me and spat. His spittle landed on my shoe.

I prayed silently. I had only the vaguest idea of what I would do next. Then words I hadn't planned escaped my mouth. "You have challenged my God. So let us see who is the greater, this idol of stone or the One who made the world. Stand aside, druids, while I approach The Bent and Bloody One."

With widened eyes, the druids slunk from the altar and the idol of Crom Cruach.

Before me, the slab of gold-covered stone stuck crookedly from the ground. But what was this? The gold overlay was separating from the stone beneath it. At the seams, on the top and on the sides, where the pieces of gold had once tightly joined, small dark cracks opened. A few cracked strips of gold testified to failed repairs.

"Lord God in heaven!" I prayed aloud. "Your power and name have been blasphemed, Your very existence questioned. Lord, in the name of Christ, Your Son, show these men and women who You are."

I raised the heavy metal cross and swung with all my might in the direction of the largest crack. At that instant, it felt like some greater force guided my arms, and it wasn't me in control, for the point found the exact middle of the crack. It struck and slid into place, going deep with a loud splintering. The front gold plate broke off, fell away.

I jumped aside as it landed with a thud and puff of dust at my feet. Beneath the plate, mold had blackened the stone, where rain leaked behind. Swimming in the mold were thousands of white worms. I raised my weapon, swung again, and the left plate and top section fell away as a single piece. I moved to the back, swung, and with a single blow that plate, too, and the smaller right plate, fell to the ground and split in two.

Dust rose in a cloud around me.

The stone's face now lay entirely exposed. The gold plates splayed over the ground on three sides. The idol's surface boiled with white worms.

"Behold your god for what he is—a spirit of evil, death, and corruption."

Silence settled over the plateau as everyone stared at the writhing, squirming tower. I saw wide eyes, crumpled foreheads, dropped jaws. The worms, the gold plates on the ground, transfixed them. They gaped at Cormag, then me, then Cormag.

Then like a wind rippling across still, calm waters, piling up waves before the coming storm, whispers and murmurings swept through them. Wide eyes narrowed, turned toward the druids. Jaws closed and lips tightened. Fingers pointed at Cormag, at Mungan, at Doiurchu—shaking, trembling fingers on hands soon turned to fists. It was anger directed not at me, but at the druids. For truth had upended their world.

Cormag's eyes, normally pink, appeared red in the firelight. His wide-eyed gaze flicked between me, the squirming white worms, and the crowd. The throng was becoming more unruly by the moment. He tried to gain control, pointed a bony finger at me, but his voice croaked. "Seize the . . . the interloper. He has . . . has defaced Crom Cruach and must die . . . he and the other one."

"Die he will *not*," came another, louder voice. Eadan's. "Taran shows us the truth. Crom Cruach is a fraud!"

"His stone's full of worms," said Bohan. "He's a fraud, a god of corruption."

"The druids are frauds," shouted a third person. "They've killed our children for, for—nothing!"

"Crom Cruach is a lie. The druids have lied to us," called another.

A voice from the past spoke up, raspy and deep. It was Gahran. "This one has destroyed our god." He pointed around his large belly at me. "He must die."

"Gahran, you're always with the druids," called a woman. "Sure now, and you've helped in this. Our children—what did they die for? For nothing!"

"For nothing, aye," said a man. "Crom Cruach is dead. He canna be the god of the sun. We've been sore deceived. By Cormag and you, too, Gahran."

Gahran opened his mouth, but the crowd's shouting grew louder, drowning him out. The throng swayed back and forth, for the storm had come and piled up the waves, toppling them over. They broke now with crashing, roiling foam, threatening to destroy anything in its path.

One after another they shouted:

"Kill the druids."

"Aye, kill them who've taken our children. And Gahran."

"Nay. Throw them over the wall. All of them."

"Aye. Give them to the Rathlin."

"Let the Rathlin have them."

The noise of the mob—aye, our clan had become a mob!—grew so loud, with so many voices calling for revenge, it was impossible to speak. They swept forward, grabbed the five druids and Gahran, and dragged them from the stone circle. I hadn't expected this, but in retrospect, the druids made it inevitable. They'd forced people to sacrifice their children, and when those deaths were shown to be for naught, when the idol upon which the people had built their lives was proven false, nothing would stay their revenge.

Like a thing alive with eyes of burning torches held aloft, the crowd swarmed from the Circle of Stones and crossed to the drawbridge. They lowered it partway then forced the six over the edge.

The Rathlin had watched these events, and when the druids and Gahran were dropped over, they were waiting. A trail of torches showed where they led the captives—to the center of their camp. Then we lost sight of them.

Back within the Circle of Stones, Eadan, Bohan, and the other parents released their children and retrieved their babies. Laurna ran up, throwing her arms around me.

The realization of what had happened settled over the Carraig Beag. After they threw the druids and their Rí Tuath to the Rathlin, they trickled back to the center of the stones where I waited. Gradually as if in unspoken agreement, everyone gathered before me. I had exposed the fraud and deposed the druids. They were left sheep without a shepherd.

I stepped to the platform where Cormag had recently stood. "Men and women of the Carraig Beag. You are my people, my *tuath*, and I rejoice that this unspeakable evil has left us. But you must not thank me. You must thank the God Most High, the ruler of the heavens, for He answered my prayers."

Then I prayed, thanking God for destroying the idol and revealing what it was, thanking Him that our children were spared and the druids' rule was over.

"Tomorrow you must choose a new Rí Tuath to lead you, a strong leader who speaks the truth, who cares more for you than for himself. One who serves the light, not the darkness. Then we must face the Rathlin, for the *tuath* is still in danger."

Many nodded in agreement. Someone said my name, and I shook my head. Other voices whispered the name of Eadan.

"But before we leave here tonight, I ask you to destroy this idol. Before we sleep, we must pound this evil stone into rubble!"

"Aye, we'll break the thing to bits," cried a voice. Others shouted agreement.

Someone took up the iron sledge meant to smash the heads of the children and, one-by-one, men began striking the rock with all their might. Black pieces fell away, exposing a white interior. Soon, another sledge appeared, and they attacked the stone from two sides. Blow upon blow fell on the crooked slab, and each man, and some of the women, had a turn. Whole chunks dropped off. The attacks increased. It was as if, by destroying the symbol of Crom Cruach, they purged themselves of the evil and darkness the idol had brought them.

The heavy blows rang and echoed between the cliffs surrounding the plain of the fort. Dust rose in a cloud until I could taste it. Soon it was no longer a towering stone, but a pile of broken rubble. Then the men pounded the pieces of rubble. What remained were only splinters, small chips. This too they beat until it became powder.

Crom Cruach was dead indeed.

But even as I gazed at the pummeled remains, I thought about the next day and the Rathlin. They were too many to fight. Eadan had said the supplies were running dangerously low. Somehow we had to convince them to leave. But how?

CHAPTER 34

The Beginning of the New

The next morning, the Carraig Beag's inner circle broke tradition and met, not in the center of the stones, but on the plateau's perimeter, under the Rathlin's watchful eyes. They decided their business quickly, speaking low while holding their spears, swords, and arrows ready. Then they gathered the clan and announced the new Rí Tuath was Eadan.

Everyone was pleased and went to congratulate him. As the men returned to their posts, Eadan approached me.

"What're we to do now, Taran? This siege must end. Our stores are almost gone. We've na any cattle or goats left to kill. Our cheese is gone. What game we bring through the cave canna satisfy all. And bringing in wood is so difficult we keep but a single fire. Twice now outside the fort, Rathlin hunting parties almost caught us. Our barley's nearly exhausted and then—no porridge. What're we to do?"

"I must go to the Rathlin."

He stared at me. "And do what? What can you do, alone, that we've na already tried?"

"I'll ask them to leave."

Eadan gave me a crooked smile. "Taran, lad, have the years made you go glipe in the head? Why ever would they do that?"

"Because I'll offer them what they want."

He opened his hands in a question. "What?"

"I'll give them the gold of the fallen idol."

He was silent a moment. "I'd have to talk with the council. What if they donna agree?"

"They must. Of what use is the gold to them now? Will they bow down to dust and gravel? Or to some gold plates on the ground? They'll never again worship Crom Cruach."

"Aye, but will the Rathlin accept only gold? They came also for slaves."

"There are ways to convince them."

"What ways?"

"Leave that to me."

Eadan reluctantly agreed, then left to regather the council for the first meeting under his leadership. For a time, they argued and discussed. Then Eadan returned. "We approve the deal, but on one condition. We're concerned that even if you convince the Rathlin to go, we face a hard winter. Our food will soon be gone. How will we live?"

"So what's the condition?"

"We keep enough gold to take to Ériu and purchase animals, grain, mead, and supplies before winter."

"Agreed. Then I go now to bargain."

After Eadan gave the orders to bring the gold plates to the bridge, he joined me. Men lowered the drawbridge halfway to the ground.

I knelt at the edge and shouted down, "Men of the Rathlin, I would discuss terms. Send me your leader so we can talk."

Soon a tall, thin man with a sparse, red beard, a helmet of hammered iron, and a chest of leather armor, stepped from the group of warriors. With him came a small, stocky man with a blunt head and a face covered with a dark beard. Unlike most of our clan, the men of Rathlin favored beards. The soldiers behind him were on alert now, swords and spears held at the ready. But this clan was unused to the bow and carried none.

The red-bearded man looked up at me and shouted, "What do you want? There's na we'd hear from you *bashtoons* but that you'd lower your bridge and surrender."

"I would talk terms of your departure."

He laughed. The others behind him laughed too.

"Sure, and you called me here to make jests? You must think me a fool."

"I'm serious. I'm prepared to offer you some of what you came for."

The humor departed from his face. "Are you having me on?"

"I am not."

"What's your name? I canna deal with a man 'less I know his name."

"I am Taran mac Teague. What are you called?"

"Faolan mac Cè. But if we're to talk, you must come down. I canna discuss this while shouting up at you."

Eadan, who waited behind me, whispered I should not, that it was a trap. But I said to Faolan, "Do you give me your word that no matter the outcome, you will allow me to return safely to the fort?"

"I give you my word."

I threw my feet over the edge of the bridge, hung for a moment by my fingers, then dropped to the ground.

As Faolan stepped forward, he eyed the drawbridge, perhaps searching for archers, then looked at me. We shook hands. Beside him was the short, dark man identified as Cathal. I offered my hand to him, but he folded his arms in front of his belly. Then Faolan drew us back twenty yards from the fort until I was surrounded by his men. They were a rough-looking bunch, indeed.

"What offer do you bring, Taran of the Carraig Beag? And now I see you're wearing the dress of the druids. Would you be a druid then?"

"I am not. I'm a priest of the one true God who created both heaven and earth."

"I know of no such God."

Cathal then spoke up in a high-pitched voice. "I recognize this man. 'Twas he we saw last night. 'Twas he who attacked the gold stone with that mighty weapon and then the gold fell away and their druids were thrown over. Beware, Faolan! There's magic afoot here."

Faolan squinted at me. "Were you the one who broke the stone and overthrew the druids?"

"'Twas I. But what I did came from the power of my God, not from myself."

Faolan frowned and looked at Cathal. "Who is this God you keep speaking of? Would I be hearing of Him?"

"Have you heard of Pátrick, the one who brought the news of this God and His Son to Ulster and Leinster?"

Faolan narrowed his eyes. "Indeed, I have. He must carry a great deal of magic to have done the deeds they tell of. What of it?"

"I walked with him. I was one of his followers."

Cathal gasped, then both men fell silent. Cathal fidgeted, hiding his hands behind his back, scratching his beard, then holding them in front, before swinging them back again. Then he said in his high squeal, "If he's walked with Pátrick, the magician, he knows his magic and his ways. I've heard of what this Pátrick has done, and I fear him, I do—if this one here can do half the same. Last night this one destroyed their god, and now I fear he comes to destroy us too."

We were silent as Faolan appeared to think. "Are you a sorcerer? Have you come to cast spells on us?"

"I'm merely a priest of the one true God. I come only to bargain."

More silence. Then Faolan said, "What have you to offer?"

"Some of the gold from the idol. In exchange, we ask you to leave this island and never return."

Faolan frowned and crossed his arms. "We came here for *all* the gold. And for slaves. And for anything else belonging to this *tuath* we desire. We didna camp here for two months to take only a wee portion."

"But I offer you a chance to take home some of that gold right now. You already have six slaves, dropped over the wall last night. Is that not enough?"

"One of them, the albino, was too old and thin—also troublesome—to be of any use to us. And I didna like his eyes. His corpse lies rotting a doddle away in the field."

Cormag. They'd killed him.

"But still, you have five slaves. Do you want to risk waiting us out and sailing the stormy seas of winter when you can have most of what you came for right now?"

Faolan was silent, perhaps thinking again. "You're a fine talker, Priest. But we must have everything we came for."

It was my turn to frown. "I warn you, I'm not here simply as a priest of my God, but as a trusted friend of Forga mac Dallán, the Rí Cóicid of Ulster." I pulled the Talisman of Ulster from my tunic and held it in front of me. "I assume you know what this is?"

Faolan took it and turned it over. His eyes narrowed. Now he frowned.

Cathal saw it and fidgeted all the more, scratching his beard and trying unsuccessfully to find a place to rest his hands. He opened his mouth to speak, but Faolan struck him in the arm with his fist and he was silent.

"I've heard of it. And this is it, I reckon. How'd you come by it?"

"Like I said, I'm a personal friend of the king. He gave this to me recently before I left Emain Macha to come here. You don't bow to him, but on the other hand, you don't want to make him your enemy. He's a powerful king with many men under his command, and his lands are only a morning's sail from yours."

"He has Forga's talisman!" squealed Cathal, unable to hold his peace any longer. "He carries the magic of the king's druids on him! He's dangerous, Faolan. Much harm can he do us. I say give him what he wants. If we don't agree, he'll use his magic, or he'll tell the Rí Cóicid, and then we'll have made a great enemy. We canna fight him."

Faolan frowned and struck him again, silencing him. "What do you offer us?"

"One half of what covered the idol. It's a goodly sum. Enough, when combined with the slaves, to make your siege worthwhile."

Faolan smoothed his greasy beard then asked me to wait while he talked with the others. From the midst of his warriors came raised voices and much waving of hands.

He returned with a scowl.

"We'll take three parts of the gold out of four. That's our demand. If it donna please you, the siege goes on."

I pretended to hesitate, noting their worn, ragged tunics. "Agreed. But after the exchange, you must depart at once. And leave us our ships."

He nodded. "We'll keep the bargain. We've no wish to make an enemy of Forga mac Dallán."

Thus, early in the afternoon, the Rathlin took their gold, broke camp, and filed down the trail out of the valley. But Eadan, ever cautious, sent observers through the hidden cave to see if they would keep their word. When the watchers reported the foreign ships had sailed away to the south, our men lowered the drawbridge, everyone rushed from the fort, and Eadan called for rejoicing.

I remember the events that followed as a blur of celebration and activity. That very night, we held a small feast, drinking half of what remained of the meager store of mead and ale. Before the assembly, I thanked God for what He had done.

After we ate our fill, Coll brought out his fiddle and the dancing began. The Carraig Beag marveled at the songs issuing from this strange, new instrument. Magical notes cut the chill mountain air and echoed away, vibrating and shimmering, carried on a crisp breeze across the valley. Then everyone, for the first time in two months, slept in their own roundhouses with their *fines*.

In the bright light of a clear, rainless morning, we found the village ill-used by the pirates. The women set about to cleaning and the men to making repairs. On the next few evenings, I preached the news of God's Son, Jesu. Having seen with their own eyes the greatness of the God who rescued them from disaster, the Carraig Beag were eager to hear the message. Much to their surprise, now they discovered, with tears of happiness, this God wished to rescue them not only from the troubles of this world, but also for an eternity of peace and joy in the next. After years of grim threats and harsh demands from the druids, it was an easy message to deliver. By the sixth day, Coll and I accompanied three entire *fines* to a mountain stream, and we baptized them.

Eadan was concerned for the approaching winter. So after waiting a week to be certain the pirates would not return, he sent an expedition to Coleraine to buy animals, food, and supplies. We normally traded with Foclut, but a village so small would be unable to part with the great sum of goods we needed. Because I knew Forga mac Dallán and the country of Ulster, Eadan asked me to go along. After just arriving, I was reluctant to leave. But for the good of the clan, I agreed. Laurna insisted on accompanying me, and I was glad for her company.

Thus did our two ships, left unmolested by the Rathlin as agreed, sail back to the coast of Ulster. There we bartered for cattle, sheep, goats, bales of oats and barley, barrels of mead and ale, and great wheels of cheese. We had to visit many *tuatha*, traveling far inland with hard bargaining to gather enough to see our clan through winter. For no one *tuath* was willing to part with much, and many were leery of gold as payment.

In the process, I was able to introduce Laurna to Eivhir and her husband, Rí Tuath of their clan. And a tall, handsome couple they made, with one young son, running bare-bottomed and imperial through their roundhouse, and a second child on the way. We had a fine reunion, complete with Coll's fiddle music, and on the evening of our departure, they put on for us a great feast.

We returned on the winds of the first winter storm, unloading animals, barrels, crates, and sheaves. We pulled the boats high on shore just as a cold, driving rain fell. The wind tore at our clothing, and the sea in the harbor beyond the breakers roiled in angry tumult.

With the men back in the village, I requested the Circle of Stones be brought down. Eadan agreed, and one day we felled a number of pines. Then we pulled down the stone pillars, rolled them over logs to the lip of the fort at the rim of spikes, and left them lying flat as additional barriers against future attack. The last remnant of the cult of Crom Cruach was gone.

In the following months, more and more people heard the message Coll and I taught, until all the *fines* believed and entered the great clan of God Himself. Each Sunday, we held a service, complete with Mass and the Eucharist. When we discovered it difficult to meet under constant threat of rain, Eadan directed the men to build a church on the very site where Crom Cruach's crooked stone once stood. Before the worst of the winter cold and rain, we had a great log building inside the fort, large enough to hold all the *tuath* at once, the first of its kind on Inis Creig.

The days lengthened, flowers bloomed, and breezes blew mild and sweet across our high valley. Then we prepared for a day of great joy—my marriage to Laurna. On the evening before the ceremony, as was the custom, Laurna invited me to her *fine*, where she cooked me a goose, stuffed with spices, onions, and sweet bread, and together we ate it.

When I returned to my roundhouse, some children had washed and brushed Raef. He met me with a wagging tail and a short bark. Even he seemed excited about the coming wedding, though maybe a bit embarrassed by the daisies they'd tied behind his neck.

The next day, everyone gathered in the church, still smelling of new-cut pine. Bouquets of loosestrife, orchids, and pennyworts stood in tall clay pots, brightening the corners of the room and filling the air with sweet perfume. Laurna was a picture to behold, gowned in white, bordered by green and gold cloth. A wreath of daisies and eyebrights topped her long, tawny hair. Rings of eyebrights bound her wrists, and a rope of tiny brass bells danced around her waist.

Coll performed the ceremony, and his normally somber face broke a smile throughout. I stood beside her, with all the clan beaming behind us while he spoke the words I had so often spoken to join other couples. I could not hold back tears as I looked deeply into her blue eyes and said, "By the power that Christ brought from Heaven, may you love me. As the sun follows its course, may you follow me. As light to the eye, as bread to the hungry, as joy to the heart, may your presence be with me, oh one that I love, 'til death comes to part us asunder."

When it was Laurna's turn, neither could she keep her eyes dry. And when Coll tied a wreath of green grasses around our wrists to seal our union, his eyes, too, were moist. Thus were we wed.

Later, as we danced to Coll's fiddle, I told Laurna we must jump when the time came, taking both of our feet off the floor without any fear whatsoever. Thereby, we defied the old superstition that the little people, the faeries, would get the upper hand in our marriage if we did. For with Christ, we could abandon such nonsense. Our Lord would protect us from such as them.

Our celebration lasted long into the night, began again the next day, and ended only on the day after that. My joy in her held no bounds. I'd almost given up hope I would ever see her again, and there I was, holding her in my arms, rejoicing in our union. She was mine, I was hers, and our life together could begin at last. For years afterward, the clan talked about our wedding, how it was such a joyous affair, and how it began a period of blessing and prosperity such as the Carraig Beag had never seen.

Thus does my tale conclude. It began when I left my island home so long ago, setting sail in a small *curragh* as an outcast, desperately seeking, then finding the truth about the one true God. It ends in the peace of God's blessing, in the company of my family, surrounded by my clan, content in Laurna's arms. And what better way to end a tale than with a wedding?

But all of that was forty years ago. To finish my tale, I must tell a wee bit more.

EPILOGUE, A.D. 483

It is late morning as I write these lines, warming cold fingers by a fire in the church we built so long ago. I have just walked in from the frosty air, still breathing hard from the hike down the high, rocky trail and the spot on the mountain where Laurna and I sometimes went to sit and talk. For that is where her body now lies buried, under wet rocks close to the clouds, perhaps a bit nearer to God. It's been five years since she left this life. Thirty seven since we stood in this church and pledged our lives to each other with such joy.

So I sit near the flames, warming old bones and nursing a melancholy that always comes after visiting her grave. It's been said of our people we have such an abiding sense of tragedy, it sustains us through our temporary periods of joy. But I remind myself I am in Christ, and try not to be that way. I will not dwell upon her death, feed my sadness, and let it grow, but instead recall the life we led, full and rich, surrounded by family, and alight with the joy of Christ. I know where she is now and this comforts me.

Laurna and I gave ourselves to each other as a man and wife should give. Out of that wild abandon came four children. Caoimhe, our oldest, arrived soon after our wedding. She grew to be beautiful, spirited, intelligent, and true. She married a son of Eadan's *fine* and is a woman and wife admired and beloved by all.

Two years later, Gilliosa followed his sister into the world. He became a devout servant of Christ and a well-regarded priest in our midst. But his is such a gentle nature; he is best suited for the priesthood, not as leader of a *fine* or the clan.

For fourteen years, we thought Laurna's child-bearing years were over. Then she became pregnant and Ceana and her twin brother, Tynan, were born. Ceana was a true child of light, graced with an all-encompassing love. She blessed everyone in her presence. Though I doted on her, God had other plans.

Tynan was a good scholar but could never sit still for books and learning. After studying only a year, he abandoned plans for the priesthood. Always, he was

291

the most popular boy in the clan. Someday, said everyone, he would be Rí Tuath. Leaving for foreign lands was the farthest thing on his mind.

Then came the tragedy that changed him forever.

Ten years ago, Ceana began a habit of walking the cliffs each morning by the sea, picking flowers, singing, humming, gathering mushrooms. Again and again, I warned her. The cliffs were dangerous. Sometimes the fog clung to them. And the rocks were so slippery. Being close to the shore brought the chance of raiders. Still she went. Tynan always accompanied her. The two were inseparable then.

But one day when Tynan was occupied, she went alone to the cliff and never came back.

No one saw a vessel. She must have fallen from the cliff into the sea. Everyone agreed. Everyone but Tynan.

Her death tore the heart from me. It nearly killed Laurna. Even now, ten years later, her passing obsesses Tynan, who clings to the notion that raiders took her away. But nay, my son, nay. We must accept the truth. Our Ceana, our child of light, is gone, her body washed out to sea. We must move on.

Tragedy and pain will try us. But with God's strength we will endure.

Nine years ago, Bohan died at sea in a fishing accident, and I, with Laurna at my side, became the reluctant leader of our *fine*. Two years later, Eadan passed away of winter sickness and everyone wanted to appoint me as Rí Tuath, but I declined. I favored instead Cailean, Eadan's son. He has since led the clan well and with honor. He and Branan mac Fionn, a friend whose wisdom on the council guides us well.

In our roundhouse, Laurna and I reveled in our two sons and Caoihme, in our grandchildren, and in all the family of our clan. In the happy times, we celebrated. In the times of death or tragedy, we mourned. Laurna filled everyone's life with joy, smiles, playfulness, and a sassy humor that never quit. Often she convinced the whole *tuath* to declare feasts for no reason, to celebrate holidays out of season, and turned unholy Beltane, Samain, Lughnasa, and even Imbolc, into affairs honoring our Lord and Savior, yet accompanied by joy, music, dancing, merriment, and of course, mead—in moderation. When she took on a part of Christ into herself, all the best in her was increased.

As if it were yesterday, I remember the tawny wave of her hair, the deep blue of her eyes, and the brightness of her smile. Aye, as if only last night she lay warm in my bed under the quilt beside me. I am comforted by the knowledge that soon I will see her again in the place Christ has prepared for all who claim Him as their own.

Five years ago when Laurna died and we buried her on the mountain, I gave my church duties over to Gilliosa—the Sunday services, the Mass and the Eucharist, the reading of Scripture, the marriage and funeral ceremonies, and all that went with servicing a church of the believers of God. The reason? Coll and I had made plans.

For years my red-haired friend and I had pondered a grand trip to Rome. We'd heard news that Leo the Great, sitting in the Lateran Palace, was writing against the Pelagian heresy. I wanted to hear this from his own lips and also understand his recent views on Christ, about how deity and humanity combined together in the Son of God. And I wanted to gather from the Roman scholars books for our island, lots of books.

But as the years passed, traders brought news. After the Roman legions abandoned Bryton, Saxons ruled the land. We heard about the hordes of Huns, those brutal horsemen, whose advance across Asia nearly conquered the plains of Gaul. Now Visigoths and Burgundians controlled major portions of that country. And who could forget the day, many years ago, when a ship brought news that Vandal barbarians from Africa had destroyed Emperor Marjorian's fleet off Cartagena? The Empire was in collapse, under attack on all sides. The once invincible Roman legions seemed powerless to protect its citizens, and in our time, travel to Rome seemed dangerous, even impossible.

By contrast, Ériu was rising in importance, prestige, and stability. It became an island of scholars, priests, and Christians living in relative peace. Recently, we learned of some monks on the continent who had packed all their books, left the anarchy of their homes in Gaul, and took refuge near Ard Macha, the center of scholarship Pátrick finally created.

Coll and Tynan were to be my companions on the voyage. Through the years, Coll and I often talked about the trip, even though he suffered from a mysterious ailment which kept him in his bed for days on end, only to see him fully recover. Despite this, he would have gone with me. But one morning, he simply failed to rise. A woman of our *fine* discovered that, in the night, he had gone to be with the Lord. For me this ended all thoughts of an adventure to Rome.

But not Tynan. He pesters me mercilessly. We must still go, he says. But not only is it too dangerous, with the Empire in collapse, I have now lost all interest. Without Coll to see it through, without my trusted and faithful companion, the trip wouldn't be the same. And as the years wear on, the difficulties of travel grow in my mind.

Instead, I will take Tynan on a journey to Ulster. It will be good to see old friends again.

It's been thirty years since Connacht raiders destroyed the Emain Macha of my youth, the home I'd known in Ulster for so many years where Forga once reigned. So our visit will be to the new Ulaid palace at Óchtar Cuillche. Many old friends have gone ahead to the Lord, including Pátrick and Forga. Now Muiredach Muinderg, Forga's son, sits as Rí Cóicid in Ulster.

We will spend time in Muiredach's palace, but also in Ard Macha with Servius. That is where he now lives and studies. In Ard Macha, Pátrick finally achieved his goal of creating a grand center of learning and Christian culture, though it never quite grew into his hoped-for town. I would like to see it before I die. The monks there have taken to living alone in small stone huts, spending time in prayer, copying and studying the sacred texts.

Aye, perhaps seeing a wee bit of the world will satisfy Tynan's wanderlust, if that's what it is. Perhaps then he will give up this nonsense about seeking a sister who is certainly dead. For the world south and east of Ériu is filled with danger and chaos.

Before me now, the sap oozes out of a log, runs down the bark, catches fire, and flares. We too are like that. We are born, we run like melting sap, full of energy and purpose, and then we die—if not in a blaze of glory, then in a puff of ash, fit only for sailing on the breeze. If our run was not for God's glory, then it was for naught. We can so easily spend our lives creating ash fit only for vanishing on the wisp of a child's breath. Or we can spread the news of Christ and create a white-hot fire of truth to endure for all eternity.

I keep thinking about the fires of Beltane. We stood on the Hill of Slane facing a distant symbol of paganism and spiritual darkness. Had the druids lit their bonfire as planned, their dark blaze would still, even now, be leading the people into darkness and spiritual death. But Pátrick lit his fire first, and it became a white-hot blaze of truth that spread across Ériu. Such is the kind of blaze we must make of our lives.

It is quiet here in the church, just me and the crackling of logs. Me and my memories, the scratching of my quill on parchment, the distant bleating of a lamb. Somewhere farther off, I hear children playing.

Our *tuath* prospers as never before. We count among us twelve *fines*, more than at any time in our history. Among the council are now many new faces, young, vibrant, and eager. Lately, they talk of sending an expedition to Inis Rathlin, where they would preach the news of Christ to a former enemy. On hearing this plan, my heart soared and I gave them my heartiest support. They have learned well. This is Cailean's doing, I know. If only I could go with them.

Only Cosgrach mac Gahran and a small number oppose him. Such men are always with us. It's rumored he pines for the old ways though I don't believe it. As long as Cailean leads us, troubled souls such as Cosgrach will have no part in determining the clan's future.

As I look back, I count too many of those I have known as passed on. But I know they have gone to Christ, to a place of light and joy. Ever do I look forward to the day when I too can see Him face to face, and again be with the ones I have loved and once known.

That time may not be far off. Each day, I seem more distracted, not by the shifting world, or by the changes in our growing, thriving clan, but by my aching bones, my dimming eyesight, and the difficulty with which each morning I rise. My travels have taken their toll. I've known others with more years than I who've fared far better. Of all things, Scripture sustains me best.

I am surrounded by my clan, yet lately I seek the solitude I find here in the church by a simple blaze of pine logs, where I can read and write. Even now, I claim whatever hardships and trials we face on this journey of life are gifts from God. For our difficulties serve only to turn us toward Him. They remind us God is God and we are not.

Ever do I realize I have been blessed more than most. Here at the end of my life, I have been blessed also with time—time to reflect and write this story of my life, inadequate though you may find it. Please forgive the indulgences of my quill.

In all that I have lived, I count two great discoveries. But I do not claim them as my own; they came only from God, through His grace, by His hand. The first is truth. The truth I found in Christ, that I helped Pátrick take to the Ériu and, in turn, brought back to Inis Creig, my home—a truth now written on the hearts of tens of thousands, enshrined in hundreds of churches, all for God's glory. The second is love. The love of Christ, and the love I found, after thinking it lost forever, in Laurna, my sons, my daughters, my family, and my clan.

Truth and love. Not a bad end for a life. I can rest well in that.

AUTHOR'S NOTES

A Personal Interest

As one who counts half his ancestry originating in Counties Cork and Antrim, I have a personal interest in the Emerald Isle. And as one who counts himself a child of God, whose destiny lies with the Christian message, I have a special interest in Patrick. After the Apostle Paul, I believe Patrick was one of the greatest evangelists in history. The results of his work were to save Western civilization and to establish a Christian enclave in Ireland that would secure the future of Christianity through Europe's Dark Age.

History versus Fiction

In all things, I attempted to make this book historically and culturally accurate. Yet certainly, writing accurate historical fiction for A.D. 432 in the time of Patrick was a challenge.

The island of Inis Creig and Taran, our protagonist, were of course, fictional. But even with them, and with the Ériu, I attempted to portray as accurately as possible the culture and way of life of the Celts. Or at least what we think we know about them.

The demon Crom Cruach was a real idol worshiped in the Irish village of Killycluggin. Today's ruins in County Cavan testify to its existence. The terrible *Oíche dar dáta Marú* of Inis Creig was based on the historical practice at Killycluggin of sacrificing a firstborn child every year on the night of Samain, the ancestor of our modern Halloween. Every time the druids sacrificed someone, it involved three deaths—by having the head smashed in, by strangulation, by the knife, or by fire or drowning. Druids in other places would often sacrifice adults, but in the case of Crom Cruach worship, they killed children. Such is the evil people do when Satan, the god of this world, claims their hearts and minds. (If you don't believe in Satan, see "Spiritual Beings," below.)

297

It wasn't until Patrick himself brought the written word to Ireland that scholars began to record accurately the history of that island. Before him, history was passed down through the tales of bards and poets. But these minstrels and entertainers tended always to exaggerate, enhance, and present their subjects in the best possible light; as historical witnesses, they are unreliable.

Even the history of the Irish kings—who ruled when and over what—is suspect. Some may disagree, but after my research, this became my chosen approach: I conclude that Ireland was divided into five main regions of related clans: Connacht, Ulster, Meath, Leinster, and Munster. Accounts differ, but I conclude that Uí Néill, in the far north, was not established until after Patrick. In each area, all the clans, or *tuatha*, were loosely associated through ancestry and tradition. Each region seems to have acknowledged its own Rí Cóicid, or regional king, who ruled over them, but again loosely. Each clan answered to their own Rí Tuath, looking to him as chief. Councils of *flaith*, or noblemen, with oversight from the druids, must have helped in this leadership. In this book, I have called the leading council of Taran's clan by its Gaelic word, *comhairle*. Contrary to some accounts, no High King ruled over all of Ireland until much later. Some have said Lóeghaire was such a ruler. But at best, it appears his reign extended only to northern Leinster, to the people of the Laigin. I believe this is as good an assessment as any.

The life of Patrick was taken from his *Confessions*, the only extant, autobiographical narrative in his hand, and from two recent influential works: *St. Patrick of Ireland*, by Philip Freeman, and *How the Irish Saved Civilization*, by Thomas Cahill. Both are highly recommended. I have also relied somewhat on *History of the Irish Hierarchy*, written in 1854, though that work must be taken with a deal of skepticism. Where its history agrees with other accounts, I have used a few incidents and characters from Patrick's life, modified to remove what appear to be fictional elements. My modifications were based in part on what the Holy Spirit did in the ministry of Paul, in the book of Acts. (See "Miracles" below.) Again, ancient Irish history before Patrick is conflicting, unreliable, and exaggerated. *Pagan Celtic Ireland*, by Barry Raftery, provided invaluable maps and discussion of existing ruins that verified locations and contents of some key villages in this story. *A Brief History of the Celts* by Peter Berresford Ellis also gave me clues to the culture of that ancient race. I am also indebted to *The Course of Irish History*, by T.W. Moody and F.X. Martin.

Throughout this work, my guiding principle was to align history, where questionable, with biblical truth. Between the two—history, such as we have it, and the Bible—a writer of fiction should be given certain freedoms.

Chapter 25, Pátrick's story, is as true a telling of his life story as I could piece together. The following, however, are speculations:

- That it was in Germany where Patrick disembarked from the ship that helped him escape Ireland. Others speculate it might have been in Britain. But the fact that the ship was carrying hounds destined for Rome suggests their immediate destination was Germany or Gaul, not Britain.
- The interval from when Patrick left the sailors to the time he returned home is speculation.
- That Victoricus, the man who appeared to Patrick in a dream beckoning him to return to Ireland, was once a fellow slave in Foclut. This would seem far more logical than that Victoricus was someone he never knew.
- That he studied at the monastery of Lérins, in Gaul, and the manner in which he became bishop.
- That Palladius's mission was an immediate failure. But this assumption, I believe, is on firm grounds. All Irish accounts say Palladius's mission was a disaster. Today, it seems popular among historians to discredit Patrick's astounding success and redistribute some of it to Palladius. But why should we try to rewrite the acclaim of the ancient Irish who were much closer to events? If they say Patrick was the major personality who—with the power of the Holy Spirit—converted the northern half of Ireland to Christianity, how can we in the twenty-first century presume to declare otherwise? Another reason for my view is that Patrick's approach to spreading the gospel follows the missionary principles given us in the book of Acts, known today as the Pauline Cycle. (See David Hesselgrave's *Planting Churches Cross Culturally*.) No wonder his methods won out over Palladius's approach.

Miracles

Patrick's *Confessions* records dreams that are most certainly true. No Christian believer can read the Bible without realizing God uses dreams and visions to communicate warnings and messages to those singled out for His favor. We also cannot assign dreams and visions from God only to the distant past. Even today, where spiritual darkness meets the light, God touches the lives of seekers and believers. As a member of a church missions team for many years, I have heard firsthand stories of how Muslims have converted to Christianity only because Jesus came to them in a dream. Fully one-third of all the converts to Christianity in modern-day Turkey have done so because Jesus came to them in a dream. How is it one never hears of Muhammad coming to a Christian in a dream, with a message to convert to Islam?

Many similar instances show us a God who is working in this day, in our age, to bring the news of Christ to those who have not heard. It shows us that God will use dreams and visions to communicate with people for His purposes. And He does so today.

Thus, Taran's dream where Jesus leads him to Sabhall is entirely plausible. And some of the miracles recorded in the various histories of Patrick are surely true. Given the exaggerated nature of the oral historical record, one must approach the subject warily. But that does not mean we should reject all of his recorded miracles.

The most common miracle the Apostle Paul performed was healing. We also have numerous tales of modern day healing where missionaries have encountered pagan worship in the "Majority World". Thus we have Pátrick and company healing the Princess Eivhir through prayer.

The miracle on Beltane I present as a plausible way God could have changed the sight of Pátrick's opponents so the believers on the hilltop holding torches appeared to their adversaries as an army of angels surrounded by light. This is similar to how Gideon won the battle against the Midianites in Judges 7.

The poisoning of Ohran and Lóeghaire's killing of Boodan could be seen as God's providence—not miracles per se, but God's hand indirectly at work to further His purposes, using the evil choices of sinful men. Patrick's history does record that druids tried to poison him. Taran's destruction of Crom Cruach on Samain could be seen as God guiding Taran to the exact spot where the idol's gold was weakest. (This incident was based on an account relating how Patrick defeated the druid worshipers of Crom Cruach at Killycluggin.) Again, God is present in this world through divine acts and by communication with His chosen instruments.

I must here also mention the tale Patrick relates about the evil spirit that held him down until a voice told him to call upon Elijah, after which he was freed from its malevolence. This came straight from Patrick's *Confessions*, which I have no reason to doubt. Theologically, of course, it's puzzling. In his *Confessions*, Patrick explains this: "I believe that it was Christ the Lord who rescued me that night and that it was his spirit which cried out for my sake."

If you don't believe miracles are possible and your wont is to disregard all reports of them, think of the universe as an open box. Consider there is something outside the box we call God. But God created the box! And this God, because He created the box, can reach inside it and perform miracles.

The atheist worldview, of course, says the universe is a closed box, that we live inside it, and outside the box there is nothing. The box and all its contents just popped into existence on its own. Even the former atheist philosopher and original thinker Anthony Flew now rejects that view and believes in God.

The final argument for miracles is if there is a God who can act, then there can be acts of God. And the greatest act of God was to create the universe from nothing. The Big Bang is not only proof of God's existence, but a miracle beyond comprehension. One moment there was nothing—no time, space, matter, energy, or laws of physics. The next moment there was—everything! (Einstein's Theory of Relativity is a proof for God's existence, concluding all time, space, matter, and energy came into existence in a single instant.) Even skeptical scientists who studied the phenomenon of Cosmic Background Radiation, the leftovers of the Big Bang, have come away awed and humbled, calling it the "fingerprints of the Maker." Robert Jastrow, founder of NASA's Goddard Institute of Space and former agnostic, said of it, "Now we see how the astronomical evidence leads to a biblical view of the origin of the world. The details differ, but the essential elements in the astronomical and biblical accounts of Genesis are the same: The chain of events leading to man commenced suddenly and sharply at a definite moment in time, in a flash of light and energy." This is not evolution—copious evidence exists against this theory that life was created by unguided processes. It is instead God's hand at work, with intentional, careful design, in creating the universe and all life.

So if we see overwhelming evidence God created the universe, we must conclude there is indeed a God who can act. How then can anyone argue that

Jesus could not perform such trivial acts as changing water into wine, or walking on water, or healing the sick? Given that, why is it not then possible that Jesus also gives this power, through the Holy Spirit, to His followers? To those like the Apostle Paul and the evangelist Patrick? So they also could heal and perform miracles? One follows the other.

If it's evidence we need, then look no further than the numerous reports, from missionaries in spiritually dark regions of the world, who have performed healing miracles today, sometimes to their own astonishment!

Thus, in times of great conflict between good and evil, where God is at work to further His kingdom, we should expect dreams, visions, and miracles.

Spiritual Beings

Genesis 1:1 says, "God created the heavens and the earth." This is not just describing the universe and the earth, it's also talking about a spiritual and an earthly realm.

Now we humans can see and hear only a tiny fraction of the electromagnetic spectrum. We can see visible light waves. We can hear sound when air molecules bump together. The instruments we have created can cleverly detect the rest of the spectrum, but we've never actually experienced it. This should point out to us that much of our world is invisible to our senses, beyond what humans can experience firsthand. As Dinesh D'Souza points out in his book, *Life After Death: the Evidence*, we believe in photons, but no one has actually ever seen one. They are just theoretical particles, or waves; we have deduced their existence only by their effects.

Then there is the problem of dark matter. No one really knows what this stuff is. All we have are theories. We think we know the physical universe, but to our chagrin dark matter constitutes some 95% of it. Think on that: We do not understand 95% of the composition of the universe! And we're only talking about the physical realm, the one we thought we had a good handle on. Thus, it is rather presumptuous of us to think God, the Creator of all that is, could not create spiritual realms beside an earthly one.

If spiritual realms exist, we should not be surprised God has created spiritual beings to inhabit them. This includes angels and demons, with Satan as chief of the demons. Jesus called him "the god of this world". Satan and his demons were once angels, of course, spiritual beings ejected from heaven due to Satan's pride and disobedience. Right now, each day, in dimensions we cannot see, demons are waging a spiritual battle with God over the eternal fates of men. (See 1 Peter 5:8-9; 1 Timothy 4:1-2; Acts 16:16-18, among others.) Demons can inhabit stone idols, perform counterfeit miracles, and through deception and lies, lead entire peoples into spiritual darkness. Such must have been the case with Crom Cruach who led the people of ancient Killycluggin to do their terrible deeds.

If the Bible is God's Word, His revelation to mankind, then this is the truth. (Copious evidence exists that the Bible is true, but we don't have room for that here.) Get used to it: A spiritual world exists populated by spiritual beings. And not all of them are nice.

The Catholic Church of A.D. 432

One major difference between the Catholic church of today and Patrick's time is noteworthy. It concerns priestly celibacy. Before the twelfth century, although the Catholic hierarchy officially forbade priests and bishops to marry, this rule was so generally disregarded that most priests were indeed married. Thus, in Patrick's Ireland, priests could marry if they wished. But as a result of the Lateran Councils of 1123 and 1139, many priests were forcibly separated from their wives. The Augsburg Confession—the Protestant declaration of Melanchthon and Martin Luther, written in 1530—complained bitterly about that policy's egregious sinful results. Some things never change.

Thus we have Taran becoming a priest while still marrying Laurna.

Note that no Pope ever officially canonized Patrick as a saint. He is, however, unofficially recognized as such and in the seventeenth century was given his own feast day, March 17.

Patrick and God's Plan For History

In my reading of history, I must conclude Patrick was an apostle just below the order of Paul himself, appointed by God to bring the Irish people out of paganism and into the light of Christ. Indeed, it seems that through Patrick, Irish Christianity saved Western Civilization even as the rest of Europe descended into the Dark Ages. While Europe was mired in war and anarchy, Irish monks, born of Patrick's evangelism, preserved the written Word, the ways of the church, and civilization itself. After Patrick, these monks went out and evangelized the Europe that others had left abandoned and in ruins.

The Bible tells us God is in control of history. He is sovereign. He alone controls events. Nothing happens, for good or ill that He has not planned or has not allowed. Everything that happens, happens for a purpose, and will eventually advance God's grand plan for history. Thus God selected Patrick for the right time and place to turn a pagan nation from spiritual darkness to light. In so doing, God preserved the church, the body of believers in Christ, and brought it through a time of great turmoil.

Because men have been given free will, there will be times of anarchy, revolution, war, turmoil, and evil. Men have used free will to further their own ends and causes in opposition to God's. The cause of all evil is the misuse of free will—man's and Satan's. (Satan, not man, was the first to choose himself above God, and thus to bring evil into the universe.) The definition of sin is doing our own will, not God's. But God has used man's evil choices and turned them for good, thus thwarting evil. In the end, God allows man his evil choices but uses them to advance His kingdom. The best example of that is Jesus' crucifixion on the Cross.

God's grand plan for history is to create a people for Himself who believe in and follow Jesus, His Son. This people will come from every tribe, language, nation, and people group on earth. He began this plan with the creation of the universe, then with the nation of Israel, charging Abraham in Genesis 12:1-3 with becoming a blessing for all the peoples of earth. The Israelites, as all of the Old Testament records, failed in this task. The responsibility then fell to the followers of Christ. God did not abandon His promises to Israel; they will eventually be fulfilled. When God's plan is complete, every people group on earth, including the Jewish nation, will have heard the good news of Christ and will have an opportunity to respond.

In the time of Patrick, Ireland was at the edge of civilization, at the ends of the earth. The Roman world viewed it as a country of uncivilized wild men and barbarians, where warriors ran into battle naked, painted blue and screaming. Yet God sent Patrick to spread the gospel, plant churches, and turn that forbidding, alien isle at the farthest reach of the world, into a key stronghold of civilization—all to further His plan for the universe.

The tale in this book is but one offshoot of that grand narrative.

Glossary of Names, Places, and Terms

- Amalgaid mac Fiachrae—historical King of Connacht until 440 AD; reigned 34 years.
- Ard Macha—[ARD mah-hah] (Macha's height) a late center of Pátrick's ministry, a town he built in the Kingdom of Ulster. In modern-day Armagh.
- *Bashtoon*—Bastards
- Beagle's gowl, a—an Irish expression meaning the distance of a beagle's howl; a long ways.
- Beltane—Also spelled Beltaine or Bealtaine. Pagan celebration of spring, traditionally held on May 1, when the spirits of the Otherworld were active.
- *Bodhrán*—[BOW-run] An Irish handheld drum beaten with a stick.
- *Bothach*—[BO-hah] lowest group on Celtic class system with no property rights: criminals, unskilled laborers, and indebted farmers.
- Bryton—Ancient Britain
- Carraig Beag —[KAR-ek BEK] ("Little Rock") Taran's clan and main village of Inis Creig (fictional).
- Celts—[Kelts] An ancient race of people existing from about 1200 BC. They ranged from Ireland and Britain through Western and Eastern Europe and even into central Asia Minor (Turkey). By AD 600, the Celts as a people were mostly confined to Ireland.
- Clabber—sticky, messy pile of mud or cow dung.
- Coleraine—a village and *tuath* near the northern coast of Ériu.
- *Comhairle*—Gaelic word for council. Within Taran's *tuath*, the inner circle of leadership.
- Connacht—[KONN-nacht] historical kingdom of west central, ancient Ériu.
- Connachta—the people and collection of clans who inhabited the Kingdom of Connacht.

- Crom Cruach—[KROM KREW-ah] historical Irish deity representing the sun god, who required the sacrifice of a firstborn child. His idol was either a large, round mound or a tall obelisk, covered in gold. Twelve upright stones surrounded the original idol. Its archaeological site is in modern-day Killycluggin.
- Cruachain—historical village holding the palace of the Rí Cóicid, or king, of Connacht.
- *Cumal*—a female slave; a standard unit of currency, equal to 3 milk cows.
- *Curragh*—[KOOR-ah] An ancient Irish boat made with a wicker frame, covered in hide, stitched with thongs. From 6 to 70 feet long.
- Danu—mother goddess of the Tuatha Dé Danann, associated with the earth and the land.
- Doddle (as in *a doddle*)—a short distance or something easily done.
- Druids—a priestly class of the Celts, worshiping the spirits of forest, mountain, and river, earth, sky, and sun. Experts in healing, judgment, and sorcery.
- Emain Macha—[YOO-wen MA-hah] historical village holding the palace of the Rí Cóicid, or king, of Ulster. Navan Fort in present-day County Armagh is a probable location for the site of this ancient fortress.
- Ériu—[AY-roo] (Modern Irish: Éire) ancient name for Ireland; also matron goddess of the land.
- *Fine*—the Celtic extended family unit, including grandparents, parents, aunts, uncles, and cousins, who all live together in a single roundhouse.
- Fir Bolg—one of the original mythical races who inhabited ancient Ériu prior to the Tuatha Dé Danann.
- *Flaith*—Celtic noblemen who acquired their greater social position due to personal skill, not inheritance. They often owned property such as fields or cattle. They had responsibilities for clan leadership and protection, including hunting and fighting.
- *Flidh*—[FLEE] Poet and keeper of genealogies. Higher on the social scale than bards, lower than druids.
- Foclut—historical village of Connacht where Pátrick was most probably held as a slave. In this story, it's also a village with whom the Carraig Beag often traded.

- Forga mac Dallán—historical Rí Cóicid, or king, of ancient Ulster, died AD 465 (?)
- *Beart Uasal*—[BEA-Art Wass-Al] ("Noble Deed") Here it is a rite of redemption, involving a great deed and repentance after grievously breaking a clan's taboo (fictional).
- Gaul—ancient name for the region of France.
- Glipe—a stupid person.
- Inis Creig—[IN-ish KRAYG] ("Island of Rocks") island home of Taran and his people (fictional).
- Killycluggin—historical inland town in north-central Connacht, home of Crom Cruach worship. The archaeological site is in modern-day County Cavan.
- Laigin—the historical people and the collection of clans who inhabited the Kingdom of Leinster.
- Leinster—historical kingdom in southeast, ancient Ériu.
- Lia Fáil—"The Stone of Destiny". A six foot-high obelisk that still exists today at Tara. It's said to have rung when the future king struck it.
- Lóeghaire mac Néill—[LOO-hair] Historical Rí Cóicid, or king, of Leinster, a son of Niall of the Nine Hostages, died 462.
- Lough (or loch)—An inlet from the sea or a large lake.
- Lugh—Irish deity and ancient hero of the distant past; god of many skills, jack of all trades.
- Lughnasa—A Celtic summer festival
- Lummox—A stupid person.
- Manannán mac Lir—[ma-na-nan mac lir] the sea deity, also ruler of the Otherworld.
- Meath—historical kingdom in south central, ancient Ériu.
- Muiredach Muinderg mac Forga—historical son of Forga mac Dallán, king of Ulster. Reigned 465-489.
- Munster—historical kingdom in southwest, ancient Ériu.
- Naoú Giall—[nah-OO GEE-all] ("Ninth Hostage") western coastal town of Connacht where Taran landed (fictional).

- *Óenach*—[WAY-nock] (pl. *óenacha*) a great fair or gathering, called every few years by the Rí Cóicid to gather the clans in celebration and sometimes to make a decision.
- Pátrick—[PAH-trick] [or Pádhraig, or Patricius (Latin)]. The Romano-Briton who Christianized northern Ireland beginning in 432. Lived 387-460?
- Palladius—bishop appointed by Rome in a failed attempt to spread the gospel in southern Ireland immediately before Pátrick.
- *Popaeg*—ancient name for the poppy plant and the drug that comes from it.
- Rí Cóicid—regional king and leader of all the *tuatha* or clans of a people who originate from the same, ancient origins. A leader standing above all the clans' Rí Tuatha.
- Rí Tuath—[REE TOO-ah] the king or leader of a clan (*tuath*).
- Sabhall—[SA-uhl] A village on Strangford Loch in northeastern Ulster, near where Patrick landed.
- Samain—(Sa-WEHN)—pagan celebration of fall, the ancestor of Halloween, when the spirits of the Otherworld were most active.
- *Sheugh*—bog.
- Stocious—state of drunkenness.
- "Stone"—a unit of weight, about 8-12 pounds.
- Strangford Loch—An inland saltwater lake on the coast of northeastern Ulster, where many think Patrick first landed.
- Tara—historical village holding the palace of the Rí Cóicid, or king, of ancient Leinster. Some say it was the seat of the High King (the Ard Rí) of all Ireland, but this is in dispute.
- Tuatha Dé Danann—[tu-ah-thah day dan-ahn] "peoples of the goddess Danu," a race of people in Irish mythology, conquering the island from the Fir Bolg. The Tuatha Dé were represented as mortal kings, queens, and heroes of the distant past.
- *Tuath*—[TOO-ah] (pl., *tuatha*) clan or tribe, a people of the same origin, composed of many *fines*.
- Ulaid—[OO-laid] the historical people and collection of clans who inhabited the Kingdom of Ulster.
- Ulster—historical kingdom of northeastern, ancient Ériu.

ISSUES FOR DISCUSSION

I. Seeking God in an Era of Darkness.

Commentary: Taran lived in a culture that worshiped the idols of demons. Yet, he knew in his heart there was something greater than his people's dark god. Instinctively, he knew good from evil, right from wrong. He knew the druids' sacrifices were wrong. He'd also heard of the One True God they worshiped in Britain. And so he rejected Crom Cruach and sought the truth. Then in Chapter 7, Taran sees Jesus in a dream. Today, we have numerous reports, anecdotes, and testimony from Muslims all over the world who converted from Islam because Jesus appeared to them in a dream.

Read: Psalm 42:1-2; Ecclesiastes 3:11; Matthew 7:7-8; Romans 1:18-20

Questions:
- a. Does each person have an innate knowledge of God buried within him, as suggested by the Ecclesiastes and Romans passages? What about the most ardent atheist?
- b. How important is it for someone, especially an unbeliever, to be seeking the truth?
- c. What is the role of the individual's seeking in a person's salvation? The role of the Holy Spirit?
- d. Is there hope for seekers living in situations where the truth of Christ is suppressed or hidden? Why or why not?
- e. What role do we, as Christians, have to play in helping people who are in similar situations?

II. The Great Commission and Church Planting.

Commentary: In Part III and in Chapter 25 we hear of Patrick's mission to take the Gospel to the kingdoms of Ériu, despite the dangers to himself. But his goal was not just to preach, it was to plant churches, create strong believers, teach them the way of the faith, and raise up leaders for his churches. This was the same mission given to Paul, chronicled in the book of Acts.

In Paul's first missionary journey, we see what David Hesselgrave calls the Pauline cycle. We can summarize this as follows:

1. *Send out* faithful men into the world to seek out the unchurched and preach the gospel.
2. *Make converts.*
3. *Gather together* these new believers into new churches.
4. *Strengthen* these believers in the faith, teaching them all that Christ commanded.
5. *Equip* teachers, leaders, and church planters.
6. *Report* back to the sending church on what was accomplished.
7. *Repeat* the process by sending out those who would plant more churches.

Read: Matthew 28:18-20; Acts 13-14

Questions:
a. What are the four parts of the Great Commission in Matthew 28:18-20?
b. How are these reflected in what Paul did on his first missionary journey?
c. Could the Great Commission be accomplished without the spread of new churches across the world?
d. Is your church participating in all aspects of the Pauline cycle? If not, where and how could it do so?
e. What can we do, individually, to further any part of this plan God has given us—to create a people for Himself, under Christ, through the church?

III. The Struggle Against Spiritual Darkness.

Commentary: Throughout the book, Taran and Patrick struggle against the spiritual darkness of pagan druidism. In today's world, Satan is working overtime to cloud men's minds and turn them from the truth. People's search for meaning has led them to New Age, Islam, various cults, and secular humanism. Some have abandoned or rejected the search for truth and turned to atheism. Others simply show disinterest and apathy toward God. Despite, or maybe because of, a deep longing for spiritual truth, too many are led astray by false ideologies and beliefs.

Read: Deuteronomy 18:9-13; 1 Timothy 4:1-2; 2 Timothy 3:1-5; Ephesians 6:10-17

Questions:
   a. What are the greatest spiritual dangers facing us today? Facing your church?
   b. How can we arm ourselves against being led astray by false beliefs?
   c. How can we strengthen our churches against false beliefs?
   d. Does this issue relate to some of the steps of the Pauline Cycle discussed in Issue #2?

ACKNOWLEDGEMENTS

In the beginning, writing a novel is a solitary endeavor. But at a certain point the advice and counsel of others is like a new hammer coming to the anvil. Thus, I give my undying thanks to Becky Isaacs and Gary Delp for reading the entire first draft and for giving such useful comments. Vicki Tiede also read the first few chapters and provided good advice.

I thank my first editor, Deirdre Lockhart at Brilliant Cut Editing, for all her red ink and encouragement. And of course, I am grateful for Amberlyn Dwinell, my editor at Lighthouse Publishing of the Carolinas, whose expert guidance and edits truly polished this work.

Without the advice and expertise I found each month at the Minnesota Christian Writer's Guild, this book would probably never have been published. That was where I discovered the American Christian Fiction Writers and the Genesis contest, in which my first two chapters placed as a semi-finalist. That, too, was where I discovered the Write-To-Publish Conference in Wheaton, Illinois, where I found both my publisher and my agent, Leslie Stobbe. Thank you, Leslie, for your support. Thank you too, ACFW, for your annual conferences where I learned about the business of publishing.

I also thank Lower Photography for providing my web and back-cover pictures at no cost. They are true servants of the Lord.

Finally, I must thank Jesus, my Lord and Savior, who gave me a gift I hope I have used to his service.